The little town of Antares in the Texas Panhandle lacked any real attraction for the new young teacher until Billy Polk appeared in his Geometry class. Mr. Harrison knew he was playing with fire each time he went skinny-dipping with the youthful Adonis out at the remote watering hole, and even more so when he persuaded Billy to pose for nude photographs at his home.

They each took small steps toward easing the sexual tension that was growing between them, but it was young Billy who took the quantum leap toward complete fulfillment of their urges.

The only person in town who had any idea what might be going on was Phil Baker: Captain of the football team, Homecoming King, built like a Greek god, endowed like a fertility statue, accustomed to receiving tribute to his extraordinary masculinity from anonymous men in a nearby city park, where he satisfied his voracious sexual appetites with them. And now he not only suspected what Billy Polk and Mr. Harrison were up to, he wanted to get in on the fun—never guessing that once he succeeded, his fellow student, the two-years-younger Billy, would take from him what he had until then denied the countless men he had been sharing sex with.

Another intensely erotic novel by John Butler, author of the best-selling STARbooks Press publications *model/escort* and *WanderLUST: Ships that Pass in the Night*, written in the same graphic language of the earlier books.

Boys Hard at Work

(And Playing With Fire)

An Erotic Novel by
JOHN BUTLER

*Florida Literary Foundation
and STARbooks Press*

Sarasota, Florida

ACKNOWLEDGEMENTS

COVER PHOTOGRAPHY

Cover model courtesy of David Butt of Suntown Studios, Ltd, London. Butt's fine photographs may be purchased from Suntown Studios, Post Office Box 151, Danbury, Oxfordshire, OX16 8QN, United Kingdom. (http://website.lineone.net/~suntown1.) E-mail at SUNTOWN1@aol.com.

A collection of Mr. Butt's photos, *English Country Lad*, is available from STARbooks Press. *Young and Hairy*, David's latest book, is enjoying huge success currently and is also available from STARbooks Press.

Boys Hard At Work © 2001 by John Butler

Printed in the United States of America.

First printing: September, 2001

This book has been made possible in part by a grant from the Florida Literary Foundation.

Library of Congress Control No. 2001-131751

ISBN-1-891855-23-9

AN EXPLANATION

This is a work of fiction, of fantasy, but the setting and the people were inspired by reality. 'Antares, Texas' exists, but not under that name; all but a few of the players in this story actually "trod the boards" in the drama of my life, but their names and distinguishing characteristics have been changed to protect their anonymity. I have attempted to portray the beauty and sexiness of 'Billy' and 'Hal' and 'Dan,' for example, but I undoubtedly fail to convey the fact that they were actually more attractive in real life because I am forced to use my limited verbal skills to portray those indescribably desirable young men.

The framework of this story is real also: The gorgeous Latin 'Danny' was certainly the sexiest, most beautiful guy I ever worked with, and if he *didn't* pluck my fourteen-year-old cherry, it wasn't because I didn't make it abundantly clear it was ripe and readily available to him. 'Les' was as well-endowed as he is limned here, and was much more than just my best friend when we were alone together in the dark. 'Jim' was a lot more than just a roommate when we locked the door to our dormitory room. The hugely-hung blond 'Earl' really did *come to call* on me often, and he always *called to come* on me—but more often *in* me. I actually taught at 'Antares,' and I did skinny-dip with 'Billy' out at 'Rodman's Pond' on a number of occasions, and he did pose nude for my camera, just as described in the following pages. This fiction fleshes out the story of what actually happened with the far more interesting story of what I also *hoped* would happen.

So, in other words, here's the real, *factual* story of what didn't happen!

DEDICATION:
For Charlie and Tom

Several years ago a well-known composer created a new work and dedicated it to the memory of a single specific *performance* of a Mahler symphony, by Leonard Bernstein and the New York Philharmonic. At the time I thought it a silly idea, but I have revised my thinking. An experience as thrilling and as perspective-altering as the one the composer remembered, or the ones I remember on this page, deserve memorializing as surely as does the beloved or respected person who is normally the subject of a dedication.

I wanted to honor the single most intense and rewarding sexual experience of my life, but found I could not decide which of two qualified, hence the dual dedication. In dedicating this work to both Charlie and Tom, I am inspired by a specific 'performance' each gave for me alone, and for which I will always be grateful.

Each real artist wields his appropriate tool—Leonard Bernstein his baton, Picasso his brush, Rodin his chisel. While the instruments Charlie and Tom brought to our encounters were natural physical and emotional endowments, they were wielded with the same artistic virtuosity.

Charlie: handsome—well-endowed—a voracious bottom—a persuasive, compelling, and sometimes almost *savage* top. During our first thrilling night together in my bed he performed with sexual intensity and versatility greater than I have ever encountered, and demonstrated greater stamina and insatiability at love-making than I would have thought possible—out-performing in real life even the most multi-ejaculatory characters in my books.

Tom: body 'to die for,' more astonishingly endowed than any man I have ever seen in person, a legendary *fuckmaster* whose sexual artistry is internationally famous. His sexual art is also his profession, and money did, indeed, change hands to bring about our meetings, but never have I spent money more wisely. The room in the San Francisco motel where we first met should have a plaque attached to it!

I hope every man who reads the following tale encounters a Tom or Charlie at least once in his life!

CHAPTERS

1.
ON MY OWN

The area where proper student-teacher relationships are most likely to be in danger is where sexual attraction is involved.

I was only nineteen when I first went to Antares. That may sound like the opening line for a science fiction story, but should you think that is what follows, let me hasten to assure you that the "Antares" I'm speaking of is a small town in the Panhandle of Texas—*not* a star in Scorpio. The star Antares is more than four hundred light-years from earth; Antares, Texas is very much on and *of* this planet, although its distance from culture and excitement might certainly be measured in light-years.

I first visited Antares when I was a freshman in college, as lacking in suavity and sophistication as you would expect a teenager to be. As a native Chicagoan who found himself in the plains of rural Texas in 1951, I might actually have been relatively suave and sophisticated compared to most of my college classmates and the local denizens; *they,* on the other hand, probably thought of me as pretentious and smug. They were tolerant and fundamentally nice people, however, and they didn't condemn me as both snob and Yankee, but figured, I guess, that I'd be all right once I wore out my first pair of shoes in Texas; by the time I had done that, I felt right at home in the Panhandle, and treasured the friends I had made there. I even thought the unbelievably flat, virtually landmark-free landscape was beautiful, even though it was at that time experiencing a drought almost as severe as the dust bowl days of the 1930's.

When I first went to Antares, I assumed it was pronounced the way I had learned in school: an-TARE-ees. As a second-semester freshman, when I was directed there to interview for a part-time teaching job, I had heard the town's name apparently mispronounced. I felt sure the Antareans would have a better handle on things *on site*, so to speak, although I knew that Egyptians would balk at the pronunciation given *Cairo* in Illinois, and Texans would blanch in horror at the pronunciation accorded old Sam's name when Atlantans or New Yorkers speak of *Houston* Street. As it turned out, the locals pronounced it there as they did elsewhere in the Panhandle, so that it sounded like something your mother's sisters might assume when they came to visit: "aunt-airs." Boyd Jenkins, the school superintendent, apparently not assuming that I was "putting on airs," smiled at my mispronunciation, corrected it gently, and offered me the job of high school band director.

It no doubt seems strange that a man who presumably had the education and intelligence to head a school system would offer a high-school teaching job to a nineteen-year-old undergraduate student. Under normal circumstances, I suppose it would be odd, but in Antares, Texas "normal" had to *give* a little bit now and then. The town at that time numbered about 600 people. It hardly "boasted a population" of 600, as the cliche would have it—a town that size would not be likely to offer anything to boast about.

The high school student body was a bit shy of 100. To justify supporting a professionally trained band director was a stretch the school board was unwilling to make. However, by employing a part-time conductor who was a music student not yet certified to teach, enough money could be saved that fans of the Antares football team—the good ol' fightin' Scorpions, naturally, since the namesake of the town is a part of the constellation Scorpio—might have something on the field at halftime to be proud of. In Texas then—as, I believe, even now—high school football was closer to religion than it was to athletics, and every town regardless of its size tried to provide all the trappings for the Friday night worship services in the fall.

While it is true I was only a second-semester freshman in college, I don't think it immodest to say that I was better qualified to accept the position offered than many college music students of whatever class standing might have been. I had attended a very large high school in Chicago, had been both drum major and student conductor of the band there, and had also played in various bands and orchestras in the metropolitan area, some of them quite accomplished, where I had also been a leader. Before going off to college I had studied music theory, and was even composing and arranging band music on my own.

When a student was needed to fill the job at Antares, my college band director, also my mentor, recommended me highly to the superintendent. Mr. Jenkins knew well how reliable my mentor was, and was almost prepared to hire me sight unseen—in fact, we probably talked no more than a half-hour before the job was mine. And I needed it. Although my college tuition was paid for through a scholarship, I had virtually no resources, and had to work as much as possible to make it through school.

The job offered was not attractive musically or professionally, but it certainly was challenging, and I was happy to accept both the challenge and the attendant salary. I did not let the fact that I neither owned a car—nor even knew how to drive—deter me, even though Antares was fifty miles away from the campus where I lived and attended classes. With *chutzpah* and stupidity ruling the day, I managed to borrow a car the required three afternoons weekly (failing to tell the owner I did not know how to drive), convinced my roommate to go with me the first several times to show me how to drive, and then—after several months of practice—got a driver's license. After my first year at Antares I bought my first car—if a 1947 Hudson can be dignified by that name.

And so for three years I drove the fifty empty miles to Antares at least three times weekly. I grew to like the little town and its very friendly inhabitants, although I had no plans to continue teaching there once I received my degree. I felt I would be well-qualified to accept a considerably more lucrative and professionally promising position at a larger school.

As Robert Burns so aptly observed, the best-laid plans of mice and men (and, presumably, college students) often go astray, and I proved to be no exception to the rule. I was due to complete my degree in the summer of 1954, but illness forced me to drop out of school for six weeks, and so

I was faced with the prospect of a new school year beginning that fall with my degree *almost* finished, and not yet qualified for teacher certification. The Antares school board was willing to overlook the incomplete status of my training, and since it seemed impractical to consider devoting an entire year to the six college credits I lacked for graduation, I elected to accept Mr. Jenkins' offer to come to Antares that fall as a full-time faculty member.

I was hired to continue directing the band program, but would also have the responsibility for conducting the high school chorus, as well as the teaching of music to students in the first six grades. This all sounds a bit more challenging than it really was. There was only one band, comprising students from elementary school as well as high school, the chorus was really a girl's chorus (no Antares *men* would have been caught dead singing—outside of church), and each of the first six grades only had to be served with about fifteen minutes of instruction each day. Naturally I also had to direct a beginner's band, teaching students to play instruments so they could enter the high school band. In all, the work was enough to keep me busy, but not so demanding that I didn't have time to devote to other interests. As it turned out, I might have been better off if I *had* been too busy for other pursuits—my life would have been much simpler that year—but a *lot* less exciting.

I had long planned to provide a home for my mother when I began teaching, and although I had not yet completed my schooling, I saw no reason to make her wait. She had devoted much of her life to raising a family in the midst of the Depression and World War II, was nearing sixty, and had earned a rest. Since a town the size of Antares could not provide a pool of houses for rent, the school board owned a number of them, for rental to faculty members; I contracted for one of these, and that August combined the tasks of moving all my personal effects from Chicago, and my mother's as well, with the delivery of a new school bus from somewhere in Michigan. As my new boss, Superintendent Jenkins, drove this yellow marvel down eleven hundred miles of Route 66, I followed in my ludicrously long, maroon 1947 Hudson—heading off into the sunset and into maturity.

This was my first house, even though it was only a rental, and it was exciting to buy furniture, draperies, etc., and to become an independent *man*. I had spent my life either living in a big city, or in a college dormitory, and the sense of *community* I found in Antares was wonderful; the people were, to a big-city boy, unimaginably friendly and welcoming, and in no time my mother and I felt we were very much "at home" there.

Once the school year began I assumed an additional, totally unexpected assignment. I was assigned (as were all the high school teachers) oversight of a study hall, and the one I presided over comprised all the members of the sophomore class. If that seems unlikely, it should be borne in mind that this was a *very* small high school, and virtually all sophomores had exactly the same schedule; the same was true of the freshmen, the juniors, and the seniors, of course.

Within days of the beginning of the fall semester, one of the students in my study hall asked if I could help her with a Geometry problem.

Although I had taken no work in mathematics in college, I had loved the subject in high school, and had done very well in it. As it was, I had no trouble in clarifying the problem the young lady had; the next day I helped two or three students with geometry problems. By the time we were a few weeks into the semester, my study hall had become a Geometry tutorial.

One of the sophomores experiencing difficulty with Geometry was Susan Jenkins, daughter of the school Superintendent. Her father came by my house late one afternoon, and as we shared a couple of beers, he told me Susan had informed him that the only place she was learning Geometry was in study hall. "I've checked with the School Board, and they've agreed to give you a raise if you'll take over the Geometry class."

"But I don't have any college training in math."

"I want these kids to learn what they're supposed to be learning. If you're the one that will make sense out of Geometry for them, you're the one I want to teach them."

"But what about Hap?" Hap Burdette was the high school coach—football, basketball, and everything else—and he was the teacher assigned Geometry that fall. "How is he going to feel about that?"

Jenkins told me, "Let me worry about Hap. He's a good man, and I don't think he'll have a problem with it."

I was flattered by the offer, and found the prospect of a higher salary something I could easily live with, so I accepted. The raise turned out to be $200 for the academic year—raising my salary to the magnificent total of $4,200! That sounds like something considerably lower than starvation wages today, but it wasn't bad for 1951. Ironically, even though I still lacked my degree, it made me the highest-paid teacher in the school system. I had not known it, but Hap Burdette and I had gone into the school year with signed contracts for identical salaries of $4,000. True to the Superintendent's prediction, Hap did not resent the new arrangement, and I was now a combined music and Geometry teacher.

I had known the band students for several years of course, and it was now one of my more pleasant tasks to get to know my chorus members and my Geometry students. At twenty-two years I was only a few years older than many of my students, but rather than feeling close to them because of the slight difference in age, I probably felt further removed than teachers older than I. I had been taught, and felt it was true, that it was important to observe an appropriate physical, social, and psychological distance between student and teacher. If proper discipline was to hold sway in my classes, I had to go out of my way to resist fraternization.

The area where proper student-teacher relationships are most likely to be in danger is where sexual attraction is involved. Should the teacher be homosexual, such a relationship is doubly dangerous, especially in a conservative rural town like Antares, since community standards are likely to be far less tolerant of deviation from the sexual norm. When teacher and student are reasonably near the same age, the possibility of breaching that gap is of special concern. Not only was I just a few years older than many of my students, I was also—as will soon become abundantly clear in the pages that immediately follow—a very active homosexual.

I was aware that I needed to be particularly "on guard," but that was an intellectual awareness: while my brain sent out the message to my glands, a breakdown in communications apparently resulted.

2

TRANSITION AND FIRST COLLEGE YEARS: JIM

*If my subsequent sex life was not anything like as active as those
introductory days had been, it was a good thing—I would never have
had time to study!*

Not at all unlike most young men my age, hormones were raging
through my body. I had led a fairly limited, but passionate, sex life
during high school, but I had encountered far greater opportunity to
satisfy my sexual hunger in the nearly four years of college just behind
me. I would say my sex life was unusually active during my first three
years on campus, and it had become *extremely* rich and rewarding
during the year just past.

I had already experienced three big "loves" in my life—one in high
school, two in college. The first two had yielded some very exciting and
memorable sexual encounters, but all three had been to some extent
frustrating. The last one had been cursed with that most difficult and
least rewarding qualification: it was purely platonic—not *my* idea, to be
sure.

I had also experienced quite a few brief affairs, of course, some of them
extremely satisfying, and several of them were *relationships* in spite of
their brevity. Most of my sexual experiences, however, had been "one-
night stands," and many of those proved to be uncommonly satisfactory
even though they held no promise of repetition.

My brief transition from high-school life to college life had promised
paradise for someone like me, one who was probably interested in sex
above anything else: I had wildly abandoned sex with two sailors on the
train coming from Chicago to Texas, and I made my debut as a
buttfucker the first night I spent on campus. If my subsequent sex life
was not anything like as active as those introductory days had been, it
was a good thing—I would never have had time to study.

I rode the famous train, the Santa Fe *Super Chief,* down from Chicago,
traveling coach class, of course. A sailor took the half-seat left when the
man who had been sitting there departed the train just after dark. The
sailor wasn't especially cute, but he was certainly sexy—sailors had
always seemed sexy to me, though. The left leg of this particular sailor's
extremely tight pants made it look like he was smuggling a salami, and
his crotch looked like he might have brought along a couple of oranges
for dessert. When they lowered the lights in the car, about 11:00, we put
the reclining seat-back in its lowest position, brought our feet up and sat
sideways on the seat, and tried to go to sleep, snuggled together spoon
fashion.

The sailor pressed himself against me harder than I thought he really
had to, but I didn't mind at all—especially a few minutes later when I
was aware that the delicious bulge in his pants leg seemed much larger,
and was extremely hard as he pressed it more insistently against my ass.
My heart was pounding in my chest as I *very* gently wriggled my ass
against this sexy sailor's hard prick. In a minute, he responded by

humping my ass very slightly and subtly. Without waiting, I responded with a more vehement wriggle, pressing my ass backward against him. He raised up in the seat slightly, so that his cock, contained in his pants leg and stretching down from his groin, nestled in between my ass cheeks. He humped more decisively—unmistakably signaling his interest. I put my arm back to rest on his side while I humped my ass backward in sync with his forward humping. He took my hand, and pressed it between us so I could feel his cock, then put his hand in front of me and began to grope my dick and balls. I squeezed and kneaded his cock, and realized I was fondling the kind of major meat I had been dreaming of since the affair with my first love, my high-school best friend Les, had ended when he went off to college. Les had been giving me eight inches of hot cock, but it felt like this sailor was offering even more.

I turned my head and whispered over my shoulder, "Great dick, man!"

He whispered, "Yours feels great too. Let's go somewhere."

We went together into the tiny bathroom at the end of the car. There was barely room for one, but we pulled our pants below our balls, and played with each others' cocks while we embraced and kissed. He was, indeed, offering even more cock than Les' eight-incher—probably about nine inches. I paid considerable attention to his balls, too—they were nothing short of enormous, and (I hoped) filled with come for me. He was also probably the most passionate kisser I had ever encountered at that point.

"I'll do you if you'll do me," he said when we took a moment to get a breath. There wasn't room for either of us to kneel before the other to give him a blowjob, so I stood on the commode, precariously balanced, having to stoop over to avoid hitting the ceiling with my head. The sailor pushed his cap to the back of his head, took my dick in his mouth in one gulp, and gave me as expert a blowjob as I had ever experienced. Everyone who had sucked me off before then had been a boy, but this was a *man*, one who obviously had plenty of time to hone his technique. He played with my ass and finger-fucked me while he sucked, and I didn't bother to warn him when I was ready to come—I knew he would want it. He continued sucking and swallowing long after I had blown my load in his throat. Then he released my cock, and I stepped down. Our arms went around each other and we kissed intensely again until he whispered, "Now eat my big dick—I wanna give you the biggest load you've ever had. Okay?"

"Oh Jesus, yes!" I gasped, and he stood on the commode as I had—his breathtaking prick jutting out and throbbing in anticipation. At first I couldn't take all of it, but the countless blowjobs I had given Les' monster cock stood me in good stead: after only a few minutes, the horny sailor was driving every inch of his formidable meat deep in my throat.

"Godamighty, I can't believe a kid like you can give a blowjob like this," he panted, holding my head in a vise grip as he fucked my mouth. "I love fuckin' your hot mouth! You gonna suck a load out of it for me?" I nodded my affirmation as I continued to nurse on his tremendous cock. I had pulled his uniform pants down to his knees when he mounted the commode, and I played with his writhing, humping, muscular ass. As his orgasm obviously neared, I began to tease his asshole with my finger, and he pressed his ass backward to open it more for me. He shoved his hips forward, driving his cock deep in my throat and trapping my finger inside his asshole. I fucked him savagely with my finger, and he fucked my mouth even more frantically. Suddenly, his asshole clamped down painfully on my finger, and he stopped humping while jet after jet of come shot deep in my throat, causing me to gag. He held my head so tightly, however, that I wasn't able to remove my mouth from his dick, and I was forced to overcome my gag reflex and keep the end of his cock and every drop of his enormous load in my mouth . . . thank God! Once his orgasm was expended, he pushed his dick back deep inside me, and continued to fuck dreamily into the hot mouthful of come he had given me. I savored his sweet discharge until he whispered, "You're gonna swallow it, kid, like I did yours."

I was happy to obey his injunction, and hungrily gulped down the delicious creamy liquid. He stepped off the commode when I released his softening cock, and we kissed a while longer before we pulled up our pants and returned to our seat. We snuggled spoon fashion again, and exchanged whispered endearments for a while.

The sailor asked me, "Can we do it again in the morning—I gotta get another blowjob before you get offa this train." He was riding the *Super Chief* all the way to Los Angeles, but I was leaving it in Amarillo in the morning, to switch to another train for a short ride south.

I whispered back, "Don't worry, I'll get you off again before I get off."

He snickered and said, "And I wanna eat another load too." He stood, and went on: "Don't go away—keep my seat for me. For us." Then he started off down the aisle. I presumed he had gone to the bathroom again—this time to use it for its legitimate purpose—but he was gone a good half-hour before he returned.

But it wasn't he who returned—it was a different sailor.

He sat next to me, and said, "My shipmate said you give a great blowjob, and I really need one. How about helpin' me out, too?" I started to say something indignant, but he anticipated that, and put his hand lightly over my mouth and continued. "I can give you almost as much dick as Wayne did. Here, feel this." And he guided my hand to his leg, where I could feel his cock straining for release. He was right; if it wasn't quite as big as the one I had sucked off in the bathroom, it nonetheless felt very promising. "And I got a roomette for a coupla hours, so we'll have privacy, and some room to work in." A 'roomette' was a small private compartment with a fold-down bed and private bathroom—a *much* more expensive way to travel than coach class. I later learned this sailor had been lured to the roomette by the older man who occupied it, and who had paid fifty dollars and yielded the roomette to him for three hours, in exchange for the privilege of fucking him.

The light was fairly dim in the car, but it was enough to show that even if the new sailor might not have quite as much dick as the first one, he had something better to offer in the looks department: he was extremely cute!

"C'mon, whaddya say, huh? Wouldn'tcha like to eat another big load tonight?" He groped my cock—I was fully erect, of course. "Feels to me like you wanna. How about it? And I promise you I'll take care of you, too." He squeezed my hard-on. "Jeez, I want to, y'know?" He looked up and down the aisle to see if anyone could see, and he kissed me. "C'mon, baby. I want those hot lips around my dick!"

Of course I went with him.

A great advantage of the roomette was that we could get naked, which we did immediately when we got inside. The new sailor—Gordy, I learned—was fairly short, was even cuter in full light, and had a great body, trim and compact, but muscular. His ass was nothing short of adorable—two rounded globes of velvet flesh. His cock was probably a good inch and a half shorter than the first sailor's—than *Wayne*'s. Still it was nice and fat, and rock hard, and tasted wonderful as I very quickly learned. Gordy lay back in the seat—the bed had not been pulled down yet—and I sucked him eagerly as his hands played with my driving head and he cooed his enjoyment of my efforts. He fucked upward into my mouth, and occasionally pulled my head from his dick to share kisses with me.

"You gonna let me fuck that pretty little ass of yours, too? That's what I really like." I assured him I would be more than happy to satisfy his wants that way. "Too bad Wayne didn't fuck you. Jesus, you know you've been fucked when he gets through with your ass, and I oughta know—Christ, what a cock." I told him there had barely been room in the bathroom to swap blowjobs. He kissed me again, "If you want, we can get him to fuck you in here. I know he wants to—he told me so. I've got this place borrowed until three in the morning, so we'll have time. Whaddya say? Think you can take a dick like Wayne's up your butt too?"

"Yeah, I'd love to get Wayne in my ass, too. And judging from the way he acted when I finger-fucked him, he'd love to take me or you up *his* ass."

Gordy laughed, "You'd better believe it—nobody like's gettin' screwed as much as Wayne does. Well, unless it's me!" He lay on his back, lengthwise on the seat. "C'mon get over me and feed me some dick while you suck me some more."

I crouched over him in sixty-nine, and drove my lips all the way up and down his cock while he sucked me from below. We each were finger-fucking the other at the same time. After a few minutes, there was a light knock on the door. We quit sucking, Gordy pulled out from below me, and we both stood. "That oughta be Wayne." He slid the door open a couple of inches, confirmed that it was Wayne, and let him in quickly.

Wayne grinned and took me in his arms, "Hey baby, miss me?" He fondled my ass. "You gonna let me inside this sweet thing? If you can take alla my dick in your mouth, I'll bet you're gonna be one helluva fine piece of ass."

Gordy was already putting lubricant in my ass, and he purred into my ear from behind. "Wayne just got a blowjob, but I haven't blown a load since this morning. I get first crack at this pretty young butt."

"Let me get naked first," Wayne said, "so he can get at my dick and have somethin' to suck on while you fuck 'im." Wayne shed his uniform, and revealed a muscular, stocky body, hairier than I like, but still damned attractive. But his dick! Jesus, I knew from first-hand experience (first-*mouth* experience, really) it was a monster, but sticking out from his naked body, it looked gargantuan!

Wayne sat on the seat, spreading his legs, his cock standing straight up. From behind, Gordy positioned me in front of Wayne, and bent my body over. My head sank to meet Wayne's prick as Gordy began to enter my ass. Both sailors grunted and gasped their pleasure as I sucked the huge prick assaulting my mouth, and humped and writhed my ass around the lesser, but still very satisfying, cock Gordy was hammering into me with brutal strokes, his balls slapping loudly against my ass as he pounded it. It was only about five minutes later that he seized my waist tightly, shoved himself as far in as he could, and cried out loudly while he froze in position and I felt his orgasm exploding inside me. It inspired Wayne to shove my head as far down onto his cock as he could, and fuck upward into my mouth even harder.

Gordy stopped panting, and reached down to pull up on my shoulders. Wayne released my head, and Gordy pulled me until my back pressed against his chest. He held me tight as he murmured, "Jesus, kid, what a great fuck you are," and began to kiss my neck passionately. I pressed back and turned my head so that we could kiss. While we did so, Wayne was sucking my cock and playing with my balls.

Wayne stood and pulled my head around so that he could kiss me. He put his enormous shaft between my legs, under my balls, and humped. "Now you're warmed up. You want some real meat up your ass now?" He pulled me away from Gordy, and embraced him while they kissed, then looked over his shoulder at me and said, "Lemme show you a little preview of what my buddy's gonna see while I plow that sweet butt o' yours. Get over there and bend down, Gordy. Gonna give it to you for a while first—just like you like it."

Reaching for the open jar of Vaseline sitting in the small wash basin, Wayne smeared it liberally over his cock as Gordy bent over the seat, and supported his upper body with his extended arms while Wayne prepared his ass. Wayne pulled Gordy's cheeks apart, and positioned the tip of his cock at the pink pucker hiding between those beautiful globes. He grinned at me, "Is this a pretty ass, or what?" Then, to Gordy, "You want it?" Gordy cried out that he wanted it very much, and Wayne began to press, saying to me, "Watch this, kid—this is what's goin' insidea you in a little while." Slowly, but without stopping, Wayne's fat shaft went in—and in, and in, and in—until his pubic hair was pressed against Gordy's ass. Watching the prodigious shaft enter Gordy had been thrilling, and my ass was twitching in anticipation of getting that lovely monster inside, too.

Wayne fucked Gordy in very long strokes, so that I could see almost all of his shaft emerging with each backstroke, glistening with lubricant, and then shoving back in with his profound thrusts. Gordy was whimpering in ecstasy, and encouraging Wayne to fuck him faster and harder. I enjoyed watching Wayne's ass grind and hump, while his cheeks clenched and opened as he drove in and pulled back. I reached down below Wayne's ass and held his immense balls in my hand while he fucked, then pulled my hand back and began to caress his driving ass, finally putting a finger all the way up his asshole, and thrusting it forward to counter each backward motion.

Had Wayne not blown an enormous load down my throat only an hour or two earlier, he could never have done what he proceeded to do for the next full half-hour without reaching an orgasm.

He pulled out, and had me stand next to Gordy and lean over. "You get it for a while next kid, then I can do some swappin' off." He did not need to lubricate me, I was still prepared from Gordy's assault, and Wayne knew it, so he thrust his massive cock deep inside me in one brutal shove. I cried out in shock, as much as in pain, but it actually felt wonderful—it reminded me of the many times Les had started a fuck that way. "Man, your ass is fulla come—you really gave him a load, Gordy!" It was true, I was full of come, but I was also full—*really* full—of dick: I'd never had this much up my ass, and it felt sensational! Although Wayne didn't need the urging, I begged him to fuck me deeper, and harder, and faster. The 'harder and faster' part he accomplished—the 'deeper part' was impossible, since he was hammering his fabulous cock into parts of my ass that had never been reached before.

Wayne grunted and moaned as he held my waist and pounded my ass. I had not touched my own cock, since I was having to use both hands to support myself while this complete *stud* gave me the fuck of my young life. But even without my touching it, I knew I was going to have an orgasm soon. I raised up and reached behind to pull Wayne's driving ass even tighter in to me, and gasped. "I'm gonna come!"

Gordy cried, "Give it to me," and quickly sat on the seat in front of me and took my cock into his mouth to suck just as it began to erupt. He savored and swallowed, while his fuckbuddy continued his furious assault.

"Get back up here, Gordy," Wayne grunted. "You're gonna get some more while I let the kid rest for a minute—he musta given you a mouthful, from the way his asshole was clampin' down on my dick while he gave it to ya." He pulled out of my ass, and I began to turn to sit down, weak in the knees from what I had just been through. His hand on my shoulder stopped me. "Stay right there, kid—I'm nowhere near through fuckin' that pretty ass."

And he wasn't. I stood side-by-side with Gordy while Wayne fucked him for another few minutes, then shoved himself back into me for another round, and so on, until after about a full twenty minutes of sharing his fuck between Gordy and me, he said, "On your back on the seat, kid, and get those legs up. You get the prize tonight." I lay as far down on the seat as I could, and raised my legs. Wayne stooped down, and shoved his cock inside me again. I rested my legs on his shoulders while he put his arms around mine and pulled me in to kiss him while he fucked me like a demon. After far too few glorious minutes, he put his head on my shoulder and all but screamed as he rammed as far into me as he could go, and I could feel his load joining Gordy's inside my body. I looked down and saw that Gordy was kneeling behind Wayne, eating his ass,

After a few minutes of silence broken only by Gordy's slurping, Wayne whispered, "Shit, kid, that was fantastic!" He reached under my upper body and I wrapped my arms around him as he stood and picked me up, with my ass still impaled on his cock and my legs wrapped around his waist. He turned and sat down, careful to keep his prick inside me, and we necked passionately for a long time. Gordy sat next to us, but I couldn't tell what he was doing, I was too busy deep-throating Wayne's tongue. Finally Wayne stopped, and smiled at me, "I'm kinda sorry you blew your load, kid. I really want you to fuck me, too, but are you gonna be able? We've only got this place for another hour."

"Closer to half an hour now," Gordy said.

"What about it, kid?" I told him there was no way I was going to be able to fuck him for a little while, and another orgasm was not going to be possible for at least a few hours. I was especially sorry, since if I had been up to it, it would have marked my first time to fuck ass, and I had long looked forward to doing to someone's ass what Les had been doing so regularly, and so wonderfully, to mine. As it turned out, I had very little time to wait before my debut, though—less than a day, as it happened.

"Looks like it's up ta you, Gordy," Wayne grinned. "I know you're always hard. He made to stand up, and I dismounted. He knelt on all fours on the floor of the compartment and pressed his ass backward. "C'mon buddy, I need a fuck."

Gordy knelt behind him and used the Vaseline to prepare them. "Give it to me hard," Wayne said, and Gordy shoved his cock all the way inside him in one lunge. Wayne cried "Yeah!" and proceeded to buck and hump, and wriggle and rotate, and in general fuck himself on Gordy's cock. Gordy didn't really have to do much work at first, just basically hold onto Wayne's waist and enjoy the ride. After a while, Gordy began humping harder and faster to counter Wayne's contortions, and soon Wayne was holding still while Gordy slammed against his ass like a steam hammer for a few minutes before blowing his load.

There was a light knock on the door, and Gordy said, "The guy's back. I'm gonna stay naked, 'cause I promised him he could fuck me again when he got back. But you guys're gonna hafta clear out." While Wayne and I dressed, Gordy admitted an attractive older man, dressed in an expensive-looking suit.

"Everything okay?" the man asked. Wayne and I assured him we had made good use of his compartment, and thanked him for it. He grinned. "Sorry I missed the fun, but I'm really interested in some more of this right now," he said as he stepped in and fondled Gordy's truly splendid ass.

Wayne said, "It's a beauty, isn't it? We kept it good and hot for ya."

I knelt behind Gordy and said, "Before we leave, I've just gotta do something I've wanted to since we got here. I held Gordy's glorious ass in my hands, and buried my face between his rounded buttocks, and tongue-fucked him for a good five minutes, while he moaned his appreciation. When I had finished, the older man smiled and said, "It's nice to see a man as young as you who can really appreciate something as truly beautiful as this," and he caressed Gordy's ass as he said it.

Wayne and I returned to our seat—amazingly, still unoccupied—and groped and snuggled until dawn, when the lights were turned back to full, and we couldn't do so any longer without shocking the other passengers.

A half-hour before we were due to pull into my station, Wayne and I went to the bathroom, where I promised I would suck him off as a goodbye gift. He dropped his pants and began to stand on the commode as he had done before, but instead sat down on it and grinned up at me. "I dunno why we didn't think of this before," he said, as he reached out and unzipped my pants and pulled my clothing below my balls. He leaned over and began to suck my cock for a while—restored to working order by then, but not quite ready for another orgasm. Wayne didn't have that problem—he was clearly ready for more action. He reached into the pocket of his uniform blouse and pulled out a small tube of lubricant, winking, and saying, "Always ready—that's me." He greased up his monster cock, then he turned my body around, and pushed a couple of fingers into my asshole. "You're still ready, ain'tcha?" I nodded—I still had a lot of Vaseline and two big loads of come inside me.

Wayne pulled me down onto his lap, and I felt his wonderful big prick slip up inside me again. He put his arms around my waist and held me tight while he humped upward, and I bounced up and down for a very long, delicious time until he gasped and blew another load in me. We sat there for several minutes while he nuzzled my neck and told me what a fine piece of ass I was. "I just wish I coulda got your pretty dick in my ass. Next time, huh?"

I stood up, and turned. Wayne stood, and our cocks pressed together one last time as I told him, "Next time, Wayne" and we kissed for a long time. I left the train without having seen Gordy again—which was too bad, since I knew he would have been more than willing to offer his ass for my use when I fucked my first butt, and it didn't seem likely that I could find one as spectacularly lovely as his when I finally did.

Sailors—I had long wanted to have sex with one, and now I had done so with two—and they had lived up to my wildest expectations. I was not to get fucked by another one until more than four years later, when I was a sailor myself.

While I had learned to suck cock and take it up the ass as a high school student, I had yet to experience the thrill of giving what I so loved taking when I went off to college, although the delights of getting a blowjob were thoroughly familiar to me. If the two sailors on the train hadn't been so busy fucking me, or if I had been able to bring a little more staying power to our encounter, I probably could have fucked one or both of them, and arrived in Texas the next day to start my new life as a man who was both buttfucker and buttfuckee.

My first night in the dormitory was to be spent alone in an empty room, since my new roommate's *old* roommate had not moved yet. Shortly after I turned out the light and got in bed, the door opened, and someone came in. It turned out to be who I had hoped and expected it might be: Richard Cross.

Richard was a handsome guy who had graduated a year earlier, and was visiting for the night. I had met him at a bull session earlier in the evening, and thought he was very sexy. I hadn't been sure, but I thought I detected some interest in me on his part, and we had exchanged quite a few sexually fraught glances during the evening. In spite of the wild sex I had experienced the previous night and very early that morning, I was seriously interested in going to bed with this sophisticated older man. (He was probably all of twenty-two or twenty-three!) When I left the bull session to go to my temporary room for the night, I had locked eyes with Richard for a long time before going out the door, and he had smiled slyly at me.

A few minutes later, as he entered my temporary room, he said that since it was too late to go home that night, he was going to sleep on the extra bed, if that was all right with me. I assured him it was great, as far as I was concerned.

For several minutes he stood in the dark next to my bed, not saying anything, clearly visible in the light coming through the window. Finally I asked him, "Are you going to bed?"

"There's no sheets or blanket on the bed," he said.

I threw back my own covers. "Crawl in here." I was sleeping in the nude, as I always did, and the light was sufficient to reveal to Richard my throbbing hard-on, which had developed during the few minutes he had stood there, and which I was holding upright for him to see. Without a word, he stripped his clothes off while he watched me stroke myself, and by the time he dropped his shorts, it was clear he was as aroused as I. And it was equally clear, when I reached up to take it in my hand, that his prick was a generous one, if not quite as spectacular as the one that had fucked me twenty-four hours earlier.

Richard dropped to his knees beside the bed, and took my entire cock in his mouth with one swoop. It was immediately evident that he was a talented and experienced cocksucker. I moaned my delight while I fondled his head, and finally told him, "Get up here so I can suck you, too." He shifted his body so that he crouched over me, and his lovely big cock hung down in my face as he continued to drive his lips up and down the entire length of mine. I opened my mouth to admit him, and we fell to our sides in a mutual frenzy of cocksucking.

His hands played over my writhing ass, and soon his finger was pressing against my asshole. I murmured, "Yes!" around his cock, and in a moment he was finger-fucking me as eagerly as he was face-fucking me. My own finger met no resistance when I began to explore Richard's hole, and his grunts and gasps were so eager as I plunged it in and out, that I soon added a second finger, and then a third. In just a few minutes, Richard stopped sucking me to moan, "If you don't wanna eat my come, you'd better stop sucking!" I made it clear how I felt about that when I stopped finger-fucking him, grasped his driving buttocks in my hands and pulled him in to me as tightly as I could, while I sucked even more profoundly—with his long cock plunging fiercely and rapidly, deep into my hungry throat. In a moment I was rewarded with a huge flow of delicious hot come flooding my mouth, which so excited me that I did not have time to give Richard the same warning he had given me: my come began to spurt deep inside his throat. It was clear Richard would have taken the same option I had if he had been given the opportunity, since he continued to suck greedily, moaning his excitement while he swallowed everything I could give him.

With our passion momentarily slaked, I reversed my body and lay next to Richard. With our arms around each other, we kissed for a very long time, both sweetly and passionately. I had lost my erection, but it soon returned; Richard's formidable prick seemed to have stayed as hard as it was when I first took it in my hand. Finally he whispered, "Do you like to fuck?"

I replied, "I *love* to fuck. Are you ready to go again already?" I was getting ready to roll on my back and raise my legs if he replied in the affirmative—as I hoped he would—when Richard surprised me by rolling onto *his* back and raising his legs.

"Then fuck me good, baby—give me another big load, up my ass!"

I was not about to tell him I had never been the active partner in anal sex, and even though I was inexperienced, I had no trouble performing the role—God knows I had enough experience as a passive observer. I knew I had Vaseline in my horn case in the room next door—soon to be my regular dorm room—but I was not about to go get it. I spit on Richard's ass and on my cock, and with one thrust, I was buried inside his voracious hole. I found that fucking butt was fully as exciting and rapturous as I had thought it would be, *almost* as wonderful as getting fucked, although I knew that nothing I had experienced could be quite *that* enjoyable.

It took me a very long time to achieve my second orgasm while I fucked Richard, but he was more than happy for that. I was so exhausted when I finally gave him my load, that after I finished I had to ask him to wait to fuck me, and we drifted off to sleep in each other's arms. During the night I woke to find Richard lying behind me, his arms around my chest, and his cock buried in my ass. If his cock had felt big in my mouth, it now felt enormous, and he proved to be as great a virtuoso at fucking as he was at cocksucking. He had dragged me to my knees by the time he palpably exploded his orgasm deep inside me, and he kept fucking for several minutes after that, never losing his erection, until I fell to my stomach. He continued to fuck me for a long time, and judging by his gasps and moans, he blew another load in me before I went to sleep again, with his exciting cock finally at rest, but still deep inside me.

And so it was that I started my first full day as a college student with my education much more complete than it had been only the day before. I also started that day by sharing another mutual blowjob with Richard, who went on home that morning, but who was to return to campus quite a number of times over the next few years to relive our experience—even long after he had married his high-school sweetheart. Most of the brief affairs I experienced over the next few years were far less protracted.

The unbelievable intensity of my three-day transition from living at home to college life was not sustained during the next few years, of course, but I managed to get enough action to keep me relatively satisfied. Before I left campus life behind me when I moved to Antares, I also fell deeply in love twice, even though my first love for Les still burned brightly. My sexual experiences with my second love, the blond, achingly beautiful Pierce Stonesifer, proved to be relatively one-sided, although we frequently shared some wonderful sex. By the time I fell in love for the third time, I had wisely given up hope of a long-term relationship with Pierce.

Still, as I went to live in Antares, I left behind no "untidy endings" in the romance department. It was true I was still in love with my third big "heart throb," Joe Corcoran, but as he was irretrievably heterosexual, I knew nothing sexually satisfying was going to result from that relationship.

For my last year of dormitory life I had roomed with Joe's brother, Jim Corcoran, and we enjoyed a very active and mutually satisfying sexual arrangement during the entire year, culminating in something of a "blaze of glory," as we shall see. Jim was Joe's younger brother—although not the youngest of the three Corcoran boys—and Joe was well aware of my sexual orientation. Still, he openly approved of his kid brother rooming with a homosexual. I believe Joe suspected that Jim and I were sharing a bed as well as a room, but that he tacitly approved of that arrangement.

The wonderful thing about my relationship with Jim was that we were not *in love* each other, but we enjoyed each other sexually as we did socially: in friendship and joy, and without jealousy. I doubt that anyone in our dormitory, other than those that one of us had shared sex with—and there were more than a few of them—suspected that after we turned out the lights and locked the door, Jim and I spent most nights in a single bed, arms around each other following active, satisfying, and passionate mutual sex.

I must admit I brought a healthy preoccupation with sex to my affair with Jim, although some might call it *un*healthy. Since puberty I had constantly been on the lookout for sexual adventure, and had managed to find a reasonable amount of it, but never enough to even *begin* to satisfy me. Even in our year together in the dormitory, when Jim and I had sex on an almost nightly basis, I was constantly scouting new "talent"—and occasionally finding it.

It was a hallmark of our very special relationship that Jim never minded when I found sexual diversion with another guy, nor did it bother me if he engaged in liaisons with others. A number of times he came into our room late to find me plugging either end of a hot young man, or being thoroughly plugged myself in the same way—and I also found him similarly engaged just as frequently.

Jim was bolder in his search for cock than I was, and had a much larger cock of his own to offer a prospective partner. With a long, fat, circumcised prick swinging between his legs as he walked down the hall to the dormitory bathroom, one which grew to over eight inches of throbbing hard meat when he soaped it up in the shower, Jim drew a lot of attention. Our relationship began, actually, as a result of his superior boldness.

During Jim's senior year in high school I went home with Joe for a holiday weekend, as I occasionally did. Joe's girlfriend, who would later become his wife, also went with us that time, so the sleeping accommodations were more crowded than they were when I had visited earlier. Normally I would sleep alone in Jim's bedroom while he doubled up with his older or younger brother. This time I hoped I might get to sleep in Joe's bed, and maybe get a crack at the adorable little ass and enormous cock he had so far denied me access to. Big cocks, by the way, were apparently a Corcoran family trait: Jim later told me that the youngest of the three brothers had well over nine inches. Bedding down at last with my beloved Joe was not to be, however; Joe knew very well what would happen if I got in bed with him, so he doubled up with the youngest brother, and I was assigned to Jim's bed, as usual—but this time with Jim in it.

I had known Jim for well over a year by that time, and had never had any reason to suspect he was anything but sexually straight-arrow, so I harbored no expectations when I climbed into his bed that night. We chatted for a few minutes before drifting off to sleep, talking about his eagerness to follow his older brother that fall to the same college Joe and I attended.

A few hours later, I was awakened by the feeling of Jim's erection pressing against my ass—presumably covered by underwear, as was my butt. His arm was casually slung over my side, and his hand lightly touched my chest. I thought nothing of it, and assumed he was asleep, probably having a dream. His cock began to hump my ass gently, and my own was in the same condition as his in only a moment. I disengaged his arm, and moved away from him, not wishing to start something the apparently sleeping boy was not inviting. After a moment, he moved closer, and again put his arm around me from behind. I lay perfectly still, and very soon felt his cock pressing hard against me. This time, however, it felt more clearly defined, and I gathered that it was no longer contained in his shorts. Such was obviously the case, since when he again began to hump me, I could feel his bare cock sliding below my shorts, rubbing against my legs. My own cock was throbbing, and I was thinking about getting out of bed to go to the bathroom and jack off, when Jim's hand lightly came to rest on my bulging crotch. I lay perfectly still, and in a few moments Jim's hand opened, and he began to grope me through my shorts.

I put an arm behind me and let it rest on Jim's side. When I let my hand rest casually on his ass, I discovered it was bare; he had apparently pulled his shorts down. I separated my legs slightly, which allowed Jim's cock to slip in between them, then I closed them again over the fat shaft, and reveled in the feel of it driving in and out, fucking me that way. Still without saying anything, he stopped stroking my crotch and put his hand under the waistband of my shorts, and pulled them down far enough to expose my balls and my dick. He fondled my balls for some time, and then his hand closed over my shaft, and he began to masturbate me while he drove his own cock between my legs even more profoundly. By this time it was obvious he was not asleep, and I was emboldened to begin fondling his ass, now writhing and driving as he humped my legs ever more eagerly. We were both breathing very heavily by this time.

He kissed my neck and whispered, "Jesus, you feel good."

I turned my head and whispered back, "So do you." I reached down and skinned out of my shorts as Jim released my cock and removed his own from between my legs. I rotated my body, and we put our arms around each other; he was completely naked already. Our hard cocks pressed together as our lips met in a long and very hungry kiss.

I reached down and took Jim's prick in my hand. I had been able to tell as he had fucked my legs that he was well endowed, but I was not quite prepared for the throbbing monster I encountered. I gasped, "Jesus, what a dick."

Jim chuckled, "It's all yours, if you want it," and reached for mine.

"Shit yes, I want it."

"Show me how much," he said, rolling onto his back, and at the same time seizing my head with both hands and forcing it down to his cock. "Open that hot mouth and eat me—I've been dreamin' about shoving my cock down your throat all day. I need a blowjob real bad . . . about as bad as I need to eat some cock myself." I was unable to reply, as my throat was completely filled with at least eight inches of fat, hard, driving dick. Not the dick of the Corcoran boy whom I was in love with, and had been wanting to suck off so desperately, but that of his high-school-age brother. But I was not complaining—Jim was proving to be an excellent stand-in for his older brother.

Most boys warn me before they ejaculate the first time I suck them off, before they learn how much I enjoy a cock exploding its treasure in my mouth, but that night Jim gave me no chance to decline to take his load that way. After holding my head while I bobbed up and down on his cock, he rolled us to our sides so he could meet my downward swoops on his cock with fierce thrusts. I played with his frantically humping ass and he fucked my mouth savagely for only about five minutes before he pulled my head as far in to him as it could go, and held it there in a vise-grip. With my lips buried in his pubic hair, and all eight inches of his fat shaft buried, unbelievably, deep inside my mouth, he let go. He held me so tightly I could not have avoided taking his load had I wanted to. The spurts of come that filled my mouth were so forcefully propelled, I came near gagging, but I managed to contain them as Jim gasped his thrill. When the last of his orgasm had burst, he began to hump again, gently, cooing, "Godamighty, John, that was a great blowjob. I guess you could tell I needed it, huh?" I was unable to reply, since he still pressed my face against his belly, and my mouth was full of the hot come that was bathing his fat shaft. Still, I nodded.

Jim continued to fuck my mouth with his still surprisingly hard cock, and apparently reveled in the feeling of his hot come enveloping it. Finally he whispered, "You want me to get up and get a towel, or are you gonna swallow that?" Still fondling his ass cheeks, I pulled his body in to me even tighter and savored the moment before swallowing his stupendous load.

I opened my mouth finally, and Jim released my head. He hooked his hands under my armpits and drew my body upward so that out lips met. Our mouths locked together and our tongues explored each other. Jim's hands caressed and fondled my body lazily, and he humped against me languorously, but my own hands were much more feverishly stroking his body, and I humped my demanding cock hungrily. Jim had just blown a huge load, after all, but I was badly in need of release.

"My come really tastes good on your tongue," he whispered into my mouth.

"God, does it ever," I said. "That was a fantastic load."

"Give me a little while, and I'll have some more for you. Sound good?"

"Sounds great, but I'm gonna have to get my gun first."

He chuckled, "I think I can help you do that. You want me to suck you off now?" I nodded, unable to speak, since his tongue was again deep inside my mouth. "I don't know if I can give as good a blowjob as you just did—you're the greatest. Damned few guys can take all my dick in their mouths like that."

"You give it to a lot of 'em?"

"Not too many, but probably more than you'd think. And they all love to take every bit of it up the ass." As he said this, he put his hand up between my legs, and began to fondle my ass.

"They'd be crazy if they didn't," I answered, and I began to writhe my ass under his caress.

He reached over and turned on the lamp next to his bed. He grinned at me as he said, "I sure was hoping you'd say something like that." His finger began to tease my asshole, and he gradually inserted the tip inside as I moaned my pleasure. We kissed again before he began to go down on me, saying, "I need some dick first." He lay on his back, and rolled my body so that I was kneeling in his armpits and he was able to service me from below.

He proved to be an amazingly talented cocksucker, knowing just when to lick and when to suck, knowing when to suck gently and when to exert intense vacuum, pausing to suck and lick my balls, sometimes making love to only the end of my cock, sometimes deep-throating it. Often he would stop moving his lips up and down my shaft while I fucked his mouth, often I fucked and his lips met my thrusts in perfect synchronization. At the same time, his hands never stopped playing with my ass, and his finger often sank all the way inside me.

Each time I began to get excited enough that Jim could tell I was near orgasm, he would slow down and say, "Make it last, I love this." Finally, after about fifteen minutes of this sheer heaven, he asked, "You wanna fuck me?"

I panted, "Oh God, yes." and he pulled out from under me. He got up and reached into the night stand next to the bed to remove an open jar of Vaseline. He grinned as he held it up, "I tell Momma it's for chapped lips." He smeared a glob of the lubricant over my cock, then reached behind himself to prepare his ass. I still lay on the bed as he knelt on all fours and looked down at me, his toes hanging off the side of the bed. "Get back there and give it to me."

I took the position he requested, standing on the floor next to the bed, and positioned the head of my cock at the opening his widely spread cheeks revealed to me. As I began to press inward, Jim shoved backwards, and buried my cock to the hilt inside himself, hissing, "Fuck my ass, John—I need it."

And he apparently did need it, since he bucked and wriggled his ass all around my cock as I fucked him brutally. Even after I had blown my load, he continued to work my dick with his ass. I remained at least partially hard for a time, until his feverish activity brought me back to full erection, and I resumed fucking him. Eventually, I had to say, "I'm not gonna be able to come again for a while."

Jim fell forward onto the bed, on his stomach, reaching behind to grab my ass and pull me down on top of him. "Stay inside me for a while anyway," he said, and we rolled to our sides and lay that way for some time, quietly enjoying the moment, and complimenting each other on what we had shared so far.

I lazily played with his limp, but still formidable, dick as we snuggled, and it slowly returned to its full glory. "You gonna fuck me with this?"

"You ready for it?"

"God yes." I reached over for the Vaseline, pulling my cock out of Jim's ass as I did so. I lubed us both up, and he lay on his back, holding his glorious shaft up. "You want me to sit on it?" I asked.

"The *first* time," he grinned, and I positioned myself over him and gradually sank down, so that my ass pressed against his pubes, and his monster was filling me. It had been weeks since I'd had quite that much dick inside me, and it felt wonderful.

My gasps of ecstasy as I rode were matched by Jim's moaned appreciation and encouragement. Sometimes I held fast over him while he fucked upward into me, more often I rode up and down the entire magnificent length of his shaft, gripping it tightly with my ass-ring as I ascended, and plunging my ass down hard to meet his stomach. After quite a long, delirious time, I knew I was ready to blow my load again. "O Jesus . . . I'm gonna come." I gasped.

Jim pulled my body forward, dislodging his prick. "Give it to me in my mouth," he whispered. I fell forward, my hands holding the headboard of the bed, straddling Jim's body. His hands held my ass as he pulled me down onto him, and I fucked his mouth while he sucked hungrily. In only a moment I gave him my second load, which he savored for a long time before he swallowed it and pushed my body away, saying, "Get back on me, I gotta give you another load."

I knelt back, re-mounted his wonderful prick, and began to bob up and down again. He fucked upward into me for only a short while before he was ready. His back arched up off the bed, and I could feel his cock erupting inside me as his hands gripped my waist so hard they bruised me. When he finally relaxed, I fell forward on top of him, and we kissed.

Jim reached over and switched off the lamp, then rolled us to our sides, so that he lay between my legs, his cock still inside me. We drifted off to sleep that way, our arms around each other.

Mrs. Corcoran's knock woke us up the next morning. By that time we had separated, and were lying on opposite sides of the bed, which was fortunate, since she poked her head in to tell us breakfast was ready.

The next night began with Jim fucking me missionary style while we necked, proceeded through my fucking him the same way, and ended with us going to sleep in sixty-nine position after having sucked each other off simultaneously. I woke at first light, and moved so that I lay with my head toward the headboard, so that in case Mrs. Corcoran looked in again, she would not get a shock.

Jim's mother did, indeed, put her head in to tell us breakfast was ready, and before we left the bed to eat, Jim asked if he could room with me that fall when he came to college. He promised me all the dick I wanted, and I not only agreed to the proposal, but offered him as much dick as I could give him. We solemnized our plans by exchanging blowjobs in the shower after breakfast.

So that fall, Jim became my roommate, and regular sex proved to be as good as we both had hoped it would be, occasionally supplemented by visiting tricks.

3

THE PRECEDING YEAR: HAL AND DAN

*I could have fallen deeply, head-over-heels in love with either one
of them—I was already heels-over-head in love with Hal. The classic
"Boy was I drunk last night, I don't remember a thing" syndrome
struck Steve the moment he woke up in my arms the next morning,
causing him to overlook our intertwined naked bodies, an open jar of
Vaseline next to his bed, and the still quite greasy condition of our
cocks and asses.*

Normally Jim and I respected each other's privacy enough to preserve
darkness when one of us found the other in bed with someone. The first
time I had found Jim having sex, I quietly turned around and left him to
his pleasure. Jim later told me the that the boy who was fucking him
when I intruded on them was one of the better-hung, more fierce and
satisfying buttfuckers he had ever had up his ass, who had expressed
sorrow that I hadn't stayed around to take him up the butt also. After
that, neither of us ever just said "excuse me" and left, to return later; we
would come in quietly and get in our own beds. We each may have
occasionally spent a frustrating hour or so in his bed, listening to the
other enjoying himself, but quite a few very pleasant threesomes had
developed that way, too.

One night Jim was threshing away with someone in his bed when I
came home, and I quietly slipped into mine and overhead the voice of his
partner expressing great appreciation for Jim's huge cock in his ass (I
knew how he felt, and had been hoping for that very thing when I got
back to the room that night). After they had finished, I later heard the
same voice asking Jim if he thought I would like to fuck him, too. Jim
called out, "Get your ass over here, John. I've got a United States Marine
who needs some more cock while I rest up to fuck him again."

I fucked the Marine twice that night, and Jim fucked him two more
times. The Marine didn't want to fuck either of us, but Jim and I both
blew him twice. In bed with him in the dark, I had been able to tell he
was well built, though not very well hung, with a round little ass. When
it became light, I discovered he was also extremely cute and boyish. We
took him back to the highway to put him on the road the next morning,
where Jim had found him hitchhiking the night before—looking sexy as
hell in his Marine uniform. He told us he was on his Boot Camp leave,
and had already been screwed over thirty times since he left San Diego
nine days earlier, racking up a dozen of those fucks in one night when
he had been picked up by four extra-horny sailors in Long Beach. He
said an ex-sailor who had fucked him when he was in high school in
Amarillo, "so many times one night, I was never sure how many loads
he blew in me," had told him he definitely would find happiness in the
Corps. So far the ex-sailor's prediction had been right on the money, and
the kid was on his way back to Amarillo to express his thanks to him in
the way he knew he would appreciate most.

Richard Cross, the first man I had fucked—on my first night on campus—came to visit only a few weeks after Jim and I began to room together. He was reluctant to admit a third party into the lovemaking we had enjoyed sporadically over three years, when he could be away from his wife—and, recently, his twin daughters. But once he caught sight of Jim's erect cock, his inhibitions disappeared, and within minutes he was riding Jim's monster, licking his lips, his eyes glazed over with ecstasy as he told me he had never felt anything quite as wonderful.

His visits to campus became much more frequent that year, and he often remained longer than the single night he had regularly stayed in the past. Richard loved to fuck Jim as much as Jim enjoyed getting it, and Richard and I exchanged fucks as frequently as ever—but there was no question it was Jim's prick up his ass that inspired his heightened interest. We also shared plenty of oral sex during his visits, but almost every orgasm Richard experienced occurred while he was impaled on Jim's big cock—even if I was blowing him at the time, or if he was fucking me when he was the middle of a 'train fuck' with Jim hammering his ass simultaneously.

After I graduated, Richard continued to visit Jim, although they had to relocate their sex-play to a motel room when Jim's new roommate was on site.

One *very* memorable night I let myself into our room and saw silhouetted in the window a tall guy driving his prick into Jim's mouth while Jim lay on his back. When I closed the door, the guy raised up, pulling his cock from Jim's mouth, and the image of it jutting out from his body was astonishing—a *titanic* instrument. My own prick sprang to immediate attention, but I said, "Sorry—I'll just get in my bed."

A voice I didn't recognize said, "It's okay, come on in—you won't bother us."

Jim's voice: "Can I turn on the light and let him see this incredible cock? I know he's going to want to see it."

The silhouetted figure took hold of his huge prick and began to stroke it. "Sure, why not." The desk lamp came on, and the largest prick I had ever seen was revealed to my admiring gaze—significantly bigger than even Jim's or Les's, or the prodigious one the sailor had given me while he made my train ride to Texas so memorable. This magnificent shaft Jim's partner-of-the-moment was wielding was as exciting as *anything* I had ever seen, and as I watched he proudly displayed it for me to admire, then plunged it back into Jim's hungry mouth and fucked a minute or so while he smiled at me. Then he pulled it out, pointed it at me and said, "You like it, John?" (We knew each other, of course.) I moved in and knelt next to the bed. "It's wonderful." It was more than wonderful, in fact—it was *stupendous*. I took it in my hand and caressed it, and bestowed several admiring kisses on its huge head before Jim reached for it and returned it to his hungry mouth. As the proud possessor of this splendid weapon began again to fuck the temporary sheath Jim's mouth happily provided, he winked at me and turned the light off.

The size and beauty of the monster cock I had been shown was truly impressive, even staggering, but even more astonishing to me was that this most admirable organ belonged to Hal Weltmann—an absolutely gorgeous, dark-haired fraternity man, who, while not as head-turningly well-built as he was handsome, was certainly no slouch in the body department, either. I had long admired Hal—*drooled* over him is perhaps a more accurate term. As seniors in a small school like ours, we naturally enjoyed a speaking acquaintance. But I had thought him to be too straight to even bother to put out feelers about the possibility of sex with him. Needless to say, I had no idea he was this well *equipped*. Hell, I don't think I'd known for sure that *anyone* was that well equipped.

I later asked Jim how he had managed to lure this *treasure* to his bed, and he told me, "I happened to stand next to him while he was pissing in the men's room in the Ad Building. I'd seen him around, but I didn't know who he was. I guess he could tell how intrigued I got when I saw how big his prick was, 'cause mine got hard as a rock, and I guess he was impressed with mine, too, 'cause as big as his had been, it got even bigger." He laughed, "And it just kept getting bigger, until, I had to start stroking mine, which made him start stroking his, and we swapped compliments, and I just asked him if he wanted to come to my room and play around. He wanted to as much as I did, I guess." I had often conducted lengthy, sophisticated campaigns of seduction, and lured *far* less exciting boys into my clutches.

I got in my bed and lay there, listening to my roommate making love with one of the most beautiful men on campus, who was probably the best-endowed one as well. All talk ceased, and only thrashing about and slurping was heard as the two sucked each other's cocks. My eyes were by then sufficiently accustomed to the dark that the limited light coming through the window and the vent in our door allowed me to see their bodies wrapped together in sixty-nine. Jim came first, and Hal apparently swallowed it. I then saw Hal crouch on all fours on Jim's bed, pressing his ass back toward him as he said, "Eat my ass before you finish suckin' me off again." (*Again? I was sorry I had arrived so late.*)

Jim's face disappeared between Hal's cheeks, and Hal gasped his joy. "C'mon, Jim—fuck me with that hot tongue. Ooooooohhh, God, that's great." Soon Hal flopped on his back, and Jim returned to sucking his cock. "Let me try to fuck you again," Hal said, and I watched as Jim crouched on the side of the bed and Hal stood next to it while he slowly inserted his gargantuan cock into him, which he had apparently been unable to do earlier. I watched Hal's ass hump, and listened to Jim beg him to take it easy. It was clear Hal was limiting his thrusts to what Jim was able to take, but he nonetheless fucked with great passion. Finally, he jerked his cock out of Jim and stroked it fiercely as he told him to get on his back. He knelt on the bed, straddling Jim's waist, still jacking off wildly, and I watched in awe as his enormous prick began to spurt white gobs over Jim's face and into his open mouth. Hal leaned down and licked Jim's face and neck clean, then kissed him. They fell together on the bed, and kissed and fondled each other.

Hal broke away for a moment to get out of Jim's bed and come to mine, where he leaned over and whispered to me, "If you want some of that, don't you jack off, y'hear? I'll be back later on, if you want."

I whispered, "I want it, and I'll be waiting for you."

Later that evening, the hugely endowed Hal crept into my bed, where

I had lain awake all the time, tingling with anticipation and forcing myself to refrain from masturbating. We kissed passionately while fondling each other, until Hal whispered, "Go down on me."

Jim was awake, and aware of what was going on, since I heard him snicker as I gagged audibly when Hal first drove himself into my throat. "Wait until he jams that thing up your butt."

Hal laughed as he replied, "Oh hell, John's gonna love takin' it up his ass, aren'tcha?" I was unable to reply, given the mouthful I was dealing with, but I nodded. "How about it, Jim—does he take that big ol' thing of yours all the way?"

"I shoved every inch of it in him the first time we fucked, and he takes every inch down his throat, too. Not many guys can do that."

"I know how they feel—I couldn't quite take it all myself, at first. C'mon John, if you can take alla Jim's cock, you can take mine." I relaxed my throat and opened it as far as possible, as I did whenever I deep-throated a really big prick like Jim's. Hal murmured his satisfaction as he gradually sank farther into me, and inspired by his fat, lip-stretching cock and my mental image of his matchless beauty, my nose was soon buried in his pubic hair. "Aaaahhh, that's it. You've got ten inches of fat dick inside your mouth, baby. *(Ten inches? Monstrous as Hal's prick was, that seemed hard to believe. Later I checked with a ruler: he had not been exaggerating at all.)*

I sucked Hal for a long time, so completely enraptured, I forgot my own needs for the moment, and it was only when Hal reversed his body—without taking his cock from my mouth—and began to suck my cock that I became aware of how badly I needed to ejaculate.

Hal was not only an extremely fine cocksucker, he was also a very skillful one, and was able to prolong his blowjob until I was in absolute seventh heaven—inspired to suck his relentless behemoth as best I knew how, my lips stretched painfully and my throat wide open to accommodate his profound thrusts. During those moments when he would momentarily stop sucking me to delay my orgasm, he expressed his happiness: "God *damn*, you're a great cocksucker. Jesus, Jim, you get this every night? You're a lucky bastard."

When my orgasm finally arrived, Hal gulped and moaned deliriously as I blasted deep inside his throat. He kept my come in his mouth for a long time while his tongue lapped at my cock, bathing it in its own discharge. Finally he swallowed, and again reversed his body, this time pulling his cock from my mouth. He crouched over me and kissed me passionately, his tongue tasting of my own come. He stopped for a moment to whisper, "Thanks for saving that load for me. Suck my dick some more, and then I wanna fuck you. Okay?"

"God yes, I want . . . " My words were cut off as his lips sealed against mine, and his tongue resumed its passionate assault.

I returned to Hal's cock with renewed enthusiasm, and this time found I had little trouble deep-throating it. Shortly after that he asked me—ordered me, really—to impale myself on his wonderfully invasive monster organ as he lay on his back. "I hate for you to stop suckin' me, but I wanna blow a load up your ass, first. Grease us up, and ride me, John."

I reached for the economy-sized jar of Vaseline that always sat on the night stand between our beds, and lubed my ass and Hal's cock with unusual care, and began to work slowly and carefully to accommodate his request. I couldn't just *plunge* my hungry ass down on him as I did with most of my sex partners, even gloriously hung ones like Jim. Years of practice taking monster cocks like those of Jim and Les hadn't *quite* prepared me for anything this big up my ass, but I was finally able, and *very* happy, to accomplish Hal's goal—*our* goal, to be sure. I soon found myself firmly seated on his pubic hair as he began violently thrusting upward with the fabulous shaft that my eager ass now gripped in all its glorious ten-inch length.

"Turn that light on again, and let me show Jim it *can* be done," Hal panted, and I complied with his request. I was so completely filled with ecstasy, as well as with his driving, magnificent cock, that just then I would have done absolutely *anything* he wanted.

Jim knelt beside my bed to watch me ride the bucking and thrusting monster shaft from up close. He continued to watch in awe for a long time, until deep within me I *felt* the explosion of the dark Adonis' copious and wonderful discharge. I was so excited I had never lost my own erection, which had flopped up and own furiously as I rode, and which miraculously, and without my touching it, began spurting another orgasm just as I felt Hal's erupt—and sprayed come all over him and me and our spectator. Hal withdrew, and we collapsed in each other's arms. Jim stood and smiled, kissed us both, and told Hal, "Give me another chance; I'll learn to take it all."

I knew that Jim was fully capable of taking *me* the way Hal wanted: he and I both might have developed saddle sores from the hours we had spent "riding" each other. But the enormous size of Hal's tool was daunting to Jim—as, indeed, it would be to almost anyone.

Hal and I licked my come off each other, and we necked for a long time, stopping once for me to honor Hal's request to tongue-fuck his ass for a while, and I fell asleep in the strong arms of Hal Weltmann—one of the most beautiful men I had ever seen, and certainly the best-hung.

Sometime before dark he shook me awake, his monster cock poking into my belly. "You wanna give me a blowjob?" I wanted to, and I did. Not surprisingly, it took him a long time to come—almost as long as it took me to reach another orgasm while we double-sucked. We both swallowed happily and drifted off to sleep. We were still in sixty-nine position, our arms around each others' asses when Jim woke us a few hours later. The condition of Jim's cock made it clear he needed service, and he stood next to my bed while I sucked him off and Hal fucked him. Neither Hal nor I was ready to shoot another load, but Jim gave me a huge one to drink.

When Hal left, probably as *drained*—literally—as Jim and I were, he made it abundantly clear that we could further pursue our delightful activities of the night just past if we would *swear* to tell absolutely no one of what we had just done. He had a lover—his roommate, he inadvertently let me know, although Jim did not apparently catch the slip—who didn't know he fucked around on him. Hal didn't want word of it to get back to him. We were both happy to comply, and saw Hal a number of times that year, even sharing him on a few occasions. Jim gladly faced the challenge of taking Hal's plunging monster all the way down his throat and up his butt, and was soon able to do so without any hesitation.

We both longed to plug Hal's ass as he so expertly did ours, although neither of us could hope to fill it to the same *extent*. However, as brilliant a practitioner as he was of *active* anal sex, *passive* anal sex just wasn't Hal's 'thing,' so Jim and I settled gladly for his eager appetite to suck cock. I might add that Hal's oral lovemaking technique was superb—he never gagged when we discharged into it, no matter how large the load nor how vehemently delivered.

The knowledge that Hal had a lover who was also his roommate was too good to ignore. The very next day I went to his dormitory—up the street from mine—to find out who it was. What I learned was decidedly in the "too good to be true" category: Hal's roommate was none other than Dan Chrisman—blue-eyed, blond, the only guy on campus who I thought might be as attractive and sexy as Hal. Both had been named "Most Handsome Men" in the college annual.

Facially, Dan was absolutely adorable, and although he was considerably shorter than the over-six-foot-tall Hal, he was much better built. Dan almost always wore tight tee shirts and even tighter Levi's around campus; the former clearly showed he was built like the proverbial brick shithouse, and the latter revealed an adorable little bubble butt. I had fantasized about sex with Dan Chrisman almost as much as I had about Hal Weltmann, and to find they were lovers was nothing short of mind-boggling.

If I had been astonished at Hal's unsuspected appetite for gay sex, I was equally dumbfounded to learn the same about Dan. Looking back on it, I have never been able to decide if the fact that the two most handsome men on campus were having sex together was a fluke, or some special magnetic attraction between two perfect specimens of masculine beauty. In any event, the thought of those two stunning men making love together was unbelievably exciting to contemplate. Hal had apparently not meant for Jim or me to know his roommate was his lover, so I kept the knowledge to myself.

One afternoon Hal stopped me on the way to class and said he wanted to fuck with Jim and me that night, but he wanted to involve someone else as well. He swore me to secrecy before he explained that his roommate/lover was Dan Chrisman, and that it was Dan's birthday, and he wanted to give him a special birthday present. He asked me if I knew Dan, and I told him I had been in a couple of classes with Dan, and not only knew him, but thought he was probably the only guy on campus who might give Hal any competition for the title of Sexiest Man in the World. Hal laughed, and declared he would award that title to Dan any day: "He's the sexiest, most beautiful guy I've ever seen, and he's fantastic in bed."

Hal went on to say he thought it would be great fun for the three of us to stage a surprise foursome with Dan, but he knew the latter would balk at it unless it was completely anonymous. Nonetheless, he assured me we could have a great time with Dan. The idea of *sharing* the two hottest men I knew, if even for one night, promised absolute paradise, and I felt sure Jim would agree as enthusiastically as I did: I knew he adored sex with Hal above all else. If he knew Dan was the fourth party, I was sure he'd be ecstatic, since he and I had often talked about Dan's sexiness and beauty, comparing them to Hal's, and deciding Hal was the hottest and sexiest man we'd ever seen, but Dan the most perfectly gorgeous one. It was a shame I would be unable to tell him who our mysterious other partner would be.

Hal said he himself didn't take it up the ass—as if I didn't know—even from Dan, but Dan was really eager to fuck ass again. Before he and Hal had become lovers Dan had been an active and eager top, but he declared he didn't want to have sex anymore with anyone but his lover, so was resigned to settling for being the bottom boy in their lovemaking, and hadn't had his cock inside a hot ass in over a year. For a special birthday present, Hal wanted to present his beautiful blond partner with not one, but *two* hot asses to fuck. Since he himself would be there, and since Dan would not know who he was fucking, nor would Jim or—presumably—I know who was fucking us, Dan should feel all right about the arrangement.

But Hal insisted on certain conditions: He was going to rent a room in the town's one motel, and I should call there shortly before eleven to find out what room they would be in; I was to bring Jim to the room, where they would be waiting for us in the dark; I could tell Jim *what* we were planning, but not the identity of the birthday boy. "Dan isn't going to know what his present is until I tell him when you guys are ready to give up your butts to him." He added there would be plenty of beer on hand, as if any inducement might be needed.

I asked, "Isn't Dan going to think something mighty strange is going on?"

"If Dan knows he's going to get my cock up his butt, he'll do anything I ask," Hal replied. *(Smug? Certainly, but I knew exactly how Dan must have felt, since I knew that I, too, would have done anything to get Hal up my butt.)* "I'll tell him we're going to have a special, super-sexy birthday party with two guys he won't know—and who won't know who he is. I'll promise him to keep the room dark and the bed hot. So you're going to have to pretend you have no idea who he is, and you'll have to avoid talking too much. I'll tell him you two are guys I used to have sex with before he and I became lovers, so don't say anything about our fucking recently, and be sure Jim understands that, okay?"

"Sure. But . . . why are you telling me who the fourth is? You know both Jim and I would agree to come *whoever* he might be, if we can get your cock too."

Hal smiled. "Look, I think Dan is the most gorgeous guy I've ever seen, and I thought I knew your taste well enough to figure that you felt just about the same way about him. Obviously I was right."

"Yeah, and I've got to admit, I've whacked off quite a few times thinking about how pretty he is, and how great his ass looks in those Levi's." I hastened to add, "But not as many times as I have thinking about you and your big cock, and how it feels inside me."

"That's what I thought, and...well, I just wanted to do something really nice for you, too. Well, for Jim, too, of course, but well . . . I dunno, especially just for you, okay?" Here he looked pointedly down at his bulging crotch as he added, "God knows you've done some *wonderful* things for me." *(I was melting inside. Could the incomparable Hal Weltmann be just the tiniest bit in love with me? I knew I could fall in love with him in an instant, if I wasn't already. But how could I compete with the perfection of Dan Chrisman?)* Hal looked back up into my eyes, and his smile turned into a huge grin as he put his hands on my shoulders and said, "Think how much *more* you'll enjoy fucking and sucking with Dan if you know who he is, and can *see* him in your mind while you *feel* him in your mouth or your butt. So that's why I want you to know who he is. Jim'll have a great time, I know, but you'll have an even better one."

It was my turn to study Hal's bulging crotch as I asked him, "Has Dan got anything like that ass-reamer of yours?"

He laughed and slugged me on the shoulder. "Hell, *nobody's* got a beauty like mine—you know that as well as anyone. But Dan's dick is big enough, and it stays hard as a rock all the time. And it's really pretty, too, and it tastes *great*—and that cute little ass of his is sweet as sugar, and it's hot as hell and tighter'n a tick."

"Hell, Hal, any *sane* guy's ass would be hot if you showed him that cock of yours—and any one of them would feel tight to you."

"Well, I'm gonna check out three different ones tonight—Dan's not gonna be he only one fucking, I promise you. You guys just be there at eleven and I want *your* hot ass to be first in line so I can get warmed up on you." He winked and walked away—and I watched in enjoyment (Hal walking away was *almost* as delightful a sight as Hal approaching), and managed to hide my raging erection as I hurried to find Jim and share the good news.

As soon as I got to the dorm I told Jim of the planned party, specifying that the fourth guy at this get-together with Hal would be anonymous. I was amazed to find that he wasn't overly enthusiastic; the idea of neither seeing the fourth guy, nor knowing who he was, seemed to 'spook' him. He said, "Hell, if I knew he was going to be as hot as Hal—or as cute as him, or Steve Counts, or Dan Chrisman, or someone like that—I'd be all for it."

I told him, "Look, I swore to Hal I wouldn't tell you who it is, but Jesus, he's *Hal Weltmann*'s lover—he's gotta be great. And take my word for it, he *is* as cute as Dan Chrisman..."

"I don't think anybody's as cute as Dan Chrisman—even Hal."

"Trust me, you'd recognize him, and you'd agree that he is every bit as cute as Dan Chrisman, believe me, and Hal tells me he's also plenty hot, and has a really sweet, tight ass."

Once he accepted those declarations, Jim became almost as excited about the forthcoming party as I was. So, at eleven o'clock that night we knocked on the appropriate motel room door. Hal first opened it a crack to be sure it was us, and then opened it fully. He was totally naked, and his cock was semi-erect, and thrilling to behold as the light from the parking lot illuminated him—it was totally dark in the room.

"Get your butts in here and get naked before I give you a beer," he said as he admitted us.

As he closed the door, I could make out the outline of Dan's beautiful body silhouetted against the faint light penetrating the relatively sheer curtains over the window. He stood in profile, and it was clear from the generous erection jutting out from his body that he was as naked as his lover. I saw Hal move to him, put his arm around him and kiss him, before he stooped down and I heard him rummaging around in an ice chest. I quickly got out of all my clothes and was ready when Hal said "I got beer here for naked guys—step up and get it while I check to see if you're ready."

I stepped forward and felt for the beer. Hal handed it to me, sank to his knees, and took my cock deep into his mouth and began to suck vehemently as he put a finger into my asshole. He declared me "ready," and apparently performed the same service for Jim. (His hands, incidentally, were ice-cold from the beer—something Hal had not foreseen; we quickly found that handling cold beer cans and having sex did not mix well, and we abandoned our drinking in favor of more pleasurable pursuits.)

After certifying Jim's and my readiness, Hal stood and said, "I want you to meet my lover—we've been ready for you guys for quite a while. Fact is," he chuckled, "he's already got a load of my come in his ass tonight, right, baby?"

"A really big one," Dan said, and they kissed. Dan stepped in to kiss me, and grope my cock as he did so. "Nice to meet you. This feels great," he said as he reached behind me and ran his hand over my ass, "and I'm looking forward to this, especially. It's been a year since I fucked butt. Hal tells me you like it." I assured him I did, fondling his generous cock and his smooth, rounded ass in return. He turned to Jim and kissed him, releasing my prick. His greeting was more enthusiastic when he took hold of Jim's cock. "Wow, what a dick. Jesus, it's *really* nice to meet you." Here he also fondled Jim's ass, and said to him, "Nice. Two hot asses to fuck tonight. You like it as much as your buddy?"

I could dimly see Jim turn around and press his bare ass against Dan, reaching back to grasp Dan's ass and pull his body in to press it against his own. "I'd say even more, but we both like gettin' fucked about as much as anyone can," Jim laughed. Hal took him by the hand and led him away to stand near one of the two beds, where they began to neck, leaving me with Dan.

I put my arms around Dan's trim body. His cock was fully as hard as mine as we embraced passionately and ground them together, and our tongues intertwined with even greater fervor. Dan was again fondling my buttocks, and I reached behind him to cup his perfect ass with both hands; it was trim and muscular, but still soft and fairly pliant. I was at last caressing the adorable ass I had craved so much and admired so often around campus—naked now, and writhing seductively under my hands. As my finger sought Dan's asshole, he began to hump rhythmically, took my entire finger inside, and "worked" it with the tight musculature of his sphincter. His finger sought me out the same way, and I welcomed it similarly. I whispered, "Am I gonna get to fuck this pretty little ass, too?"

Dan whispered, "It's my birthday—everybody here fucks my ass tonight. Your dick feels great, and it's gonna feel even better up my butt, but I gotta admit, I'm really looking forward to getting your buddy's big dick inside me. You get that all the time?"

"Just about every night," I replied.

"Lucky boy," he snickered.

"*Me* lucky? This from the guy who Hal Weltmann fucks all the time?"

"Good point. But don't worry ..." here he kissed me. "... I'll bet he fucks you at least once tonight, too. But I get to fuck you first—and I'm really looking forward to it."

We continued to kiss and embrace for a long time, humping each other hungrily. Jim and Hal were similarly engaged; they had fallen onto the bed, and were all wrapped up together. It certainly sounded like they were enjoying themselves.

Although there was no light burning in the room, my eyes had become accustomed to the darkness, and there was enough light coming through the drawn curtains that I could clearly make out Dan's beautiful face, his adorable, cleft chin, and the trim, beautiful body I had so long admired and craved. I sank to my knees to study Dan's cock, and found it as beautiful as his face and body. As I was kissing the tip of his prick, I opened my mouth, and Dan drove himself all the way into me, in one fierce plunge. His hands took firm hold of my head, and he fucked my mouth slowly and as deeply as he could, grinding his buttocks while I kneaded them. His cock was well above average in both length and girth, probably seven inches long, and I was able suck it profoundly, without having to make the adjustments needed when I serviced Hal's monstrously large shaft. Dan's prick *tasted* wonderful to me also, even more wonderful knowing what a perfectly beautiful young man was driving it eagerly into my worshipping throat.

Dan said, "I want to suck you, too," raised me to my feet, and led me by my cock over to the empty bed, where he told me to lie on my back. I did as he told me, and he straddled my head as he faced my feet. He fell forward over me, and with one gulp took my cock completely into his throat and began sucking with perfect technique; having practiced by eating Hal's challenging cock regularly had certainly engendered a master cocksucker.

I engulfed Dan's pretty, hard tool as it hung down temptingly over my mouth, and we spent a long time passionately sucking and finger-fucking each other, and generally slurping and grunting with total abandon. I could clearly hear Hal and Jim having a helluva good time doing *something* on the other bed. Judging by the fact that I rarely heard words—mostly gasps and moans of pleasure—I assumed they were sucking each other off as Dan I were doing. At one point I heard Hal say, "*Yes*. That's all of it at last." I assumed Jim had finally mastered the technique of deep-throating Hal's ten-inch lip-stretcher; Jim later proudly confirmed that he had.

I released Dan's cock from my mouth, and moved my head upward to kiss and lick his magnificent ass. I put my tongue inside his tight sphincter, and began to invade him with it. "Oh Jesus, I love it," he gasped, as he stopped sucking me and raised to his knees, keeping my busy tongue inside him. He sat backwards over my face and moaned, "Eat my ass . . . oh God, that is so *good.*"

I ate Dan's ass for quite a while, until he fell forward and again began to suck my cock. I returned to his, and we fell to our sides and sucked in sixty-nine while we finger-fucked each other for some time more.

Before either Dan or I was near orgasm, Hal told us to get up and change partners, and just before letting go of me, Dan declared, "I want to fuck your ass, *soon.*"

Jim overheard this as he moved in to embrace Dan, and told him "And I want this cock of yours up my butt soon, too."

"I can't wait to give it to you." Dan replied. As he and Jim fell together in sixty-nine, he added, "Aaaahhh—give me that big dick."

I moved into Hal's arms, and his magnificent prick pressed into me as we began passionate kissing and groping. While Jim and Dan threshed around in noisy and apparently uninhibited lust, Hal and I lay on our sides together on the other bed and double-sucked joyously. He fucked my ass with one or two fingers as we nursed, and even briefly allowed me to penetrate him with an entire finger—more than he had ever allowed before. As I began to fuck him with my finger, however, he backed away from it, saying "I can't do that, but I sure as hell want to stick this hard dick of mine into you." He reached somewhere and produced enough lubricant to grease me up thoroughly. We lay on our sides, with him behind me, and I began to glow with wonderful warmth as he gradually sank the entire length of his magnificent tool deep into my always-hungry ass, filling me, as always, with indescribable *warmth* and satisfaction.

While Hal was hammering my ass—passionately, wonderfully, as *deeply* as only this stud could fuck—I could make out Dan's ass crouching over Jim's head, with Jim's face buried between the perfect rounded cheeks. Dan's head was bobbing up and down over Jim's dick. Hal held my body tight in his arms, fondling my chest and biting my neck, and continued to plunge his huge shaft so deep in me that I was crying out in ecstasy. After a wonderful interval of this delicious reaming, he pulled out and got off the bed. "It's time for the special part of this party," he announced. Jim and Dan disengaged and sat up on the other bed.

Hal told Jim and me to kneel side-by-side on one of the beds. He said, "You know I don't take it up the ass, and my baby here loves to fuck butt. But he doesn't screw around on me, so he hasn't had his dick up a butt in over a year. He knows I used to fuck both of you, and I've told him how much you both like to take it up the ass, and how good you are at it. So now I want you guys to both give him a special double birthday present: your asses—but as a present from me to my baby." Dan stood and Hal's arms went around him while they kissed.

"Thank you, Hal. I love you," Dan said.

"I love you too, baby, but just for tonight it's open season. You can bet while you're fucking one, I'll be fucking the other, and so forth, and if you want either of them up your ass, go for it."

Dan laughed, "If I don't get that cock I've just been sucking up my butt before tonight's over, I'm gonna be really disappointed."

It was Hal's turn to laugh. "Hell, the first time I sucked it, I damn near strangled on it."

"Now you know how I feel when you're shoving that incredible thing of yours down my throat," Dan said lightly, then very seriously added, "but I love every inch of your cock, and every inch of you, Hal." They kissed again.

"Tonight everybody gets every inch of everybody wherever he wants it," Hal said, "except up my butt. Only tongues in my ass, but I sure hope no one forgets to give those to me."

"If we forget, I'm sure you'll remind us," I said.

"You won't need to remind me," Jim added.

"C'mon, let's give my baby his birthday present," Hal said. I turned my head and watched over my shoulder as he greased up Dan's cock and Jim's ass. It was easy to see clearly in the darkened room now. Hal's cock and my ass were already well prepared from the reaming he had been giving me. He patted my ass, and spoke to Dan. "Here it is for you, baby. Nobody's ass is as hot as yours, but I recommend this one highly. I just checked it out for you, and it's ready. Fuck it hard."

I might have minded being discussed as though I were a piece of meat, if it were not for the special circumstances; if I could be having sex with Dan Chrisman and Hal Weltmann at the same time, I wouldn't care about anything at all. I was especially looking forward to doing to Dan what he was getting ready to do to me.

Dan took my waist in his hands, and Hal guided the tip of his prick to my opening, and said "I got him warmed up for you baby—go for it." Dan plunged himself completely into me with one hard thrust; I suspect Hal may have shoved him. Whoever did it, it felt wonderful. Jim, kneeling next to me gasped and cried out as, apparently, Hal drove his fat monster into his ass with a similar thrust.

Dan held me close and began to give me a glorious fuck, gasping and groaning with passion and telling me how much he loved it. If his cock wasn't an ass-reamer like Hal's or Jim's, it was extremely satisfying, and he wielded it like the virtuoso *fuckmaster* I discovered him to be that night. He plunged into me furiously, sometimes fast and sometimes slow and gloriously deliberate, slapping his pubes against my ass loudly, but he alternated that with sweet, slow, profound thrusts, accompanied by gentle kissing and sucking on the back of my neck. At one point he was kissing my ear as he rested for a moment—his cock planted deep inside me—and he whispered very softly, "God, John—you feel so *fine*." With his stomach pressed against my back, he began again to fuck me slowly and deeply, with long strokes. I could imagine what a thrilling sight his beautiful ass would be as he did that. I wished Jim could see, but knew that was not possible at the moment, since Hal had led him to the other bed after fucking him side-by-side with Dan and me for about ten minutes, and it was clear from their very vocal lovemaking they were preoccupied with their own activity. I could clearly see Jim lying on his back just then, with Hal kneeling between his upraised legs and kissing him while he pounded his ass as only he could do.

I turned my head and whispered to Dan, "You recognized me?"

Dan kissed me on the lips, then spoke into my ear again, "Yeah, I recognized both of you guys when my eyes got adjusted after you came in. Do you know who I am?" I shook my head in assent, and he whispered, "I thought so. Are you hot for me? Do you like my prick in your ass? Have you wanted to fuck me for a long time? Will you fill my ass with come like Hal does?" I had eagerly whispered yes to each of his questions, as Dan grunted in pleasure and fucked me gently. Then he reared up and returned to his exciting, savage mode.

Hal and Jim stopped their noisy fucking, and Hal said it was time to switch partners. Dan had not yet shot his load into me, since his wonderful technique had allowed him to prolong his lovemaking. I turned my head so Dan and I could share kisses as Jim returned to kneel beside me, with our toes hanging off the side of he bed, and our bodies lightly touching. No further lubricant was needed as Dan pulled his prick from me, took a step to the right, and drove himself into Jim's ass, saying "Here's what you're gonna do to me with that big fat prick of yours after a while."

Hal leaned over me and pressed his chest to my back. He kissed my ear, his huge dick pressing between my legs, and chuckled, "My baby's a pretty hot fucker, huh?" I groaned my agreement, and he added, "You ready for this big ol' thing of mine up your sweet ass again?" He didn't wait for the reply he knew he would get, but stood up, took my waist in his hands, and slowly, but inexorably, slid his incomparable monster in me all the seemingly endless way to the hilt.

Hal and Dan kissed each other a lot as they stood side-by-side behind Jim and me, plowing our asses and muttering things to each other like, "Oh God, baby, this is great, isn't it?" Jim and I, kneeling side-by-side while the two astonishingly beautiful lovers fucked us, also shared kisses and expressed similar sentiments.

Hal's fucking had become ferocious when he pulled out of me and gasped, "Roll on your back, I'm going to shoot my load on you." I barely had time to get in position before I saw and felt his prick discharging its hot contents all over me as he screamed, "Aaaaahhhh." I held my mouth open wide, hoping to catch at least some of the divine offering Hal was providing. Mercifully, one jet landed on my lips and tongue; it was as hot and delicious as I could possibly have wanted.

Dan cried, "Oh Jesus, Hal, what a big load," and began grunting as he hammered into Jim's ass with brutal strokes. "I'm about to get mine, too."

Hal's cock was still huge, and he was still stroking it as he groaned, "Pull out, baby, and let me see you blow your load on top of mine."

Dan looked like nothing less than a god as he withdrew from Jim, threw his head back and masturbated furiously. Hal stepped to the side and Dan took his place as his cock began to shoot on my chest and stomach, adding his own love-offering to Hal's in six or eight generous spurts. I held my mouth open again, and the thoughtful Adonis blowing his load on me leaned over and directed one of his last copious blasts directly into my mouth—nectar, granted me by a god.

Dan leaned down and kissed my come-covered lips, as he took my cock away from my own stroking hand and said, "Let me finish you off; I want you to come for me now."

I heard Jim cry, "I'm about to get my load, too...." and I knew my own orgasm was nearing.

Hal said, "Get over here and shoot it on top of ours." Jim quickly stood, and Dan pulled back, still stroking me. Almost immediately Jim's big prick was blasting its contents on me, and on Dan's busy hand.

Dan cried, "What a great dick." and leaned over to suck Jim's prick long before it had apparently stopped discharging.

Dan continued to suck Jim, still jacking me off, and Jim humped into his mouth until I gasped, "I'm coming." Dan's golden head immediately left Jim's cock, and plunged over me in time to catch every drop of my load in his mouth. I watched Hal position himself behind the stooping Dan, and, judging by the moan of delight Dan murmured around my cock, shoved his stupendous endowment inside his lover's perfect ass.

"Jesus, what a stud," Jim said, and knelt behind Hal to eat his driving ass. I watched Hal fucking Dan, and reveled in the thrilling heat of my own come on my dick as Dan used his tongue to bathe it with in his mouth.

Dan finally removed his lips from my shaft, and leaned forward to kiss me. As he did so, he trickled a generous portion of my come—and, presumably, some of Jim's—into my mouth. I murmured my pleasure, and our tongues played in the viscous mouthful. Finally, Dan sucked the come back into his mouth, and swallowed it. He grinned down at me, "That was fantastic, but I've got the biggest dick in the world banging my ass—maybe I should pay some attention to it." He rose to his feet and said over his shoulder, "C'mon baby, fuck me hard."

Hal held Dan's waist in his hands, and fucked ferociously for a few more minutes, grunting, "God I love your ass, baby." Finally his arms went all the way around Dan, and he stopped humping and kissed his neck. "I've gotta rest a few minutes, though." Jim rose from behind Hal, where he had apparently been tongue-fucking him all this time.

Dan turned around, and put his arms around his lover. They kissed and embraced for a moment. When they broke, I said, "Will someone get me a towel? I'm covered in come."

Hal laughed. "Time for refreshments for the birthday boy, He already blew one candle out. Excuse me, I meant he blew one candle." He leaned over me, and used his hand to scrape the gobs of come on me into a single pool at my navel. With his finger he mixed the combined loads together, then licked his finger and smacked his lips, saying "Yeah, I think it's ready to serve, but you've got to let me serve it to you my way." He dipped three fingers into the thick liquid, and smeared it on Dan's cock. "Now feed it to your guest," he said, taking Jim's head in his hand and forcing it down to Dan's crotch. Jim sucked Dan's come-covered prick clean. Jim stood, and Hal applied more semen to Dan's shaft. "Now the other one," and I bent over to suck him clean again. Hal smeared more come on Dan's dick, and this time he, himself knelt to suck it off.

Hal stood, and took the rest of the pool of come and smeared it over his own dick—there was ample room to do so, of course. He licked his fingers and grinned at Dan. "Now blow the biggest candle of all."

Dan kissed him, and said, "God I love you." as he sank to his knees and began to suck. He took every inch of Hal's cock inside. Watching that much cock go into a mouth was astonishing—it didn't seem possible there would be room. I was proud of my ability to take it that way—and now, presumably, Jim's as well.

Dan stood, and he and Hal kissed. They moved to lie on the bed next to me, continuing to kiss, as Jim lay next to me on the other side, and put his arms around me; we shared kisses as well. The four of us spent a considerable bit of relatively quiet time that way, changing partners occasionally. It was difficult to tell who was the best romantic kisser, Hal, Dan, or Jim: they were all superb. But for frenzied, passionate, 'tongue-deep-down-your-throat' kind of kissing, Hal was by far the best of the three, certainly the best I had ever known up until that time, and—along with the two dedicatees of this book, and '90s porn star Brenden Knight—one of four best I have *ever* encountered.

Refreshed, we all pretty well stayed hard, and Hal masterminded us through a renewed round or two of passionate fucking and sucking. He had each of us, himself included, kneel one at a time before the other three as they all stood side-by-side to be serviced orally. He made sure Jim and Dan and I each fucked the other two, but in all these activities, he told us to avoid coming. Hal, of course, usually had his prick buried in the one of us not involved in a fuck at any given time, screwing all three of us as thoroughly, as deeply, and as magnificently as only one so wonderfully endowed can do.

Fucking Dan's ass was astonishingly thrilling and satisfying. Until I saw the perfection of the young Texan whose story is the crucial one in this book, it was quite simply the most beautiful, most utterly perfect thing I had ever seen. To actually be able to fuck it was an incomparable privilege, and I made sure I let Dan know how I felt while I screwed him. He was also unbelievably tight, but not so much so that it was painful to fuck him—which was something I have encountered several times when beginning to fuck a virgin ass, or fucking a straight boy who doesn't think he wants to get fucked, and resists until he realizes how eminently delightful *The Wonderful World of Buttfucking* really is. How Dan could have been so tight when he regularly took Hal's gargantuan shaft inside him was a total mystery.

Just before Hal directed that Jim take my place in Dan's ass, as we lay there and I fucked the blond Adonis in missionary position while we kissed passionately, Hal knelt behind me and drove his cock all the way inside me, and fucked me so hard he was driving my prick brutally into Dan—in effect, fucking his lover, but using me as an instrument to do so. It was the highlight of my life until then: my cock inside the most perfect ass I had ever seen, kissing the most beautiful boy I had ever seen, with the most breathtaking cock I had ever encountered slamming into me. I had not yet blown my load when Jim succeeded me in Dan's ass.

Jim hammered Dan's ass for a long time with his tremendous dick, eliciting almost continuous cries of ecstasy from Dan, and culminating in a scream from Jim as he emptied his load in the perfect blond boy. I had never seen him deliver a more inspired fuck, and I had been on the receiving end of an enormous number of truly memorable ones from him.

Hal then took Jim's place and screwed his lover like the consummate *fuckmaster* we all knew him to be, complimenting Jim on the hot liquid lubrication he had left inside Dan. The culmination of Hal's plowing came in a hugely vocal orgasm while he was planted deep inside Dan's adorable butt as the latter knelt on all fours to receive the final phase of the fuck. As he lay over Dan's body, Hal panted, "Okay John, Jim and I filled this baby's sweet ass with our hot come, now get in there and top 'im off." He pulled out, and relinquished the beautiful blond to my eager tool. As I entered I was unusually excited by the hot liquid enveloping my cock, and was moved to say, "Jesus Christ, you are so full of come. I couldn't imagine anything feeling better than when I fucked you before, but this is unbelievable."

I took pains to make my contribution to the love-offering inside Dan relatively slow in arriving—I was enjoying this enormously. As I was fucking Dan, I could see Jim and Hal cuddling and kissing, so I knew I wouldn't be overheard as I whispered into Dan's ear, "My God, Dan, I've been dying just to get a glimpse of you naked, and here I am with my cock inside your hot, perfect ass again, and fucking you in Hal's come—can you imagine how wonderful this is, or how perfect and beautiful I think you are?"

He turned his head to kiss me and whisper back, "You're sweet, John, and I love to feel you inside me—I can't wait to feel your come shooting inside me too."

Dan didn't have long to wait. With great force, I shot my load deep inside him. When I was completely finished, I withdrew, and Dan rolled on his back and began to masturbate wildly, saying "Who wants this?" I fell on top of him and took his cock into my mouth just in time to feel huge spurts of his load erupting into my throat. Dan held my head tightly as he shuddered with orgasm, then fell limp while I sucked him dry, bathing his cock in my mouthful of his come, as he had done for me earlier.

I kissed Dan, squirting a bit of his own come into his mouth, stood, and went over to Jim; I kissed Jim, and slipped some of Dan's come into his mouth. I next went to Hal and deposited even more of that precious offering in his mouth, and then swallowed what was left, as Hal and Jim grinned and followed suit.

As Dan lay there on his back, Hal knelt between his legs. Dan raised his legs and took his lover's enormous cock into him. Hal leaned over and kissed him very sweetly, and said, "Happy birthday, baby." Looking up at us, he said, "I'm gonna plug my baby's hole so he can keep what we all put in him inside—at least for a while. Let's call it a night."

"Thanks, guys, for giving me the best birthday present ever," Dan said, "and since Hal slipped up a little while ago, I might as well say thanks John and Jim."

I laughed, "Hal didn't even need to slip up about your name—you know, it's pretty light in here. But anyway, nobody's got an ass like yours, *Dan*. I think I'd recognize it in complete darkness, by feeling alone. Thanks both of you for letting us be a part of this. You're the luckiest two guys in history: both gorgeous, both sexy as possible, and a perfect match of the most amazing cock in the world and the prettiest ass in the world."

Jim echoed my sentiments, and we turned a light on so we could dress. Dan lay smiling in Hal's arms, impaled on his lover's matchless tool. He was unthinkably beautiful. Jim and I dressed and kissed both Dan and Hal goodbye before leaving them—both rolled on their sides, with Dan's legs up around Hal's waist, and Hal's ass humping slowly and sensually as he plunged himself lovingly and tenderly into his perfect lover.

Back in our room, Jim declared it had been the most exciting night of his life, and I had to agree. He said he had known almost right away that it was Dan in the room with us, and declared that Dan's ass was as perfect as Hal's cock—an opinion I quickly confirmed as my own. We were both too tired to fuck, but we spent the night lovingly cuddled in each other's arms, as Hal and Dan were presumably doing.

Hal and Dan: what an incredibly, perfectly beautiful couple they made. Given any encouragement, I could have fallen deeply, *head-over-heels* in love with either one of them—I was already *heels-over-head* in love with Hal.

Only three or four times after that, when Dan was out of town, Hal visited Jim and me again for a night-long threesome of wild and wonderful sex, although he and I, or he and Jim, shared impromptu quickies when the opportunity presented itself. Before the first of those night-long visits, I asked Hal if he would consider scheduling a repeat performance of our foursome with his lover, but he smiled and said, "That was a very special birthday present for Dan. I couldn't let him fuck my butt, but I'm glad he got to fuck my friends while I was there to watch. And it really got a lot *heavier* than I had planned for it to, but it was still great. But we're not gonna do it again.

"I guess you probably think I fuck around with other guys besides you two, and guess what? You're right—there are three or four others I meet with alone now and then. You know Shane Vaughan? He's one of 'em." Shane Vaughan was a star of the football team, not especially handsome, but built like the linebacker that he was—and as *macho* as they get. I was astonished. "You might wanna check Shane out," Hal went on. "He loves to get fucked, and has no trouble at all takin' me up his butt or down his throat. He's dyin' to fuck me, but no way. Even if I was to let someone fuck me, it wouldn't be Shane—his prick is almost exactly as long as mine, and even fatter. I can hardly stretch my mouth wide enough to get his dick inside it, and I sure as hell can't take all of it like I can Jim's, but I can take enough that he has a fine time, and he always blows me a mouthful big enough to choke a horse. Shit, he'd split me wide open if I let him fuck me. You and Jim could have a fine time ridin' ol' Shane's dick, though—and he'd love ridin' Jim's, especially.

"But you know, when Shane, or one of my other 'regulars,' or you and Jim and I get together we fuck and we suck—but that's all we're doing. Dan and I may *seem* to be doing the same thing, but we're actually *making love*, okay? I have to keep 'making love' special for Dan." Wise words, and sweet ones—from a uniquely beautiful and exciting man.

The memory of Dan's incomparable beauty still haunted me. He had been friendly each time we exchanged a few words in passing after his birthday party, but when I tried to talk about the experience we had shared, he changed the subject, and cut our conversation short. Finally I asked him, "*Please*, Dan, just talk to me for a few minutes about it—what can it hurt?" He decided it probably couldn't hurt, so we went to a fairly secluded booth at the Student Union, and talked over a cup of coffee.

Dan began by saying, "Look, I'll do absolutely *anything* Hal wants me to do. If he wants us to get together again with you, or Jim, or both of you, he'll tell me. I'd like it, sure—hell, I'd *love* it, I had a wonderful time with you guys. And I'd really love to fuck you again, and get that big thing of Jim's inside me again, but I'll only do it if it's what Hal wants. I love him, and I *belong* to him, so you'll have to ask him."

"Dan, it's just that . . . well, look, I'm only speaking for myself now, not Jim, and it's not just about sex. It's about something like . . . oh Jesus, it's hard to explain. Dan, there's something so very *special* about you. You're a really nice guy, and that's fine as far as it goes, but what makes you so special is your face and your body and—I hope you don't mind me putting it this way—your ass. I think you're the most completely beautiful person I have ever seen in my life. The way I feel about you, it's like you're physically perfect—I mean really, truly *perfect*—and I want to . . . *worship* you. Sex with you was amazing, and especially with Hal there—God, he's such an incredible man—but even if we can't ever do that again, I just desperately want to see you, and touch you—*all* of you—in private, where I can try to show how deeply I admire you. Dan, I can't stand the thought of never being able to really let you know how much I . . ."

"Look, John, the only reason I'm not blushing, or telling you to quit bullshitting me, is that I know you're serious. I could tell that night at the motel there was something different, something extra in the way you felt about me. The sex was absolutely great, and I know you loved it as much as I did, but I knew somehow that what you were feeling was something more than just sex when we were making love together, one-on-one. The way you kissed me and touched me—it was like you said, like you were worshipping me, too. I gotta tell you, I was more than just flattered—I also felt really *glad* thinking you felt that way, you know? I know Hal loves me, and I've been with other guys in the past who were in love with me , but Hal is . . . special—like you said you feel about me. Right now there's no one else for me but him. But I don't think anyone, not even Hal, has ever felt the way about me you're saying you do—or said anything about it, anyway."

"I can't understand why everybody doesn't feel that way about you, Dan," I said. "I think you're the most beautiful thing I've ever seen. Really. Your face, your body . . . God, you're just *perfect*."

"Jesus, John, that's pretty heavy! But it's also mighty ... mighty *moving*, I guess I should say. Look, you really want to spend an hour or two just . . . I feel really stupid saying this, but, *worshipping* me? No strings attached?"

"I'd give anything to, Dan. You tell me what I could do to convince you to let me do it—and only that, if that's all you'd feel right about."

He thought a few minutes, then looked up at me and smiled. "Okay, here's the deal. Figure out someplace where we can be absolutely alone for a couple of hours, and give me your schedule. I'll compare it with mine and Hal's, and I'll tell you when we can meet. This is only gonna happen once, understand?" I nodded my solemn agreement. "And no one—not Jim, not Hal, absolutely *no one*—is to know, before or after. And I won't suck your cock or fuck you, and I won't let you fuck me, 'cause I'd feel that was cheating on Hal. I don't know why I feel that way—shit, I know he fucks around behind my back. For example, he told me he used to fuck with you and Jim before he and I got together, but I know Jim didn't even start school here until a little while after that. But still, I know he loves me, and I can't cheat on him—I don't want to, I love him too much. I guess you could suck me off, or jack me off, and eat my ass if you wanted to. Listen to me—*if* you wanted to." He chuckled and briefly laid his hand on top of mine. "I know you want to, and I know how good you are at that. We can kiss and hold each other, and stroke each other without holding back. And you can see me and touch me all you want, like you said you wanted. In other words, I guess I'm saying you can *worship* me, and I don't even think I'll be embarrassed, because I can tell how sincere you are about that. And because of all that, I'm not gonna feel like I'm being untrue to Hal. What do you think?"

I agreed fully, of course, and didn't even harbor a secret hope that Dan would relent and fuck me or suck me off, or let me fuck him—well, not *much* of a hope, anyway, but I must admit I planned to bring a tube of lubricant just in case. I didn't quite follow his reasoning that I could suck him off, for instance, and he would still be faithful to Dan; he could fuck my mouth, but not my ass—was there really that much difference in the significance of the two? I certainly didn't argue with him, though—I was deeply grateful for what he was agreeing to. And I was genuinely moved by his feelings for Hal, and I admired and respected him for that. I gave him my schedule, and a week later, on a beautiful Tuesday morning in April we drove out to Arroyo Grande State Park, about ten miles from campus, and spread blankets on a smooth patch of sand in an extremely remote branch of the arroyo I had scouted out. There, under a brilliant blue sky, I worshipped the peerless blond god, Dan Chrisman.

When we had hiked back into the secluded place I had found, which would be shaded from the sun for another two hours, owing to the steepness of the arroyo walls that enclosed it, I arranged the blankets to provide an appropriate altar for my worship, I kicked off my shoes, and stripped completely while Dan took off his cowboy boots and socks. I had asked him to let me undress him.

I stood next to him, gently touching every angle and surface of his beautiful face as I studied it in admiration before putting my lips to his and sharing a very long, very gentle and chaste kiss. I stepped back, and slowly pulled his tight white tee shirt over his head. His body was nothing short of miraculous: broad shoulders, an expansive chest tapering to a narrow waist, and muscular arms. His breasts were wide and rounded, his nipples small and copper-colored. His flat stomach was hard, with abdominal muscles clearly defined. His navel was small, and very low on his body, almost hidden by the belt of his low-slung, but still very tight Levi's. Aside from his close-cropped blond mane, the only hair visible on his body was dark: his eyebrows, the thick, long eyelashes over his emerald-green eyes, the fairly sparse thatches in his armpits, and an inverted "v" that began at his navel, and disappeared into his Levi's.

I ran my hands lovingly over every surface of his upper body, and he gazed warmly at me and smiled as I did so, revealing very white teeth—obviously as perfect as the rest of his body—and displaying adorable dimples. I bent my head and kissed his nipples, then gently took one in the fingers of one hand and the other in my mouth, and sucked and fondled them, alternating sucking the two. His hands took my head, and he gently caressed it as he murmured, "Jesus, John, that feels so good." I raised up, and our arms went around each other, and we pressed our chests together and kissed for a long time, first gently and purely, then more boldly, our tongues exploring each other's mouth, but still not with anything like lust.

I sank to my knees and unbuttoned his Levi's. I was pleased to note, as I began to pull them down, that he wore no shorts. When I noted how exciting that was to me, he said, "Unless I'm dressed up, I'm always naked under my Levi's, or shorts, or whatever—it excites me to feel my cock rubbing against them."

I pulled his Levi's down, exposing the dark hair over his cock. As the waistband cleared the end of his cock, it sprang up and trembled at my lips, bobbing very gently in semi-erection. I looked in wonder at the perfection my limited view of it had masked in the darkened hotel room where I had first seen it: circumcised, light in color, with an only slightly darker head, which was considerably larger than the shaft—a 'mushroom' head. The shaft was perfectly smooth along its entire length, and as I gazed, and as Dan's hands gently moved to hold my head, his cock gradually stretched out and reached its full length without my ever touching it, about seven inches long and fairly fat. I pressed my lips to the head of this divine cock, and as I kissed it lovingly, I could feel it throbbing against my lips. I whispered, "That's the most beautiful prick I have ever seen in my life."

"Thank you, John," Dan said, simply. "Worship it in any way you want."

I opened my lips, and slowly, pressed them forward to grip the shaft lightly just below the head, and I lapped at it inside my mouth before pressing further to take all of his cock. His hands pulled my head in tightly, and my lips were buried in his pubic hair. Having learned to suck cock with Les's eight inches when we were in high school, having honed my art by swallowing all of Jim's eight-plus inches almost nightly all that year, and having recently mastered the challenge of deep-throating the ten-inch wonder of Hal Weltmann's behemoth, swallowing all of Dan's cock was relatively easy. Nonetheless, I thrilled to it as if it were the biggest cock I had ever sucked. Given my level of comfort in sucking it as deeply as possible, I was able to exercise subtleties of the art of cocksucking that an outsized monster like Hal's generally would not permit. Dan repeatedly voiced his approval and appreciation of my service as he fucked my mouth slowly, but profoundly.

I could not say how long I sucked Dan's cock initially; it was a long time, but our deliberate, tender approach to giving and receiving a blowjob would not precipitate an orgasm, nor did I—nor, I suspect, Dan—especially want Dan to shoot his load at that point. Plenty of time for that.

When I stopped sucking Dan's cock, to return to my exploration of his entire body, he leaned over and kissed me sweetly, without saying anything. I pulled his Levi's to the ground, and he stepped out of them and kicked them aside. I raised his cock and studied his balls: not large, drawn up against the base of his cock just then, and covered with a very fine fuzz of hair much lighter than that above his cock. I licked down the underside of his cock, and kissed and licked his scrotum, then took it inside my mouth to suck.

I sat back on my heels and looked up at Dan, who was smiling down at me. My voice trembled as I said, "Show me your ass, Dan." I continued to look up at his face as he smiled, folded his arms, and turned around. He looked upward at the sky, and my gaze drifted downward over his v-shaped back, and came to rest on the sheer embodiment of physical beauty and perfection: Dan Chrisman's ass. I actually gasped as I saw it: two smooth almost complete hemispheres of golden flesh, flanking a deep chasm that hid the entrance to heaven I had breached so unforgettably in that motel room. His buttocks were amply rounded, and the fact that the muscular, well-formed legs they surmounted were unusually long, added to the look of rotundity. Dan's face was absolutely sublime, his body was glorious, and his cock—although not as big as the one his lover regularly fed him—was divine. His ass . . . was quite simply the most overwhelmingly beautiful thing I had ever seen.

I don't know what I said to Dan, but I know I somehow tried to voice my complete awe as I looked at his ass. Dan reached behind himself, and ran his hands lightly and seductively over the soft golden velvet of his down-covered buttocks as he whispered, "Kiss it John, lick it . . . put your tongue inside it and fuck me that way."

I did as I was told, and as I would have done anyway, had he said nothing. After kissing and licking all over, I pressed my face between his cheeks. He leaned over and used his hands to spread them, revealing his beautiful pink pucker, which I penetrated with my tongue as deeply as I could. He moaned in ecstasy and wriggled his ass as my tongue danced and thrust deep inside the torrid chute, gripped tightly by the muscular ring guarding it. Hal Weltmann's immense cock regularly invaded this chamber and stretched this muscle—how could it still grip me as tightly as it did? I did not ask myself this question at the moment, I simply gave in to my complete joy as I ate out this Adonis' perfect ass.

Dan lay on the blanket, and I simply sat or stood next to him to study his perfection visually for a long time—with him lying on his back, and then on his stomach—before lying down with him, taking him in my arms, and beginning a session of kissing, embracing, and fondling that may have taken ten minutes, or may have taken an hour. I have no idea how long it took, I was in a state of complete rapture. Our kisses and fondling ranged from sweet and loving, to voraciously passionate, and our cocks stayed fully hard all the time. Dan finally whispered in my ear, "I'm gonna have to come soon. That doesn't mean we have to stop, but I've just gotta get my load for right now."

"Can I suck you off?"

"Yes, please. And share it with me, okay?"

I knelt between his legs and bent over him to take his prick in my mouth. He immediately began to hump upward into it, fucking me voraciously. I held his hips, and rolled us over, so that I lay on my back, and his groin was directly over my face as he continued his fierce mouth-fuck. My hands fondled his wildly thrashing ass, and just as I managed to get a finger inside his asshole, he fell over my face, burying his cock as deep inside me as it could go, while his hot come spurted violently, deep in my throat. When he had finished, he resumed fucking, but slowly and deliberately as he murmured, "God, I needed that." His asshole worked my finger, and he did not indicate I had overstepped the bounds of what he had allowed for this meeting by putting it there.

Remembering his injunction to share this load with him, I kept it in my mouth while his prick drove in and out of the mouthful of hot syrup he had given me. He pulled his cock out, and moved his body downward over mine, so that our lips were only inches apart. He smiled at me, and put his arms around me, pulling us to our sides, He pressed his lips to mine, and sealed our mouths together. I opened mine, and he thrust his tongue into the come I had saved for him. We passed it back and forth several times while our tongues intertwined, and while we sucked them. Finally, with all the load in my mouth, he pulled his head back and smiled warmly and lovingly. He put one finger on my nose and said, "That was wonderful. Now you can swallow it—I want you to have it."

I swallowed, and we again kissed and cuddled for a time, until Dan said, "Don't you hafta get off, too?" I assured him it was imperative that I do so very soon. "I'm sorry I can't suck you off or let you fuck me. I really want to, John, and I'm tempted to, but . . . well, you know how I feel."

"It's okay, I understood the rules when we came out here, and being able to make love with you the way we have been is so fucking wonderful, I don't really care."

We were lying on our sides, and my cock was pressing against his, which had wilted only somewhat after his discharge. He spread his legs, reached down, and put my cock between them. Closing his legs over my dick, he said, "No reason you can't fuck me this way if you want." I pressed his body to me and fucked his legs for all I was worth. He worked with me, gripping my cock with his legs, humping back, moaning his excitement, and encouraging me to get my load. It wasn't long before my orgasm was obviously imminent. Dan pulled away and rolled to his stomach. "Blow your load on my ass, and then lick it off, okay?" I quickly knelt between his legs, and placed the shaft of my cock between his buttocks, then fell over his back and fucked him that way until I knew I could hold off no longer. I raised to my knees and began to masturbate furiously, looking at the golden, glorious target he presented as he raised his ass high. He reached behind to spread his cheeks, and looked over his shoulder to watch me jack off. With a loud cry of rapture, I directed my copious load into the crevice that framed the entrance to heaven, which he had revealed when he spread his cheeks for me. Dan's cries were almost as loud as my own: "Yes, John—oh God, yes. Shoot your come on me."

When I had finished ejaculating, Dan let his body fall flat, closing his buttocks and trapping much of my come between them. His ass continued to writhe in excitement as he panted, "Suck it out, John—eat it outa my ass." I first licked up the come that had dripped down onto his balls, then dove between his cheeks, which pressed against both sides of my face. I sucked and pressed further inward until my mouth was buried up against his asshole, and was fairly well full of come. I tongue-fucked Dan for a few minutes, and then squirted part of my load into him. I pulled away, and rolled him to his back.

I lay over him, our lips touching. He pulled my head down to him, and opened his mouth, admitting my come into it. Again we passed a load between us, but this time it was he who swallowed. "And you managed to give me some inside my ass, didn't you?" he asked. I grinned and admitted I had. He didn't object, but only smiled sweetly and said, simply, "Thank you."

The shadow of the arroyo rim was leaving the blanket where we lay. It was about 11:00, so we moved the blanket to a smooth spot closer to the wall, where we would be shaded by a rock overhang—something I had considered when I selected this spot. We had another couple of hours before we would need to worry about Dan getting a sunburn that he would probably not be able to explain to Hal. I had brought a large Thermos of iced tea, which we shared as we took a break, propped up side by side, talking easily, brushing our hands and fingers lazily against each other, and often stopping to kiss. Our touching and kissing was sexy enough that we never really lost our hard-ons.

Dan finished his iced tea, and lay back on his stomach, resting his cheek on his arm, his eyes closed. His body was so beautiful, and the mounds of his ass so perfect, I began a very slow exploration of his entire dorsal side—kissing, licking, worshipping every square inch, leaving his ass for last. After pressing my face against the velvet of his buttocks, I kissed into the crevice between them, and he raised his ass slightly to allow my tongue to penetrate him easily. He had occasionally groaned in pleasure, or whispered my name as I had been kissing and licking; now he groaned in passion, "Oh John, that is so *good*. Put it as far inside as it'll go—I love it."

I tongue-fucked my god again, profoundly and reverently, while my hands played over his arms and shoulders, and especially over the seemingly cool golden velvet flesh of his ass cheeks. He began humping the blanket and rotating his ass while I ate, and presently he rolled over on his back, putting the sacred temple where I was worshiping out of reach. He raised his head to look down at me and smile. "If you keep that up, I'm gonna come again, and I want this to last longer." I raised my body and lay over him, kissing his lips as he whispered, "And I will come again for you—just don't make it happen too soon. Will you come again for me?" I promised him solemnly that I would.

We embraced and kissed tenderly for a while, Dan's hands exploring my back and ass while I held his head. I raised up and began to accord his ventral side the same kind of body-worship I had shown his dorsal, paying special attention to his swelling breasts and sensitive nipples. His smooth skin was completely flawless, front and back. I left the best for last again, and finished by kissing and licking his balls, and the very hard shaft lying on his stomach, pointing toward his chin. Opening my mouth wide to admit his mushroom head, I raised it with my lips, and then sank them down the shaft into his pubic hair. Dan's hands fondled my head as I licked and sucked the beautiful shaft in my mouth, and I drove my lips up and down it entire length, slowly and reverently at first, but gradually becoming more passionate. Dan again whispered his satisfaction, and as I sucked more lustfully, he began to fuck upwards into my mouth. and his hands held my head tightly to receive his thrusts.

He pulled my head off his cock, and said, "I'm gonna shoot again any minute if you keep that up. I wanna see you come again first. Kneel over me and come on my face."

I knelt with my knees in his armpits, and jacked off deliberately—I didn't want to rush this. Dan voiced encouragement, and frantically embraced my sides and my ass while I stroked. My cry of ecstasy as I ejaculated was accompanied by Dan's equally excited one of pleasure, His mouth was open wide as he cried out, and most of my first jet went into it. He kept his mouth open, and some more of my discharge went inside as I sprayed my semen all over his forehead, his cheeks and lips, and even his neck. He had shut his eyes when I began to shoot, and it was fortunate that he had, for a large rope of come crossed one eyelid. I guess he knew as well as I how much semen in one's eye can sting. When I had finished, and sat back on his chest, he scraped the come off his eyelid, and opened his eyes. He smiled and licked his lips, ingesting a considerable portion of my ejaculate. "That was so hot, John! I want to do that to you. I wanna blow my load in your mouth, but don't suck it out—I want us both to see while I'm shooting in you." He snickered, "and I'll be sure to miss your eyes."

I smiled down at his come-covered face. "Want me to lick you off?"

"No, clean me up with your fingers and smear it on my dick. Then you can suck it clean before I give you my load." He grinned, "Of course, you can suck it for a long time after it's clean, if you want. I'm in no hurry to feed you my load—I wanna make it last."

I cleaned his neck and face off with the sides of my fingers, and smeared my come on Dan's prick. I kissed him again before I opened my mouth to welcome his cock, now coated with my own semen. I don't know how everyone who has been given the opportunity feels about the taste of my come, but a lot of guys have told me they loved it, and it's always tasted great to me—especially when someone is feeding it to me from his mouth, or when I'm licking it from some gorgeous guy's skin where I've blown it. Sucking it from Dan's prick was especially wonderful, since I was also sucking *the* most gorgeous guy's prick at the same time.

Dan spread his legs, and I lay between them, my head over his cock, and sucked and licked his cock and balls with all the adoration I could muster. I spaced my efforts out so it was not until fifteen or twenty minutes later that Dan began fucking upward into my mouth urgently, saying a couple of minutes later, "I'm gonna come soon. Get on your back." I rolled to my back, and Dan straddled me, stroking his cock furiously. "Open your mouth, John—I want you to have it." I opened wide, and in a moment, the beautiful mushroom head inches above my lips began spurting thick white gobs directly into my hungry mouth. Aside from a little on my nose and chin, every bit of Dan's love-offering found its target. When he had finished, he shoved his still throbbing prick into me, and said, "Suck me some more, but don't swallow yet."

I sucked Dan's prick lovingly, as he lazily humped it into my mouth. Finally, he pulled it out and leaned over me so we could kiss and share the mouthful of treasure he had given me.

We lay clasped in each other's arms, kissing and caressing for some time before Dan said, "I really hate to say this, but I've gotta get back to town." He raised his head and looked very seriously into my eyes. "Thank you for this, John. You made me feel so . . . I dunno, so admired, and so *wanted*. I'm grateful to you for showing me. You're a very special guy yourself, you know. If it wasn't for Hal, I could . . . oh hell, why talk about it, I love Hal so much."

"But you're saying you *could* love me?"

"Oh yes, John. I could love you very much, but it's not possible while I'm with Hal, and I hope I'll be with him always. I know you'll find someone else to love the way you do me, someone who can return it—and you are in love with me, aren't you."

"Of course I am Dan, I know you know that. I don't just love you, I'm *in love* with you, but I've accepted that it's hopeless. I'm just so grateful to you for letting me show you that this afternoon."

We dressed and went back into town. It had been probably the four most deliriously *romantic* hours of my life, but it could lead nowhere. Still, I had that time with Dan to treasure all my life.

A couple weeks later, I ran into Dan, and he again told me how meaningful our session out at the park had been for him. He hinted that he would like to repeat it, if I was interested. I was, of course, and I spent another wonderful half-day worshipping my special god, in almost exactly the same way I had earlier.

Less than a week before he and Hal were due to graduate, Dan called me after supper, and asked if I was doing anything. I wasn't, and he asked me to meet him in front of the dormitory in fifteen minutes. He picked me up there in his car, and we drove out into the country, and hiked a half-mile or so from he road, to a grassy clearing, where we spread the blanket he had brought. The moon was intensely bright, and I could see his perfection clearly while we made love—but this time it was even more special than before.

"As far as I can see, this will be the last time we'll ever be together," Dan said as we lay together, kissing. "I want to make you fully happy at least once. Hal will never know, and I'll always know I was just expressing my gratitude for your love and admiration in the best way I can, not betraying the man I love. So tonight, for this one final time, we're really together, John. I'm all yours to do whatever you want with me, and I want to do what I really wanted to do those two times out in the Arroyo."

Our lovemaking that night was nothing short of *epic*, to my mind—not wild and unrestrained, but leisurely and gentle and completely *loving*. Only as we approached orgasm each time did lust take over momentarily—otherwise it was all romance and tenderness. Each of us fucked the other twice, always in missionary position, so we could kiss while we did so. We sucked each other singly, and in sixty-nine, and we ate each other's asses the same way. We lay together in the warm moonlight until almost one in the morning. I was as rapturously happy as I had ever been. And I never saw the perfect Adonis, Dan Chrisman, again.

When the college annual had come out a few weeks before my last lovemaking with Dan, I first turned, as I always did, to the pictures of those five young men whom the annual staff had selected as "Most Handsome Men on Campus" for 1954. For an unprecedented third year, the number one man was Hal Weltmann. I later kidded Hal about this accomplishment, and he winked and grinned as he told me, "The faculty adviser for the annual saw me wearing a whole lot less than I've got on in those pictures the first year it happened—in fact, the only thing I was wearing at the time was the biggest hard-on he said he'd ever seen. The last two years he's called me to come by his office so he could check out my qualifications again just before they made the selection for the year."

The number two "Most Handsome Man" that year turned out to be none other than Dan Chrisman, also a holdover from the previous year's list, where he had been number five. Hal said, "I told the adviser they should pick Dan for number one this year if they really wanted to pick the most handsome guy, but Dan wasn't about to put out for him," and he ginned widely as he added, "like number one did, so I guess number two was as high as he was gonna get."

The boy I first fell in love with on campus, the blond and almost-as-beautiful-as-Dan stud, Pierce Stonesifer, was the fourth "Most Handsome Man." Not surprisingly, Pierce was the third holdover from the previous year.

The most astonishing thing, however, was that I had also had sex once with the fifth man, Steve Counts. Of five men selected as 'most handsome' that year, I had fucked two of them, sucked off four, and had been sucked off and fucked by those same four.

Pierce fucked me many times, but would never let me fuck him, although cocksucking was high on his list of favorite activities we shared. Hal, of course, had resisted my urgent desire to plow his pretty ass as well. The luscious Steve I had encountered in the dormitory shower fairly late one night, vigorously stroking an ample hard-on, which was quite as attractive as the extraordinarily handsome man who was sporting it. He did not seem to be drunk when I had first observed him, unseen, but as soon as he became aware of my presence he began acting so, and stopped jacking off. I had already developed a hard-on of my own while I watched him, and when I started stroking my dick, he resumed his own masturbation. We talked for a few minutes about being really horny, and after watching each other beat our meat only a few minutes longer, he 'drunkenly' suggested it might be fun if we could "help each other out." We went to his room and helped each other a great deal, spending the remainder of the night sucking and fucking each other in every imaginable position. The classic *"Boy was I drunk last night, I don't remember a thing"* syndrome struck Steve the moment he woke up in my arms the next morning, causing him to overlook our intertwined naked bodies, an open jar of Vaseline next to his bed, and the still quite greasy condition of our cocks and asses.

Number three on the list was a boy whom I barely knew, but considering the enormous bulge his Levi's always displayed, to say nothing of his remarkable beauty, I had often wished to know him better. Perhaps the faculty adviser for the annual did.

The night before graduation, Hal called me and said he was coming by in a minute. When he arrived he said that Dan had actually sent him over to say goodbye to me and Jim. He told me, "Dan said he'd already said goodbye to you. What does that mean? Well, anyway I'm sure he meant I should give you both a goodbye fuck. I'm pretty sure he knows we've been carrying on, but he's not gonna say anything about it. Where's Jim? I've only got two hours."

Jim had already left for the summer, so for two hours I enjoyed the sheer ecstasy of Hal Weltmann's stunning dick and glorious lovemaking all by myself.

Hal and Dan both graduated at the same time that spring, and they left to find work and live together in Dallas, where, I was sure, Hal would soon be distributing his largesse—his very *large* largesse—as liberally as he had been for the previous four years. How long those two gorgeous men remained lovers, I have no idea, but it would be nice to think Hal is *still* sinking his magnificent shaft into Dan's adorable little butt today. Certainly the two remained lovers for over a year more, because my contact with Hal was (thank God.) not yet over, and he later apprised me of the status of their continuing relationship as lovers—paradoxically enough, sharing this information with me on occasions when he and I were sharing sex.

In the fall of 1954, with a new school year starting and a new roommate for Jim, who was still on campus, and a new home for me—living fifty miles away, with my mother on the premises—Jim's and my *regular* sex became basically a thing of the past. When time and occasion permitted, we shared each others' bodies and cocks and asses with the old abandon and delight, and our passionate lovemaking was that much sweeter for its greater rarity. Jim's new roommate was either straight—as Jim swore he was—or, if he was sharing his bed with Jim, had sworn him to secrecy concerning their sexual activities. Judging by the eagerness and *passion* Jim brought to our occasional meetings, I didn't believe he was "getting any" in the dormitory.

4.
SKINNY-DIPPING WITH TEMPTATION: BILLY

Unfortunately, my brain doesn't always rule my actions—an organ considerably to the south of that one too often directs me along other paths.

If Jim wasn't "getting any" from his new roommate, I knew him well enough to know that he'd be giving and getting cock somehow, somewhere, aside from the fucking he was guaranteed when we visited together.

The college was small, only about 1,700 students, the majority of them male, but he was still living there among more than a thousand college-age boys, horny guys in the full bloom of their first sexual maturity, ready and willing to fuck about anything if the circumstances were right—and away from home for the first time and finally able to indulge their sexual appetites with relative freedom. A good many of those boys were also now *relatively* free to explore those *forbidden urges* that had been troubling them. I felt sure Jim would continue to be a lead scout in exploring sexual territory for those latter types, when he found them. And with his boldness and his superior endowment, he'd continue bagging plenty of the first variety, the ones whose urges had not been of the forbidden sort—and probably convince a considerable number of those that there was plenty of enjoyment and satisfaction to be found in both giving and taking a cock in a hot mouth or up a hungry ass.

That pool of a thousand horny boys also promised anonymity for high school boys, ranch hands, cowboys, businessmen, hitchhikers, etc., who visited it to indulge their taste for cock. I knew that most of the gay, potentially gay, and even some of the straight boys and men who discovered what a very talented and *large* cock Jim had to offer would continue to return for more. It was a shame that his charitable works would be curtailed considerably because he apparently was now living with a straight boy, and would no longer be able to provide a ready place for his partners to go with him for sex at any time of the day or night, as he had when we roomed together.

For me, in my new situation, regular sex with my roommate and all those frequent short-time partners on campus was no longer a ready option. Unrequited love for Joe and the now-only-sporadic sex I enjoyed with his brother was not enough. I was used to a lot more, and I needed more—or, to be perfectly frank, I guess I really just desperately *wanted* more. Was it possible to find a new conquest in Antares, someone to regularly share my voracious appetite for sex?

The cultivation of satisfactory sexual liaisons in my new home town seemed highly unlikely for several reasons. For one thing, there was no army of horny guys looking around for dick, like those who visited my college to try and hook up with some of the thousand horny-young-studs-ready-for-action on campus, where they could probably find someone to screw with. Also, Antares was a terribly small community, and everyone seemed to know what everyone else was up to, and who was "doing what, and with which, and to whom" (to quote the old limerick). Finally, there seemed to be no local pool of attractive men or boys to tempt me anyway.

There was not one adult male in the town whom I found attractive, but that in itself was not surprising, since, with few exceptions—like Richard Cross—I had not since high school and the first year or two of college been attracted to men older than I. As for the high school boys in Antares, I could *almost* say I found none of them tempting, but there was one "possible" and one "definite" who caused vague (in the first case) and decided (in the latter) stirrings in my shorts. To be sure there were several good-looking and really well-built boys in the high school, and I would gladly have gone to bed with a number of them, but they were, to me, only attractive, not irresistibly *tempting*. Again, this was not surprising.

I had always found that boys or men who *really* appealed to me sexually were relatively rare. I was no prize, I know—probably something like average in looks, stature, dick size, and all the things that really count in the gay world—so I can offer no excuse for my unwarranted selectivity, nor can I explain it. Many years later, when advancing age forced me to settle regularly for sex with guys who might not have been my first choice, I discovered they were often—if not usually—better in bed than the 'dreamboats' I favored.

As I have observed earlier, the area most fraught with danger to an appropriate student-teacher relationship is the possible involvement of sexual attraction. With luck, neither of the *only two* really tempting boys in town would have been in any of my classes; while that would not obviate any possible difficulties, at least it would not threaten my effectiveness as a teacher. As luck would have it, *both* the rather-tempting boy and the extremely-tempting one were sophomores, and therefore both in my Geometry class.

The less attractive of these two sophomore standouts was Joe Don Griffith, and I really find it hard to say why he was at first attractive to me. He was not, in fact, terribly handsome, nor was he unusually well-built. His body had yet to take its fully mature form, so his physique would no doubt develop further. Still, he had a reasonably well-muscled, trim body, and was of relatively diminutive stature (5'7" or so), although he could possibly gain another inch or two in height. He was crew-cutted (as were most boys in Antares High School in 1954), with dark hair and a fairly low hairline. His eyes were deep-set, his ears protruded somewhat, and his face was even a bit asymmetrical—features that really made him look interesting, rather than detracted from his appearance.

Part of what made Joe Don attractive was that there was an air of cockiness about him that was, to me, extremely engaging. He swaggered a bit as he walked, and his language and speech bespoke one who wants to be sure his masculinity is not at all in question. I suppose, basically, those characteristics are to be expected in almost any teen-aged boy seeking to *belong* in a rural environment, so there was more to it than that. He also exuded an air of eroticism. I couldn't at first explain how I sensed that, but I knew he *wore* his cockiness like a new suit, and simply *was* sexy. His sexiness was not long in manifesting itself clearly.

Whether Joe Don was "coming on" to me or not, I couldn't tell. He made it a point to approach my desk frequently, and invariably positioned himself so that the crotch of his always-tight Levi's rested on the edge of the desk-top, where it bulged appealing—and at the time I didn't know if he really intended to *display* his bulge that way, or not. Whether he noticed me eyeing that tempting bulge I didn't know, but I suspected he did. His voice was hoarse and his speech slow and sexy, and no matter what he said, he generally spoke as if he were somehow sharing a really filthy story that *he and I together* wouldn't want anyone to overhear for fear they might misunderstand our relationship. I couldn't say why, but to me he even made a question about Geometry seem like an erotic suggestion. He had something of a crooked smile, which he used a lot, and he always gazed fixedly in my eyes as we spoke. Although only reasonably attractive physically, his sexy voice, deep stare, and generally sexy manner, combined to make Joe Don tempting.

He was always "Joe Don," I might add—never just "Joe," certainly never "Joseph," although that was part of his full Christian name: Joseph Donald. The phenomenon of the compound male nickname seems to be endemic to the American Southwest: Bobby Ray, Sam Bob, Jim Pat, Joe Bob, Billy Jack, *Joe Don*. The feminine counterparts are found more generally in the deep South as well as the Southwest: Betty June, Jo Beth, Bobbie Jo, Peggy Sue, etc.

Outside of class, Joe Don also seemed to be *around* a lot, and even then it seemed he always managed to prop his bulging crotch up on something as we talked. I thought I was surely mistaken, but there always seemed to be just a suggestion of his *humping* the fence rail, or the car hood, or whatever he rested his crotch on; he even seemed to be doing it to my desk, in front of the entire class. He frequently draped an arm over my shoulder as he spoke sexily to me when we talked outside of class, rather like we were old buddies. I didn't object—frankly, I enjoyed the contact—and although he didn't say anything to specifically suggest it, I always felt he was about to ask me to go off somewhere and do something with me that we probably shouldn't do. *(Like fuck?)* He never became so familiar as to use my first name, but rather than calling me "Mr. Harrison," as the other students did, he always called me "Mr. H.," and the name was invariably accompanied by a suggestive smile—like we were really close friends *("Fuckbuddies" perhaps?)* keeping up the pretense of a student-teacher relationship.

Fortunately, I was able to restrain myself from making improper remarks or suggestions to Joe Don. He was my student, and he was only a sophomore. If I had been planning to spend another three or four years in Antares, and Joe Don had continued his *apparent* "come on," I suspect I would have begun to lay the groundwork for later possibilities. All things considered, however, I felt I could resist Joe Don's sexiness.

But Billy Polk . . . that was going to be an entirely different matter.

Billy wasn't just the most attractive boy in Antares High School, he would have caught the eye of anyone attracted to young men wherever he might have been found. He certainly caught mine.

In stature and build, Billy was almost a twin to Joe Don. He was maybe 5'8", perhaps an inch taller than Joe Don—but still below-average in height—and had the same body type: trim, with excellent natural musculature. In his basketball uniform, where his legs, shoulders, and arms could be clearly observed, the play of strong muscles beneath his smooth skin was—to me—almost unbearably erotic. His waist was very narrow, his chest quite broad for his basic body type, and his pretty ass would have stopped traffic. That *adorable* ass—the only way to describe it, really—was, as he was, small, but it was beautifully rounded, displaying the two perfect globes of the classic "bubble butt," and it struck me as so desirable that I longed to bury my hands, my face, my cock, my *anything* deep within the cleft that separated those two magnificent swelling buttocks.

Facially, his beauty perfectly complemented his fine young body. His dark blond hair was short and straight, and flopped carelessly on his forehead. He had wide-set, sparkling gray-green eyes, with wonderful crinkle lines that formed any time he smiled. Rather than the normal arched eyebrows, Billy's described an inverted, flattened "v," skewed to the outside, and were considerably darker than the hair on his head. His cheekbones were high, and subtle, but adorable dimples also appeared when he smiled. And that same smile displayed extremely white, even teeth when he flashed it—and he flashed it often. The total physical "package" Billy presented was breathtaking.

I had not been aware of Billy during the previous three years, when I had been commuting to Antares and teaching only part time—then, I had basically known only the band students. Now, finding him in my study hall/Geometry class, I observed him closely. The first day I was struck with his facial beauty and the sight of his sweet young ass, and he seemed to grow more attractive daily. By the end of the first few weeks of school, I was totally smitten with him, but not just with his beauty.

Billy evidenced a degree of the cockiness and swagger that Joe Don displayed, but that was only natural: he was on both the football team and the basketball team, as was Joe Don. Although the *majority* of male students at Antares High School played either football or basketball, or both, they were all idolized by their fellow students and the townspeople—especially during a winning season, of course—so if they *swaggered* a bit, it was to be expected. I found their swagger rather appealing, and if the swaggerer was as attractive as Billy Polk, it was downright *sexy*.

The swagger was only in Billy's walk, though. As I came to know him, I found him to be soft-spoken, extremely polite and respectful of authority, considerate, and generally *sweet*—but completely masculine and self-assured (read: "sexy".). He was unusually well-spoken, considering his background, seemed to be intelligent, had a slightly impish sense of humor—which I later found to be more than slight—and had a mature sense of *perspective*, considering his tender years. He was always well-groomed, and although he dressed in the standard Levi's-with-tee-shirt-and-cowboy-boots ensemble of the 1950's Texas, his clothes were always clean and fresh-looking. He did not wear the extremely tight Levi's a good many young men did in those days—and given the perfect rotundity of his cute little ass, I *cursed* that deviation—but they were never sloppy or drooping. His clothes accentuated his perfect body, but did not exaggerate it.

Beautiful, sweet, intelligent, sexy: Billy would have been a standout in any setting. At Antares he was a brilliant light shining in an otherwise ordinary environment. But his fellow students didn't seem to see in Billy what I saw. He was, of course, popular, but the girls weren't falling all over themselves to be near him, and he seemed to be only "one of the pack" with the male students. I could not understand why he wasn't *The Shining Star* of the school—I certainly viewed him as such, as the reader has no doubt by this time concluded.

Was there *anything* wrong with him in my estimation? Yes . . . oh, yes, indeed. The things wrong with him, however, were simply conditions, a catalogue of obstacles standing between me and Billy as a love object/sex partner (take your choice): Although there was only a six-year difference in our ages, that is a serious gulf when the younger is only a high-school sophomore—and at his age he would probably be considered 'off limits' for even those a few years younger than I was. He was also a student of mine, and professional ethics militated against any emotional or sexual involvement with him. Finally, his sexual orientation seemed to be completely heterosexual—a far cry from my own. Even had he been of legal age and not my student, I assumed I would stand no chance of sexual dalliance with this sexy, sweet, beautiful young man.

Intellectually, I knew I must not pursue Billy, that I should even go out of my way to avoid an unusual degree of contact with one who was both terribly attractive to me and terribly 'off limits' as well. That was what my *mind* told me to do. Unfortunately, my brain doesn't always rule my actions—an organ considerably to the south of that one too often directs me along other paths. And so, knowing full well it was unwise, I cultivated Billy's companionship and hoped some kind of friendship would develop. Was I subconsciously hoping that I would end up with him in my arms, in my bed, in my mouth, in my ass? Of course I was, and I fear there was even a considerable *conscious* component to my campaign.

Billy was a good Geometry student, but he did occasionally come to me with questions. Naturally I always took special pains to answer his questions thoroughly, and at length—and if my hand occasionally found its way to his back as he leaned over my desk, or if my hand rested on his arm as I explained something, where was the harm? It didn't seem to bother him—but it certainly bothered me each time I touched him. I frequently had to stay seated after a chat with him, until my erection subsided.

Finally, one afternoon just after the last period of the school day, he came into my room. "Mr. Harrison, I really am having trouble with this Geometry assignment," he said. "I spent the whole study hall working on it, but it's not making sense to me."

"Sit down, Billy, and let's see if we can't make sense of it together." My heart was beating just a bit faster than usual as he stood next to me in the deserted classroom—the first time I remember being completely alone with this beauty.

"That's just the thing—I've got to get to football practice. Is there some other time we can go over it?"

Heart now beating a bit faster still, I said, "Well, if you want, come by my house tonight. I'm not going anywhere, and we can take all the time you need."

"Gosh, Mr. Harrison, that'd be great. Is eight o'clock okay?"

I told him eight o'clock would be fine, told him where I lived, and that I'd see him then and there. Watching his incredibly pretty little ass as he left, my heart was beginning to *pound*.

My mother was, of course, home when Billy came by that night, but that presented no problem; she almost immediately went to her bedroom, where she spent most of her evenings, watching television, with the door closed. She could have left the door open, since I was certainly not planning to attempt a seduction there in the living room—certainly not that night, anyway.

Billy and I sat side-by-side on the sofa, and he spread his Geometry book and paperwork on the coffee table in front of us. I often innocently *(Hah.)* put an arm around his shoulders as I explained things, and if our legs were pressed rather firmly together as we sat there . . . well, that could have been his doing, couldn't it? *(It wasn't.)* After forty-five minutes or an hour, we seemed to be about finished, when the phone rang. After answering the phone, I returned and stood next to Billy, watching over his shoulder while he worked, and casually kneading the muscles of his neck as I examined what he was doing. I stood a bit behind him, so he couldn't see the swelling in my crotch.

"That looks fine, Billy, I think you've got it down."

"Thanks, Mr. Harrison, and thanks for rubbing my neck. That feels great—Coach Burdette worked us out pretty hard this afternoon."

I took his neck and shoulders in both hands now, and turned his body a bit so that he was facing entirely away from me as I massaged him vigorously. He groaned in contentment, and murmured, "Gosh, that feels *so* good."

I agreed, it felt very good indeed, and as I extended my massage to include his back and the sides of his upper torso as well, the swelling in my pants grew painfully hard. I told him, "Lie down there on the couch, I'll pound your back." He did as instructed, and I studied the perfect roundness of his delectable ass while I pummeled and kneaded him vigorously. He writhed with pleasure under my hands, and I would *swear* he even humped the sofa a bit as he did so, although that was probably wishful thinking on my part. Finally, I slapped his pretty butt and told him to get up. "You've got to get to school in the morning, I've got to get to school in the morning—get out of here." I rose, and held my teacher's-edition copy of the Geometry textbook in front of myself, hiding my very full erection behind it—like a high-school boy smuggling his hard-on down the hall.

Billy stood up and worked his neck with his hands while he rotated his shoulders and upper body sensually. "Wow, that felt good. I really do appreciate your helping me like this."

I put an arm around his shoulders as I led him to the door and said, "Billy, I'll help you any way I can. I think you're a very special guy." I tossed my book on the table next to the door—he was standing too close to see that my cock was straining for release—and put a hand on each shoulder as I inclined my head and looked into his eyes. "Just let me know what I can do for you . . . any time."

My hands were still holding his shoulders, and I was still studying his eyes when his one free hand came up and cupped the back of my neck as he looked seriously into my eyes, and said, "You're a really good guy, Mr. Harrison. Thanks again." And with that he was gone.

My mother did not hear Billy leave, nor did she see me go directly to the bathroom to masturbate—my senses drunk with the sight, the feel, and even the *smell* of this beautiful youngster as I discharged my load violently. Following orgasm, returning to sensual sobriety, I told myself *that* was as far as I was going to let my pursuit of Billy go.

Yeah, right.

The next morning, as I sat working at my desk before school began, Billy came into my room—smiling broadly, and looking glorious. He flexed his arms and shoulders and said, "Muscles feelin' great, got that Geometry down pat—both thanks to you. It's gonna be a terrific day." He walked over and squeezed my shoulder. "Thanks again—you're a pal." He turned and began to leave. *(Oh God, that cute ass!)* As he was leaving, I called out, "And good morning to you, Billy." He turned around, and his grin was huge as he winked at me and left the room. A little caress, a big grin, and a sexy wink from a beautiful young boy is always a nice way to start a day.

Aside from my normal day-to-day contact with Billy, in class or casually in the hall or the lunchroom, I did not really have a chance to interact with him for another week or two. Then one day I passed back a set of Geometry papers, and Billy's had been unusually bad—terrible, in fact, although his work was normally quite good. As I handed it to him, I said, "Stay after class for a minute, Billy, so we can talk about this." He rather sheepishly said, "Yes, sir," and when class was over, he waited until everyone else was gone before he came to my desk.

"It was really terrible, wasn't it?" he said.

"Billy, I know you can do this work better than that. What happened?"

"I've been busy, and I've got some problems, and . . . well, I just let it slip, and I really am sorry. I know I should do better work for you."

"What sort of problems, Billy? If there's anything I can do to help, let me know. Remember I told you I'd do anything I could for you."

"I don't want to bother you, you've already gone out of your way to help me. And besides, it's . . . oh, you don't want to know about that sort of thing."

"Billy, unless you think I'm sticking my nose in where it's not wanted, let me help you if there's any way I can. But if it's something you don't want to talk about, don't be afraid to tell me that."

He studied me for a few minutes before replying. "If you really *don't* mind, I would like to talk to you about it."

"Name the time—I want to help."

"I get out of football practice around five today; could we meet then?"

I told him I'd pick him up in front of the gym when he finished with practice, and he flashed an adorable smile as he thanked me again and hurried off to his next class.

I actually arrived at the gym a few minutes early, and Billy was already standing there, waiting for me. He got in the car, and I asked, "Where to?"

"Do you know where Rodman's Pond is?" I admitted I had no idea, so I followed Billy's instructions as we drove. He told me about the pond as we traveled fifteen or so miles out into the country. "It's really a stock-watering pond, where a creek is dammed up on Mr. Rodman's ranch. I work for him in the summer, so he doesn't mind if I use it. I come out here a lot, to swim, and sometimes even to study, but usually just when I need to think about things. There's never anyone out here, so you can be all alone."

"Sounds like a great place to talk. And you can go swimming out there? I didn't think there was any place to swim around Antares. Hey, it's warm enough, maybe we can even get a swim in this afternoon. Should we go back by my house and get bathing suits?"

Billy laughed. "You sure don't need a bathing suit at the pond. There won't be anyone out there, and I've seen a guy's pecker before. Shoot, I've got one myself, you know."

I began to get both nervous and excited. The idea of seeing Billy naked was very appealing to me, but I also knew I'd get a hard-on, and how would I explain that to him? "Maybe I'll just watch you swim. Besides, someone might come along."

He laughed again. "You can see a car coming out there ten minutes before it gets there." He was no doubt right; the incredible flatness of the landscape made the usual cloud of dust boiling up behind any car visible for many miles. "And if I'm going swimming, you're going swimming, okay?" And as he said that he put his hand on my right leg and left it there. That *really* made me nervous, but it felt great, too.

"Well, okay, but first we do what we're going out here to do: we talk about what's getting in the way of your work. Deal?"

"Deal," said Billy, and his hand squeezed my leg and patted the inside of my thigh before he let go. We chatted about nothing in particular, and eventually arrived at the pond, at the end of a one-lane dirt road, two or three miles long—truly in the middle of nowhere, and not a soul in sight, as promised.

The rectangular pond was maybe a quarter-acre in size, and was formed by a raised earthwork dam. The water was basically a dirty brown, and didn't look very appetizing, but it felt warm enough for at least a quick dip. A crude diving board had been rigged up at one end—basically an anchored two-by-twelve plank. I got an old blanket out of the trunk of my car and we spread it on the dirt next to the diving board. I smiled as I did so, remembering how unforgettably Dan and I had used this same blanket when we said goodbye—and thinking how wonderful it would be to share it the same way with the fledgling blond Adonis at my side. We flopped down, and I said, "Okay, what's the problem?"

Billy sprawled out on his back, put his hands beneath his head and grinned, "There isn't any problem—I just wanted to get a ride out here so I could go swimming."

"You'd better be kidding," I said, as I sat down next to him. He rolled to his side and propped himself up on an elbow, and his look turned serious.

"Sure I'm kidding. But you know what feels strange to me? I feel like I *can* kid around with you. Is it okay if I feel that way?"

I reached over and rumpled his hair. "Billy, of course you should feel that way; I *want* you to kid with me, just like I want to help you. I know you're a student and I'm your teacher, but I'd like to be your friend, too."

He put a hand on my leg again. "I don't know how, but I just knew we were going to be friends. I like you, Mr. Harrison—and, well it's funny, but I can tell you really like me, too. You do, don't you." The last wasn't stated as a question—he knew.

"I like you a whole lot, Billy." I turned my body a bit toward him, and rested a hand on his hip, hoping he would regard my touch as casual, and would be unaware that my heart was racing, and my hand trembling very slightly. "And I want to help you because you're a student of mine, but I especially want to help you because I'd like to think of you as a special friend. Look, I know I'm a lot older than you . . ."

His hand left my leg and he rested it on my arm as it extended toward his hip. "Hey, I *need* a friend I can talk to who's older than me, and I really feel I can talk to you and you'll listen. And besides, you're not *that* much older anyway." He reached up and rumpled *my* hair. "And I want you to kid with me, too." His hand moved to cup the back of my neck and he looked into my eyes for several seconds and said, "So we're really friends, right?"

I removed my hand from his hip, and reached over to cup his neck in return. I smiled at him, and said, "We're really friends, Billy." And I did want to be a friend to him, and I genuinely *liked* this young man—this *very* young man—but I also *wanted* him. I fought hard to keep from pulling his head in to mine, and kissing him.

I knew I was playing with fire. I knew I should back off and keep my distance. I knew I should discourage his completely trusting offer of close friendship. But as I looked into that beautiful and (yes, even at his young age) *sexy* face, I felt the electricity that our hands resting on each other's bodies engendered. And I also felt the pressure of my throbbing erection in my pants, I knew I was hooked. I released his neck, sat back, and asked, "Okay, now, what's the problem?"

He again lay on his back as he began to tell me about the things that were troubling him. He lived with his mother—his father had left when he was an infant—and she had to work very long hours to support herself and her only child. He wanted to work more than just the summer work and the few hours he put in on weekends helping Mr. Rodman so that he could be of more financial assistance to his mother. She insisted he devote his time to school, though, so he could go to college. He was worried about meeting her educational expectations for him—not sure he was a good enough student for higher education, and worried about the increased financial burden of college. Also, most of his friends seemed to be developing interests that bothered him: smoking, some drinking, minor vandalism and hell-raising, and a refusal to talk about anything much but sports or sex. More and more he felt he had little in common with those old friends, and seemed to want to be by himself, or to find friends with interests more in keeping with his own. "But how can I find friends like that in Antares? I already know everybody, and none of 'em are really what I'm looking for. I know that makes me sound stuck-up or something, but it's really the way I feel."

"That'll change when you get to college, Billy. But what about girls? Do you date a lot? Do you have a special girlfriend?" By this time I, too, had sprawled on my back, and with my hands under my head, was looking at the sky. He raised himself up and looked down at me.

"Girls are okay, I guess, but they just seem so silly to me, and there aren't any I know that I really want to date yet. I just don't think girls are my problem. Not yet, anyway."

I reached both arms around him and pulled him close to me, saying "You'll have plenty of time for girls to get to be a problem." And I began to wrestle with him, hoping to divert his mind from the question that had probably begun forming in his mind: *Is this guy queer, and is he going to try to kiss me?* If he had been thinking something along those lines, my diversionary tactic apparently worked, since he giggled, and we tussled on the blanket for a few minutes, until we both fell back laughing Then he sat up and said, "Okay, now a swim," and he began to take off his clothes. He pulled his tee shirt over his head, and took off his boots and stockings. He stood, and unbuttoned his Levi's and pushed them down to his feet, so that he stood in front of me in only his skimpy, dazzlingly white briefs.

His body was absolutely adorable—as beautiful as I had expected it to be—which meant very, very beautiful indeed. He had surprisingly broad shoulders for his trim frame, very nicely defined arm muscles, an unusually narrow waist, and his flat stomach boasted an incipient "washboard." His legs seemed longer when he was stripped, and they too displayed well-defined musculature—and the crotch of his shorts looked delicious, if not bulging quite as much as I had hoped it might.

I was astonished when he turned his back to me, began to wriggle his adorable little "bubble butt," and tantalized me by pulling the back of his shorts down to reveal his bare ass as he did so. He stopped gyrating, pulled his shorts back up, and looked back over his shoulder at me. He bared his perfect little golden ass again, but this time he leaned forward and crouched slightly, so that he actually *pointed* it at me when he started to wriggle it—all the time grinning back at me over his shoulder. I couldn't believe this was happening. I knew he was just 'horsing around,' but my cock was so hard I was ready to explode. With a big laugh, he turned around, and very casually dropped his shorts down to where they rested on his puddled Levi's, and stepped out of them. He stood with arms akimbo, and laughed, "So, you ready to get naked and get wet?"

This incredibly beautiful youth now stood before me in all his astonishingly sexy glory. I could not take my eyes off him, but I tried to seem casual. His large, almost hairless balls formed a cushion for a prick that was as beautiful as I could have dreamed—not especially large, but certainly ample, and long in proportion to its girth. It looked like a perfect pink velvet tube with a light-colored plum adorning its end. Not at all hard, but not completely soft either, it stood out a bit as it drooped downward—the whole surmounted by a small patch of sandy-colored pubic hair. Aside from that, and small thatches of hair under his arms, his body was hairless. He was a somewhat less mature version of the perfect Dan Chrisman—a Ganymede, an Adonis almost grown into an Apollo. It was all I could do to restrain myself.

He threw both hands high in the air and *intoned* in a deep voice, "I shall now demonstrate my world-famous swan dive." And he trotted over to the makeshift diving board, and stepped out to the end. "Observe." He pantomimed preparation for an elaborate dive, but ended by simply jumping high in the air, cupping his balls and prick, and performing a 'cannonball,' shouting with joy as he broke the water. He surfaced, laughing, and told me to get in the water.

"It's cold, isn't it?" I asked as I sat there. He got out, came over to me and began to drip all over me as he started to undo my shirt buttons. I stood and said, "Okay, I'm coming in." As I stood, I had to stoop to conceal my erection. I had my shirt, shoes, and socks off when Billy went back and jumped in the water again, giving me an opportunity to quickly get out of the rest of my clothes and hurry into the water to conceal my hard-on. The relatively cold water quickly shriveled the visible evidence of my interest in the boy splashing and cavorting nearby.

As I stood there in waist-deep water, Billy laughed and called out: "I saw that."

"Saw what?" I asked, knowing full well what he was talking about.

He floated on his back, exposing his prick and balls, and while he back-paddled idly with one hand, the other grasped his cock and he masturbated lazily. "There was something wrong with your peter, Mr. Harrison. It musta got bit by a wasp or something—it sure was swelled up." All the time he continued to masturbate, and his own prick was now fully hard—and *much* longer than I would have thought it would become. He had a fairly thin, but wonderfully long, and totally tantalizing, beautiful, desirable, *edible* young prick. He stopped stroking his cock, waved it around, and giggled, "Oh no. I must have got bit, too." I leaped for him, pulled him underwater, and we wrestled in the waist-deep water for a while.

We finally stopped, and wound up laughing as we stood together, arms around each other, prick-to-prick. Fortunately, given the water temperature, neither of us then still had an erection. I said, "Are we going to swim, or are we going to fuck around?" He pulled me close and ground his groin into me and whispered passionately, "Maybe we should fuck around."

I pulled him close, reached down and cupped the cheeks of his perfect little ass and ground my cock into him until it grew hard again, After a sexually charged minute during which I continued to press and grind against him, I felt his cock growing hard again as he continued to grind it against mine. I knew I was very close to stepping over a line that might prove dangerous, so I said, also in a passionate whisper, "Maybe we'd better swim." Billy reached down and cupped my ass in his hands and began to hump his hard prick against me—there was no question but what we were both distinctly hard now. He put his lips to my ear and whispered into it, "Maybe you're right."

Again, astonishment: He hugged me to him, and quickly planted a kiss on my lips—not a kiss of passion, by any stretch of the imagination, but not just a quick peck, either. He actually *kissed* me. With that he pushed himself away from me, and dove into the water.

We swam around for a while, then got out and lay together on the blanket. We had no towel, so it was necessary to "air dry" in the fading sunlight. Billy lay on his back, while I lay on my stomach, trying to conceal my raging erection. Nothing was said for a while, and finally Billy rolled onto his stomach and snickered, "That wasp sting still bothering you?" I rolled over and sat up and said, "I guess wasps don't bother you." Billy glanced at my obvious hard-on and began to hump the blanket we lay on, his gorgeous little ass writhing in both circular and up-and-down motions that *really* made my erection rage as I watched it. It was all I could do to refrain from stroking my dick. He said nothing as he studied me and continued to hump until he said, "Sometimes they sting me, too, I guess." And he rolled over, and his pretty cock was hard again. "See?"

It was all I could do to keep from bending over him and taking his beautiful long shaft in my mouth. Instead, I mustered all my strength, and reached over to his far side to roll him back on his stomach, and put temptation out of the way—but only partially out of the way, since I was now presented again with the golden mounds of his utterly delicious ass. I let my hand rest brazenly on one of his swelling buttocks as he looked over at me and began to fuck the spread again, saying, "Oh no. That wasp bite stings so bad." He giggled, and stopped humping, and I left my hand on his ass for a long time. He began to grind his ass again, this time slowly and sexily, obviously enjoying the feel of my hand on it. "You want to give me a massage again?"

"Billy, if we stay here five minutes more, we're going to get in trouble. We'd better get back into town."

He sat up and again cupped my neck with his hand. "I guess you're right—massage next time. Friends?" I leaned over and kissed his lips lightly as I replied, "Friends." and I pulled back and looked closely into his eyes for a moment before leaning over and kissing him again, a bit longer this time, and added, "The best of friends."

He smiled and gave me another quick kiss before he said, "Thanks." He stood up, and his incredibly pretty cock was still fairly hard—standing out long and thin as he began to gather his clothes. He was apparently devoid of self-consciousness about either his nudity or his erection; I was *very* conscious of both, of course.

I stood and faced away as I began to dress, so I could avoid the very strong urge to sink to my knees and yield to the temptation that this sweet young beauty was presenting: consciously? subconsciously? playfully? seriously?—I didn't know, and my heart was pounding in my chest. Billy dressed also, singing something like *"Gotta hide our big old wasp bites."* to some sort of tune as he snickered.

We said almost nothing on the way back to town, and Billy sat fairly close to me. He put his left hand on the inside of my right thigh, and left it there as I drove. I desperately wanted to grope him. I knew if he moved his hand up and cupped my hard cock I would have returned the gesture—and I had already come close enough to letting things get out of hand at the pond. So, I drove, and Billy innocently kept contact with me, and I felt wonderful. *Horny*—but wonderful.

About a block from his house, I pulled up in front of the Courthouse. (Antares is the county seat of Goodnight County—named after Panhandle cattle pioneer, Col. Charles Goodnight.) I turned, and looked seriously at him for a minute. "This afternoon has to be strictly between you and me, Billy. Promise me you won't tell anyone *anything* about it."

He returned my gaze just as seriously, and said, "I don't *want* anyone else to know about it; this afternoon was just for us." He gripped the inside of my thigh for just a second, and then released it as he slid away from me on the front seat. I dropped him off at his house, wondering how I could have let myself become so smitten with a teenage boy who was also my student.

That night my mind was a complete turmoil. Could Billy's brief kiss, his playful masturbating, the youthful caricature of blatant teasing all have been innocent? I really couldn't say. I knew there had been a *charged* sexual atmosphere between us. I knew it had been serious on my part—however inadvisable—but couldn't tell how much of it had been the result of coltishness and innocent flirtation on Billy's. It struck me as significant that he had sat very close to me while we drove out in the country, unobserved, but in town he had been careful to put the proper distance between us.

I could not erase from my mind the sight of his ravishingly beautiful young cock as it had briefly bobbed and danced before my adoring eyes that afternoon—long, hard, and unbearably tempting. The only thing I really *knew* was that I desperately wanted to be holding him in my bed that night, with that long, slender prick deep inside me, or my own raging cock buried in the heaven that lay between the twin, velvet mounds of his perfectly formed ass—and sharing the deep, passionate kind of kisses our quick ones had only suggested.

My confusion was not alleviated when I saw Billy the next day. He was as friendly as always, but not unusually so, and he seemed to act as though nothing meaningful had transpired between us the afternoon before. Perhaps it had only meant something in my mind?

I was grateful for what he had let me share with him out at Rodman's Pond, but also grateful to him for something else. He *could* have taken advantage of the intimacy of that afternoon's encounter in our teacher-student relationship, but I saw absolutely no sign of it. He performed well in class and on tests and quizzes, continued to treat me as a respected teacher, and unfortunately—actually, perhaps fortunately—said nothing that would indicate he expected us to repeat that provocative scene. I was in a confused limbo of mixed relief and disappointment, and experiencing, I must admit, a touch of hurt.

5

PLAYING WITH FIRE — SEXUAL PRECOCITY AT THE OL' SWIMMIN' HOLE

I knew two things were going to be very, very hard the following afternoon: (1) controlling my natural desire to make fully passionate love to this beautiful boy, and (2) my cock. ... I knew that if our affair went any further, I would find myself hopelessly in love with a high-school sophomore.

A couple of weeks went by without any special communication between Billy and me. I saw him regularly, of course, and he was as friendly as he always was, but no occasion seemed to throw us together. I was beginning to think that our afternoon swim was going to prove to be a one-shot affair. Then one especially warm Saturday morning, as I was washing my car in my driveway, Billy pulled up in his mother's pickup truck. I waved to him, he parked behind my car and got out. He was grinning as he came up to me and said, "If you've got a bathing suit or some shorts I can wear, I'll help you wash your car."

I put the sponge on the hood of my car and smiled at him. "I'm really glad you're here, and I will accept all the help I can get. Let's find you a bathing suit." We went into the house, and back to my bedroom.

Once inside, Billy himself closed the door, and as I rummaged through my dresser, he took off all his clothes. I turned to look at his totally nude, totally desirable young body; he held out his hands to me and said, "Look familiar?"

"It looks very familiar." I stepped up to him and put a hand on his shoulder. "And to save you asking, it looks great. It's also great to see you this way again." He grinned hugely, and I think I blushed. "I mean just you and me, alone together. I've missed being with you. Not that it's not good to see you naked, you're a great-looking guy—as if you didn't know."

He stepped up to me and put both hands on my waist. "I enjoyed our afternoon out at the pond a lot, Mr. Harrison, and I've wanted to be with you again, but I've really been busy. But I'm here now, and I don't have anything I need to do today." He turned around and pressed his beautiful bare ass against my crotch. "Do I get my massage now?" He leaned forward and gyrated his ass suggestively while he pressed it against me. Looking back over his shoulder he wiggled his eyebrows and said in a low, mock-sexy voice, "Or do we pick up where we left off?"

I put my hands on his waist and turned his body around, then moved them down to cup his adorable velvety buttocks and pull his body in to me. I replied in the same kind of voice he had just used, my lips no more than an inch from his, "If we pick up where we left off, my car will stay dirty. Put on the bathing suit." Washing my car was *not* the thing I most wanted to do at that moment, needless to say, but I controlled myself, and reluctantly relinquished my embrace.

He snickered and took the bathing suit. As he put it on, he said, "Okay, we wash your car. But we will not wash my pickup—and you know why?"

"Okay, I'll bite, tell me why."

"Because I want to drive out to the pond to go swimming, and it will just get all dusty. But there's something I need before I go out there—and you said you're my friend, and you've got to give it to me."

"Billy, I told you I'd do anything for you I could. What do you need?"

"I need a good friend to keep me company—and unless you've got something else you've gotta do, I really want you to go along. How about it?"

"I'd love to go with you, and I'll be sure you get that massage this time."

Billy put his hand down the waistband of the too-large bathing suit, and pushed it forward in the crotch, making an enormous bulge. His eyebrows rose, and he assumed a look of abject innocence as he said, "Do you suppose those wasps will still be out there?"

"They will be, *friend*, if you attract them like that."

He laughed and we headed outside.

Billy looked incredibly cute with the bathing suit hanging off his trim, sexy body, drooping so that it *almost* revealed his pubic hair in front, and the crack of his ass in the back. If his adorable little 'bubble butt' hadn't been quite so rounded, I think the bathing suit would never have stayed up. He put himself so fully into the job that he was pretty well soaked when we finished; I stayed relatively dry, but that was probably because I spent more time studying and admiring my beautiful helper than I did on the task at hand. Finished, we went back in the house. Billy grabbed his clothes and headed for the bathroom to dry off while I dressed. I told my mother we were going out in the country to swim, and we took off in his pickup.

We stopped and bought a couple of sandwiches and soft drinks on the way out to the pond, and had finished them before we arrived. We pulled up near the pond, where Billy jumped out, and fished a blanket out from behind the seat. "Observe. I am prepared." He quickly spread it out on the ground near the water, and began pulling off his clothes. When he was left in only his briefs, he stopped and told me, "Off with the clothes." I had been so fascinated watching him strip, that I hadn't even started to undress. He turned around, and as he had done here before, leaned forward and wriggled suggestively while he bared his cute ass, and said, "Or do I have to do my dance again to get you naked?"

I walked up behind him and pulled his shorts down to his ankles—placing my face within a few inches of his tempting young ass as I did so. I stood, put my hands around him and cupped his breasts. "Please, no dance, I'll get naked." Billy ran for the diving board and jumped in while I got out of my clothes, and again tried to hide my raging erection as I entered the water from the bank. The air was very warm that day, but the water was a lot colder than it had been a few weeks earlier. We both laughed about the temperature, and stayed in for only a few minutes.

We lay on the blanket and talked for quite a while. Billy and his naked body were so beautiful I could hardly take my eyes off him. I think he was aware of how frequently I studied him, but he said nothing about it, and did not seem embarrassed; I rather think he enjoyed seeing *my* enjoyment in looking at him. Except for the few minutes in the cold water, my erection had been constant since Billy had begun to remove his clothes, and I really couldn't hide it from him most of the time. So, I simply gave in and let him see it hard; he made no comment about it for a while.

Billy rolled on his stomach and said, "Okay, now I want that massage you promised me." I knelt next to him and began kneading his shoulders. He said, "No, get over me and do it right." I straddled his body and worked on his shoulders and back, pinching, punching, and massaging his muscles. He groaned in pleasure, while I almost groaned in frustration: my hard cock was resting on the beautiful cheeks of his rounded little ass, and I dared not put it between them, where I so wanted it to be. I directed my manipulation lower on his body and massaged his buttocks, then down his legs and calves. I tried to underplay my massage of his ass, as I knew I would lose control if I got too involved. I moved back up, and was again at his neck and shoulders, when he rolled over under me.

With his eyes closed, he murmured dreamily, "Do my shoulders and my chest that way." I was actually sitting on his cock as I did what he requested, but it was not hard, and I avoided any excess movement to stimulate him—although I desperately wanted to. I worked down to his waist, and he smiled and opened his eyes, "That feels so great. You really are good at this."

Than Billy raised his head and looked at my cock—which was standing straight out. "You know, you really do have a problem with that peter of yours, Mr. Harrison. Is it hard all the time?"

I leaned down and put my face right against his as I whispered, "Only when it's around you, Billy." He laughed and propped himself up on his elbows, and then obviously turned serious as he said, "You can do something about it if you want to—I don't mind."

My heart was pounding. "What do you think I should do about it?"

Billy's reply was not the one I *most* wanted to hear from this gorgeous, sexy youngster that I craved so much, but it was a lot better than nothing: "Jack it off."

"Billy, I don't think I should . . ."

"Oh, Mr. Harrison, we both jack off—why can't I watch you?" He pulled out from under me and knelt facing me. "Go ahead and jack off and let me see you shoot; I really think you've got a great peter, and I want to see you jack it off. I wish my peter was like yours."

"Billy, you've got a wonderful cock—really long. It's longer than mine; why would you want one like mine?"

"Because it's nice and fat." He put a hand on my chest, and said very seriously, "And because it's yours." He surely must have felt my heart pounding. "And do you really think my peter . . . "

"Your *cock* Billy—you're a grown-up now."

"Do you really think my . . . [a big grin here] my *cock* is wonderful?"

"Yes, Billy, I think everything about you is wonderful—you're a terrific guy. I wish I had *your* cock—I really do."

Another big grin lit up his face as he took hold of his cock and began to stroke it. As he did so, he turned serious. "You can have it any time you want."

My heart was threatening to burst with excitement, but I guess I was still exercising *some* control. I said, "You know that's not what I meant."

"No, but I meant what I said, Mr. Harrison. You're my special friend—I'd give you anything I could, and I'd do anything you wanted." His long prick was now fully hard, and his fist moved up and down the entire length of the shaft. "You said you'd do anything for me I wanted, and if you *really* want—"

"Billy, this is getting out of control . . ."

Billy reached out and took my cock in one hand, while his other continued to stroke his own. "Please, jack off your peter—your *cock* for me. I want to see it shoot."

I took over for him saying "Okay, but you'd better let me do it though."

He sat back on his haunches and stopped masturbating, and watched closely while I began to jack off. I was terribly excited looking at him studying my efforts. He divided his attention between my cock and my face, seemingly as interested in seeing my feelings while I jacked off as he was in my actual masturbation. Every time his eyes met mine, I stared into them for a moment, then pointedly looked down at his cock. When I did, he would resume stroking it for a while. Finally I told him, "Stop jacking off. Just watch me, because I want to see you do this, too."

Billy grinned, and raised to his knees to give me a quick kiss and said, "Great—I'll save it for you."

I was now grunting with passion, and my fist was stroking at a frantic pace. As I neared climax, I panted, "Where shall I shoot this, Billy?" He put his hands on my shoulders and pulled my body close to his, all the while looking down at my cock and my busy fist.

"Shoot it on me, Mr. Harrison." He was panting also. "Yeah, that's it—keep jackin' it off and shoot all over me. I want to see your big cock shoot a really big load of come."

I was about to explode, panting, "Oh Billy . . .Billy . . . this is for you. I'm going to come, I'm going to . . ." My cock discharged a massive load all over him, erupting in five or six spurts of considerable velocity. His hands tightened on my shoulders as my come splattered on his beautiful young chest, even his chin, and down onto his hard cock. "Oh Billy, take my come—take my hot come."

"Yeah, Mr. Harrison—give it to me. Shoot it all on me, I want it from you." As I finished discharging, and began to cease my violent panting, Billy put his arms around me and held me tight, saying passionately into my ear, "That was fantastic. It was really exciting to see your come shoot on me—and it felt great. Thanks for doing that for me.."

I released my prick and put my arms around Billy as I panted, "Thank you, Billy, you inspired me. It felt extra great because you wanted me to do it."

He released me and sat back, then began massaging my come into his neck and chest. "Let me show you how much you inspired *me*. Sit back and watch this." He put his hand on my chest, and scraped off some of my come that had ended up there during our embrace. He spread it over his prick, then scooped more of my come from his own chest, and further lubricated himself. He started to stroke, and panted, "Your come feels so good all over my peter." He was now masturbating frantically, and he gasped, "Yeah, I'm gonna come for you now. I wanna blow it all over you. You want me to?"

"Jesus yes, I want you to Billy—*cover* me with your load. I want that big, long prick of yours to shoot it all over me." I was fully hard, and was again jacking off wildly. "Come on, give it to me, Billy. I'll bet you're gonna give me a gallon."

"Oh, Mr. Harrison, take it, take my load—here's my come for you." Stroking frantically, he closed his eyes and raised his face to the sky in a look of absolute rapture, and a moment later I watched great spurts of white come shooting out of the end of his precious long cock—a *much* bigger load than mine had been, and mine had been plentiful. His come landed in my hair, on my face, my shoulders, my chest—it was complete ecstasy. He continued to stroke long after he had finished, but eventually began to pant and sag—still with his eyes closed in bliss.

Finally, he calmed down, opened his eyes, and smiled at me. "Was that a good load, Mr. Harrison? Did I give you what you wanted?"

"It was wonderful, Billy. You gave me exactly what I wanted—and you gave it to me all over."

He laughed and looked at the come in my hair and on my face. "I guess I *did* coat you with it, didn't I? He put his arms around me again—our chests were sticky with come—and he did his famous sexy whisper, "Do you want to try for a second coat?"

"You've got to be kidding—you *couldn't* have any left in you."

"I don't, but it wouldn't take long to build up another charge."

"Another time Billy—if you want."

"Another time, Mr. Harrison. *I want.*" He kissed me quickly on the lips, then pulled back and looked steadily at me for a minute; very slowly his lips approached mine again, and he gave me a long, very serious, very *tender* kiss. We held each other tightly and kissed for quite a long time. My lips opened, and I tried to put my tongue in Billy's mouth, but he wasn't ready for that yet. I certainly didn't mind—I was enjoying his sweet, romantic kiss as much as anything I could imagine.

We finally stopped kissing, and continued to hold each other tightly. He put his lips to my ear and said, "You don't need to tell me not to say anything about what happened today. This is just between us—Mr. Harrison and Billy Polk, very special friends."

I kissed him again, then whispered in his ear, "Very special indeed, Billy Polk."

He ground his body against mine. "It really feels good to rub my peter against you like this."

"Billy, that's no peter. When it gets as big as yours, and shoots like yours does, it's a cock—a prick, or a dick, maybe—but little boys have peters." I kissed him again. "With all this come you shot on me, it's pretty clear you're no little boy."

Billy moaned, and whispered urgently, "I've never felt this good before." He kissed me, this time passionately, and although he didn't open his mouth to admit my tongue, he opened it enough that our tongues did meet and dance together briefly at our lips.

I fondled and caressed his ass, and said, "You do feel mighty good, I know that." I had cupped his ass before that, but I had never before really felt it this way. He seemed to purr as he held me more tightly, and wriggled his ass very slightly under my hands—apparently enjoying it a great deal.

He broke the moment, finally. "Hey, we're going to get stuck together if we don't clean off. Everybody back in the pool." He jumped up, got in the pond, and stood there sponging off his chest.

I waded in after him, saying "I've got a lot more cleaning up to do than you." I stood there and made sure he saw me scoop a generous sample of his come off my shoulder, and lick it off my finger. "Mmm, tastes like my friend Billy."

He laughed, and said, "That's *disgusting,*" and jumped at me, pulling me under the water. I came up, and he giggled as he vigorously began to scrub at my hair. "Hey, there's some of Billy here, too."

We splashed around for a while. Finally, Billy came up and put his arms around me. I returned his embrace, and he said, very seriously, "We can't come out here and do this again."

My heart sank a bit, but it was to be expected: *I had gone too far.* I smiled ruefully, and said, "Okay, Billy, it's entirely up to you."

"You know why?"

"No, Billy, tell me why."

"*Because it's too darned cold.*" He laughed and pushed me backwards into the water as he ran out of it. I laughed, too, and followed him.

We flopped down on the blanket to dry, side-by-side on our backs. His hand found mine, and we held hands. We didn't talk for quite a while, just enjoyed being there together. Finally, Billy said, "We'll find someplace else, if you want to."

I propped myself up on an elbow and looked at him steadily; I gathered my courage, and put a hand on his soft cock—the first time I had actually touched it. I desperately wanted to fondle it, but I simply let my hand lie there. "There's no reason we can't come back here, is there? We just won't get wet."

He put his hand over mine where it lay on his cock, and left it there while he said he agreed with my reasoning. He pressed on my hand and said, "No one else has ever touched me here before, and I'm really glad you're the first one. You know, it took a long time before you touched my peter—I was afraid you didn't want to."

"Billy, I want to do a lot more than just touch it, but we've got to let this happen more slowly. Okay?"

"Sure, Mr. Harrison—we can take as much time as you want, but your hand feels so good on my peter, it's turning into a cock again."

And his cock *was* growing again—and I fought hard to avoid grasping it firmly and re-commencing our love-making. His hand still pressed mine to it as it lengthened and hardened under my touch. "One thing you can be sure of, Billy, is that wherever it might be, I want very much to meet with you again like this soon." I reluctantly withdrew my hand and gave him a quick kiss.

Billy put his hand on my cock—which was very hard, of course—and said, "Great. And as hard as you are, maybe you should give *me* a second coat."

He started to stroke my cock, and I got up, laughing. "We'd better let well enough alone for today. Let's get dressed." Definitely *not* what I wanted to say or do, but since I had relieved some of the pressure on my libido when I blew my load on this adorable boy, I was able to resist temptation a bit better than normally. We put on our clothes and drove back to town.

As we drove back, I told Billy he needed to stop calling me "Mr. Harrison" when we were by ourselves. "Don't you think after what we just did, that *Mr. Harrison* is a bit formal?"

Billy said, "I know your first name is John, but you're still my teacher, too. So *John* isn't right for my teacher, and *Mister Harrison* isn't right for my special friend. I don't know—I'll think of something."

"Okay, you do that. I don't want to have to start calling *you* "Mr. Polk."

He laughed and said, "You'll have a new name soon. And don't worry, I know that I'll still have to keep calling you 'Mr. Harrison' at school and in town."

I patted his inner thigh and said, "You're a helluva guy, Billy Polk."

"And you're a helluva guy, *Mister* Harrison."

That night, thinking about the afternoon with Billy, I was completely torn between rapture and guilt. The sight of his beauty, the sight of his long cock shooting its load on me, the taste of his come as I licked it from my finger, the feeling of his pretty cock as it grew hard in my hand, and especially the wonderful sweet kissing—all those things were unbelievably exciting and precious to me. I knew that if our affair went any further, I would find myself hopelessly in love with a high-school sophomore. I knew I was already *in lust* with him, and could not go to sleep that night until I had masturbated again, shooting my load with Billy's beauty in my mind and his name on my lips.

The next day was Sunday, and I heard nothing from Billy. I rather hoped he would come by or call, so that I could see if he was having second thoughts about our encounter of the previous day—it had, after all, been extremely passionate for an uninitiated teen-ager. Not hearing from him made me think that he might have regretted letting his emotions go as he had. I didn't dare call him at his home, of course.

As he entered my classroom the next morning, he was his usual friendly self, and was his normally alert self as the class progressed.

As he was leaving, he smiled and said "'Bye, Mr. Harrison."

I stopped him and said, "Let me talk to you for a minute, Billy," and went over to my desk and opened my grade book, so that if any of his classmates had observed my detaining him, they would assume I wanted to talk with him about a grade, or something to do with Geometry. He followed me to my desk. By this time the classroom was empty. I turned and looked seriously at him. "Billy, are you all right about Saturday?"

"Mr. Harrison, Saturday was the best day of my life. I really had *fun* with you." He looked steadily at me for a moment. "And I want to do it again just as soon as we can—if you still want to."

"I worry that things are happening too fast, Billy. I want to do it again as soon as we can, too. I just want to be sure you don't feel that I'm pushing you to do anything you don't *really* want to do."

"I felt I was pushing *you*. I know I enjoyed what we did, and I knew before we went out there that I wanted to do it with you." He turned, looked at the door to be sure we were alone, and said very quietly, but intensely, "When you jacked off on me, and let me jack off on you, it was really *fun* . . . but it felt like it really *meant* something, too. Do you know what I mean?"

"I know exactly what you mean, Billy—it meant just as much or more to me. I don't think we did anything wrong, or anything that we should feel guilty about, but I just want to be sure you feel the same way."

Billy grinned. "Believe me, the only thing wrong with what we did was that we had to stop too soon. I've got to run to class, Mr. Harrison, but we'll get together as soon as we can. Look, I told you that you could . . . well, that you could have my peter—my cock—any time you wanted, and I want yours again as soon as I can have it. In case you haven't noticed, mine is thinking about you." He looked down at his crotch, and his Levi's clearly showed a bulging erection. "And I'll bet your is doing the same thing mine is."

"Believe me, Billy, I'm in the same condition. Now get to class, and let me know when we can get together again, so we can do something about it, okay?"

A big smile *(those perfect teeth—that angelic face.).* "Soon, *Mister* Harrison?"

"Soon, *Mister* Polk—real soon." He grinned and headed out.

I knew I was becoming obsessed with this beautiful youngster, as I could have easily become over Dan a few months earlier, if Dan had offered me any encouragement. Given Billy's looks, his sweetness, and his sexiness, my interest in him was easy to understand, and I was beginning to think there might be something serious developing. I was not *actively* in love with anyone at the moment, and I was beginning to think Billy could easily be the next big love of my life, if circumstances permitted.

I knew I was still in love with Pierce and always would be, just as I would always be in love with Les, and with Joe—Jim's brother. Distance and other commitments had brought about a break-up of my affair with Les, and Pierce had decided he wanted no more of our relationship. Nothing overtly sexual had ever passed between Joe and me, but I still loved him also. His brother and I had fucked and sucked each other endlessly, of course, but my love for Joe was, unfortunately, unsullied by sexual contact.

Almost two years earlier, Joe had divined the collapse of my affair with Pierce, and had actually offered to let me have sex with *him* on a regular basis, to see if I could "get over" wanting to go to bed with guys: naive, to say the least, but still very sweet and thoughtful. I had at first declined Joe's magnanimous offer, too depressed about losing Pierce, and still too much in love with him to want anyone else yet, even though I found Joe attractive. Coming to really appreciate Joe's amazing offer, and knowing Joe had a big, beautiful, wondrously *fat* cock, helped me come to my senses and I began to consider what wonderful solace I could fine with Joe's fine, juicy monster inside me on a regular basis. By the time I had fallen in love with Joe, he had apparently come to regret his rash promise to give me all the sex I wanted—he was, I am positive, completely heterosexual—and he had decided we should just be friends, and so our love remained Platonic—dammit.

Over the years I had regularly fueled my masturbation fantasies with dreams of my love objects and sex partners. For the last couple of months, except for occasional visits with Jim—one of them a spectacularly satisfying threesome with him and Richard Cross at the same motel where he and I had celebrated Dan Chrisman's birthday so unforgettably—I had had *only* my masturbation fantasies to enjoy, whereas earlier they had merely been a *supplement* to my active sex life. I knew I needed to find another lover, or at least another regular sex partner. I had not had to rely solely on fantasy since about thirty seconds after I first caught sight of Les's enormous raging hard-on when we were both high-school sophomores—Billy's age.

Prior to my fascination with Billy, I had mentally conjured up the faces, the bodies, the cocks and the sexual prowess of my earlier lovers and occasional sex partners while I masturbated, remembering especially the intense and feverish lovemaking: my times in bed with Les, my first-love/best high-school friend, who was the first boy whose prick I sucked, and who was the first to suck me off, who also became the first to show me the delights of getting fucked—by a master with a master tool, who took my cherry with a cruelly large cock that sent me to heaven once I got over the shock; sex with Pierce, the incredibly beautiful blond who provided me with my first taste of come from someone I truly loved, and who often after that filled my ass or my mouth with his hot discharge; the ultimate thrill of Hal's gargantuan shaft slamming into me to deliver his priceless load, or watching in awe while he did the same thing to Dan's perfect ass; kneeling to service both Hal and Dan, and getting fucked at both ends simultaneously by the two Adonises; getting fucked savagely by two anonymous horny sailors as we traveled through three different states; the literally hundreds of times Jim had satisfied my hunger while I satisfied his; the many brief encounters of special excitement, like the insatiable young Marine Corps hitchhiker Jim and I had shared.

Paradoxically, in spite of the fact that I was relatively dependent only on memories for sexual stimulation now, my fantasies lately had grown increasingly of a milder, more romantic nature. I often dreamed of the tender days I had spent worshipping Dan in Arroyo Grande, and the unforgettably romantic night under the stars when he had given himself over completely to my reverent adoration. But especially I thought of an adorably cute high-school boy with a trim body and a nice, long cock, taking my exploding ejaculate all over his sweet body, and then giving me his in the same way—and then lying with me in loving and tender embrace.

I knew that the urgency of my love and lust for my former lovers and sex partners was fading—at least for the moment—replaced by growing depth of feeling for my adorable young Billy. Far *too young* Billy, of course, 'off limits' Billy—but beautiful, sweet, loving, tender, *sexy* Billy.

I didn't have to wait long to be with the new object of my obsession again. After class on Wednesday he lingered at his desk for a few moments, apparently so that he would be the last to leave. He came to my desk and said, "No football practice tomorrow afternoon. Want to go out for a swim and not get wet?"

"I'd love to. I hope we'll get a *little* wet, though."

Billy grinned and said, "I'll bet we do, at that. If you unreel your hose the way I want to unreel mine, I'll bet we get plenty wet—but I'll bet it won't be cold." *(A rural teenage master of the sexual* double-entendre, *no less.)*

"It'll be hot as hell, Billy. My *hose* is ready right now, but I guess it can wait until tomorrow."

"Mine's pretty much ready now, too. Would you like me to prove it to you by demonstrating the famous Joe Don Griffith *desk-fuck?*" Here he put his crotch—bulging with an obvious erection—on the edge of my desk, and began to hump. "You recognize this?" he snickered. "Looks to me like Joe Don likes to entertain you this way a lot." He snickered, "But don't get the idea he's picking on you specially—I've seen him do his desk-fuck in a lot of classes. Shoot, he came over to my table in the lunchroom the other day, and propped his dick up on the corner of it and fucked it while he asked me about an English test."

"I've certainly seen it, that's for sure. But you do it a whole lot better—I'd rather watch your version any day. And hey, I've never heard you say *fuck* before. I oughta wash your mouth out with soap."

He deadpanned, "You're my special friend, you can wash my mouth out with anything you want."

I thought, *Jesus. Is he making with the* double-entendres *again? Is he suggesting he wants to give me a blowjob, or is he just being sweet?* My *hose* was throbbing painfully by then. I smiled at him, nervously. "That still doesn't tell me when you started saying 'fuck.'"

"Since I started thinking about it a lot lately—since we first went swimming together. And I'm going to think about it tonight, looking forward to tomorrow afternoon."

"Billy, you make me feel so . . . I don't know, Billy, I want so much to . . ."

"Don't say it. So do I, and we'll really talk about it tomorrow. But think about it tonight after you go to bed, okay? I'll be thinking about the same thing at the same time." He grinned crookedly—a sweet, innocent youngster's version of a leer—and added, "And I'll bet we'll both be doing the same thing, too. Sweet dreams, Mr. Harrison," and he turned to go. Before he got through the door, he turned back, still grinning. "I mean . . . sweet dreams, Pete."

"Pete? I don't . . . What do you mean?"

He walked back to my desk and put both hands on it as he leaned over and assumed the adorable, sexy, deep voice that had announced his so-called diving exhibition out at Rodman's Pond: "Tomorrow, *The Great Billy* will explain all."

"I'll look forward to hearing it—and you *are* great, Billy."

He was still leaning on my desk as he said, quietly, and without any suggestion of kidding around, "So are you, and I really wish I could *kiss* you right this minute, but it'll have to wait—but I'll kiss you that much longer and harder then." A sly grin took over: "*Everything* will be longer and harder then."

"I can't wait, Billy."

"Neither can I . . . *Pete*. Gotta go." He turned and left, and I studied his ineffably sweet young ass as he left the room, and had to sit there for several minutes before my erection subsided enough that I could also leave.

Pete? Well, I guessed I'd find out the next day, and I *knew* tomorrow was going to be another incredible day with my sweet . . . what, lover? Hardly. Certainly not yet—but it was beginning to seem I *might*, indeed, have a new one soon. But, oh God, so young. But also so sweet, so attractive—so unbelievably sexy.

And here was the really strange thing: Billy seemed to be working harder at realizing the seduction than I was. Of course, even though I felt sure he was aware that we had to proceed very carefully, he still had far less to lose if word of our involvement became known. I had gone this far toward some kind of 'relationship' with trepidation, knowing that I must move slowly—if at all. Yet, he was so extraordinarily attractive that I was almost powerless to stop myself from getting very close to him, at the very least. But he seemed to anticipate every tentative move I made to reach that objective by taking a larger step closer to me. I knew he was an innocent—I could *not* be mistaken about that—but nonetheless he seemed clearly bent on our relationship becoming more and more intimate. The sexually *charged* atmosphere of our first meeting out at the pond had become an aura of barely controlled lust during our second one. What would happen there tomorrow? Would the "barely controlled lust" become out-and-out *sex*? I wanted it to, desperately, but I also knew that since we were playing with fire, we had to keep that fire under control.

I felt sure Billy wasn't really *teasing* me, that he was probably prepared for, and even anticipating, full-blown sex with me soon. I had to hold back, though, let him lead the way, and give him plenty of opportunity to back down if he found himself "in over his head." As much as I wanted him sexually, I did not want to hurt him or lose his respect and friendship—this was a very nice, very sweet young man. Of course, there was a very slim possibility that I was reading him wrong, that he was actually just kidding around with me. If that were the case, and if I came right out and went for full-blown sex with him—not just some sexual horseplay or mutual masturbation—he might react very badly, and I could find myself out of a job. Or worse. I doubted my character was strong enough that I would be able to exercise the enormous mental discipline needed to avoid turning "*if* I came right out and went for full-blow sex with him" into "*when* I came right out and went for full-blow sex with him," and I was worried.   I knew two things were going to be very, very hard the following afternoon: (1) controlling my natural desire to make fully passionate love to this beautiful boy, and (2) my cock.

By a very fortunate coincidence, my mother announced that afternoon that she was going up to Indiana to stay with my older sister in East Gary for several months. My sister was experiencing some difficulty in pregnancy and, although she was three months away from the expected delivery date, her doctor had advised bed rest. My mother planned to go up and assist her during that final time, and probably stay a few months or so after the baby was born—to be of further help, and to revel in the grandmotherhood she was probably beginning to suspect she would never know as a result of my actions. She planned to fly to Chicago early the next week.

The first thought that crossed my mind when I learned of her plans, of course, was that the house was going to be empty, and Billy could very well visit me there. My mother apparently never overheard any of the sometimes fairly noisy lovemaking I engaged in with Jim when he visited, as she had also not heard anything, or turned a deaf ear to, the many times Les and I had made boisterous love when I was in high school. Jim or Les sleeping in my bed was one thing—perfectly natural in my mother's eyes—but a high-school boy, a student of mine doing so would be quite another matter.

The planned meeting tomorrow would still be out at Rodman's Pond, but the next one might very well be in my bedroom. Would Billy be ready? Would I be ready to see if he was willing to allow us to *go all the way*, as I desperately wanted us to?

That night I hit on a plan that might ease us into an all-out sexual encounter, if one was going to develop—as I was pretty sure it was—and one which could serve a corollary purpose as well.

I wanted some pictures of Billy that could provide focus to my fantasies about him, pictures that would show his facial beauty as well as his stunningly attractive body—which I could look at and fantasize over as I masturbated. The only photographs I had of him were in the previous year's high school annual, the Antares *Starscape,* and while he looked absolutely adorable in them, they were decidedly not sexy, and he looked much younger: one year makes a lot of difference at that age. Furthermore, masturbating over pictures of a high school sophomore was crazy enough, but the boy in those pictures was a freshman. I could have taken regular snapshots, of course, but I wanted something *special*. What I *really* wanted was a set of pictures showing a totally nude Billy, with his adorable, long cock fully erect. I knew this was completely out of the question, however; I had no darkroom facilities, and no photo lab I had access to would process what I wanted, even if Billy would agree to pose.

I decided I could sneak a set of "artistic" nude pictures of my young Adonis past a commercial developer if I was very careful in taking them—and if Billy would pose for them, of course. I suspected Billy *would* agree to pose for me, but I was uncomfortable telling him why I really wanted the photos—even if he knew for sure I was queer and had the hots for him, both of which, I felt pretty sure he at least suspected. "*I want some naked pictures of you so I can look at them while I jack off, Billy.*" I didn't think he was ready to hear that any more than I wanted to say it to him just then.

I decided I would use a subterfuge, and explain it to him the next afternoon when I approached him with the idea. The gorgeous Billy Polk, naked and alone with me in my home and posing for sexy pictures. Who knows where that might lead? I knew where I hoped it would take us.

Thursday was a long day, as I eagerly awaited my time with Billy. Leaving class that morning, he told me he would meet me at the parking lot at the end of the school day, and we could leave from there. When I arrived there only a few minutes after 3:30 he was already standing beside my car— beautiful, *sexy*.

When I walked up to him, he smiled and said quietly, "Hi, Pete."

"Still Pete, huh? You *are* going to explain that, right?"

He grinned and nodded, saying, "I'll explain on the way. Ready to head out and see if we can get wet again?"

My turn to nod and smile. "Let's go—I'm *ready*."

As soon as we cleared the town limits, Billy slid over in the seat to sit close to me, and put his left hand on my crotch, openly groping it and massaging my immediately-hard cock through the material. "I've been really looking forward to doing this."

I put my right hand over his. "That feels so good, Billy. I've been looking forward to it too."

"You're really a lucky man, Mr. Harrison. Do you know why?"

"I know when your hand is holding me like that I'm very, very lucky, Billy, but why else?"

"Because you've got two cocks. You've got this one . . ." Here he squeezed my cock with his hand, and then he reached over with his right hand and moved my right hand to his own bulging crotch. His cock was obviously hard, and he pressed my hand into it. " . . . and this one belongs to you too."

"My God, Billy, that feels so wonderful, and . . . well, hell, *you're* wonderful. And you've certainly got two cocks, too—you know that, I think—the same ones that belong to me."

"I *knew* you were going to say your peter was mine. I just knew you would, and that's why I want to call you Pete—you're my very own special peter."

Billy used both of his hands to open the fly of his Levi's, and to take his hard cock out. "Put you hand around it, Pete—feel how much it wants to be with you." I took his beautiful prick in my grasp—it felt wonderfully exciting and *fine*—and his two hands encircled and pressed my own hand around it as he began to hump upward, fucking my fist. "I've gotta use the word *fuck* now Pete—I'm fucking your hand, like I really wanted to be doing when I was jacking off on you."

"Billy, slow down. That feels so damned good I'm liable to run off the road. Keep that big prick of yours hard and ready for me, but we have to wait until we get out to the pond."

"Okay, but I want my special peter ready for me, too." He began to unbutton my pants, and pulled my prick out. Grasping it in his hand, he kissed my ear and murmured, " . . . my own special *cock.*" He began to stroke my cock; I still held his, and he was still fucking my fist.

"Hey, we've got to slow down—we're going to be through before we even get there. Billy, I want this afternoon to be long and wonderful—just like this beautiful cock of yours is long and wonderful. We've got all the time we need to enjoy ourselves, and to share our cocks, and our *come*, and . . . and just see what happens, okay?" I reluctantly released his throbbing, driving prick. "We'd better put 'em away, until we get out to the pond. And besides, there are other cars and trucks out here once in a while; we don't want anyone to see."

I well remembered one time when I had been driving out in the country near school, with Pierce Stonesifer riding next to me, his pants pulled down, and me stroking his cock while his head lay in my lap and he sucked me off. I had been so preoccupied with the wonder of the moment, that I was taken by surprise when a pickup truck passed us on the left, and the man in the passenger seat looked down into my car, and saw what was going on. Amazingly, the man only smiled and winked at me, and I returned his salute in kind. I didn't tell Pierce what had happened until after I had blown my load in his throat, and he was ready for me to pull over for a while and give him a blowjob in return.

Billy kissed my ear and then my neck, released my cock, and moved away from me a bit, and began to restore his cock to his Levi's while I fumbled to stuff mine back out of sight. "Okay, I'll put it away for now. And you're right—it is gonna be a wonderful afternoon—and long, like you said, but like *your* cock. If I can be with you, and if we can share our cocks, it *has* to be a wonderful afternoon, Pete. My very own Peter." He took my hand in his and brought it to his lips and kissed it, then moved them both downward so they rested on the seat, and we continued to hold hands.

"God, Billy, you're so damned special. I shouldn't be doing this with you—you know that as well as I do—but I want to so much that I just can't help myself."

"I can't help it either. I want to be with you more than anything else in the world."

"We're together, Billy. We're very, very special friends, and we've got time to let *everything* happen between us that can happen. Do you know what I mean?"

"Sure I know what you mean, and I dream of doing *all* those things with you."

"We've just got to take it a little slower. I want you to be absolutely sure *you* want something to happen between us before we try it. Okay?"

"Okay . . . Pete." He chuckled, "It still seems a little funny to call you anything but Mr. Harrison, but I especially like calling you Pete now, since you know what it means."

By this time we had arrived at the pond. I parked the car, got out our blanket, and spread it on the ground. As I was doing so, Billy came up behind me and put his arms around me. I turned around and returned his embrace, and our lips met in a kiss that began tenderly, but soon became extremely passionate. When my tongue tentatively sought entrance into his mouth this time, he opened wide and took it inside, and drove his own into my mouth. Later that afternoon, Billy told me had never given anyone a 'deep-kiss'—girl or boy—but for a maiden effort, it was glorious, and we stood there for a full five minutes, all but eating each others' faces, until I whispered, "Let's get undressed."

Billy said, "Okay, but I hate to stop. I didn't know kissing could be so terrific—that was almost as exciting as feeling you shoot your come on me. Do you mind if I watch you undress? And will you undress *sexy* for me?"

"I was about to ask you the same thing. Let's just undress each other, and we'll do it as slow and sexy as you want." I stepped up to him and began to pull his tee-shirt out of his Levi's; he began to unbutton my shirt, and slipped it back over my shoulders and let it drop to the blanket. We kissed lightly and he pulled my tee shirt out of my pants. Once each of us had pulled the other's tee-shirt over his head, we embraced again, pressing our bare chests together. Billy whispered, please kiss me again, Pete."

We resumed our fevered kissing as I put a hand down the waistband at the back of Billy's Levi's and shorts, and fondled his ass. Both of his hands cupped my ass through my pants and he pulled our bodies even closer together, and began to grind his cloth-covered hard dick against mine. I returned his motion, and reveled in the feel of his adorable naked ass writhing under my hands while he humped. Nothing further was said as we caressed and kissed for a very long time.

Finally, Billy stepped back and knelt in front of me. I raised one leg at a time as he removed my shoes and socks. Then he unbuckled my belt and unzipped my pants, pulling them down around my ankles, and I stepped out of them. My cock was painfully hard inside my shorts, of course. Billy's hands reached up to cup it and massage it. "This feels *so* good." He pulled my shorts down, exposing my hard prick, which sprang out as soon as it was released. Billy studied it, and his hands went around me to fondle my ass. I was both hoping and afraid, in about equal parts, that he was going to take my dick in his mouth. I began humping my ass as he held it, and my cock bobbed and swayed in front of his face. "And this *looks* so good. My special peter looks so wonderful."

I took hold of his shoulders, and raised him to his feet, stepping out of my pants as I did so. "I want to see *my* wonderful big peter." I knelt and began to take off his boots, which took considerably more effort than taking my shoes off had cost him. With his boots and socks off, I unbuttoned his Levi's, and slowly pulled them down to his ankles. His very white Jockey briefs were bulging hugely, but rather than caressing his bulging basket, I turned his body around, so his adorable little behind filled my vision. I tugged on the elastic of his shorts, and pulled them down to rest atop his Levi's, exposing the twin globes of his incredibly desirable ass. I felt exactly the same reverent awe I had when I had begun to worship the holy perfection of Dan Chrisman's ass.

From behind him, I ran my hands over the sides of his legs, his torso and his firm, flat stomach, upward until I began caressing his chest and tweaking his nipples as I laid the side of my face up against the velvet smoothness of his gorgeous young buttocks. It felt so wonderful it was all I could do to refrain from spreading his cheeks and pressing my face between those divine mounds, and sinking my tongue into him. "My God, Billy, you have a beautiful ass. It feels so wonderful."

"How does this feel?" he said as he turned his body around, and his long, hard prick slapped up against the side of my face. I resisted my first, *predictable*, impulse, and moved my head backwards. I took the throbbing shaft in one hand and stroked it, while with my other I cupped his large, almost hairless balls.

He pulled me to my feet, and stepped out of his pants as we again spent a long time in kissing and caressing. We each played with the other's ass and our hard, bare pricks ground into each other as we kissed and humped, standing together out in the wide open prairie with nothing around us for miles, under a clear blue Texas sky—I felt as if I had gone to heaven.

I pressed him down to the blanket, on his back. I propped myself up over him, and continued to kiss him while I caressed his chest, his stomach, and his cock, while his hands fondled me. He murmured contentedly, often telling me how wonderful it felt. I told him to just lie still there for a minute, so he closed his eyes, and let his hands lie at his sides. I began to kiss and lick the unblemished, velvet skin of his shoulders and his chest, and continued moving down to tongue and kiss his stomach—worshipping this beautiful youth as I had that other sublime Adonis, Dan Chrisman, and on the very same blanket.

I bypassed the tempting prick as I kissed and sucked the entire length of his legs, and began working my way back up, on the inside of his legs. As my lips and tongue reached his balls, I stopped, and propped myself up again—my mouth only a few inches away from the beautiful tip of his throbbing hot prick, which I had taken in my hand, and was holding in an upright position. He raised his head, and he watched me study his cock, I gently took it in one hand and bestowed a very long series of tender kisses on the end of it. He lay perfectly still, although I could feel his body trembling.

I looked up at his face and said, "You're the most exciting and beautiful boy I've ever seen, Billy, and I want to take you in my mouth—as much as I've ever wanted anything." Still holding his rock-hard shaft in my hand, I moved my body up so that we were face-to-face, and his arms went around me. "But only when, *and if,* you tell me you want to take me that way, too. Okay? You don't need to decide right now; if you feel the slightest hesitation, you shouldn't decide right now. I can wait." I smiled down at him, "God knows you're worth waiting for. And if you decide that's not what you want, I'll understand, and I can deal with it. I may have been reading things wrong since we started seeing each other. Maybe you're not interested in . . . "

He placed his hand flat against my mouth to stop my words. "No. I'm interested, Pete. You *know* that. I want to be inside you, and soon—and I want to be . . . well, *all the way* inside you. I mean . . . do you want my cock inside you more than just in your mouth? You know what I mean."

His last statement was not a question. He knew I was aware of what he was talking about—and I wasn't really surprised that he was contemplating more sophisticated lovemaking than just a blowjob, although given his innocence, I would also not have been surprised had it never occurred to him. "Yes, I know what you mean, Billy, and yes, I want you *all the way* inside me."

"Just give me time, Pete, 'cause I've never done anything like this before—well, not really. I've jacked off with some of my buddies before, but that was kid stuff—but . . . " he laughed nervously. "Wow, you're right about this happening fast. And the thing is, I want you to be in my mouth and all the way inside me, too—I want us to really *share* what we do. And that's a big step, isn't it?"

"It's a very big step. Look, Billy, if we never do more than what we've already done today, it will be wonderful, and I'll always think I was the luckiest guy in the world for being able to hold you like this."

He hugged me close, and rolled me on my back. As his face hovered over mine, his lips barely touched my own as he said, "*We're* the luckiest guys in the world." He kissed me gently, then his mouth opened, and his tongue began to explore my mouth. Our tongues intertwined, and we spent a passionate period of the hottest kind of kissing—and although he was a novice kisser, he seemed to be a naturally talented *master* of the art. It was hard to believe a naive high-school boy could be so accomplished. He finally pulled away, and said, "If I don't jack off soon, I'm gonna bust."

"I'm needing to do the same thing, Billy. How do you want to do this?"

He stood, and pulled me to my feet. "Jack off all over me again—that was so exciting last time. Better yet, let me jack you off." He pressed himself to me, I enfolded his body in my arms, and with one hand he played with my ass, and with the other he began to stroke my cock. He sank to his knees in front of me, and masturbated me fiercely—the tip of my prick only inches away from his face. My hands cradled his head and I moaned with passion.

I had maintained an erection for so long, that my orgasm was actually quite a bit slower in coming than usual. Finally, almost delirious with excitement, I moaned, "Oh God, Billy, I'm getting ready to shoot. Fuck my cock with your fist. Billy, you're so hot—make me come on you."

"Pete, shoot your come all over my face. I want your jizz all over me again.."

I cried, "Billy—take it Billy." as I erupted, and I could not see where I was shooting—my eyes were closed with ecstasy, and Billy was directing my emission where he wanted it to go.

When I had finished, and was literally shaking with spent passion, I looked down to see my come all over Billy's hair, his forehead, his clenched eyes, and even on his lips. He was panting with excitement, and his mouth was wide open, but I could not see that any of my emission had gone into it—he had probably instinctively closed it tight when I began to discharge, as he obviously had his eyes. I was still clutching the hair on his head, as I had during my orgasm; I released it, and wiped the come from his eyelids. He opened his eyes and looked up at me with the look of an angel in rapture. His look also bespoke naivete and trust and *love*. It's difficult to imagine how a face covered with semen could suggest all those tender things, but that's what I saw.

I raised him to his feet, and said, "Billy, you're the most wonderful guy I've ever known," and I kissed him very tenderly. My come coated our lips, and as his mouth opened to me, we shared the taste of it on our tongues as well. But it didn't deter Billy, and we kissed and hugged tenderly for a long time.

Finally, we broke, and I told him, "I quess I got my come in your mouth. You said that was disgusting." He smiled at me and used a finger to remove some of it from his forehead. He put his finger in his mouth and sucked it clean. "Maybe it's not so bad after all."

I kissed him again, and sank to my knees. "Turn around and let me kiss your sweet little ass while I work on you." He did as directed, and even leaned forward a bit. I studied this fine example of anatomical perfection, running my hands lovingly over the rounded cheeks, and murmuring, "God, Billy, you are so beautiful—your ass is absolutely divine!"

Billy spoke over his shoulder: "My ass is yours, Pete, just like my cock is. Everything I have belongs to you."

I kissed and licked the fine, smooth cheeks of his perfect young ass while I reached around his body and masturbated him slowly. Finally he turned around and, again placing the tip of his outthrusting cock directly in front of my lips, said, "Do it hard—I want you to jack me off on your face."

It was his turn to hold his masturbator's head tightly as I frantically picked up the pace. Soon he was moaning in passion, and said, "Here it comes, Pete—take it." I grasped his prick tightly in both hands, and Billy fucked frantically into the tight sheath. Soon I could feel the come boiling up along the considerable length of his prick as I held it tightly with one hand while I quickly reached through his legs and played with his ass, putting it in between his wildly humping cheeks, and letting my fingertip press against his asshole. As Billy screamed "Aaaaaaahhh." and his asshole clenched the very tip of my finger, I was rewarded again with the gratifying sight of his perfect cock shooting copious streams of hot come, and I opened my mouth wide to direct as much of it inside as I could, but he was shooting so forcefully that a couple ropes of it also crossed my face and landed in my hair, and I even saw one jet shoot well past the top of my head. My first impulse, of course, had been to engulf his erupting cock with my mouth, and suck every drop from it, but I had resisted—and it had been especially rewarding to watch those thick white jets spurting from that beautiful prick.

I glanced up at his face, and saw that he had his head thrown back and his eyes squeezed shut. He milked his prick until the last small spurt of come dripped from it, and he panted in relief. Finally, he shook his cock, spattering my face with a few further drops of his ejaculate, then he opened his eyes, and smiled down at me. I looked up at him in adoration, and swallowed the generous load he had given me to drink, then licked off the drop of come still trembling on the end of his cock.

He raised me to my feet and held me in his arms. "You're so wonderful," he said, and he leaned forward and licked his come from my face, and then kissed me deeply. He knew as well as I that he had blasted six or eight large spurts onto me, and I doubt that he thought that many of them had shot over my head—as one actually had. With evidence of only two or so of his jets on my face, I suspect he knew where I had taken most of them, but he said nothing about it. The come on his tongue was still warm when he kissed me, and tasted perhaps even a bit better—if possible—than what he had blasted directly into my mouth, since I sucked it from his tongue. It was as sweet as anything I had ever tasted.

"Oh God, Billy, your come tastes so fine, your prick looks so great when you're coming, you feel so good in my arms, and your ass is perfect. I've never known anyone like you. Thank you so much for wanting to share yourself with me."

"I don't want to just share myself with you—I want to *give* myself to you, Pete. I said I *belong* to you—I mean it. Do anything you want with me."

"What I want is what *you* want, Billy. I guess this might sound a little strange to you, but . . . I love you. I love you very, very much. I've never known anyone who makes me so horny, but makes me feel so good, and so warm at the same time. I more than just love you, Billy—I'm actually *in love* with you." I hadn't planned to make that declaration—in fact, I hadn't completely realized I felt that way until just that moment. "I don't know how you want to handle that—or even if you *can* handle that—but it's honestly the way I feel, and I want you to know"

"I'm really glad you said that, because I've been afraid to say it to myself. I'm in love with you too, Pete. I want to be with you, I want to do everything with you, I want us to kiss and make love all the time—I want us to *fuck*, Pete. I want to be *inside* you, I want you to be inside me—and we're going to do that soon. We will. I *want* you, and I really, really *love* you. Lately, I think about you and what we do all the time. Every night I jack off thinking about us. Shoot, yesterday as soon as I left you I had to go to the boy's room and jack off, thinking about seeing you today." He grinned and said, "But I didn't jack off last night—I wanted to save it up for you. Could you tell?"

"I could tell you had a whole lot to give me, Billy, and it was fantastic."

"I hate wasting it when I jack off—I want to be giving it all to you. God, Pete, I love you so much."

"But I'm your teacher, and . . ."

"No, in school you're my teacher. When we're together, you're my special friend—you're my *lover*, I guess, and I'm . . ." Here he gave me a very tender kiss. ". . . I'm whatever you want me to be—anything I can give is for you to take, if you want it."

"I want you to be my lover, just like you are. I want to hold you, and to kiss you, and . . . yes, Billy, I want to fuck you and I want you to fuck me, too. I want your wonderful long prick all the way inside me. I want to do more than just see it shoot its load—I want to *feel* it shoot inside of me."

"It will . . . and soon, Pete. I know I *want* the same thing, but . . . I'm just not quite ready yet, I don't think."

"I understand, Billy. When you're ready, I'll be ready. Just let me know." I took his face in my hands and looked into his eyes. "And by the way, I beat off a lot thinking about *you*. When I remember how you look and how you feel, I get too excited to save it all to give to you." I pulled him down to the blanket, and we lay together for a long time, saying absolutely nothing—just kissing and embracing.

Our passion temporarily slaked, we talked about a lot of things—both trivial and important. Billy declared he was feeling more and more remote from his friends. "I don't seem to have anything much to talk about with them anymore, and lately I think about being with you all the time."

"Billy, we can't be together all of the time, you know that. I've got to work, and you've got your school work, and football, and everything else. Besides, we have to be really careful that nobody suspects what we mean to each other. You do realize, don't you, that if *anyone* found out about what we're doing, we'd both be in really big trouble? Me a lot more so than you."

"Sure, I know. And don't worry—nobody's ever going to know. But Pete, tell me . . . No, never mind."

"Go ahead, ask me anything you want."

"Well, look, I guess you've done this before with a lot of other guys . . . "

"I'm not going to lie to you, Billy. I have done this before, with other guys. But there haven't really been that many of them, and there's never been *anyone* I thought was as exciting and wonderful as you." This wasn't entirely true; actually, there'd been a large number of guys in the past, although not nearly as many as I had wanted. A few of them had actually meant an awful lot to me, and I *might* have found them as exciting and wonderful as I did Billy—who can equate such things? Certainly I had never known anyone so completely sweet and trusting as Billy, and combined with his beauty and his sexiness, he presented a very potent candidate for "Most Attractive Lover" status. The gist of what I said was true, though: I did think Billy was unbelievably exciting and wonderful—and I was in love with him, crazy as that seems, given his age. "And before you ask: no, I've never done anything like this with a girl. Look, I know . . I know what that makes me in your eyes, but it can't be helped. I've had sex with different guys, I've never fucked a woman, and I'm in love with a beautiful high-school-aged . . . man. I almost called you a 'boy,' but when you're in my arms, I know I'm holding a young man, not a boy. And when your hot load shoots all over my face, that could only be coming from a man—and the way it thrills me, it could only be coming from a man I love very much."

He pressed me to him and kissed me for a long time. "I've never been with anyone like this—a boy or a girl. Even when I jacked off with my friends we never really touched each other. Some of my friends made me a lot more excited when I jacked off with them than when I did with other ones, but even with the ones who made me extra horny, I didn't touch them. Sometimes some of the other boys would want to touch me while I jacked off, but I never let 'em—told 'em it was queer. Now I want to touch you and do so much more—I guess that makes me the same way you are, doesn't it?"

"I think it's way too early to tell, Billy. You may find a girl someday, and even soon, who you're really attracted to, or there may some day be another guy who . . . "

"No other guy, Pete, I promise you."

"Look, you love me, I love you, we want to be with each other—that's all that really counts right now. What it's *called* is for someone else to worry about. We'll just call it making love, okay?"

He nodded and laid his head on my shoulder. "Making love." And we lay there for another delicious, long, loving time.

Soon we were both hard once more, our caressing got more passionate, and we were grinding our hot cocks into each other again. Billy rolled me on my back and knelt over me—his hard prick standing straight out and looking gorgeous—and my prick nudged tantalizingly against the *sanctum sanctorum* of his cute little asshole. He said, "Can I jack off on you again?"

I smiled at him and held his prick as he began to fuck my fist. "Of course you can—I'm eager to have more of your come on me." I reached up and played with his nipples as he beat his beautiful long cock frantically. He backed up a little, and said, "Can I shoot my come on your cock?"

My hands went to his face. "Shoot your wonderful come anywhere you want, as long as it's on me, or in me—and remember, that's *your* prick, you don't need to ask." His eyes again closed in ecstasy, and his head went back as his come discharged all over my prick, my balls, and my stomach.

"God, I love you Pete. Take my load." As he relaxed, he fell on top of me and buried his tongue in my mouth—our two cocks pressed together, soaked in his delicious hot emission. After a few minutes, he straightened up and took my prick in his hand. "Your cock is so hard, and I want to beat it off while it's covered with my come." He began to masturbate me furiously.

"Billy—roll on your stomach, and let me shoot my load on your beautiful ass. I want to look at it while I shoot—it turns me on almost as much as this big hard prick."

He murmured, "Oh God, yes." and rolled on his stomach. His perfect, rounded ass was magnificent as I played with it, and stroked my cock even harder. Billy reached behind himself, and guided my free hand to the crack of his ass, and pressed it against his asshole. He began to move his ass from side to side, and up and down as I fondled it passionately "Cover my ass, Pete." I pulled my hand away from his asshole, exposing it to view, and shot my load all over it, and the beautiful cheeks that framed it. Billy continued to writhe, moaning in passion, "Oh Jesus, your come feels so hot." He reached behind, raised his ass in the air, and used his hand to rub my come over his cheeks, and with one finger he forced some of it into his asshole. "This feels so good—Pete, I want you to put all of your load in here the right way for me someday soon." Together we continued to rub his asshole and his cheeks until my come was all worked in. He rolled on his back and looked up at me very seriously. "I think I want it that way. Can we do it, Pete?

"We'll do it, Billy. I'm going to shoot my come so deep inside you, you'll feel like I'm exploding—but I don't want to push you. We'll do it when you're ready, and not until then. And I want that sweet long cock of yours shooting all the way inside me as soon as you're ready, too."

"I'll be ready for it someday soon, Pete—I will." He pulled me on top of him, and we kissed and caressed for another long while.

It was getting late, and we dressed—lingering for a lot more necking.

Starting back to town, I approached Billy with the plan I had in mind to take photographs of him. I told him I had a friend who was an artist who needed nude pictures of a young man to use as studies for paintings. I asked Billy if he would consider posing for them. I told him they would not be "dirty" pictures—that his prick and balls would not show in any of them, and that there was no way anyone in Antares would ever see them. He asked, "Will you be taking the pictures, or will there be someone else there?"

"There won't be anyone there but you and me. And there's some really good news too. My mother is going to be leaving early next week, and I'm going to be living alone for several months."

Billy grinned. "So we can take the pictures at your house, then, and have a really good time, too." He put his hand on my leg and moved very close. "A really good time."

"Great, Billy. We'll do it next week, after my mother leaves. But we'll get all the pictures taken before we start any kind of 'good time,' okay? That way we'll get them made; if we start having a good time too early, we'll get distracted."

"It's a deal. And you're going to make love to me in your bed, aren't you?"

"I am, and it's something I've wanted to do for a long time, Billy. I've shot my load so many times in that bed wishing you were with me—it's going to be fantastic to actually have you there with me when I come."

"Pete—stop the car."

Not knowing what was the matter, I pulled off the road suddenly, and stopped. "What's the matter?"

He put his arms around me and kissed me deeply. "There's nothing in the world the matter. I love you. I love you more every day—and I just had to kiss you one more time." I held him to me tightly, and returned his sweet, yet passionate kisses. I needed to say nothing; he knew how much I loved him.

6

MOVING IT INDOORS

*He walked into the living room, totally nude... Actually, he was
naked, I guess. 'Nude" means wearing no clothes; 'naked' means
you're unclothed, but doing something about it. This sweet, beautiful,
naked boy held out his hands to me and grinned seductively, "Look
good?" Watching him ride me, with his eyes closed and head thrown
passion of this high order in one so young.*

I took my mother to the airport several days later, and told Billy the
"coast was clear" for the photo shoot and our next meeting at my house.
He seemed as eager as I was for our next session, and we set Friday night
to get together, since it wasn't a 'school night,' and he would be allowed
to stay out until midnight, or even a bit later. Friday morning he attached
a note to the homework paper he turned in: "I am really looking forward
to posing for pictures—can't wait to see what *develops.*" I was pleased
to get his note, but not pleased that he had attached it to a school
paper—especially one that *could* get someone curious about what might
be going on between a teacher and a student.

After class he told me he would come over to my house around 7:00,
if that was all right. I told him I could hardly wait, and he replied that he
felt the same way. I chided him about the note, and he promised never
to do anything like that again, looking very serious and penitent. Then
his face lit up, and he grinned, "Big night, Pete." His ass looked so cute
as he left, I wanted to jump him right then and there.

A few minutes before seven, the doorbell rang, and I opened it for
Billy. Closing the door behind himself, he threw his arms around me and
favored me with a huge, deep kiss, which I returned with equal passion,
and we stood there for some time necking, fondling, and grinding our
hard cocks together. I pulled Billy's beautiful, rounded, and *writhing* ass
tight to me and held him still. "We've gotta get these pictures out of the
way first, and if your prick is as hard when we try to take them as it is
now, we're going to have trouble. Go on in the bedroom and strip, and
I'll pull the shades."

As I began closing all the drapes and curtains, Billy went to my
bedroom, saying, as he did so, "I'll pull the shades in there." When I was
finishing in the front part of the house, he walked into the living room,
totally nude, with his pretty, long prick standing straight out. Actually,
he was *naked*, I guess. 'Nude' means wearing no clothes; 'naked' means
you're unclothed, but doing something about it. This sweet, beautiful,
naked boy held out his hands to me and grinned seductively, "Look
good?"

Pointedly staring down at his hard cock as I walked up to him, I said,
"It looks good enough to *eat*, that's for sure."

He put his hands on my head and looked straight into my eyes, very
gravely, as he pulled me in for a kiss. "Are you gonna eat it for me, Pete?
I want you to, you know, if that's what you want."

"You know what I want. I just don't know how I'll hold off until we get these pictures taken."

"Do you want me to eat you?"

"I want you to do what will please you, Billy. You don't have to do something because I want you to do it."

"I'm *dying* to, Pete. I want you inside me." He hugged me tight, and whispered in my ear, "I want to *suck your cock.*" He pulled back and looked very sober again as he added, "I want it in me as much as I want to put mine in you."

I kissed him. "We'll do it Billy—we'll be inside each other and make love to each other soon. Right now we've got to calm down and get these pictures taken, okay?"

He pulled away and smiled, "Okay, but let's get it over with."

"I never thought I'd say I wanted to wait before we did something together until you lost your hard-on, but if that pretty cock of yours is sticking out like it is now, we won't be able to hide it in the pictures, and I won't get 'em back from the developer. Sit down, and we can keep our hands off each other and talk about something besides sex for a while." I laughed, "I doubt if I can see you sitting here naked, and not stay hard, but it doesn't matter how hard I am."

I went to the kitchen and opened Cokes for us. Billy sat on the couch while I sat on a chair near him—but not too close—and we talked about trivial things for a while. Finally, his beautiful cock was no longer hard, and we began to take pictures.

I spent about forty-five minutes photographing Billy, posing him in every way imaginable, showing his perfect body and ass to greatest advantage, and doing my best to capture the *angelic* quality of his face. I had him hold his legs or body in such a way that his balls, prick, and pubic hair never *quite* showed; in a number of pictures he held something in front of him to conceal his pubic area—something which *barely* concealed it. Most of the poses were extremely seductive, and many of the sexiest of those were suggested by Billy himself *("Does this look good?"*—accompanied by a very sly grin). Billy practically *seduced* the camera as we took pictures; he knew very well he was seducing me at the same time—as if that weren't a *fait accompli*. He looked especially appealing as he knelt facing away from the camera, looked back over his shoulder, and smiled—his ass as perfectly beautiful as his face.

Finally, I posed him leaning over a table, his legs spread wide, and his ass presented to me. I told him his balls were showing, to hold them up out of the way. He did so, and I took several pictures, from different angles. As I knelt directly behind him, taking a close-up of his ass, he stood up and turned around; his prick was incredibly long, and standing straight out—seeming longer than I had ever seen it—and it bobbed directly in front of my face. Billy moved his hips so that his cock swayed and dipped even more temptingly. "Either take a picture of this, or let's go in the bedroom and do something else with it."

"I'd need a *really* wide-angle lens to take a picture of that. Let me take just a couple more pictures with you hard." I shot a few pictures of Billy wearing his white Jockey briefs, his hard prick obscenely bulging inside, pointing to the left. Then I shot a final group of a half-dozen shots with his hard cock covered only by a very flimsy, white cloth dinner napkin, which, like the Jockey shorts, did more to *reveal* the glory it covered than it did to conceal it. In all those last shots, with the briefs and with the napkin, his long prick was so clearly outlined by the thin material it was easy to tell he was circumcised.

The final picture was the *piece de resistance*: one of him standing in profile, with his prick jutting straight out, and the napkin draped over the top of it, barely concealing his balls, and *not* covering his pubic hair. I felt sure I would never get *that* one back from the film processors, but if I did, I would have one of the most amazingly *sexy* pictures ever taken.

I put the camera down after I shot that last picture, and took Billy's hips in my hands, drawing him to me as I knelt. I whisked the napkin from his prick, so that the tip of it was only inches away from my eyes. "This is so beautiful, and *you* are so beautiful, and I want this more than I can tell you." I took his cock in my hands and kissed the head of it very slowly and gently.

Billy pulled me to my feet. "Oh God, Pete, I can't wait any more. Get out of your clothes. I want to see you this way."

We went to the bedroom, and as I began to strip off my clothes, Billy flopped onto the bed and watched me. Now naked, and with my prick as painfully hard as it had been for almost an hour, I approached him; I knelt at the side of the bed and looked into his eyes, putting my hand on his stomach. "I love you, Billy Polk."

He put his hand out and cupped my chin. "I love you, John Harrison. Lie down here beside me." I got on the bed and our arms went around each other. We began to caress gently and to kiss tenderly and sweetly. Gradually, we began to heat up, and our hands were feverishly exploring our bodies, our asses, our assholes, and each of our tongues was eagerly fucking the other's mouth.

I rolled Billy on his back, and began kissing and licking his chest and shoulders, and sucking each of his nipples as he moaned in passion. Working my way down to his belly, I buried my nose in his pubic hair as I kissed the base of his cock, and with one hand explored his ass The other hand took hold of his throbbing shaft, and I moved down and took his balls into my mouth and sucked them. Wonderful. I positioned my mouth over the tip of his prick, kissed it, and then looked up at him. "Put your beautiful cock all the way in me, Billy; make love to my mouth—I want to suck my beautiful lover's wonderful hard prick."

I opened my mouth, and very slowly took the entire length of Billy's cock deep into my mouth, while he groaned a long sigh of ecstasy, "Ooooooooonhh ... *Jesus*, Pete!" I buried my lips in his pubic hair, and sealed them over the base of his cock. His cock felt fatter than I had expected it would—its greater-than-normal ratio of length to girth made it appear long and thin to the eye, but to my mouth, it felt as fat, if not quite as long, as the last one I had sucked—Jim's. It tasted as delicious as any I had ever had in my mouth—even Dan's.

Billy held my head in his hands, and began to hump, driving his prick in and out of my mouth. With such a mouthful of cock, I couldn't speak, but Billy provided a litany of sexual fervor while he fucked my face: "Oh, Pete, take my dick. . . . your mouth feels so *good*. . . . nothing has ever felt like this . . . suck me hard . . . my prick is right where it belongs . .

. I love to fuck your hot mouth . . . love my cock the way I love you, Pete," and more and more of the same—each expression more wonderful to hear that the one before. And he humped and fucked my mouth frantically at times, but also took time to fuck very slowly and deeply as well. Finally he pulled my head away from his prick, and drew my face to his. "If you keep that up even another minute, I'm going to shoot come inside your mouth."

"Billy, I want you to blow your load in my mouth. I want to feel that hot jizz shooting in me, and I want to suck you as hard as I can while you shoot, so I can get every drop of it. I've already tasted your come, you know—and I want as much as I can get."

"I want you to suck me off—and I want to give you every drop I have. But let's wait; I don't want this to be over—ever. And I want your dick in my mouth first." He rolled me on my back, and began to kiss his way down my body.

I held Billy's head as he was kissing my body. "I want to be inside you, more than I've ever wanted anything, but are you sure you want to suck me?"

"He stopped and again kissed my lips as he whispered, "I know that makes me a *cocksucker,* but I don't care, I want to suck your cock." He resumed his ministrations.

"Billy, you're not a cocksucker, the way you mean it, and neither am I—it's just making love." And with this, Billy's mouth opened, and he *devoured* my prick with one gulp, beginning to suck it profoundly, while he also manipulated and exercised my balls. That I had taken all of Billy's long cock inside my mouth the first time I sucked it was understandable—I had had lots of practice sucking cock, with such challenging dicks as Les's and Jim's and Hal's to develop my technique. But this was the first time Billy had ever taken a cock in his mouth, and he had no trouble at all deep-throating me. It was clear he was naturally talented at what he was doing, but he was not faced with as formidable a challenge as his cock presented to a potential cocksucker. I'm pleased with, and reasonably proud of what Mother Nature endowed me with in the cock department, but it isn't a great challenge for most guys.

On my maiden voyage as a cocksucker Les shoved eight inches of fat dick all the way down my throat and fucked it like a savage. I tried to resist, thinking he would choke me, but he persisted—ignoring my gagging, and gasping words of encouragement while he assaulted my throat with his monster tool—and I learned quickly enough to welcome the first of the countless loads he shot into my throat over the years. And I wasn't in love with him—not at that point, anyway, just in love with his prick—but by the time he hammered that prodigious monster up my virgin ass a while later, I loved everything about him, and would have welcomed him that way even if he had been hung like Hal. But Billy was in love with me already, so I suspect he would have performed well even if I had lot more dick to give him—and love conquers all, we are told.

I groaned in delight as I fucked Billy's mouth. "God, baby, I love you so much, and I've wanted to be inside you for so long—you're just wonderful." He gagged a few times, and I told him to relax his throat; he did, and he was soon able to suck me as deeply as I could have wanted.

As he sucked, he reversed his body and crouched over me so that his lovely, long prick was now hanging down over my face. I sucked his balls for a while, and then opened my mouth and took his cock in, and we spent a long time in delirious sixty-nine, fucking each other's mouths as passionately and lovingly as possible.

Finally, Billy pulled his mouth off my cock and said, "Pete, I'm going to come soon—are you sure you want to suck me off?"

"Give it to me, Billy, and don't stop until you give me every drop of come you can feed me." He again reversed his body and knelt with his knees in my armpits and his hands braced against the headboard of the bed. I grasped his ass as he thrust his prick deep into my throat and began to fuck my mouth furiously. In a minute I was rewarded with the gush of his hot come as it literally exploded from the end of his prick into my throat, in copious and repeated spurts. "God I love you, Pete. Take my load!" I swallowed and sucked all the more eagerly as he continued to fuck me and gasp his joy. Soon he cradled my head in his arms and pulled our bodies to our sides, all the time keeping his cock buried in my mouth, and he panted and humped with slowly subsiding passion. Not a word was said for a long time as he continued to hold my head and very gently fuck my mouth with his now limber, but still long prick.

Finally, very, very quietly: "That was the most wonderful thing that has ever happened to me—I love you even more now than I did before, and I didn't think that was possible."

I relinquished his prick and moved up to cradle him in my arms. "Anything for you Billy. I love you more than I can tell you. I love holding you, I love kissing you, I love sucking you. I love your face, your body, your incredible ass. I love everything about you."

"I want something even more wonderful now, Pete. I want you to come in my mouth.

"Billy, are you sure? You don't have to—"

"Of course I'm sure. I want you to fuck my mouth and fill it the way I did yours. I want to drink your come, Pete—I want *you* inside me." He began to move down, and took my prick in his mouth. With my cock still buried in him, he pulled me, on my back, to the side of the bed, and he knelt on the floor while he spread my legs and buried his lips in my pubic hair. His hands frantically explored my chest and my ass as he moved his adoring mouth up and down the shaft of my prick, sucking deeply. Soon I could hold back no longer, and I frantically fucked his mouth as my come discharged into him. He sucked all the harder as I shot into him, and he continued to suck and swallow until I was completely spent.

He got on the bed with me, and we embraced and kissed as he said, "I knew that would be even more wonderful. Oh Pete, your come tasted so *good*, and I can't believe how exciting it was when you shot it into me. We really *are* lovers now, aren't we?"

"No two people could be *more* lovers than we are Billy. You're the sweetest guy I've ever known, and I enjoy being with you, and making love with you, more than anything I know. My come is inside you right now; your come is inside me right now—that's the way it should be.

We're in each other's arms, and we love each other. I feel so lucky I can't believe it."

"I feel the same way. I just feel like I want to shout and tell everyone how much I'm in love."

"Billy."

"I know, I can't tell *anyone*."

"No, you really can't, Billy. The only person you can tell is me, and so I want you to tell me all the time how much you love me."

Not much later our hard-ons had returned, and soon we were sucking each other's pricks again. Billy said: "It felt so good when you shot your load on my ass last time. Will you do it again? And can I shoot on yours, too?"

"I'd love to cover your beautiful ass with come again. Roll over." He did, and sooner than I would have thought possible, I shot my load on his ass, and especially between his beautiful, rounded cheeks. He wiggled his ass and humped the bed as he said, "Massage it into me, Pete." I began to work my come into the smooth skin of his ass, and into his asshole as well. He humped his ass harder as my finger teased him with the slippery come. "*Into* me, Pete. Work it into me." The tight ring of muscle grasped my finger as I gently inserted it into the delicious heat of his young asshole—well lubricated by my come He writhed as I carefully fucked him with my finger.

"Pete, that feels so *good*. It hurts, but it's also really exciting. I don't know if I can take it, but I want you put your cock in me and fuck me that way."

I had to laugh. "Baby, I just shot one load in your mouth, and another one on your beautiful ass. I'm gonna have to rest a while before I do anything." I fell over his back, and whispered into his ear, "Billy, I want to fuck your ass—and I will, if you really want it, and if you'll promise me one thing."

"Anything, Pete. What is it?

"That you will fuck my ass as deep and as hard and as long as you can with that amazing prick of yours."

"You know I will. Do you want me to do it now?"

"I want you to shoot on my ass like I did on yours, and work your come into me. Then next time, we can start out by fucking each other in the ass, when neither of us has blown a load for a while—'cause I want you to give me such a big one I'll be able to really *feel* it shooting up inside me."

I got on my stomach and spread my legs. Billy knelt between my legs, frantically beating off, until I was rewarded with the feel of his hot come splashing onto me. He held his prick very near my asshole, where he had deposited most of his discharge. With his hand he used his come to lubricate my asshole, and soon was working it into me and fucking me very hard with a finger. "Give me a couple of fingers, Billy." Soon he was fucking me with two—then three—fingers, and I rolled on my side as he finger-fucked me, and I told him "Beat me off again while you fuck me that way."

I would not have thought myself able to come again so soon after having just deposited one load *into* my young lover, and another *onto* that beautiful stud, but I was ready again, and as Billy's fingers fucked my ass, I shot again. "Billy, this is going inside your ass next time. Billy, I love you."

Billy cried out passionately, "Oh God, Pete, I can't wait." And he rolled me back on my stomach and with one violent thrust drove his very long prick all the way into my still come-lubricated asshole, and began to fuck me fiercely. "I've got to fuck you—I love you!" I spread my legs to better take his cock inside, and he fucked me savagely, and at enormous length. He braced his arms on the headboard of the bed, and grunted while he humped. I gasped encouragement, and he gasped his love and lust while he slammed into me. His prick felt as wonderful in me as Hal's had—better, really, because I was in love with this beautiful young stud who was fucking me so ardently.

Billy's debut as a buttfucker was a long, spectacular one. Having just blasted his *second* load on my ass a very short while earlier, he was able to pound me for an extremely long, absolutely thrilling time before his third orgasm approached. After what must have been ten or fifteen minutes of his frantic, profound fucking, he called out, "Here it comes again. Oh Jesus, Pete, I love you so much." And I *did* feel his wonderful long prick erupting for the third time that evening, deep inside my body." Billy Polk: boy *stud*.

He was completely exhausted when he had finished, and collapsed on top of me, panting heavily. He made no move to take his cock out of me, nor did I want him to. I reached behind him to hold his gently gyrating ass in my hands while my asshole gently worked his prick, until his breathing subsided. We lay there immobile for several minutes until he whispered into my ear, "I'm sorry, I couldn't help myself. I *had* to fuck you."

"You did the right thing, Billy; no one has ever done a better thing. That was the best fuck anybody ever got. Are you *sure* you've never fucked anybody before?"

"Of course I haven't, Pete. That's the first time I ever fucked anyone in the ass. Gosh, until I fucked your mouth an hour or so ago, I'd never fucked anyone anywhere. Why?"

"Because you're so incredibly good at it. You fuck like you'd been practicing for years. Thank you, Billy—it was really, really wonderful. *You're* really, really wonderful. It means an awful lot to me that I'm the first one you fucked."

"And you're the first one that ever fucked me in the mouth, and you're going to be the first one to fuck me in the ass, too. I don't care if anyone else *ever* fucks me, as long as you do." Billy pulled out, rolled me on my back, and pinned my arms down as—in a sudden, complete change of mood—he laughed, put his face right in mine, and said, "And you're going to fuck my ass so hard next time I'm not going to be able to sit down for a week. Deal?"

"Deal." We began to wrestle playfully. "But you may not have a chance to sit down anyway—I'm going to keep you busy filling *my* ass all the time."

"I'll keep it full all right. Fingers, cock, come—you name it, I'll shove it in there."

We wrestled and giggled, and finally subsided, wrapped in each other's arms, and again quietly told one another of our love. *Our Love. My love*—for the most beautiful and sweet young man I had ever known, and he was still just sixteen. Sweet sixteen, and soon to be not just kissed, but *fucked*—as he had just so thrillingly fucked me.

I longed to hold Billy in my arms all night, but he had to get home, and it was getting late. He made me promise that I would fuck his ass very soon, and that *somehow* we would work things out so that he could spend an entire night with me; I ached for it as badly as he. Kissing him goodnight, I desperately wanted to take him back to bed and never let him go.

I didn't have to wait long before we were able to spend the night together. Just a few days later, Billy stopped me in the hall at school and told me his mother was going to Oklahoma that day to visit her brother, leaving him at home alone—and giving us an opportunity to spend a whole night in each other's arms. Because his mother might conceivably phone home while she was away, Billy suggested we spend the night together in his bedroom, rather than mine. The idea was particularly appealing to me; it would be especially exciting to be in the room where he grew up, in the bed where he regularly slept (and masturbated.), and to make love to him surrounded by his boyhood belongings. The room would *be* Billy, and that was very arousing in itself.

He had a basketball game that night, and we agreed that I would come to his house about nine. After the game I took my car home to leave it there, and I walked to Billy's house; it was night, so no one would see me going there—Antares had no street lights—and my car would not be parked outside, causing anyone to wonder why it was there. The house was dark when I arrived, and I wondered if Billy had been delayed. Nonetheless, I knocked, and in a minute, the door opened. Billy stood there—completely naked, and stroking his hard cock.

He grinned at me. "If you like what you see, come on in and see how it tastes." I walked in, slammed the door behind me, and dropped to my knees. Billy seized my head and rammed his cock deep into my mouth and began to fuck it slowly and deeply. "Oh God, Pete, that feels so great—I couldn't wait to do this to you."

I stood, took him in my arms, and kissed him as he began to unbutton my coat and shirt. I quickly shed my clothes and we fell to the floor locked in each other's arms, writhing together, frantically caressing each other's bodies, and kissing passionately. Billy was on his back as I reversed my body and knelt over him so that when I took his prick in my mouth, he did the same for me, and our arms locked around each other as we double-sucked wildly. Billy released my cock and began to suck my balls; I lifted his body a bit as he lay below me so that I could perform the same service for him. As we licked and sucked balls, I gently began to probe Billy's asshole with my finger, and taking his cue from me, he was soon plunging his entire finger in and out of my ass. I kissed Billy's beautiful ass as I probed him, and told him, "Let's go in your bedroom and slow down—we've got all night ahead of us."

He moved into my arms and kissed me. "I want you to fuck me in my very own bed—and I want to fuck you there. And I want to suck you, and I want you to come on me, and inside of me, and I want to make love all night long and shoot my load a dozen times with my lover."

"Billy, you're the most exciting guy I've ever known—and if I can't shoot a dozen loads for you, I'll come as close to it as I can. Take me to your bed." Billy led me to his room and turned on the light.

"This is where I lie awake at night thinking of you and jacking off." He took my hand and drew me down on top of him on the bed. "And this is where I want you to put your cock inside me. Fucking your ass in your bed was the most exciting thing I've ever done—and I know that you fucking me in my own bed is going to be even better."

"Sometimes it really hurts the first time, Billy, and I don't want to hurt you—but I want to fuck your beautiful ass so bad I can't stand it. I brought plenty of Vaseline to make it easier."

"I've got some too; I've been practicing, using my finger, and it feels really good. I just know that your big prick is going to feel wonderful inside me."

"Let's go slow and build up to it; I want to explore every square inch of your perfect body before I fuck you. Stand on the bed.

"What?"

"Stand up on the bed, and let me worship your body."

He kissed me and giggled. "Okay—if that's what you really want." He stood on the bed, legs spread, hands on his hips, and smiled down at me. "You like what you see, Pete?"

"I *adore* what I see." I caressed, kissed, and licked his perfect young body all over. He responded with murmurs of approval as I did so—especially when I licked the underside of his long cock, sucked his balls, and gently took the entire length of his prick deep into my throat. I turned him around and licked and kissed the incredibly smooth, perfect globes of his ass—he leaned forward and used his hands to spread his cheeks as I began to kiss his asshole.

He reached behind and began to probe his asshole with his finger. "Put something in here, Pete—it's so hot for you." I removed his finger and substituted my own, which I began to fuck him with rather energetically. He humped my finger and groaned with pleasure as I did so. "So good. So *good!*" I pulled my finger out, pressed my face between his rounded buttocks, drove my tongue as far into him as I could, and began to tongue-fuck his wildly gyrating ass. He reached behind and pulled my head in tightly as I continued. He groaned, "That's the greatest thing I've ever felt."

After a frantic few minutes of this, I pulled Billy down on top of me on the bed. "I've never done that to anyone in my life, and I never thought I would, but your ass is the most beautiful, perfect, exciting thing in the world. I can't get enough of it." I saw no need to trouble this sweet boy with the truth: that I was no stranger to eating ass; I had, however, been extremely selective in making love that intensely personal way, doing it with a handful of only the very select, most beautiful or irresistibly sexy partners .

Billy rose to his knees and teased his own asshole with the end of my prick—almost admitting it into him. "Put your big cock in it, Pete, and fuck me like you've never fucked anyone before. I want my lover all the way inside me. . . I want you to fill me up with your prick and with your load."

"Lie on your side and let me grease you up, Billy. I'll get behind you—that's the best way to do it first."

"Is that the way you got fucked first?"

"Yes, and the guy who fucked me first had a really huge prick—I didn't think I'd be able to take it, but I did, and once it was in me, it was the greatest thing I'd ever felt."

"I'm going to love it, Pete. I don't care if it hurts at first, I want you to fuck me like I fucked you the other night."

I liberally lubricated his asshole and my prick, and positioned us on our sides. Pressing the head of my cock tightly up against his hole, I said "Work yourself down onto me gradually—you set the pace, and let me in slow and easy. Once I'm all the way inside you, I know I'm not going to be able to control myself—I'm going to fuck my beautiful baby for all I'm worth."

Billy began to undulate his ass, and very gradually pressed against my prick hard enough that the tip began to slip in. The muscular ring of his asshole was incredibly tight as he slowly wiggled and humped against me. "Oh, God—that hurts. It hurts—but I want it." He continued to press back and hump, and little by little—in spite of his protestations of pain—my cock slid into his incredibly hot and tight young ass. Finally, I was all the way in.

"Pete. Oh Pete, I love you so much! You feel so good inside me, and I want you to fuck me. I've never felt this wonderful in my whole life. Fuck me—*love* me." He put his hands back and grasped my ass, pulling me even more tightly to him as I began to fuck him very gently.

"Billy, you feel so wonderful . . . you're so tight and so hot. I've wanted to fuck this perfect ass since I first laid eyes on it. At last, at *last.*" And I began slowly to fuck him in earnest.

For every forward thrust of my driving prick, Billy countered with a backward movement of his ass. He proved to be as much an absolute *natural* at getting fucked as he had shown himself a prodigiously natural talent at fucking when he had impetuously drilled my ass a few nights before.

We had by this time moved so that he was on all fours, and I knelt behind him, holding his waist in my hands while he pulled me in to him and gyrated his ass wildly. "*Fuck me, Pete. Fuck me. Fuck me. Fuck my ass!*" He suddenly rose to his knees and said, "Jack me off—I'm going to come." I put one arm around his chest and held him tightly, and as I stroked his long, throbbing cock with the other hand and continued to fuck him, Billy shot spurt after spurt all over his bed. His head was thrown back in rapture, and he moaned loudly, "Come inside me Pete." And he turned his head to kiss me as I continued to fuck his wildly driving ass.

Soon I could hold it no longer. "Take it, baby." and I erupted inside him. He pulled me to him as tightly as he could. "Fill me up with your come, Pete. I can feel it shooting inside me." I continued to drive myself into him long after I had finished my orgasm, and he continued to move in rhythm with me. Finally, he fell forward on the bed, pulling me with him so that I lay on top of him, and my prick stayed buried inside his ass.

We lay there in absolute silence for several minutes, until finally Billy whispered, "Nothing in the world has ever felt so good."

"Only one thing has ever felt better."

"What could possibly be better?"

"When you did that same thing to me a few nights ago"

"I wish I could do it to you every night for the rest of my life—and you could do it to me. I love you so much I feel like I could burst." I slowly removed my cock from his ass so he could turn around, and we held each other tightly and kissed sweetly and silently for a very long time. We finally became aware of the fact that we were lying in Billy's come, which by then had grown cold—and we were getting cold as well. He suggested we get in the shower to warm up.

In the shower, we immediately began kissing and hugging under the hot water, and our pricks were immediately poking into each other. Billy knelt and began to suck me as he fingered my asshole. I murmured, "I want your prick inside there very soon, baby."

He sucked me for a long time before he stood and replied: "You can bet I'm going to put it there, and I'll show you I'm no baby."

I turned around, spread my cheeks, and backed up to his cock. "Show me now—put that long, beautiful thing of yours all the way in me; fuck me as hard as you can."

Billy took the soap and lathered my ass, and soon was pressing the tip of his prick into me. Very slowly he worked the entire, considerable length of his cock into me, kissing my ear and murmuring endearments—quite a change from the first time he entered me. "I don't want to fuck you as hard as I can—I want to fuck you with as much love as I can." He put his hands on my shoulders and bent me forward, and began to fuck me with the longest strokes he could—*almost* emerging from me with every movement backwards, and then plunging back in as far as he could—which was very far indeed. I reached behind to cup his beautiful ass in my hands as he fucked.

"Oh God, Billy, I want you to shoot your come in me, but I wanna suck it out of you."

"I promise you if you let me come in you this way, I'll shoot again in your mouth soon—but I want you to come in my mouth at the same time. Okay?"

"More than okay—that's perfect. Keep fucking me—fuck me *hard* now . . . and explode in me." Billy stepped up his strokes, and was soon savagely attacking my ass. He began to grunt wildly as he hammered himself as deep as he could, and finally, with a huge cry of passion, he clasped me to him, buried his cock as deeply as it would go, and began to erupt way up inside my body.

The water was still pouring down on us as Billy relaxed, turned me around and kissed me for a long time. Finally, he whispered, "I think I gave you as much come in you as you put in me." I laughed and agreed with him. He added, "And I want you to put more in me right now."

He knelt and took me in his mouth and began to suck frantically. I held his head in my hands and let the water play over us as I fucked his mouth as fast and as hard as I could, and I was soon shooting my load deep into his throat, even though I had filled his ass only a short while earlier. Billy murmured "Mmmmm." as I continued to fuck his mouth long after I had stopped coming. Finally, we both calmed down and he stood and kissed me. "Can you taste your come in my mouth?" I admitted I could. He held my head tightly a few inches from his face as he wiggled his eyebrows *a la* Groucho Marx and giggled, "Tastes great, doesn't it?"

I grasped his head and answered him the same way, "Not as good as yours—and I'm going to taste some of that tonight if I have to go in the bedroom and lick it up off the bed where you wasted it."

He laughed and clasped me *very* tightly in his arms, and whispered hoarsely in a deep, mock-Russian accent, "Don't vurry, comrade—Billy Polk alvays has much, much more love juice for his Pete." Then in a sultry, *non*-Russian whisper directly into my ear: "I'm going to shoot so much come in your mouth it's going to be squirting out of your ears."

"What? I can't hear you, I've got come squirting out of my ears."

We laughed, got out of the shower and dried off. Back in the bedroom we quickly got under the come-splattered bed covers and held each other tight, kissing, and talking a great deal about nothing at all except the wonder of loving each other. (*Yes, he was only sixteen—but I was only twenty-two.*)

Eventually we drifted off to sleep. I woke as it began to get light; I shook Billy and told him I had to get back home before full light, as it would not do for anyone to see me leaving his house in the morning. He came fully awake, and agreed we needed to be careful. "But you're not going until I make good on my promise." He took my head and guided it down to his cock, which was already hard. I took it in my mouth and began to suck as he re-positioned his body so that he could suck me at the same time.

Lying on our sides, we held our arms around each other tightly as we sucked deeply and fucked each other's mouths wildly. Eventually Billy panted around my cock, "Here it comes." Then as he started to suck me again, his beautiful ass drove his cock deep into my throat, and I was rewarded with his delicious, *copious* load. I didn't say anything when, just a minute or two later, I delivered my load into his throat, because I wanted to hold his come in my mouth as I gave him mine. We both savored each other's offering for some time, finally breaking to lie head-to-head and exchange the taste of come in our mouths.

In a few minutes, Billy put his finger in my ear, then tasted it. "Hm. I think I taste come." He looked pointedly into my ear and laughed, "Oh no. It's squirting out of your ears. We giggled and wrestled for a few minutes.

"I've *got* to get out of here, Billy. This has been the most wonderful night of my life—and I love you—but I *have* to go." I began to dress.

"I feel the same way, Pete—will you fuck me again soon?"

"Don't worry, I will—and in case you hadn't thought of it, you've still got some other new ways to fuck me before we start repeating them."

"I promise to fuck you every way possible, if you'll do the same for me. My butt hurts this morning, but it was so wonderful getting fucked by you I'll be ready for more right away."

"As soon as possible, baby."

"No baby."

"Billy, when you're inside me, there's no doubt I'm getting fucked by a real man—but you're still my baby." I kissed him, checked to be sure the coast was clear, and hurried home.

During the several days his mother was gone, and Billy had no one to answer to for his time, we managed to get together almost every day or night. And as he was a fine student in Geometry, he was an "A+" student in lovemaking. The first time we met after I initially fucked him, he was eager for me to sink my cock into him again—and often. Late in the afternoon of that day, Billy came to my house, and we ate dinner together naked—feeding and playing with each other in almost equal parts.

After eating, we lay on my bed and necked for a long time. Then, with Billy on his back and the Vaseline liberally applied, I positioned my asshole over his hard cock while I squatted and then settled down on it. As he entered me, he groaned with delight, and I said, "Here's another way for you to fuck me." He began to hump and I began to bounce up and down, riding his lovely prick in absolute ecstasy.

He discharged his load violently into me, and with his prick still in me as it softened, we kissed tenderly. He whispered into my ear, "I can't *wait* for you to fuck me like that. Lie on your back now." I rolled over, and Billy greased us up and settled himself on me. His asshole was incredibly tight as he began to ride me, but he enjoyed it as if he had done it every day of his life. He bounced up and down so energetically, my prick came out of him several times, but he invariably forced himself back down over it and recommenced his wild ride. He cried, "Oh God, Pete, it's like I'm fucking myself with your prick." And at the same time he masturbated his own prick with equal enthusiasm. Watching him ride me, with his eyes closed and head thrown back in ecstasy, I marveled at beauty and passion of this high order in one so young—to say nothing of the magnificence of the body I was plumbing.

It didn't take too much of his wild enjoyment of my prick before my come exploded inside his ass—but he only rode the harder, "I feel you shooting in me. Fuck me, Pete ... Oh God, I'm going to come again!" Although it had been a very short time since he had shot a load inside me, he now began to spurt another generous one all over my chest and face.

I scooped his come from my chest and began to eat it and smear it on my face. "Billy, your come tastes so damned good." He fell on me and began to lick his discharge from my face, after which we kissed and shared his load, and snuggled for a very long time—my soft cock still inside my young lover.

After a "cooling down" period, we were both hard again, and although I had a meeting to go to, we sucked each other off before we had to part. Billy had already come twice shortly before that, but his latest load still seemed to fill my mouth—and according to him, I challenged his swallowing ability as well.

About a week later I got the pictures I had taken of Billy back from the Kodak color processing lab. Amazingly, they returned all of them—even the one where his hard prick stood straight out as it supports the napkin barely covering it. There was even one that had been taken when I was apparently unaware that while Billy was posed in profile, with a leg raised to conceal his cock, his big balls and a couple inches of his prick hung down in plain sight. The photos were all color slides, instead of prints; I suspect if they had been prints, at least a dozen of them would have been 'censored' and destroyed.

When I showed the pictures to Billy, I confessed to him that there was no 'artist' who needed pictures of a young man. He laughed, and said, "I thought they were for you when you asked me to pose. Then when you started taking pictures of my hard-on, I knew. I'm glad you took 'em, Pete, and I want you to keep 'em near you all the time, so even if we're not together I'll still be with you. I wish you had pictures of me sucking you off, or getting fucked—so you could look at 'em any time and be reminded how much I love you."

I still treasure those pictures today, more than forty-five years later. I have often looked at the slides over the years, and much later, when it became easy to find a photo shop that would process nude pictures—and even outright pornography—I had prints made of all of them, and keep them in a special album. When I look at them, I'm always astonished at how extraordinarily beautiful young Billy Polk was at that age. I still think the profile shot with the cloth draped over his jutting erection is as sexy as anything the porn studios have ever produced, and I have a framed, eleven-by-fourteen print of that, which I have only worked up the courage to hang in my bedroom in recent years. When I picked up the prints at the Atlanta photo shop, the owner told me, "That's one of the prettiest, and sexiest boys I've ever seen." I feel sure pictures of Billy Polk—nude in the earlier shots, *naked* in the last group—can be found in at least one home in Atlanta.

Even after Billy's mother returned, we managed to find time for continuing sexual exploration. Within a few weeks we had fucked each other in every conceivable position. Kneeling on all fours in my living room, in the same spot where I had earlier photographed Billy's perfect young ass, my own ass was penetrated by his lengthy young prick as he frantically drove it into me and erupted thrillingly. A few minutes later I matched his eruption as he knelt on the sofa while I stood behind him, held his waist in my hands, and fucked him as savagely as he had just serviced me. Lying on my back on my kitchen table, with my legs raised high, I again received the thrill of Billy's explosion of come inside me—shortly before he declared me to be "lunch," and leaned over me to dine on my cock and suck it dry.

An especially warm day permitted another trip out to Rodman's Pond, where my young lover and I kissed and reminisced as he lay on his back and I fucked him "missionary position" for the first time. That same day we knelt face-to-face by the pond while we masturbated and shot onto each other in homage to our first sexual encounter there—climaxed this time by a much more satisfying 'finale,' as each of us licked his own come off the other's chest and shared it with the other's hungry mouth by means of a passionate kiss.

On one occasion as we showered together—Billy having come to my house directly from a particularly sweaty football practice—he said he needed to get out of the shower for a minute to pee. I told him he could just piss in the tub as we showered—I wanted to watch his long, beautiful cock as the piss streamed from it.

He smiled sexily and stepped back a few paces, facing me; "How's this, Pete?," he said as piss began to course from his cock.

I impulsively knelt before him. "Cover me, Billy ... I want your hot piss all over me." He directed his spray, and I positioned myself so that he would know I wanted him to piss even on my face. I had never even considered doing something like this, but it was an incredibly erotic experience for both of us. In fact, there was only one other time in my life when I did that.

About two years after the day Billy pissed on me, when I was in the Navy, I spent an afternoon on a deserted beach in Guam with a cute, unbelievably sexy little blond sailor/shipmate of mine, whose enormous cock I had been begging him to give me for a long time. He said he would let me suck him off if he could piss on me. I agreed, and when he pissed on me, his cock grow even larger and apparently harder than I had seen it before—decidedly in the Hal Weltmann class—and I sucked a load out of it commensurate with its size. Before we left the beach that afternoon he had me kneel on all fours while he pissed on my back, just before he knelt behind me and plugged my ass with his monster dick—and though he never pissed on me again after that day, I sucked him off and took him up the ass dozens of times before I left the ship. I learned the blond stud had a lover, a musclebound, burly Sergeant in the Marine contingent aboard the ship, who threatened to beat me up if I didn't stop screwing with his partner. The blond sailor didn't, thank God, stop feeding me dick—he claimed that even though his Marine 'sea pussy' had the hottest ass he'd ever fucked, I did a lot better job of sucking him off—but he was more careful about keeping his boyfriend from finding out about it after that. He often drilled my hungry ass while I leaned over a railing at the fantail of the ship when we were out to sea at night—usually with a half-dozen or so pairs of sailors on either side of us enjoying themselves the same way. Several times, while I was making love with some other sailor back there, I saw my blond fucking his Marine boyfriend, and twice I saw the Marine crouch before him and get pissed on before he got fucked. It was a horny ship, to say the least.

Billy's prick was hard by the time he finished urinating, and I sucked the last drops of pee from his cock as he fucked my face for a few moments and murmured, "God, that was exciting." He pulled me to my feet, turned me around, and bent me over. He soaped us up, and his cock seemed even longer than usual as he savagely fucked my ass—and he passionately praised mine as I drove it into his writhing body only a few minutes later while he bent over to receive it.

We never slackened the pace of our oral attention to each other as we explored the wonders of fucking each other, though. I sucked and licked Billy's balls almost as often as I thrilled to the taste and feel of his long prick deep in my throat—and he always returned the favor with as much fervor as I brought to it. I caressed, kissed, and generally worshipped his perfect ass, often tongue-fucking him for very long periods of time, an action he declared he enjoyed as much as I did—meaning he had a helluva good time when I did it. We sucked cock standing, kneeling, lying on our backs or our sides—and most especially as one of us straddled and tightly grasped the other's head while 'fucking face' to deliver a hot load of come to a loving mouth. We both loved 'sixty-nine,' of course, and I *especially* delighted in it, since it afforded me a close-up view of his perfect ass as it writhed in passion when he delivered his love-offering to my mouth.

And Billy's ass *was* perfect—and his prick was perfect—and his body was perfect—and his face was that of an angel—and his love-making was astonishingly precocious. It seemed unbelievable that a high-school sophomore could be such an accomplished lover, but I knew when his prick delivered its hot, explosive load to either of my adoring orifices that he was all of that, and more.

I had rarely been as sexually satisfied as I found myself just then. In the developing stages of my affair with Billy I had relied on Jim to provide occasional relief—he often drove up to visit me, or I drove to campus to see him—and we sucked and fucked with the same old fervor we had known as roommates/fuckbuddies. When I visited him, we occasionally shared our lovemaking with a third party Jim recruited for the occasion. Fortunately, I did not *love* Jim, so I didn't feel I was really being untrue to my growing love for young Billy when Jim and I had sex. That was specious reasoning, to say the least, but I was becoming so wrapped up in my sweet young lover that I really didn't much *want* to fuck with anyone else; I could have a wonderful, beautiful, passionate young man whom I loved, as often as I wanted—I could have Billy.

Characteristically, Jim didn't have his feelings hurt when our sexual relationship gradually all but ground to a halt; he told me he was finding an ample number of guys to fuck with on campus—he continued to be remarkably successful at locating eager sex partners. I must admit I suffered a special twinge of jealousy when he told me of a couple of visits from the *hottest* sex partner he had ever, in my estimation, discovered: Hal Weltmann, of the voracious monster cock. I would be lying if I said the thought of having *that* magnificent organ driving into me, and quite literally *filling me* with joy again, did not challenge the concept of my not wanting anyone other than Billy. At least Dan had not accompanied Hal when he visited with Jim, so my envy was not compounded.

There was more than just sex and lovemaking to Billy's and my relationship, however. He often came to see me, both at school and at home, to ask me to help him do school work. Sometimes it was Geometry—he was still in my class, after all—but it was also English, Spanish, or History. He never asked me to do work *for* him; it was usually my help in making suggestions for re-writing or re-thinking that he sought, and which I happily gave. He often helped me, too—yard chores and handiwork at home, for instance, and logistical help with arrangements for the band and the all-girl High School Chorus I directed. He and I were often seen together, and no one seemed to think that was odd—and that was important, since it was inevitable that he would often be seen around my house. Mrs. Polk even came to my house once to deliver a pan of brownies and to thank me for all the help I was giving her son. She said she regretted that Billy had no father or older brothers to help her in raising him, and was grateful I took so much interest in him. She thought he regarded me as an older brother. If she had been *aiming* for irony, she couldn't have been more successful.

It is a comment on the naivete of the time or the place—more likely both—that no one seemed to think it peculiar that a young bachelor teacher who was apparently not dating any girls took so much time to befriend an incredibly attractive high school sophomore—one who also wasn't dating. I was, admittedly, the youngest teacher in the school system, but I was still a teacher, and Billy was still a student.

A variety of factors made it possible for us to enjoy our closeness without comment. It was a very small town, so *everyone* was fairly close to *everyone else,* but these people respected privacy. Neither Billy nor I—I hope—evidenced traits of femininity, the sure sign those days of homosexual leanings or activities. I doubt, really, that anyone in Antares thought there could be such a thing as homosexuality *there*—that was some kind of big city perversion. Billy and I were both highly visible in separate contexts, as well—he as both football and basketball player, I as band and choir director. Billy *never* presumed on our relationship in class and at school—he was an obviously conscientious student in my Geometry class, and outside of class he always accorded me the respect and formality local people felt was due a teacher.

Was the achievement of our relationship dumb luck on my part? Much of it was, of course—finding Billy, and winning his love—but the really important factor lay in Billy's character. He was as intelligent as he was beautiful—well, perhaps not *quite* as much so, since that would have made him a genius of the highest order—and was therefore able to gauge how he had to act if we were to continue our relationship. He also had the emotional stability and will power to control his *wonderful* raging hormones when he had to—but I thanked God he often let them rage unchecked when we were together. I appreciated my good fortune almost as much as I enjoyed the feel of his muscular young body in my arms or his long prick deep inside me, the texture of his velvety ass as I caressed it, the wonderful grip of his asshole as I fucked him, or the indescribably sweet taste of his kisses and his come—or, best of all, his frequently uttered words, "I love you, Pete."

As Christmas time approached, it became clear that Billy and I would be separated for a couple of weeks. I had to go to Indiana to visit with my family, and Billy had family obligations as well. During the first few weeks of December, we would have stepped up the pace of our love-making in order to "tide us over" during our separation, but it really wasn't possible to increase the frequency or intensity of our sexual encounters: we were meeting and fucking at every possible moment, and at absolute fever pitch. I couldn't get enough of Billy's sweet kisses and his wonderful prick inside me, and he apparently felt the same way about me. Nonetheless, as school let out for the Christmas break, we had to part company for a while—and we knew that even telephoning would be awkward, so it really was "goodbye" for a limited time.

The night before I left to drive north, Billy spent the entire night in my bed. He told his mother he was staying over at Joe Don Griffith's house, and he had pledged the latter to "cover" for him if need be. I was concerned about the danger of someone finding out about us—perhaps even *especially* the sexy, 'desk-fucker'—but Billy swore that Joe Don had agreed to ask no questions, saying he would probably need the favor returned some day. Furthermore, Billy was sure his mother would never check up on him anyway. I reluctantly agreed, and as it turned out, there was no problem.

The sexual details of our last night together before Christmas need not be rehearsed here; everything we did we had done before, and is described in this account already—the frequency of our orgasms and the profundity of our passion *were* remarkable, however. As hot as Billy had always been, he was at something like 'meltdown' temperature that night—the length of his cock-stroke as he fucked my ass or my mouth seemed especially exciting, and the speed and force behind it seemed unbelievably impassioned. And he almost *screamed* his "Fuck me, Pete." and his "God I love shooting my load into you." and other endearments of that sort. I did a creditable job of matching the special fervor and dedication he displayed.

In all, during the twelve hours or so that he spent at my house that night, we fucked each other in every conceivable position; we sucked cock in every way we could think; our kissing was as wild and wonderful as it had ever been; I tongue-fucked Billy's asshole every time before penetrating him (which drove him *wild*); we kissed and licked each other generally, concentrating especially on balls and tits; I worshipped Billy's body—and especially his glorious ass—with my hands; and we cuddled, and whispered endearments to each other for hours and hours. I shot my load twice into my lover's ass, and twice in his throat that night—a total of four orgasms. Billy not only matched me, but went me one better: as we prepared to settle down and sleep for a while, he plunged his prick into my ass yet again and declared he was leaving it there while we slept. Naturally he began to fuck me, and shortly deposited a *third* load into my already twice-blessed ass—and he did leave his beautiful prick in me as we slept, bathed in his own wondrous love-juice.

As we awoke the next morning, we got in the shower together, and each of us knelt before the other to suck a final load out before parting. After a makeshift breakfast, Billy put on his coat to go, but as he was halfway out the door, he slammed it shut, turned to me and dragged me back in the bedroom. He pulled down my pants and pushed me so that I leaned over the bed. Standing behind me, he plunged his prick into me again and began a final wild fuck. After shooting another load into my appreciative ass, he clasped me tight from behind and said he didn't know how he could stand to be away from me for two weeks. He pulled me to my feet, turned me around and knelt, and said, "One more load to hold me, Pete." Grasping my ass, he swallowed my prick and commenced to suck my cock as eagerly as I fucked his mouth. My *sixth* orgasm in the *one* half-day of the evening and morning we made love was not as copious as some of the immediately preceding ones, of course, but Billy licked his lips after swallowing, and declared it wonderful. We finally parted, and I hit the road an hour or so later.

7.
FLASHBACKS: DANNY AND LES

Danny looked magnificent standing there on the hilltop,
naked, erect, beautiful. I knelt before him and returned to the work
I had begun in the bushes.
Dean grinned at me. "You give a mean blowjob, and I really enjoyed
it . . . now let's get out of
here before somebody comes." He laughed, "Before somebody
else comes, I mean."

While I loved my family, the prospect of two weeks alone with them was daunting, to say the least. I was pleased to find on arriving at my sister's home, however, that Les Coston had called to leave word that he was going to be in Chicago for ten days, and wanted me to come in to the city and spend some time with him; he was midway through his first year in the Air Force, and would be home on leave. The prospect of visiting with Les promised to enliven and alleviate my enforced separation from Billy considerably, because of our wonderful history together; I had learned much about what was exciting in life as Les and I knelt in front of, and sometimes over each other to suck cock, or as I lay below him or knelt with him behind me, impaled on the thrilling bulk of his eight-inch ass-reamer.

Les had not been the first guy whose cock I sucked, however. That honor went to Danny Morales, a boy I first met when he came by the apartment in Chicago where my mother, my sister and I lived, to take my sister out on a date. He and my sister knew each other from high school, where they were both Juniors. I had never seen anyone I thought was quite as handsome as the sexy Latino who picked up my sister that night—and in spite of my youth, I knew very well what I was attracted to, and I was never more jealous of my sister than I was that night.

I was working in the neighborhood drug store at that time, and the next time Danny came over to take my sister out, he asked if they needed any help there—he wanted a job, and said he would appreciate my putting in a good word for him. My sister—bless her—had suggested he ask me when she learned he was looking for work. I campaigned for Danny's employment—*very* anxious to be given a chance to work side-by-side with him—and he got the job.

Danny was very dark—of both Latino and, I think, Indian heritage—and had a wonderfully muscular figure, even though he was fairly trim. His sculpted chest and broad shoulders showed to wonderful advantage in the tight T-shirt he customarily wore, and his even tighter Levi's displayed a perfectly rounded little ass. Two other things had fascinated me about Danny the first time I saw him—his breathtaking handsomeness, and the fascinating bulge that he sported in the crotch of those tight Levi's.

I had been having orgasms for well over a year by that time, and once I had met Danny, he appeared in more of my masturbation fantasies than anyone else. I already knew it was guys' pricks I wanted, not the girls' pussies I was *supposed* to be craving, and Danny was not only the most handsome, suave older guy I knew, but his Levi's promised *heaven,* if heaven could be thought of as a big cock—and somehow I knew even then there was a statistically significant correlation between the two.

Danny became a "soda jerk" and I was a delivery boy, but we still worked side-by-side quite a bit. I felt sure he was aware of the frequency and intensity of my admiring glances, as well as my propensity to rub up against him at every available opportunity. One night, about a month after we started working together, he showed me he had received the message clearly.

He and I were left alone to do the cleaning-up after closing. We were in the back stockroom when Danny declared he had to 'take a leak.'

"C'mon with me" he said, as he ruffled my hair and strode off for the employees' bathroom. Framed in the doorway, he stood by the commode and began unbuttoning his Levi's. I watched him from just outside the door. When he unbuttoned his jeans, I noticed he wore no underwear, and while that excited me, my heart began to race when instead of just pulling his cock out to pee, he pulled his Levi's down to his knees, revealing his adorable golden ass and his cock and balls—an incredibly stimulating sight to me. He waved me inside the bathroom, "Get in here, don't you have to pee too?"

My beating heart went into overdrive and I actually began to tremble with the thrill of his invitation to join him while he displayed his beauty. This was the first time I had really seen a mature prick up close, and I stepped into the doorway, unabashedly staring in both fascination and admiration at the large and tempting equipment hanging below his tee-shirt. Danny laughed, and let the flaccid tube of his tempting meat lie in the palm of his hand as he turned to me and presented it for closer inspection. "Don't be afraid to look at it, it's okay. What do you think—have I got a good dick?"

Gulping, heart *pounding,* I stepped into the bathroom and looked up into his smiling, handsome face . "You've got a *great* dick, Danny—really *big,* too."

"Go ahead, you can touch it if you want to." I stood next to him and stared at his prick. "Don't you want to?" he asked. "Go ahead, take ahold of it," and he released his prick and thrust his hips forward, causing it to jut out from his body, and pulling his tee-shirt up in front as he did so, giving me a view of the thick, black pubic bush above it, and his almost hairless balls hanging below. I reached out and very carefully put my hand around his cock and began to stroke it gently. I could feel it pulsing and swelling in my hand. And my own cock was throbbing inside my pants by that time also, and had grown as hard and as large as it had ever been. Danny grinned as he said, "Hell, John, it ain't gonna break. *Work* on it—you jack off, don't you?"

"Sure . . . sure I do—a lot." This was certainly a truthful answer. In fact, I frequently masturbated fantasizing about *exactly* what was happening at the moment, and with the same cast of characters: dark, sexy Danny . . . and me.

As I stroked Danny's cock it grew hard and, to my young and inexperienced sensibilities, *enormous.* "That feels great, John, keep doing it . . . and play with my balls." I put my other hand beneath his prick so I could cup his wonderful big ball-sac. His nuts were tightly drawn up when I grasped them, but as I massaged them, the sac loosened, and they began to move around freely inside it. He began to hump his cock into my stroking hand, and soon I had my fist closed tightly around his shaft while he fucked my hand seriously. He grinned at me, and put a hand on my head as he whispered, "You're doing fine—that really feels good." He dropped his pants and shorts to his ankles and then pulled his tee shirt up over his head, and threw it onto the water tank part of the commode. "How do I look?"

"Jeez, Danny, you look terrific." It was obvious that Danny had observed how fascinated I was with his body, and it seemed he enjoyed displaying it for me to admire. His entire, muscular body was now visible to me, and he looked even more beautiful and exciting than he had in my imagination.

He took hold my shoulders as I continued to massage his balls while he fucked my hand, and very solemnly asked me, "You want to see me get off?"

"Oh yeah, Danny, I want to see it, I really do."

"Do you get off yet?" He reached down and cupped my hard prick through my pants. "I'll bet you do—you sure are hard. Take your pants down and let me see your dick." I reluctantly released his cock and balls, and did as I was told. Danny took my hard prick in his hand and began to stroke it. "That feels good, doesn't it?" I murmured my delight. "You want me to get you off first?"

"More than anything I want to jack you off. Your dick is so big and hard—it really feels great." I was by then stroking his cock and playing with his balls again.

Danny again held my shoulders and fucked my hand vigorously. "Mmmmm . . . that feels great. His eyes were closed, and he was lost in pleasure. He opened his eyes and smiled at me. "Let me show you something that really feels great," he said, and knelt before me. With his face directly in front of my cock, he took it in one hand and began to masturbate it, while he fondled my ass with the other. "You want me to take it in my mouth? It feels really terrific." I panted that I very much wanted my prick in his mouth. He moved in close, then looked up. "Do you want to take mine in your mouth too? Have you ever done that?"

"I never have, but I want to with you—Jeez, I like you so much, Danny, and you've got such a terrific dick."

"Ah, it's just a prick. But yours is really nice, too. Tell me how this feels." And he opened his mouth and took my entire prick inside—all the way to its base. He applied wonderful suction to me, and I grabbed his head and began to fuck his mouth eagerly as he sucked. He stopped for a minute and looked up at me. "Feel good?"

"Oh God, yes. That feels better than anything I've ever felt."

"But don't go blowing your load in my mouth, okay? If you're getting ready to shoot off, pull out or make me stop, okay?" I nodded agreement, and he began his wonderful lovemaking again. He sucked very hard, but alternated with gentle periods of tongue massage, so that the process didn't end with a quick orgasm. Finally he stood. "Want to do that to me now?" I knelt and took his prick in my hand. He cradled my head in both his arms and said, "Now let's go real slow—you just let me do the work at first, okay?"

I opened my mouth and he inserted only an inch or so of his beautiful cock into me, and fucked me very tentatively, and in a slow tempo. "Oh God, John, that feels good—you suck real hard, 'cause I really want to *fuck* your mouth with my big prick. You want me to? You like it?" I continued to suck as I nodded and murmured my assent. Danny introduced his prick into my mouth gradually; he surely knew I was inexperienced, and would have trouble taking it all—but by the time my lips were more than halfway down the shaft, he was holding my head tightly and fucking me in earnest, a bit farther into my mouth with each thrust. Each time I gagged, he would pull back somewhat, but after only a few strokes, he would again be plunging deeply into my throat. Although I wasn't able to take his cock completely when I began to suck it, before long my nose and lips were grazing his pubic hair each time he jabbed his shaft into me.

Danny's passionate cradling of my head, and his very vocal enjoyment of my efforts inspired me to give a much better blowjob than you might expect a totally inexperienced youngster to manage. I later calculated that Danny had about seven inches of cock, and for a cocksucking debut, that's challenging enough.

While I sucked, I reached behind him and fondled his humping and gyrating ass-cheeks, thrilling at the feel of his muscles at play beneath the cool velvet skin. The beautiful, ultra-sexy Danny Morales, my *god* at that point in my life, was fucking my mouth and I had his ass in my hands—I had never been so thrilled or delighted. I had dreamed of something almost exactly like this for a long time, and I was almost crying with happiness.

Finally Danny's rhythm grew frenzied, and he pulled his prick from my mouth. "I'm about to get it—jack me off and watch me shoot." He held my head by the hair, about a foot back from the end of his prick as I reached up and began to masturbate him and fondle his balls again. Soon he shouted, "Oh, God . . . here it comes." I felt his ball sac draw up, and he fucked my still masturbating fist as his hot come began to spurt bounteously from the beautiful object I was worshipping. Much of it went past my head, but a lot went on my face, my chest, and in my hair. He still held my head tightly, and when I looked up, I could see that his head was thrown back, and his eyes squeezed shut, while his chest heaved with passion.

I was panting almost as heavily as he was, but his labored breathing finally subsided when he whispered, "Oh, Jesus, John, that was great." He opened his eyes and smiled down at me like an angel. He raised me to my feet, reached for his tee-shirt, and began to clean his come off me. He grinned as he said, "Man, I got a lot on you, didn't I?"

He had got a lot on me, indeed, and while I had been looking up in adoration at his frozen, post-orgasm, godlike beauty in adoration, I had licked his come from my lips. I had, of course, sampled my own discharge before that, and it had tasted fine, but Danny's tasted like sheer ambrosia. "I loved it Danny, but you're getting your shirt all messed up."

"I don't mind getting my shirt messed up that way; it was in a good cause, right? That felt terrific—and you did a really great job, too; I've been hoping for a long time you'd want to do that with me." He smiled crookedly, "And I was pretty sure you did. Guess I was right, huh?"

"Oh God, Danny—*yes*." He was so unbelievably handsome. I desperately wanted to kiss him, but I restrained my impulse. As young and inexperienced as I was, I sensed even then that kissing was much more intimate than cocksucking, an axiom I later learned was true.

"You want me to jack you off now?"

"Oh please, Danny—or I can do it myself. I'm about to explode I want to shoot off so bad."

"Well, we can't have that happening, can we?" And he stood behind me and began to stroke my prick as he reached around. With his other arm he pulled me to him. I could feel his semi-erect prick pressing against me, between my ass cheeks, and I put my arms back to pull his ass in to me. His strokes grew in frenzy, and I could feel his cock getting hard again, and poking between my legs. Soon I cried, "Here I come." and Danny continued to stroke as my come shot out, the first few jets reaching the wall, the rest hitting the floor. Danny had been nibbling my ear and whispering, "That's good, John—shoot your load for me." As he had done so, his then fully hard cock was fucking me between the legs.

We stood there in embrace for a few minutes. His ass felt wonderful, and his hand still held my prick. He continued to hump his own cock lazily between my legs as we shared the dreamy afterglow of our shared sex. I whispered, "That was fantastic, Danny. Thank you."

He released my cock and pulled his from between my legs. I turned around, and he hugged me to him with both arms, and said, "That was fun, but we've gotta finish cleaning up." He turned me around and looked closely into my eyes. "Look, you can't tell *anyone* about this. Okay?"

"Oh, I won't Danny—never. This was just between you and me."

"That's good—and if you want to, we can do it a lot. But you *really* can't tell anyone—*ever*. You've got to promise. If anyone ever finds out, I won't give it to you any more."

I put my arms around him and hugged his exciting body to me. "This is our secret, Danny—and I want to do it as often as you'll let me, okay?"

Danny hugged me tightly, broke the embrace, and grinned widely as he waggled his now almost completely flaccid prick at me. "You're going to see a lot of this baby." And he winked and pulled up his pants, donned his come-soaked tee shirt, and we finished cleaning the store.

Danny proved to be as good as his word, too. I did see a lot of his prick for the next year or so, until he graduated from high school. I remember it seemed wonderfully large to me when I sucked it, and its seven-inch length was something I was soon able to accommodate easily in my throat. It also prepared me well for Les's much bigger tool—the next major one "around the corner" for my developing, precocious libido. Whatever the size of his prick, Danny was a terribly handsome, well-built young man, who bestowed his wonderful sexual favors on me at a time when I wanted and needed them desperately.

We got together for sex three or four times a month, usually in the drug store when we shared cleaning-up duties alone—as when we had our first sexual experience together. He would indicate to me that he wanted to play by telling me to reach under his long apron at some time during the evening while we both stood behind the cash register, where we could only be seen from the waist up. When working behind the soda fountain, all employees of the drug store were required to wear a heavy, starched white apron that reached from the waist almost to the ankles. After our first sex, any time Danny got me alone when we were working together at night and asked me to reach inside his apron, I knew what I would find: his fly would be open, and his bare prick would be hanging out of it. He would let me stroke it and massage it for a minute before he made me stop. He would wink, and say something like "Can't let it show," or, "Better put it away for right now," and restore his cock to his pants before he returned to the soda fountain; it was his special—and delightful—way to signal that after the store closed, we would be left alone to clean up, and he wanted us to engage in our sex play. That always involved me sucking his prick, and often included his expertly performing the same service for me. I liked it best when he spread a tarpaulin on the floor, and we both got completely naked and lay on it while we made love. Then I knew we were going to suck each other's cocks in sixty-nine.

On only the second occasion we had sex together, when Danny was about to come while I was sucking his dick, he asked me if I wanted him to shoot in my mouth. I did—desperately—and he held my head firmly as he blasted a generous load into my hungry throat. Every time after that, I either sucked him off that way, or he would watch his come shooting into my open mouth, or he would lie on his back and jack off during the last moment or two before orgasm, and then watch while I lapped the come from his belly and chest. It was impossible to say which way I preferred to eat his load—I loved the sensation of his cock erupting inside my mouth, but I also loved watching it spurt its thick white feast. In either event, I always got to eat his delicious discharge.

He never sucked me all the way off—he always managed to pull his mouth away at the last split second before I began to ejaculate—but he loved to watch me come. He usually enjoyed playing in my semen, spreading it on his cock and his stomach or chest, and rubbing it in while he murmured how good it felt. He would smile dreamily when he did that, and even if he had already given me a load, his cock would be rock hard, and I would suck it some more. On those occasions he frequently made me keep sucking until he gave me another mouthful.

Other times, if the two of us didn't clean up alone when the drug store closed, he would walk home with me after work, around eleven-thirty at night—passing through Chicago's Lincoln Park, and stopping off in the bushes to play. I especially enjoyed making love with Danny outdoors: a feeling of freedom and daring added to the joy of our sex, just as years later, my first sexual encounters with Billy—outdoors, and in the even-more-exciting full daylight—had been particularly stimulating for that reason. Danny always conveniently forgot to leave his apron back at the drug store when we headed for the park after work—so it always served as a spread to protect us from the grass and dirt as we played. The apron was also often used in "mopping up" operations after Danny had spurted his load on me in a place my tongue could not reach, or if my own load had ended up somewhere that would not allow him to rub it into his skin—like in his hair. In our park encounters, we would both get completely naked if it was warm enough, and that was, as always, particularly gratifying to me—especially if the moon was bright enough for me to enjoy the sight of his beauty while we made love.

Danny had a really magnificent body, and I loved feeling it and looking at it as I knelt before (or over) him, or as he stood and displayed himself to me. And Danny really did like to *display* his golden-brown body for me. Usually when we got completely naked in the back of the drug store, he would walk around me, posing like a bodybuilder perhaps, maybe rubbing his hands all over his body while he moaned sexily, standing with legs wide-spread and pelvis thrust forward while he stroked his hard prick, leaning over and spreading his cheeks so I could see his asshole, lying face down on the tarpaulin, and undulating his beautiful, muscular ass as he fucked the floor, etc.

When Danny paraded himself for my admiration, he would ask me, "Does this look good?," or 'What do you think of this?," or similar questions designed to elicit my praise. I invariably praised whatever part of his anatomy he was showing me, or expressed my joy in watching whatever sexy action he was taking, and I was always sincere. My spoken praise was often accompanied by more tactile demonstrations—my hands and lips often fondled and caressed every inch of his magnificent body. If the groans of satisfaction he uttered at those times were any indication, he especially enjoyed my sucking his nipples while I put a hand between his legs and played with his ass.

Once as he lay on the tarpaulin putting on a show for me, grinding his prick into it while I watched him, I became too excited by the beauty of his ass and its gyrations to wait for him to suck me and jack me off, as he usually did. I knelt between his legs, and shot my load onto his writhing buttocks. Danny cried, "Oh shit, John—that is so fuckin' *hot*." He reached behind himself, and massaged my come into his cheeks, and down into the crack between them, all the time humping and grinding his cock into the canvas below him. He raised his ass and pointed it at me. "Lick my ass clean and then suck me off." I leaned over and licked all my come from his velvet cheeks, and tongued down against his asshole, which drove him wild. Finally, he rolled over, and I drove my lips all the way down his cock; he grabbed my head tightly, and almost immediately, he began to discharge into my hungry mouth, with a huge cry of passion. I kept his ejaculate in my mouth, and rolled him back over and drizzled it onto his cheeks and his asshole. He panted his approval as I licked him clean again. Before we dressed that night, he held me tight in his arms as he told me how much he had enjoyed it—and his lips were only an inch or two from mine when he said it. I thought that *at last* he was going to kiss me, or let me kiss him, but it didn't happen.

One of our more memorable encounters happened one summer night in the park. We were lying on the ground in the bushes just east of where Wilson Avenue ends as it meets Lincoln Park, and I had been sucking Danny's prick at great length. As he was holding my head tightly in his hands and fucking my eager mouth, he said, "Come on, I've got a really great idea. Get your clothes." We both gathered our clothing, and—both of us totally naked—we walked out into the clearing and up to the top of a small hill nearby, Danny leading me by the hand until we stood atop the hill, where we dropped our clothes and embraced. I stepped back a few steps, so I could look up at him framed against the night sky. "I'm King of the Hill, John—I want you to pay tribute to your king."

There was little moonlight, but the apartment buildings and the traffic on nearby Lakeshore Drive added to it, so we could see each other clearly. Danny looked magnificent standing there on the hilltop, naked, erect, beautiful. I knelt before him and returned to the work I had begun in the bushes. I felt wonderfully *free* as we made love out in the open like that—as I paid tribute to my very own beloved king.

I don't know if anyone saw us on top of the hill that night—probably not—but if they did, they got an eyeful. My euphoria was even greater when Danny had me stop sucking his cock, raised me to my feet, and knelt before me to return the favor. He caressed my ass as he sucked me almost to the point of orgasm. "Don't shoot now, John—not yet."

"I'm real close to coming, Danny."

He stopped sucking me and stood. "That really feels good, doesn't it? I really love it when you suck me. Nobody else sucks cock like you do." I agreed it felt *almost* as wonderful to be sucked by him as to be sucking him—and it did, but not quite, since he was the most exciting, beautiful *man* I had ever seen, and servicing him gave me enormous pride and pleasure. I wondered about 'nobody else' sucking his cock as well as I did. Who else was he giving it to, and how many of them? I was never to learn.

He put his arms around me and pulled me close. "Keep your legs together—I'm going to fuck you." Since he was considerably taller than I , he had to squat slightly to put his stiff prick between my legs, under my balls. My own prick lay against his stomach as he began to fuck me between the legs. I reached down and caressed the magnificent twin globes of his hard, *driving* ass as he clutched me tight and fucked harder and faster, until finally I was rewarded with his cries of "Take it, John—here's my load." and the feel of his prick squirting its precious contents between my legs, and against my ass. He continued to caress me and hump his pretty ass until he calmed down. Then he released me, put his hand between my legs and scooped up his come. He held his hand in front of my mouth and told me to lick it clean. When I had finished, he again put his hand between my legs, and reached back to caress my ass and run a finger over my asshole as he *purred*, "That was so great—why don't you do that to me?"

I tried to duplicate his method of fucking me, but the difference in our relative height made it unworkable. If I stood before him and put my prick between his legs, it was about three or four inches below his balls—not up next to his magnificent cock, where it felt best for both of us—and if Danny squatted slightly to allow my prick to nestle against his balls, his legs parted, and failed to provide a tight sheath for me to fuck. After several attempts to find a way, Danny said, "I'll lay down, and you can fuck me that way."

He lay on his back and I inserted my prick between his tightly clenched legs, under his balls, and into the crevice between his cheeks. It fit perfectly, and I was soon fucking my precious sex-god as hard and as fast as I could. Danny held my ass as I fucked, and said, "You sure are good at that. I'm all hard again." I took hold of his prick and stroked it as I fucked. As I neared orgasm, I pulled out, took my prick and Danny's together in my fist, and masturbated us both together. Soon my prick was shooting all over my hand and Danny's belly, and he said, "Don't stop jacking us off—I'm going to come again." and as promised, his prick very shortly added its load to mine. I continued to hold our pricks together as Danny scooped up a load of come from his belly and began to massage my asshole with it. I released our pricks and got some of our come on my hand, and boldly massaged Danny's asshole with it as I knelt over him. Finally, I collapsed on top of him.

Neither of us said a word for some time. Finally he arose and pulled me to my feet. He hugged me in his arms and said, "We do have a good time together, don't me?" We dressed and left the park. It was the closest I ever came to fucking Danny before he left for college.

I probably had sex with Danny fifty or sixty times in the year or so between out first encounter in the drug store bathroom and his departure for the University of Illinois at Champaign-Urbana. I always sucked his prick a great deal, and he usually sucked mine. We often re-created our leg-fucking activities in the park, there, and in the back room of the drug store. I especially enjoyed it when Danny lay on top of me to fuck my legs; at those times, when he was humping most profoundly, and especially when he was actually ejaculating, his lips actually brushed mine, and we *almost* kissed. Each time we had sex, he invariably fed me at least one large load of come, and I shot at least one load—usually on him somewhere. Although Danny liked playing in my come, and massaging himself with it, he was never moved to taste it—even when it was mixed with his own. He often stopped sucking me and released my prick at the last possible second before my orgasm, and I frequently blasted my load onto his face, but I never observed him licking his lips.

I began high school at the same time Danny left for college. He came back to visit the drug store a few times, and although I made it perfectly clear that I desperately wanted to have sex with him again, he always declined.

I suppose I should have been heartbroken at Danny's lack of interest in continuing our sex play, and aching and restless at missing him after he left. However, I was finding new, exciting guys in high school to admire. Sexual activities in my first year or so of high school were disappointing, especially after the wild, extremely satisfying relationship I had enjoyed with Danny, but one has to make do with what is available. Until Les entered my sex life late in my sophomore year—about a year after he entered my life more generally—the guys I "made do" with were splendid, but the activities seriously limited.

All through high school, Eddie Wingo and Dick Stone were in my "home room," and I thought both were cute and endlessly sexy. Both were fairly thin, both wore extremely tight Levi's. Eddie was tall and rangy, with dark hair cut in a 'crew cut,' and sparkling black eyes that mirrored his irrepressible sense of fun. Dick was of only slightly above-average height, with tight blond curls, cropped fairly close. I cultivated their company, but couldn't seem to get close with either of them away from school. I made it a point to try to be in the boy's room with Eddie or Dick as often as possible, and standing next to him when he peed. I invariably got a hard-on watching, and always played with it a bit as I stood side-by-side with either of them. It took only a few times before Eddie was also playing with his prick and getting it hard when we peed together, but Dick took a while longer to get into the spirit of things. Eventually things heated up further, and it came to be fairly common for me to stand next to either of them in the deserted boys' room as we stroked not just our own dicks, but each others' as well—and if time and privacy permitted, we stroked ourselves or each other until we blew our loads.

The boy's room was configured in such a way that we could not be seen from the entrance as we played, and had ample time to separate if we heard someone else enter. On rare occasions, the three of us met there—and once I was jacking Dick off with one hand and Eddie with the other, when they both blew their loads, at almost exactly the same time. Eddie had been working on mine in the meantime, and in a minute or two he directed my eruption against the back-splash of the same urinal where his and Dick's loads were still oozing downward.

Neither had an unusually big prick, but Eddie's was considerably longer than mine or Dick's, and I especially found my mouth watering for it. Eddie's cock was, I believe, almost exactly the same size as Danny's, and I desperately wanted to do the same thing to it I had done so often to that of my gorgeous Latino coworker. But until one memorable night just as we began our final semester in high school we never got past playing with each other's pricks and jacking ourselves or each other off to orgasm.

Eddie and Dick were cute; Dean Henderson, on the other hand, was quite the most beautiful guy I had ever seen—eclipsing even the wonder of Danny Morales' beauty. Dean was a senior when I was a freshman. Tall, with golden blond hair, an incredibly sensitive face, and a trim body, he usually wore tight, faded Levi's with a fascinating bulge prominently displayed at the crotch. I drooled over him constantly, but had no occasion to even speak to him. We moved in completely different circles, but I was totally in awe of his beauty and desirability, so I just followed him whenever I could, gazing adoringly at his face and his body. Any time I saw him head into the boy's room I went in and hoped to position myself next to him so I could see, in the flesh, the cause of that bulge in his pants. I often saw Dean's cock while I stood next to him at the urinal, and it was big and beautiful, and tempting in the extreme. I always played with my prick if we were alone together, but was never emboldened to make a "pass." Dean seemed to ignore me—boys playing with their cocks in a high school bathroom is not at all unusual—but he must surely have become aware of my attentions and the frequency with which we "happened" to share the boy's room.

Eventually my persistence paid off, but far too briefly. Toward the end of my freshman year—Dean's senior year—I stood two urinals down from him and played with my hard prick, and I saw that he was having trouble starting to urinate, because his prick was rock hard, standing straight out in front of him—and it was long and it was unthinkably beautiful. He looked around to be sure we were alone, then looked at me and said, "Do you like what you see?" He approached me, his hard cock jutting out from his fly, and bobbing and swaying as he walked. "You're always looking at it, but this is the way you've been wanting to see it, right?"

I could hardly speak, I was so enthralled. I barely managed to gasp, "You've got a wonderful dick."

Dean stroked his cock, and said, "Then why don't you help me with it. C'mere." He walked over to a stall, and stepped inside, turning around and saying, "Get in here if you want it." I went in the stall, and locked the door behind me. He unbuttoned his Levi's, and pushed them and his shorts down to his ankles. His cock looked even bigger and more mouth-watering as he said, "Get down there and suck on it. I'll give you a load if you want it."

I knelt before him, and he grasped my head fiercely and sank his shaft into my adoring mouth." I buried my lips in his golden pubic hair—I had learned well under Danny's tutelage—and began to suck profoundly as I cupped his butt cheeks in my hands and he began to fuck my mouth. "Wow, that's fantastic—you've done this before, huh?" His cheeks writhed and humped under my caress, and he shoved his cock fiercely in and out. At times he thrust his cock so deep into me that I gagged, but each time I did, he kept fucking just as savagely, and cried "C'mon, take it." I began masturbating almost as intensely as he was fucking me. Eventually, he pulled my head in and held it tight against his belly as his cock began to fill my mouth with his hot come. Instead of blasting deep in my throat, as Danny's had always done, Dean's come flowed from his cock, and after his climax was complete, he continued to hold my head and fuck my mouth, but gently, as he murmured, "Shit, that felt great. You're a great cocksucker, you know that? You swallow all of it?" I nodded, and he added, "Good boy."

As Dean's come had begun to flow, I had stopped jacking off, and returned my hands to his ass, to fondle it while I reveled in the sensation of his orgasm. When he had finished coming, I again returned to working on my own cock. Dean said, "You can keep sucking my dick until you shoot."

It took very little time after that before I blasted my load. When I had finished, and my gasping had subsided, Dean pulled his cock from my mouth and chuckled. I bet you got your come all over my shorts. Did you?"

I saw that I had apparently shot most of my load between his legs, and against the commode, but there was some semen on his shorts, and on the fly of his Levi's. "Yeah, a little."

"Well, you gotta clean me off before I pull my pants back up. Guess you can eat a little more come, even if it's your own."

I licked the come from his Levi's, but basically had to suck it from his shorts, where it had been blotted up. My come tasted good, but *sucking it from Dean Henderson's shorts* was a special thrill.

When I had finished, I stood and we both pulled our pants up and buttoned them. Dean grinned at me. "You give a mean blowjob, and I really enjoyed it, but it ain't gonna happen again, understand? That's not my style. Now let's get outa here before somebody comes." He laughed, "Before somebody *else* comes, I mean."

I turned around and unlocked the door, and we left the stall. A student I didn't know, and never saw again, as far as I know, stood at the urinals with his pants undone, masturbating furiously and staring at us. He had obviously heard most of what had gone on. Dean and I looked at each other and giggled, and watched our spectator jack off for a minute, until he turned around and blasted a load into the urinal. We left the bathroom before he turned around again.

I still followed Dean into the boy's room when I got the opportunity, but except for once, when we had a virtual repeat of our first encounter, he always ignored me, as if nothing had ever happened between us.

My only other *determined* campaign was even less successful; Don Shuman, with the very tightest Levi's in school and the most beautiful, perfectly rounded ass I had ever imagined, completely eluded me. He was cute, he was sweet, he was friendly, I knew him at school, and I even tried to grope him once, but I never even came close to seeing his prick, much less beholding in the flesh what I thought at the time was the most perfect ass in the universe.

Les Coston, on the other hand, became the first big "love of my life" without my waging any kind of campaign. We initially became friends through shared church activities, and only gradually did he begin to interest me sexually. He was good-looking, but not exceptionally so, and he had a good build, but, again, nothing special.

Les's outgoing nature won me over when he urged me to share his enthusiasm for swimming, and to learn to play tennis with him. I was not much interested in athletics, although I was reasonably fit and coordinated, but Les was so friendly, and I liked him so much, that I was more than willing to take an interest in what he wanted to do, just so I could be with him—and he reciprocated, going with me to the concerts and plays I especially enjoyed. He quickly became the best friend I had ever had, and we were at each others' houses frequently—a kind of closeness with a friend I had not shared since I had moved to Chicago from Minneapolis, at the age of eleven.

It was in the shower room at a YMCA swimming pool that I discovered that even though it was not hard at that moment, Les had a really huge prick, and I began to hope for an even more meaningful relationship than the already rewarding, but non-sexual friendship we shared. In retrospect, I'm surprised we took so long in getting around to having sex with each other, since Les talked and kidded about it a lot, and I, of course, was preoccupied with it. At any rate, we eventually got around to it in a big way.

The first time I got to see Les's cock in its full glory was in a tent, when we were camping out on a bicycle trip. We had both stripped to our shorts, and had lain there for some time talking, often about sex. Les said. "I've really got a hard-on, you wanna see it?" I had been stroking my own erection for some time in the dark, hoping that our sex talk would inspire Les to suggest we play with each other. I was thinking about Les's big cock often by then, and was hoping to find a way to open sexual negotiations with my friend—but without offending him, and risking the loss of his treasured friendship. I expressed my keen desire to see his cock hard, and when he played a flashlight over it, I almost gasped in awe.

The sight of it thrilled me; his erect cock was enormous—and he not only showed it to me with more-than-justifiable pride, he encouraged me to play with it. It was unimaginably rigid when I first grasped it, and larger by far than any cock I had ever seen, much less felt—fatter, and significantly longer than Danny's. I began to stroke it and study it as he held the light on it, and soon I was unable to resist the temptation to suck it. As my mouth closed around the end of Les's gigantic cock, he propped up the flashlight, so it would provide some illumination, and took hold of my head, which he slowly began to drive up and down his lip-stretching shaft. "I was hoping you'd want to do that." I managed to accommodate all of his challenging endowment—God knows, I had practiced enough with Danny.

Les pulled his shorts off, and I followed suit, so we were both naked. He lay on his back and I knelt over him while he fucked my mouth hard and deep, but also—somehow I knew—lovingly. "Man, Johnny, you do that really great." Les was, incidentally, the only person who ever called me "Johnny" regularly.

Later, at his request, I rolled onto my back while he knelt with his knees in my armpits, and lay over my head and fucked my face for a very, very long time. Les pulled his dick from my mouth and moved back, so he could play with mine. He sat back and stroked my cock and manipulated my balls for a few minutes before he reversed his body so that he crouched over me in sixty-nine, took my prick into his mouth, and began to suck wildly—I, of course, sucked his just as fiercely, while I played with his ass.

Les slurped and murmured his pleasure loudly as his tightly-held lips drove all the way up and down my cock, and he sucked prodigiously. My best friend was a very talented cocksucker—and it had taken me something like a year to find out. At the same time I *feasted* as he hammered his monster tool down into my ravenous mouth. I had loved sucking Danny's prick, and my brief taste of Dean's pretty tool had been wonderful, but this was *major meat*.

It had been a year since I had sucked a dick, and even though that cock had been the divine Dean Henderson's, it had been a long, dry spell since. My masturbatory play with Eddie and Dick had helped keep my libido in check, but I was starved for cock—and Les was feeding me a banquet.

He knelt over me while we sucked each other, and soon I told him I was about to shoot my load. He stopped sucking me and focused the flashlight on my prick, and said "I want to see you come." I continued sucking his huge tool as I began to masturbate. Les took over for me, and soon his driving fist brought the come shooting from me as I moaned and sucked his prick even deeper and harder. He continued to hold my prick as he said. "That was great, Johnny—I really liked seeing you get your load.

I stopped sucking him long enough to tell him I wanted him to shoot all over me. He turned around so that he knelt over my chest and faced my head as he continued to fuck my mouth. "I can't do that yet—but I really want to. Keep sucking, maybe I can come this time." I found it astonishing that such a sexy guy, with such a gargantuan prick, one who loved fucking my mouth, and one who sucked my cock like an expert—although admittedly my cock offered far less challenge than his did—was unable to do what I had been doing for several years. Furthermore, Les was actually six months older than I.

I was thirsty for come, and had been hoping to drink from Les's fabulous dick, but it didn't distract me from enjoying what I was doing, and I kept sucking him happily for a very long time. Finally he told me to quit, that he wasn't going to be able to shoot. Truthfully, my throat and jaw were so tired from sucking, and his prick had stretched my lips so much, I was actually relieved to stop.

We lay together for a long time, holding each other—more as friends than as sex partners, I believe—talking about what we had just done, and who else we had done it with. I told Les about Danny, and my limited experiences with Eddie, Dick, and Dean. Les told me that aside from some rather juvenile sex play on Boy Scout trips, his experience had been limited to a couple of encounters with Bob Glass.

Bob was on our school swimming team with Les, and I knew him because he had been in several of my classes. I had never thought too much about Bob in a sexual way—although he seemed nice enough, and was reasonably attractive. But when Les told me that night that Bob had the biggest prick he had ever seen—he referred to it reverently as a "purple monster"—Bob suddenly seemed *much* more attractive to me.

Les told me all about his two experiences with Bob:

They had found themselves left alone together in the shower after swimming practice one afternoon earlier in the year, and had begun to compare their unusually impressive endowments. One thing led to another, and they were soon both hard and playing with each other. Les told me they adjourned to his house to continue their play without fear of being interrupted. Les's parents both worked, but even when they were home, his bedroom was isolated enough, and they respected his privacy enough, that he was free to do anything reasonable in his own room.

In Les's bedroom, they got naked again, and showed each other how big their pricks could *really* get. They began to masturbate each other seriously. Les asked Bob if he had ever had his dick sucked, and Bob admitted he had been getting blowjobs since he was in grade school.

Les laughed nervously, and said, "Yeah, but I'll bet you never gave one, didja?"

Bob laughed outright, and said, "Don't be too sure of that. Givin' a blowjob is almost as much fun as gettin' one." He was holding his stupendous shaft out in front of him and stroking it as he added, "You wanna get down there and find out?" He didn't have to extend a second invitation.

Les knelt in front of Bob, and he stroked the enormous shaft while he kissed and licked the cock-head before opening his mouth *wide* to feast on the biggest cock he had ever seen.

"Johnny, I could hardly get my lips around it, but I stretched 'em, and when he started to fuck my mouth, I thought I'd choke."

"But you didn't make him stop, did you?"

Les laughed, "God, no—I was enjoying hell out if it." He returned to his story.

Bob fucked Les's mouth happily for several minutes, then pulled him over to the bed, where he lay on his back and told Bob to get over him in sixty-nine position, so they could suck each other at the same time.

I interrupted again. "How did Bob take yours? It just about choked me, you know, like his did you."

"He sucked cock like a champ. I don't see how he got it all in his throat, but every inch of me was all the way inside of his mouth. And he could really give me some suction, too—like you did, Johnny." Here he patted my ass and pulled me to him. "You suck cock like a champ, too."

"So do you, Les. I really liked it when you sucked me—best ever, really."

"You ready to do it again?"

"I want to hear about you and Bob first, but I sure want it again after that."

"Well, we sucked each other for a long time, and finally Bob said he was gonna shoot, so he knelt over me and just about covered me with come. Man, it looked so hot shootin' out of that purple monster of his. Then he sucked me some more, and finally he got hard again, and I sucked him some more. I barely got his prick out of my mouth before he shot another big load on me—splashed all over my face this time. It really was hot, Johnny—I wish you had been there with me."

"God, me too. But you didn't get your load when you were with him?"

"I wish I could, Johnny . . . but one of these days, y'know? Anyway, Bob said he was disappointed, but he didn't mind since he got to give me a second load."

"You said you fucked with him another time."

"Right. The second time was one night after a swim meet. We went to his house that time, and we sucked each other in his bed for a really long time. Then he climbed on top of me and was fucking my mouth when he reached over to the night stand and got a jar of Vaseline. And he reached around and put some in his asshole and covered my prick with it. Then he put his asshole over the end of my dick, and started to slide down."

"You mean you put your prick inside his ass?"

"Yeah, and it was fantastic. He just kept twitching his ass and moving down a little at a time until my dick was all the way inside him, and then he started to bounce up and down on it. It felt better than anything I've ever felt. He rode my cock like that for about five minutes, and I kept jacking off his big ol' prick all the time, and pretty soon he sat down real hard on my prick and shot his load all over me. Man, it was so hot I couldn't stand it. He cleaned my dick off, and started sucking it again—and after a while he was ready to blow again, and he beat off like he did the first time.

"When he blew his load that time, I was jackin' off like crazy, and had my mouth wide open, tellin' him to give it to me, and a big gob of come went right inside."

"Wow. What was that like?" I asked—knowing only too well how wonderful it must have been, but anxious to know how Les felt about it, hoping he had found it exciting, so he might be willing to do for me what Danny had never done, and what I had done for Danny so many times.

"I don't know. It kinda surprised me, I guess—but it wasn't too bad. I spit it out, and Bob looked sorta disappointed. Maybe I shoulda given it another taste, 'cause Bob leaned over me and licked all his come offa me and swallowed it, and it looked like he loved it."

I grinned at him, although he couldn't see it in the dim light. "Well, I told you how much I loved eating Danny's load. And besides, you oughta give it another try—my mother always says you should try new foods."

Les was grinning when he answered, "Yeah, well, maybe sometime. And maybe one of these days I'll give you something good to eat, too." He had been reaching behind me, and gently inserting the tip of a finger into my asshole, working it a little more energetically as his description of fucking Bob grew more heated. "Could I try to fuck your ass, Johnny?"

"I don't think I can do that—but I really wish I could."

He took one of my hands and put it on his cock—still hard and huge—and said, "Just think how good that would feel up your ass. And fucking it would feel really good to me, Johnny. C'mon, be a pal. You've always done whatever I wanted you to do. I really wanna fuck you in the ass. You liked me fuckin' your mouth, didn'tcha?"

"God, yes, Les. I'll try, okay? But not tonight—next time, when I haven't got my rocks off before we start. But I can't promise I can take this big thing." His finger was still probing, and he had most of it inside me by that time—it felt *extremely* good, and I was beginning to think taking his cock there might be feasible, after all.

"C'mon, if Bob can take it up the ass, so can you." His full finger was now slowly plunging in and out of my ass. "Doesn't this feel good?"

"It feels great, Les—but it's a big jump from your finger to this" There I squeezed his throbbing tool. "We can try next time—but I really can't promise I'll be able to take it."

He looked into my eyes. "But we'll try next time, okay? Promise me that, anyway." I nodded agreement. "Just *kinda* sit on it now, and let me jack you off again, okay?" I got on top of him, and his huge prick filled the crevice between the cheeks of my ass as I clenched them around his shaft and bobbed up and down. "That really feels good, keep it up—Jesus, I wanna be inside your ass." He masturbated me with very fast and long strokes, and soon I shot my load on him as we both panted and grunted in passion. He pulled me down on top of him and whispered savagely into my ear, "I want to fuck your ass soon."

I went down on him, and kissed the head of his cock, "I really do want this inside me any way I can get it. It's so big and hot." I sucked for a long time, but he was obviously not going to come, so eventually we went to sleep. I had never slept like this—with someone I'd been having sex with—and it was wonderful, even if our bed was only a pallet in a tent. I woke up several times during the night, and snuggled against him. I didn't want to disturb his sleep, and it was all I could do to keep my hands and mouth off him.

I would undoubtedly have begun pursuing Bob Glass to get a taste of the famed "purple monster" for myself, but my burgeoning affair with Les consumed my sexual attention. Furthermore, Les had sworn me to secrecy about Bob, so there was no easy way to open the subject with him. I did manage to see Bob's prick in the boy's room one time when he was pissing—and even though it was soft, it was incredibly impressive, looking like it hung down to his knee. Bob Glass's cock was probably as big as Hal Weltmann's, and many times, over the years, I dreamed of it, and regretted never having experienced the delights of that stupendous organ. Unfortunately, only dreams.

As far as I *know*, Les and Bob never got together again to match their magnificent cocks—at any rate, if they did, Les said nothing about it. As I soon came to know, the sensation of Les's massive tool up the ass was addictive—surely if Bob had enjoyed it once, he would have pursued further encounters; God knows I did.

After our wonderful sexual *debut* in the tent, Les and I became regular sex partners. We sucked each other at his house after school, or on those occasions when we were so unusually horny we cut a class or two to work in a midday blowjob (Les's house was close to our school). I often slept over at his house, but he only came over to my apartment for lovemaking occasionally—it was harder to hide our activities from my mother than it was from his parents. Les's prick, huge as it was, soon felt right at home when buried in my throat—as his hot mouth felt *just right* when he sucked mine.

Les worked as a lifeguard at a hotel swimming pool, and I frequently helped him clean up after closing, when we would indulge our love of cocksucking. It was in the locker room there one evening, as I stood on a bench, with Les standing before me and sucking greedily, that he did not pull back when I warned him I was about to shoot, and he finally ate my load. He kept it in his mouth and swished it around for a moment before swallowing. He grinned and declared it was not only edible, but delicious in the extreme, and he sampled more of that same *cuisine* later that same night in his bed. He regretted not having *dined* more fully when Bob Glass had blown come into his mouth—and I always suspected he and Bob got together at least a few times after that so he could rectify that failure. I knew I would have.

By that time I was in love with Les. I had loved Danny, of course, but I always knew there was no hope of him feeling about me as I did about him. But Les became my whole life, and even though I kept up my studies and musical activities in school, and continued to work twenty or thirty hours a week at the drug store, I thought about him all the time, and spent every minute I could with him—even if we weren't having sex. I loved him when we weren't having sex, but I *adored* him where we were—and my adoration was about to grow into near worship.

Les had been continuing his campaign to fuck me in the ass, and I pursued the same with him. He had come to enjoy the feeling of my finger fucking him, as I enjoyed his, and we occasionally tried to insert our cocks into each other, but we were both put off by the pain. He always made his attempts to fuck me before I had shot a load, assuming I would be more receptive and eager, but it hadn't worked. Finally, one night when I was sleeping over with Les it finally happened. When we had first gone to bed, we had tried to fuck each other, unsuccessfully, but had serviced one another orally, and Les had eaten my load with his newfound enthusiasm. As always, I had spent a great deal of time sucking and masturbating Les, still hoping to finally achieve the eruption of magnificent, hot come that I knew he would some day give me. It hadn't happened, of course, and we finally drifted off to sleep.

Sometime in the middle of the night he woke me—his hard prick fucking me between my legs—and asked if he could try to fuck me again. Of course he could try. And of course I wanted him to. Wielding the Vaseline, he liberally coated his cock, and used his fingers to line my asshole very thoroughly before beginning his assault. He fucked me rather thoroughly with one finger, then added another. He managed to add part of a third finger before suddenly replacing his fingers with the head of his huge prick. It hurt terribly, but I wanted him in me so badly that I relaxed as much as I could, and felt the head of his prick slip past my sphincter muscle. The pain was intense, but Les was *cooing* encouragement in my ear (we lay on our sides, with him behind me) and he very gradually pressed until his shaft was sliding slowly into me. It hurt, but it felt wonderful at the same time, and the joy gradually overcame the pain. I felt flushed with excitement, and experienced the most wonderfully *full* feeling I had ever known.

Les began a very shallow fuck, which made me feel even better, and I began to press my ass backward in counter-rhythm, to meet his forward thrusts. I cried out in pain at first, but also encouraged him to keep invading me. His thrusts became more energetic, and his shaft drove in an out of me with increasingly long strokes. I was by then seized by complete rapture.

Les was gasping in pleasure, and crushing me to him as he kissed and nibbled my neck and ear. He assured me he would take it as easy as he could. Soon his entire shaft was buried inside me, and we lay there unmoving for a long moment, basking in the incredible warmth of being locked together in this most special and wonderful way. Les whispered, "Jesus, Johnny, that feels so *good*. Do you like it?"

"I *love* it, Les." I reached behind and fondled his ass. "I love *you.*"

Les whispered back, "I love you too, Johnny." For the first time, just as Les first began to fuck my ass, he whispered the words I longed to hear from him, and which we would exchange many times after that. It was very early in the morning on Wednesday, November 15, 1950, in the Coston house on Ridge Avenue near Glenwood Avenue in Chicago, Illinois—not a time or place I am likely to forget. And there was yet another wonderful "first" to be reached that glorious morning.

I had dreamed of taking a dick up my ass for a long time—I had somehow always *known* it was going to be wonderful—and I was ecstatic as Les began his loving invasion. I was finally getting fucked, and by the boy I loved, and who loved me. But my God, what a prick it was for my initiation as a bottom. If I hadn't been in love with Les, I doubt I could have taken his immense cock in me that night.

He was gentle at first when he began to fuck me, but as I gradually began to thrill to the wonder of him, we picked up the pace to the point where I was bucking and driving back onto Les's huge tool as wildly as he was thrusting it forward into me. He continued his assault for a very long time, and I was as delirious with sexual excitement as I had ever been, or even dreamt of being. Les had been playing with my own cock while he fucked me, but I had been holding back, knowing that once I climaxed—which would be the second time that night—I would feel the pain more than the ecstasy. Finally, I could hold it no longer. "Oh God, Les, shove it all the way in and roll me on top of you—I've gotta come."

He penetrated me as deeply as he could (very deep, indeed) and rolled on his back, with me still miraculously impaled on that throbbing, thrilling cock. He masturbated me savagely, and my come was soon spurting on his hand and my belly. "God, Johnny—this is great. I wish I could be *eating* your come right now."

The pain of his penetration did, indeed, return to some extent following my orgasm. I asked him to please take it out slowly, and he was especially gentle as he did so. Then he rolled me over so that we were face to face, and my come was still slippery on his hands as his arms pulled me tightly to him, and his lips were only an inch from mine when he whispered, "I do love you, Johnny." I assured him I loved him more than anything in the world, and I achieved another milestone: for the first time in my life I really kissed a man—and he returned my kiss with the same sincerity. We held each other close, fondling and kissing each other—mostly tenderly and sweetly, but also with great passion when our tongues danced together and Les ground his still-hard prick against me before we went back to sleep.

I was head-over-heels *in love* for the first time in my life. I had had a huge crush on Danny, of course, and had been terribly attracted to Eddie and Dick, to say nothing of that gorgeous Mount Everest of Beauty, Dean Henderson, but this was something else; the way I felt about Les was real, it was deep—he was the man I *loved*. I didn't know whether Les was saying "I'm *in love with* you" when he told me "I love you." That was certainly what I meant when I said it to him. I didn't care; he loved me, and that was enough—and I was now able to show my love in the way he wanted me to.

Les immediately equipped his locker at the hotel swimming pool with a large jar of Vaseline, and we each kept a jar convenient to our beds in our respective homes. Every time we met for sex—and we met more and more frequently—Les fucked my ass endlessly. He loved the sensation, apparently, as much as I.

I especially enjoyed kneeling on all fours on the diving board at the deserted, after-hours hotel swimming pool where he worked, while Les stood straddling the board and grasped my waist tightly as he fucked me—or while he lay on his back on the diving board and I stood astride him to ride his cock. Those were the ways we both liked to fuck best when we were feeling especially hungry and horny, wherever we might be; when we were in a more romantic mood, I would lie on my back with my legs wrapped around Les's waist so he could fuck me in the missionary position, and we could share kisses at the same time. We enjoyed the boisterous kind of fucking best when we made love by the swimming pool, because the cavernous space had an extremely resonant acoustic, and our cries of passion were echoed and amplified, and ricocheted all around us at a high decibel level. Les's cries of joy in fucking me were all the more exciting when they surrounded me that way, and increased the thrill I derived both from his hammering that marvelous big cock deep into me, and from the highly vocal expressions of his obviously enormous delight in doing so. My echoing cries of "I love your cock, Les." of "Fuck me harder." seemed to stimulate my lover to even greater heights of passion.

If only he had been able to come, and if only he had been able to take me in *his* ass. It seemed unthinkable that such a wonderfully endowed *fuckmaster* as Les Coston should have been unable to shoot a load from his formidable cock, to experience the ecstasy of ejaculation. Moreover, his fucking me was so unbearably exciting, I grieved that he could not know the thrill he gave me when his prick entered my hungry ass, and plunged in and out—although my cock wouldn't be anything like as thrilling to him as his monster was to me.

He really tried to reach orgasm when we made love. He fucked me endlessly, often continuing to drive his cock into me long after I had come, or long after I was ready to stop. He urged me to keep sucking him long after I was too tired to want to continue. He occasionally *forced* me to keep sucking him or keep taking his cock up my ass even when I begged him to stop, and while I'm nothing like a masochist, I must admit I enjoyed extra thrills when he did that. We both masturbated his beautiful cock at such length that at times it was almost bruised. All this in the wonderful cause of orgasm—but still without results.

I wanted desperately to drink his come as he drank mine, and he certainly wanted to feed me what I craved. He experienced an occasional wet dream—unfortunately, never when I was sleeping with him. Even if I were to miss eating it when one of those spontaneous orgasms actually arrived, I would have been thrilled to clean up after him that way: the thought of the gigantic load that must have been building up in that huge prick was staggering.

He was also very eager to get fucked—and he seriously, conscientiously tried to take me into his ass; he knew very well how thrilling I found his prick inside me, and he was anxious to experience the thrill himself. But however much Vaseline we applied, however diligently we tried, he always sorrowfully made me stop before I ever got more than the head of my prick past his sphincter. He enjoyed getting fucked by one finger, and "rode" it enthusiastically. If he was particularly excited, I was able to put part of a second finger in him, but no dick in Les's ass yet. He often had me shoot my load directly onto his ass, and massage it in with my finger. I know he really wanted me to fuck him, but he maintained it just hurt too much.

To make up for not being able to take my load in his ass, Les took special pains to take it in his mouth. We never got together that he didn't have me shoot my load into the depths of his throat as he sucked me at least once—and often more than once—but I managed to spew a lot onto his face and body as well. He particularly enjoyed lying on his back while I knelt over his face and masturbated, so we could both see me shoot into his open mouth. He frequently shared my load with me as we kissed passionately following my orgasm—and I must admit, I tasted damn fine.

8

FULFILLING FIRST LOVE'S PROMISES

He whispered, "Gonna miss that hot ass of yours." I told him, "And I'm gonna miss that big dick of yours." I knew by then that he was going into the Marine Corps in a few weeks, so I added, "Think of me every time you fuck some Marine's ass."
Eddie laughed, "I guess I'm gonna be thinking of you a lot."

Les went off to college a semester before I did—to a university in Wisconsin. After his departure, my sex life was *relatively* dull, although not stagnant, thanks to the charms of the sexy Dave Elton, and sudden revived interest from an unexpected quarter.

Dave was the younger brother of Mike Elton, one of my two best friends in the school band. He was two years younger than I, and I had known him a couple of years by the time Les graduated. Dave was not especially handsome, only nice-looking, but he had a really splendid body, and I had been hot for it for since I'd first seen him. He was tall—at least six three'—with extremely long legs and a cute little bubble butt. He had a massive chest, tapering to a very narrow waist, and his arms and shoulders were heavily muscled—he enjoyed lifting weights, and it showed. His upper body was not at all out of proportion, though; nature had obviously given him a fine build, and he merely defined and toned it in his basement gym. Dave in a tight T-shirt, or stripped to the waist, was an awesome sight.

A few weeks after Les left for college, Dave and Mike and I shared a tent one night on a weekend boating trip to Fox Lake, about fifty miles from Chicago. It was the very same tent where I had first seen Les's cock erect, and had first sucked it. I was hoping the tent might prove lucky again, and it did.

When the three of us stripped down to our briefs and retired for the night. I made sure I slept in the middle, between Dave and his brother. I let a leg press against one of Dave's while we all talked and joked for a while, and he didn't move his away. Getting bolder, I reached down and scratched my left leg, as it pressed against his, and let my hand remain down there, resting on both our legs, where they touched. Dave apparently didn't mind that either, and when I gradually began to ease my hand toward the inside of his leg, he rolled to his side, facing me, and I could feel the crotch of his briefs pressing against my arm. I pressed my arm into it, and he began to hump slowly.

I rolled to my side, facing him, and reached down to grope the bulge in his shorts. His prick was hard as a rock, and when I began to massage his balls, his hand came over and began to fondle my crotch—I was, of course, fully hard by that time, myself. I reached inside the waistband of his shorts, and began to stroke his cock. He stopped playing with me, and pulled his underwear down to give me free access. I pulled mine down as well, and we reached for each other simultaneously, each of us grasping a cock obviously ready for action.

Mike was, by that time, snoring heavily, and oblivious to what Dave and I were doing. Oddly enough, Dave's brother was *much* more handsome than he, but I was not attracted to him—he wasn't sexy like Dave, and he didn't have the glorious body that Dave had. I had slept with Mike on several band trips, but I had never been tempted to make a pass at him. If Dave had been in the band also, I'm sure I would have arranged it so I could have slept with him instead of his brother. This was the first opportunity I had found to sound him out—and, hopefully, to feel him up.

I was propped up on an elbow while I played with Dave, so I had only one hand free to explore. I soon stopped stroking his cock and fondling his balls with it, and began to run it over his exciting shoulders and chest. He continued to stroke my dick—actually masturbating me by then. I pulled his head in to me and whispered very softly into his ear—I didn't want to wake Mike up—"C'mon outside."

I pulled up my shorts, and backed out of the tent on my hands and knees. I watched for a few minutes, and began to wonder if Dave was going to follow me, but he finally crawled out, head-first. He stood and whispered, "I wanted to be sure Mike was still sleeping." We had pitched our tent in a grassy clearing, and I walked over to stand at the edge of the clearing, above the tent. The tent flap opened out into the middle of the clearing, so I went to stand where Mike would not immediately see us if he woke up and poked his head out to see where we had gone. Dave followed me. I dropped my shorts to my ankles and stepped out of them as Dave approached.

The moon was very bright, and I could clearly see Dave drop his shorts and stand there looking at me. His body was nothing short of magnificent, and his cock stood straight out from his body, quivering in full erection. His cock wasn't in the same league as Les's, or even Danny's, but it was still very tempting; it was probably a bit over six inches in length—about the same as my own. I stepped in to him and took it in my hand. He reached down and took mine as I whispered, "I wasn't sure you'd come"

He snickered quietly, "I haven't come yet—but I will. I'm so horny I'm gonna have to come pretty soon, no matter what happens." He released my dick and pressed his body tightly against mine as he took my waist in his hands and ground himself into me. "You wanna help me?"

I released his cock, and put my hands around his body to cup his buttocks in my hands. "Can I help myself at the same time?"

Dave's ass writhed in my hands, and he reached down to hold mine, and we ground our cocks together. "You can help yourself to anything I've got—you gonna do the same for me?"

"You can bet this pretty little ass I will." I put my arms around him and fondled his back and shoulders. I was astonished when he not only returned my embrace, but held the nape of my neck in one hand, pressed his lips to mine, and drove his tongue deep into my mouth.

We necked for a long time, our hands playing over each other's bodies and asses. Coming up for air, Dave asked, "Surprised?" I nodded. "You know, I've been watching you check me out ever since you started coming around the house—like, I'd watch you talking to Mike, but I could see you were sneakin' a peek at my butt at the same time. And when I'm only wearin' shorts or my bathing suit, or even just have my shirt off, you look like you wanna eat me up. I can't believe that Mike doesn't notice once in a while, anyway."

"I didn't know I was so obvious," I said.

"Oh, you weren't obvious, but I was watching close, to see if you were interested—'cause I was interested in you. I was so glad when you started playing with me tonight—I didn't think you were ever gonna make a pass at me, and I was afraid to put a move on you until I was sure." He kissed me again, "Now I'm sure you're interested, and I guess you can tell I'm interested, too." He humped his cock against my belly when he said the last.

I began to fondle his broad chest, cupping his breasts as he murmured his satisfaction. "Suck 'em," he gasped, pressing my head in his hands, and pushing it down toward a nipple. "I love that." I sucked his large nipples in rotation, at the same time reaching behind him to caress his busy ass with one hand, and up between his legs to fondle his balls with the other, while he humped his cock against my forearm. "God, John—that's fantastic." He moaned in pleasure while I sucked. "I love gettin' my tits sucked almost as much as I like gettin' somethin' else sucked."

I raised my head to kiss him passionately, and then whispered, "I wanna suck anything you want sucked."

"I'm glad to hear that—I need my dick sucked in the worst way. And it's not gonna be a one-way deal. You want a blowjob, too?" He gave me a quick kiss, and chuckled. "A little sixty-nine sound good to you?"

"Oh hell, yes, Dave. Please."

He fell to his knees. "Well, since you asked so politely . . . " he said, and engulfed my cock in his mouth in one swoop, as his hands cupped my ass cheeks and he pulled my body tight against his mouth. It was clear he was no novice. I held him by the hair and fucked his mouth, and he drove his head down my cock in perfect sync each time I thrust it forward, all the time sucking prodigiously.

He would occasionally stop bobbing his head and sucking, and hold my ass still while his tongue played eagerly all over my cock, inside his mouth. It was during one of those moments I said, "I'm gonna come soon, Dave. If you don't wanna take . . . "

He groaned around my cock, "No, I want it—gimme your load." And with that he returned to his sucking with renewed vigor. It was clear he was eager to get my load, and in a moment I gave it to him. He murmured his approval all the time I was erupting inside his mouth—and I gave him a *lot* of what he wanted. He lapped at my cock with his tongue, bathing it in my own discharge for some time before he swallowed, and stood. He kissed me, and I could taste my come on his tongue. "God, John, you musta been saving that up for me. What a mouthful."

I whispered into his mouth, "It's been a long time since I got sucked off. You gonna give me a mouthful, too?"

He laughed quietly, "Well, I got sucked off last night, but I'll still have plenty to give you—I've been wanting to give some to you long enough."

I was somewhat startled. I had always thought of Dave as shy, and more than likely relatively inexperienced sexually. "Who sucked you off last night?"

"We had a Scout meeting. If they gave merit badges for cocksucking, about half our troop would have a chest full of 'em—but our Scoutmaster would have the most. He taught me everything I know about it. Did he do a good job?"

"He did a great job," I answered. "I'm not a Boy Scout, but I managed to learn a lot on my own. You want me to show you?"

Again he pushed my head down—but this time he also pushed me to my knees. His cock was jutting out from his flat stomach, the tip trembling at my lips. "Yeah—show me, John. I need it."

Dave's cock fit nicely into my throat, and even his most savage thrusts didn't gag me when he fucked my mouth. I sucked for a long time before he bent over, pulling his cock from my mouth, and kissed me, then whispered into my ear, "I usually like to *tell* a guy who sucks dick as good as you do what a good job he's doing, but we sure-as-shit don't wanna wake Mike up. You want me to blow in your mouth, too?"

"Oh yeah. But I hope you're not ready yet—I'm really having a good time."

"I'll hold off as long as I can—I'm not anxious for you to stop suckin' me, either. But when I shoot off, keep my come in your mouth, okay? Then you can drizzle it over my tits and suck it off of 'em. A lot of the guys I screw around with like to do that—and it *really* turns me on." *("A lot of the guys I screw around with."? I wondered how many that might be.)* He rose, and stepped over to the makeshift clothesline we had rigged to dry our towels and bathing suits. He brought the towels back with him and spread them on the grass. He whispered, "We can lay down here—'n then my come'll stay on my tits while you suck on 'em. I'll give you an extra thick load, like I always do. How's that?"

"Sounds great, but c'mon, I wanna get back to your dick." I lay down on my back on the towels, and pulled Dave over me. He knelt straddling me, and laced his fingers behind my neck, then pulled my head into an upright position and shoved his cock into my hungry mouth.

He fucked my mouth almost brutally, occasionally whispering "Yeah, eat my big dick. or "God you're good at this." or "C'mon and suck me dry." Finally, after about ten solid minutes of his ferocious mouth-fuck, he hissed, "Here it comes—remember not to swallow any of it." And with that his come began to spurt forcefully into me, and he continued to fuck as hard and as deeply as he was able until he was entirely spent. He pulled my head even tighter in to him, and I could feel his chest heaving with passion. He whispered, "That was amazing. You still got it in your mouth?" I nodded, and he pulled his cock from my mouth and leaned down to kiss my lips. "Good boy. Now squirt it all over my tits."

He lay on his back next to me, and I leaned over to deposit his come on his swelling, rounded breasts. He had promised me a mouthful, and he had promised an extra-thick load; he made good on both counts. His thick white come remained on his chest, even when it slowly oozed down there from the mounds of his breasts. He breathed, "Oh God, yes—that's so fuckin' hot." while I was drizzling my mouthful over his tits, and when I began to suck it from him, paying special attention to his large, hard nipples, he panted and writhed under me, saying "Suck 'em for me, John—Jesus, I love it."

I did not swallow as I lapped up his thick come, and when I had all of it, I held my head over his and kissed him. He opened his mouth, and I let the come flow from mine into his. He rolled to his side, and we embraced while we kissed hungrily, and passed the tasty mouthful back and forth. At last he closed his mouth when all his come was in mine, and whispered. "You get to swallow it." I did so, and we lay together necking for some time, not saying anything, but communicating our feelings nonetheless.

Dave's cock was still fairly hard, but mine was almost painfully erect again. Dave raised a leg slightly and said, "Put your dick between my legs and fuck me," and closed his legs tightly to provide a sheath for my cock as I began to obey his request. I fucked his legs for a long time, and after five or ten minutes his fully hard cock was poking into my stomach so eagerly that I opened my legs for him to fuck me that way. Each of us fondled the other's ass while we fucked, but when I began to put a finger into Dave's asshole, he said, "No. I don't do that—sorry." I was sorry, too—but I understood. Two years ago, when I was his age, I hadn't had a dick up my butt yet, either. He had a lot to learn yet—wondrous, and unbelievably satisfying things.

When my orgasm seemed near, Dave rolled to his back. I lay over him and continued to fuck him between the legs, just as I had done with Danny, but just as my panting signaled an imminent discharge, Dave whispered, "Blow it on my tits." Without thinking, I rose to my knees and knelt between Dave's legs as he spread them for me, and I braced myself with one hand while I seized my cock with the other and jacked off until the come began to spew—and I again directed it over that exciting broad chest of Dave's. Dave gasped his approval, and when I had finished, he whispered, "Suck my tits again."

I cleaned him off again, just as I had done before, except this time the load I forced into his mouth when I kissed him was my own, and we swapped it back and forth until this time he was the one to swallow. We were lying on our sides, embracing, and he said, "Roll on your other side." I did as he asked, and he put his cock between my legs and fucked me that way from behind, reaching around to fondle my tits—nothing like what he offered for me to fondle—and biting my neck as he fucked furiously. I frequently reached behind me to take his cock and tease my asshole with the tip, but he didn't try to put his cock into it, as I desperately wanted him to do. He would fuck between my ass cheeks for a while before returning to my legs. I knew it was only going to be a short time, however, before he would be lying behind someone this way, and fucking him properly—hopefully, it would be me.

He fucked my legs for a long time before he blew a load in between them. His come seemed as thick in his second orgasm as in his first—I was to learn that his come was always unusually thick—and it remained on my legs as we lay there cooing our satisfaction, and whispering our admiration for each others' abilities.

After a long, delicious period while we nestled in the warm afterglow of our sex, Dave whispered, "We'd better get back inside the tent before

Mike wakes up and finds us gone." He moved backward, causing his now-limp cock to slip from between my legs. He swiped his hand between my legs and scooped up his come, then rolled me to my back. He knelt straddling me, and rubbed his come over his swelling breasts, which made them glisten in the bright moonlight as he ran his hands sensually over them. "God, my come feels good," he whispered.

"You want me to suck it off your tits again?"

"No, I wanna rub it in this time." He worked the come into his skin, as if he were rubbing on skin lotion—he was, in a way—and I enjoyed the sight of him caressing his broad chest in such a sexy manner. When it seemed he was through, he leaned over me. "Now you can suck 'em some more."

I sucked his tits for a while, and we lay side-by-side and necked again before we decided we had better call it a night. "We never got to that sixty-nine," I said.

"Next time for sure," Dave whispered, and stood. We put on our shorts, stood there and shared just a few more kisses while he promised to make that 'next time' as soon as possible.

Mike woke up momentarily when we got back in the tent to lie down, "Where've you been."

"Hadda pee," I answered, and that apparently satisfied his curiosity, for in a minute he was snoring quietly again. Dave and I held each other and kissed for a long time before we drifted off to sleep.

The sixty-nine Dave promised me was not long in coming, although it was not easy to find occasions when we could get together for sex, much less sleep together, but we managed enough that I was not terminally horny during that summer and the semester after Les graduated. We always sucked each other off, but I never got to fuck Dave's ass—although I often tried—nor would he fuck mine, however much I urged him to. We always fucked each other's legs—fucking by proxy, in a way—and Dave always wanted me to suck his tits, and pay special attention to his chest. I almost felt I was worshipping Dave's chest when we had sex, but given the chest he had, that was appropriate.

I made love with Dave when I was home for Christmas and summer vacations until he graduated from high school and went into the Army—not following Mike into college—and he eventually settled in California, where he was stationed during most of his military service. Shortly before I went to Antares, I saw a set of nude pictures of him in a copy of the magazine *Physique Pictorial,* put out by the Los Angeles-based Athletic Model Guild. His hair was longer, and his face more mature—and he had become very handsome. His body was even more magnificent—his chest even broader, and his waist apparently as narrow as ever. I wrote him in care of the magazine, but never heard from him.

Much later, when hard-core gay pornographic movies were beginning to flood the market in eight-millimeter prints, I saw an ad for one featuring Dave Elton—and he was actually using his real name there, as he had in the physique magazine. I bought a copy, of course, and found that even though Dave was in his mid-thirties, he looked far more handsome than he had in high school, and his body was as stunning as it had appeared in the Athletic Model Guild photographs. It was clear from Dave's part in the movie that he still loved having his tits worshipped, but it was also clear he had learned a few things over the years. He sucked cock fully as well as I remembered—and his partner sucked him off and deposited Dave's come on those still-magnificent tits before he lapped it up and swallowed it (this was a pre-condom film, of course). But Dave also fucked no fewer than three different butts in the one film, and in every way imaginable. His cock was quite impressive, longer than I remembered it, and he threw his legs in the air before the movie ended, and took it up the ass like a man who truly enjoys that sport—and he took it from a cock that would have outstripped even Hal Weltmann's monster. I wrote to him again, this time in care of the movie company, but still without any response.

I was due to graduate high school in January, and my home-room classmates decided they wanted to have a picnic and wiener roast to celebrate the beginning of our last semester together—the semester when Dave Elton and I would be 'going at it' hot and heavy. Eddie Wingo, one of my old jack-off playmates, had worked at the Tuohy Avenue Beach on Lake Michigan as a lifeguard during the summer season, and he got special permission from the Parks Department to have the party there on the first Friday of the semester, even though the beach had closed officially a few days earlier, on Labor Day.

The boy's room jack-off sessions I had shared with Eddie and Dick Stone had tapered off and all but stopped by the end of our junior year, and I hadn't really missed them—by that time I was having *real* sex with Les. But on the first day of school that fall, I happened to stand next to Eddie at an adjacent urinal, and we talked about the party coming up Friday night. We both stroked our cocks as we peed, and Eddie suggested that he and I and Dick might want to spend a little time in the lifeguard station after the party, for what might very likely be our final jack-off session together before we went of to college; he had a key to the station, and we could be safe from discovery. I agreed enthusiastically with the idea, of course, and Eddie promised to clue Dick in on his plan. We agreed that he and I could have a good time together, even if Dick wasn't interested.

Eddie stepped over to me and took my hard dick in his hand and suggested we beat each other off right then, 'for old time's sake.' I was more than willing, and began to stroke his. I realized then that Eddie's cock had grown nicely during our high-school years—it now felt almost as big as Les's ass-reamer. Moreover, Eddie's body had filled out, and he had grown even cuter, and now had the reputation of being a cocksman. Dick looked about as he always had, still as cute as a button.

Eddie jacked me off, and directed my discharge into a urinal, while I continued to masturbate him, and he discharged into my hand. I stepped over to a lavatory to wash his come from my hand, but I surreptitiously licked most of it off before I turned on the tap—the only time I had ever tasted come from either of my two home-room jack-off buddies. It tasted as fine as I had hoped it might.

I hoped Dick was going to be interested in meeting with Eddie and me in the lifeguard station after the picnic that Friday, and, given the fact that we could get naked and not have to hurry for fear of discovery, I even more fervently hoped something more than just jacking off might develop. If it turned out to be just me with Eddie and his big dick, however, I probably stood a better chance of getting more of his come to eat without having to hide it. Les had been gone for six weeks, and I was missing the special eight-inch excitement he provided, and which Eddie could come close to supplying, if he was willing.

We built a bonfire on the beach that Friday, just as it got dark, and the thirty-or-so of us sat around laughing and talking, and remembering good times during our almost four years together. Dick had whispered into my ear that he was looking forward to meeting Eddie and me in the lifeguard station later.

It was a very warm night—almost like summer, even though the lake water was beginning to get too cold for comfortable swimming. We roasted hot dogs and marshmallows, and even sang. By ten o'clock, a few of our classmates had already drifted off, and soon almost all were gathering their things to go home. Eddie had to stay until last to see that the fire was completely smothered, and Dick and I generously agreed to stay and keep him company.

Finally, it was just the three of us on the beach—except for a few 'steady ' couples who had spread blankets in the sand at the far end of the beach, and were lying together, making out; they were too engrossed in what they were doing to pay any attention to what anyone else was up to.

We smothered the fire, and went into the lifeguard station. It was a wooden building, about ten feet square, with the lifeguard perch on top. It was intended for the lifeguards' use in storing personal items when they were on duty, changing clothes, etc. There was a lavatory in one corner, but no toilet facilities. There was no light fixture in the room, since it was not intended for night-time use, and a louvered window allowed plenty of light during the day. There was a black cloth hung over the window when we went inside that night, and Eddie switched on a battery-operated lantern he had apparently put in there earlier, when he had draped the window. We all wore only our bathing suits, and Eddie pulled his down and stepped out of it, giving me not my first glimpse of his cute ass—we had shared gym classes together—but my first look at the *new and improved* Eddie Wingo ass. Like his cock, it was now a stunner. He said, "C'mon you guys, get naked and let's *do* it."

Dick was shedding his bathing suit as he added, "And for once we don't have to worry about anybody catching us." If Dick's cock had grown any, or if his ass was any sexier, I didn't observe it—I'd seen his ass in the locker room before, and it had always been adorable, and at seven-or-so fat inches when erect, his prick was a very satisfactory handful that I hoped would prove to be a very satisfactory mouthful or assful that night.

"I pulled my suit off as I added, "Yeah, and for once we can take all the time we want."

We began to play with each other. My cock was fully hard by the time I removed my bathing suit, and as soon as Dick reached for Eddie's, his own rose until it was standing straight out from his body. I stroked Dick's hard-on and watched Eddie's prick grow to its now very impressive size in Dick's busy hand. Eddie took my cock in hand, and began to stroke as Dick murmured hoarsely, "Jesus, Eddie, your dick is really big."

Eddie snickered, and said, "And your ass is really cute, Dick."

Dick blushed, "Oh c'mon, Eddie."

Eddie continued using one hand to stroke my cock, but reached behind Dick with the other, and caressed his ass. "Well, it is."

"C'mon, Eddie, quit messin' around," Dick said, and stepped back, releasing Eddie's cock, and putting his ass out of range of Eddie's hand—and his cock out of range of mine.

"Well shit, guys, we're naked for the first time while we're doing this," Eddie said. "We might as well do something besides just jack off like we always did in the bathroom. That was kid stuff." He released my dick and took his own dick in his hand and flourished it. "Does this look like it belongs on a kid?" Eddie grinned and turned to stand directly in front of me. He put both hands behind me and cupped my ass as he pulled me in to him. His big cock was poking into my stomach. "How about it, John? You've got a cute ass, too."

I almost hoped Eddie could feel how hard my heart was pounding, how excited he was making me. "You want my ass, Eddie?" I boldly put both arms around him and began to grind my cock into his. "What do I get out of this?"

"Jesus, you guys." Dick said. "Quit foolin' around."

Eddie turned his head toward Dick. "Hell, Dick, I thought we came here to fool around." He turned again to grin at me, "So let's fool around. Whaddya say?"

"You really want my ass, Eddie?" I asked.

"Okay, for the sake of argument, let's say, sure, I wanna fuck you in the ass."

I could tell he was as serious as I was. "Okay, for the sake of argument, let's say I let you. What do I get from you," I replied.

He squatted slightly, and pressed his hard cock up against my legs, just below my balls. I squatted for a moment and his cock slid nicely in between my legs, which gripped it when I stood. He began to fuck me, as he said, "You get eight inches of big, hard cock from me, but I'll blow you, too."

"Dick cried, "God *damn*, this is gettin' outa hand."

Eddie turned us around so he could look at Dick while he spoke to him over my shoulder—we were in full embrace by then, and Eddie kept fucking me between the legs while he spoke. "Shit, Dick, look at you. I don't see that you've lost your hard-on. Looks like you're as hot to do something with it as I am. You mean to tell me you've never done more with another guy than just jack off?"

"Well . . . well hell, sure. But I've never taken it up the butt."

"Neither have I," Eddie said, "but I've plowed quite a few asses before, and I'm not gonna let a friend suck me off or let me blow my load inside his ass unless I give him something in return—unless it some old geezer who can't get enough, like Coach or Mr. Novotny."

Dick and I almost chorused, "Coach and Mr. Novotny?" Mr. Novotny was the school Guidance Counselor.

"Hey, forget it. You didn't hear it from me," Eddie laughed. "But what the hell, if it's with a friend, suckin' dick can be fun, too." He withdrew his cock from between my legs. walked over to Dick, and put his hands on his shoulders. "I've had a whole helluva lot of blowjobs, and I don't mind admitting to you guys I've given a few, too." He winked at me and grinned as he spoke to both of us, "And they haven't always been friends, and sometimes I didn't even know who they were, but if I liked 'em, and they blew me or let me fuck 'em . . ." He shoved his cock between Dick's legs and grabbed his ass as he began to fuck him. "C'mon, let's have some fun. When're we gonna get another chance like this?"

Dick had been standing rigidly until then, but at last he relaxed and put his hands behind Eddie to fondle his humping ass. "Oh, what the hell. Yeah, I've swapped blowjobs a few times. But I've never fucked a guy."

"Same as fuckin' a pussy—only tighter, and I think guys like it better. And there's not all the bullshit to put up with. But are you sure you don't want it, too?" He was running his hands lovingly over Dick's buttocks by that time. "I meant it when I said you had a cute ass. What about it, John—isn't this a cute ass?"

"I've always thought so," I said. I had often dreamed of doing all sorts of exciting things to Dick's ass, in fact. Dick seemed surprised at my declaration.

Eddie was still fucking Dick's legs and playing with his ass as he grinned at him. "C'mon, Dick, this would be a good time to take it up the butt for the first time." But Dick declared his intention to keep his ass virgin, and Eddie returned to hold me. "So, how about it, John. You really gonna give me some ass tonight?"

I turned around and pressed my ass against his hard-on. "Sure, Eddie. Sounds like fun."

He reached around to stroke my cock, and cooed into my ear, "It will be fun, I promise you. How about Dick? You interested in takin' both of us on? You want some of this ass, too, don'tcha Dick?"

Dick gulped audibly and confessed he was definitely interested in losing his cherry as a buttfucker with me. I told them I was interested in helping both of them out, but I expected them to get my rocks off this time some other way than jacking me off, as they had always done in the past. Eddie laughed, "I'll suck you dry, John—so will Dick, right?"

"Sure," Dick agreed, finally laughing—although nervously.

"Let's spread some towels around here so we can lay down and get comfortable," Eddie said. "We've got plenty of time, so might as well work up to it." There was a stack of clean towels in the corner, and we covered the floor with them. Eddie stood in the middle, still erect, arms akimbo. "Let the games begin."

I knelt in front of him, and opened my mouth. He took hold of my head and slipped his dick all the way down my throat—slowly, but decisively. When it was in all the way, Eddie gasped, "Wow. Not many guys have been able to do that for me in the last couple of years. Yeah, suck it, John—make love to that big prick." Dick came to stand beside us, expressing his amazement at my ability to take that much cock in my mouth. In a moment I moved over to his cock, and alternated sucking the two boys for several minutes. I was sucking Dick when Eddie lay down and pulled me down on top of him, head-to-toe, so that our mouths loomed at each others' cocks. Eddie began to suck me, and I returned to sucking him.

Dick knelt next to us and watched our sixty-nine for a few minutes before saying, "Open up, and let me in." Eddie and I moved our bodies so that we lay in a rough triangle, and I again sucked Eddie, while he began to suck Dick's prick and Dick began to suck mine. We reversed out bodies several times, so that I could suck Dick's cock while he sucked Eddie's and Eddie sucked mine. Both Eddie and Dick were obviously experienced cocksuckers, and Dick was a talented one as well, but Eddie was a virtuoso.

Eddie pulled away, and went over to fumble in his beach bag. He came back with a tube of lubricant, and grinned, "Get on your knees, John—time for the main event."

The two talked about who was going to fuck me first, as though I wasn't even there, but I didn't mind. I had often been fucked twice or more in one night, but never by two different guys, and I was looking forward to it. Moreover, given how horny Eddie was, I wouldn't be surprised if I got fucked at least three or four times that night. It was decided that Dick would go first, and warm me up for Eddie—which made good sense, actually, since Eddie's cock was a lot bigger than Dick's.

I knelt on all fours, and Dick lubed us both, then knelt behind me and began to enter me gently. "Go ahead and shove it in, Dick," I cried, "I want it." His hands grabbed my hips, and with one fierce thrust he was all the way inside. He began to fuck me like a demon, panting and telling me how good it felt. I panted and returned his compliments.

Long before I wanted him to, Dick neared orgasm. It was clear to Eddie that Dick was near, since he said, "Blow a big load in him, Dick—I wanna fuck him in your come." And in a moment Dick slammed himself in as far as he could, and held himself there, while he uttered a loud, wordless cry and I felt his cock erupting inside me in six or seven palpable spurts. He began to fuck again, slowly, apparently draining the last of his orgasm.

Dick fell heavily over me, pushing me onto my stomach, and he lay still, his chest heaving, his cock still inside me. "Jesus Christ, John—what a *fuck*."

Eddie asked him, "See what I mean about fuckin' butt?" Dick nodded and gasped, and Eddie rolled him off me, saying "Get back on your knees, John. I gotta get some of that hot ass now."

I again knelt. Eddie positioned the tip of his cock at my sphincter. He was apparently already lubricated, and I didn't need to be. He began to whisper endearments to me as he gently began to insert his prick into my ass. I drove my ass backwards with one fierce shove, and took Eddie's entire enormous shaft inside me in one stroke. I cried out in ecstasy—it felt like Les fucking me again—and Eddie's cry drowned out my own. "Fuck, what a hot ass. I'm gonna fuck you within an inch of your life."

He began to hammer me savagely, panting his joy and his appreciation as I assured him of my own.

Eddie's fuck lasted a lot longer than Dick's—for which I was grateful. He stopped fucking to prolong it several times, whispering his appreciation into my ear while he rested. Several times Dick expressed his admiration for what we were doing, and during one of Eddie's pauses, he lay on his back and slipped under me, lying so that I could suck his still-hard cock and he could suck mine while he looked up to watch Eddie fucking me, from a much closer vantage point. Eventually, Eddie could hold back no longer, and with a series of insanely frantic thrusts, his cock began to unload palpably inside me, and I began to unload in Dick's mouth at almost the same moment. Dick continued to suck, but gently, as Eddie and I calmed down, and he finally swallowed my discharge—not the first load of come he had eaten, I assumed.

We rested from our happy labors for a half-hour or more, chatting casually about things that were going on at school, and wondering who might be doing what we had just been doing, and with whom. Eddie and Dick both talked about girls they dated, and girls they screwed, and I lied about a few affairs of my own with girls. Dick went over to the lavatory to pee in it at one point, and Eddie whispered into my ear, "I don't believe for a minute you're screwin' any girl—you're too damned good at suckin' cock and takin' it up the ass. But I don't mind—it's none of my business, and besides, I really like it when you're doin' it for me. "

Dick returned to lie beside us, and noticed that Eddie's cock was fully erect again. We had been playing with each other the whole time, but very casually, and without passion. Dick snickered, "Looks like somebody's ready to get back to what we were doing."

Eddie grinned and pulled Dick's head down to his cock. "Why don't you start things off?" Dick cheerfully began sucking Eddie's huge cock again. Eddie lay on his back, enjoying Dick's ministrations as he pulled me over to him, so that our faces were inches apart. "You wanna get fucked again?"

"Any time—and as often as you want," I replied.

"Good boy," Eddie said, and surprised me by planting a fairly serious kiss on my lips before moving his own down to suck my tits, lick my stomach, and take my dick back in his mouth again. Keeping my dick in Eddie's mouth, I raised to my knees and knelt, straddling him and picking his head up in my hands to fuck his mouth. He sucked ravenously and played with my ass, driving a finger or two into me as he sucked. I was aware that Dick lay at my back, still feasting on Eddie's cock.

Eddie pushed me away, "C'mon and give us some more of that ass. Dick—you wanna fuck John first again?" Dick wanted to, and he did—for a gloriously long time before he gave me another load. I lay on my back this time, with my legs on Dick's shoulders, and with Eddie kneeling at my head, his cock jutting out for me to suck while he played with Dick's tits. When Dick's orgasm finally neared, he fell over my chest and put his arms under me, kissing my neck feverishly as he humped faster and faster, moaning "Jesus, John, you're a fantastic fuck." He cried, "Take it." and rammed into me as far as he could go, freezing in that position as he bit my neck and I felt his cock exploding in me again. Then suddenly his lips were pressed hard against mine, and his tongue was driving hungrily into my mouth.

"Fuckin' hot." Eddie cried, and I looked up as he raised Dick's shoulders and leaned forward to take Dick in his arms. Dick returned the embrace, and they shared a long, very passionate kiss, fully as hot as the one Eddie had just interrupted, and *much* hotter than the one Eddie and I had shared earlier. "Get outa the way, Dick, and let me in," Eddie said, and nudged Dick aside, and knelt where he had been. I raised my legs and spread them, and not five seconds after Dick took his cock out of my ass, Eddie's had taken its place, and he was hammering it into me. "God damn, John—you are fuckin' *full* of come." And it was true: you could actually hear Eddie's prick squishing as he drove it in and out of me. "Man, this feels unbelievable."

Eddie fell over me, and I locked my legs behind his back. He moaned, "Oh Jesus, John . . . what a great fuck." And it certainly was a great fuck, with long strokes, savage thrusts into me, grunts and moans of joy—but the kissing was almost as good as the fucking. Eddie did not hold back this time, he locked his lips to mine, and we tongue-fucked each other's mouths ravenously. He put his arms under my shoulders, and began to lift my body. Without stopping kissing, and with his cock still in me, he rolled us over, moving his legs so that they were flat on the floor behind me, and I was sitting on his cock. He stopped kissing me, and fell to his back. "Ride my prick, John—I wanna watch while you fuck yourself on it."

I bobbed up and down on Eddie's prick, my cock flopping wildly, and he humped upward into my ass while he fondled my chest. Dick came over and knelt astride Eddie's body, facing away from me, and clearly began to fuck his mouth. Eddie held Dick's ass, and I reached between Dick's legs to play with his balls while he humped.

"Turn around, Dick," Eddie said, and Dick shifted so that he was still straddling Eddie, but was now facing me. Eddie pulled Dick down until he was apparently sitting on Eddie's face. I watched Dick's face while I continued my wild ride. His expression went from a look of surprise to a look of utter bliss. He closed his eyes and smiled, murmuring complete joy, and I knew Dick Stone was getting his ass eaten for the first time. He opened his eyes—glazed over with ecstasy—smiled at me, and took me in his arms. We shared the same long, passionate kind of kiss Eddie and I had shared shortly before. Dick released me and sat back, and he continued to revel in feel of Eddie's tongue in him—no doubt darting all around inside his asshole. His face was a study in rapture—he had always looked cute, but he really looked astonishingly *beautiful* at that moment. Eddie pulled Dick's body back a bit, and I could see Eddie's chin and lower lip, and occasionally the tip of his tongue, as he sucked and licked Dick's balls—then back a bit farther, and Dick's cock was in Eddie's hungry mouth. Dick fell forward, and took my dick in his mouth, and sucked hungrily.

We were three very happy guys at that moment: Eddie was fucking my butt and sucking Dick's cock; Dick was sucking my cock while Eddie sucked his; I was riding Eddie's enormous cock while Dick sucked mine.

After a moment or an eternity of this—I had no idea which—Eddie said, in a voice apparently muffled by a mouthful of dick (or a mouthful of Dick, if you prefer), "Don't suck him off, Dick. I wanna do that so he knows how much I love fuckin' his ass."

Dick sucked me only a while longer, then sat to the side and watched while Eddie finished fucking me. Eddie reached up and pulled our chests together as his orgasm approached, and he fucked my mouth with his tongue again, matching the thrusts his big cock was making into my ass. He quit kissing me when he finally blew his load, all but *screaming* with lust, and I could feel him exploding inside me fully as forcefully as he had the first time.

His panting subsided finally, and he kissed me again, this time tenderly. "Great fuck, man. You ready to give me a load?" I assured him I was, and I asked him how he wanted it. "Why don't you fuck me?" he grinned.

I grinned back. "Okay. But I thought . . . "

Eddie laughed. "You didn't let me finish my sentence. Why don't you fuck me . . . in the mouth."

I pulled up off Eddie's cock, and as I did so, a stream of come flowed from my ass onto it. I knelt in his armpits, my cock trembling over his lips. He raised his head and opened his mouth. I cradled his head in my hands, and began to fuck him. He murmured his satisfaction around my cock, and his hands busily fondled my chest, my back, and my shoulders. He didn't play with my ass, because Dick was very busily doing that—fondling it, and driving a finger or two in and out of it to counter my thrusts and withdrawals into Eddie's mouth. Sooner than I wanted, I was ready, and I cried "Take it, Eddie." as I pulled his head tightly into me, and began to fill his mouth. He sucked and lapped eagerly, until I had finished, then swallowed and whispered around my cock, "Great load, John."

I leaned down and kissed him lightly. "Great blowjob, Eddie. Thanks."

The three of us lay there a few minutes longer before Dick jumped up and said, "Holy shit—it's way past one in the morning, and I was supposed to be home by midnight. I gotta go, right now." Eddie said he and I would close up, so Dick dressed quickly, and with a quick kiss for each of us, and an assurance that he had enjoyed the night a lot more than he expected to, he was gone.

When the door closed behind him, Eddie grinned and asked me. "You gotta get home, too? I wish you'd hang around with me a little while longer."

"Sure, Eddie, but I don't think I can come again, and . . . "

He laughed, "Neither can I, for a while, but I kinda hate for tonight to be over, y'know? Just lay here and snuggle with me for a while. He gently pushed me down on the floor, on my back, and knelt between my legs. "Your butt has gotta be sore—Jesus, you got fucked four times."

"Yeah, it's sore all right, but I feel great."

"Just let me put my dick in you while we lay here, okay? You feel so fuckin' good. And you really are a great piece of ass, John—best fuck I've had in a helluva long time—guy or girl."

"Thanks, Eddie. I'm really glad I pleased you—and between both you and Dick, I've never had sex like tonight."

Eddie wasn't really erect when he entered me—he had to hold his cock tight around the base and push to get it in. Surprisingly, it hurt when he did that, although it had felt nothing but wonderful when he shoved it in me with one hard thrust when it had been larger, and fully erect.

He kept his cock in me for something like an hour and a half, occasionally humping it lazily in and out, keeping it semi-erect. We talked about our sex lives, and at his urging, I confessed that I was strictly queer—which didn't seem to bother him at all. "Thank God for queer guys—where would I be without 'em? I love to fuck 'em—and they give the best blowjobs, too." He told me he didn't think of himself as queer at all, but he did like fucking ass, and admitted he enjoyed sucking cock almost as much: "I always tell myself I'm just doin' it to show my appreciation to some guy who let me fuck him, but between you and me, I love to suck cock and eat come. But that's strictly between us, okay? Don't even tell Dick."

I agreed that I would keep his sexual appetites secret, as he agreed mine would be.

Our talk was pleasant, and the feeling of his cock inside me was wonderfully satisfying. But best of all was the kissing—and we shared tender, affectionate kisses all the while. Eddie suggested we had better be going, but he began to hump me a little more enthusiastically as he said it, and I could feel his cock growing and hardening inside me. He asked, "Can I fuck you one more time before we go?"

"God yes, Eddie," I replied, and our kisses grew passionate as his cock, began to thrust in and out of me with increasing force. Soon he was fully hard, and he was fucking me with the same ardor he had shown earlier in the evening. It took a very long time for his third orgasm to arrive, but it was time very, very well spent, in my mind. Eventually, he blew another load in me, and spent a long time sucking me off—and I managed to give him yet another load myself.

We restored order to the lifeguard station, and locked up. Eddie said he hoped we could find ways to get together once in a while, and I promised him we would. He drove me home; I had taken a bus to get to the beach—I neither had a car of my own, nor even knew how to drive one at that time. We held hands all the way, and we sat in front of my apartment building, kissing and groping each other for ten or fifteen minutes before we said goodnight, just as if this hot stud was bringing me home from a date—which I guess he was. And what a date, and what a hot stud. The night had been one of the real highlights of my life. It had been my first threesome, and it had been a great one—even if I still hadn't got to fuck anyone in the ass. It would also prove to be the only threesome I would have before my memorable train ride as I left for college. Although I got together with both Eddie and Dick individually after that, we never managed to meet as a trio again.

Eddie was fairly aggressive in getting together, and we shared sex another five or six times during that semester. We even double-dated for the Senior Prom in early January, and after we took our dates home around dawn, we went back to his house and made love in his bed until noon the next day.

On the other hand, Dick was hesitant about approaching me for sex. He and Eddie and I saw each other every school morning—we were all in the same home room, after all—but while Eddie seemed to enjoy sharing secret looks and key words recalling our relationship, Dick seemed to shy away from any hints I dropped about our getting together again. I assumed Dick wasn't interested in another sexual tryst, until one night just before closing he showed up at the drug store, and asked if I wanted to go out for a Coke when I finished work. I had no idea he even knew I worked there, but I was glad to go with him. We went in his car, and when he asked where I wanted to go, I told him it was his choice. He admitted that what he really wanted was to go to the park and sit in the car and talk. I agreed.

When we parked, we made no pretense about going there to talk. We immediately got in the back seat and got naked, and Dick fucked me, not a hundred yards from the hill where Danny and I had made love out in the open on that special night years earlier. After Dick had blown his load in me, and sucked me off, I told him about what Danny and I had done there, and we got dressed and left the car to go to 'the scene of the crime.' It was far too cold to walk around outside naked, and it was also too cold for people to be wandering around in the park that late, so even though the moon was very bright that night we didn't worry about privacy. Standing atop the hill, Dick pulled his cock out, and I knelt there and sucked it. Then he dropped his pants and turned around, and I knew what he really wanted—I had seen his face when Eddie had been eating his ass. I buried my face between his swelling cheeks and tongue-fucked him for all I was worth, while he moaned and cried out in joy. I stood, and pressed the head of my cock between his cheeks, and whispered into his ear, "Let me fuck you—just think how good that would feel."

He turned around and kissed me, saying, "I can't. I'm sorry," and it sounded as if he really was sorry. He knelt and gave me the consolation prize: a very impassioned blowjob, and a good one, I might add—much better than the one he had given me in the back seat of the car. I wondered if he had been practicing, and, if so, with whom? He swallowed my load and stood behind me. Then I bent over and he fucked me again—out in the open in the bright moonlight. Back in his car, we kissed for a long time before he drove me home. He did not hold hands with me, nor did he kiss me goodnight when he dropped me off, but it had still been fun—just not as much fun as screwing with Eddie was.

Dick and I got together several times more, always at my house, with my mother away at work. He fucked me each time—usually twice, but *three* times on one occasion—and he always wanted me to rim him, which I was happy to do. We sucked each other individually and in sixty-nine, and he eagerly swallowed every load I could give him. The last time we were together was during Christmas vacation, and we made love under the Christmas tree in my apartment. He seemed especially romantic that night after he fucked me the first time (perhaps it was the Christmas tree), and our kissing was much more affectionate than it usually was, and when we sucked each other in sixty-nine, I blew my load in his mouth and kept sucking him until he fed me one that way. He had blown his load up my ass probably a few dozen times, and I had often sucked his big cock, but it was the only time I ever actually sucked him off, and he seemed to feel good about that—but then, so did I. But it didn't stop him from giving me another load up my ass shortly after that, even though it took quite a while longer—and I felt good about that, too.

Following our graduation ceremony in late January, everyone was hugging everyone else, so no one thought it odd that Eddie and I embraced for a relatively long time. He whispered "Gonna miss that hot ass of yours."

I told him, "And I'm gonna miss that big dick of yours." I knew by then that he was going into the Marine Corps in a few weeks, so I added, "Think of me every time you fuck some Marine's ass."

Eddie laughed, "I guess I'm gonna be thinking of you a lot," and he patted my ass, and actually kissed me, although quickly. All the guys in our class were kissing all the girls, but I think I may have been the only guy to be openly honored as I was—and if anyone noticed, they didn't mention it.

I completely lost track of both Eddie and Dick after graduation. Dick went to Wesleyan University, and never seemed to be home when I was in Chicago, and Eddie was always gone, playing Marine. Dick was decidedly the less demonstrative of the two in our homosexual play, yet I sensed that he was actually gay. And I felt sure that Eddie was heterosexual, albeit a heterosexual who loved to kiss boys, and to fuck butt and suck cock—and given sufficient inspiration, to eat a cute boy's ass.

I saw Les only rarely during our years in college, although we corresponded with some regularity. When our vacation visits home coincided, we had sex, of course, and it was wonderful to feel him inside me again—nothing is ever quite like first love. On those occasions we always caught each other up on our sexual adventures.

In Les's junior year at Wisconsin he and a fraternity brother struck up a sexual relationship much like his and mine had been, although he said their lovemaking was not nearly as intense as ours. I wondered if that were true, though—after all, what else could he say?

The Christmas vacation of 1954, when I had to forego beautiful young Billy's love for a couple of weeks, still promised to be especially exciting, since Les had worked things out so would have three full days (and nights.) together. Since I was visiting my sister's house in Indiana, I drove to Chicago, and was invited to stay at Les's house—sleeping in that wonderful bedroom of his where we had first really made love, and where we had shared so many ecstatic moments. Les had finished his Basic Training for the Air Force, as well as Flight School, and was getting ready to go to his first regular duty station.

We spent a lot of time getting caught up the first afternoon we were together, and even though I was in love with Billy and missing his beauty and sweetness, to say nothing of the great sex we shared, I was excited about seeing the man who had introduced me to so many things that were important to me—sexual and non-sexual—and to sharing lovemaking with him again. I was especially intrigued by what he had told me on the phone when we were making plans to meet: "I have a couple of surprises for you that I know you're really going to like."

After dinner, with Les's parents going out to a party, and *finally* leaving us alone together in the house, we went to his bedroom. As soon as we were in his room, Les said "Get out of your clothes—we've got a lot of catching up to do." He stripped while I followed his order, and in less than a minute we were both naked.

"What are the big surprises you've got for me?

"You're going to love both of them, Johnny, but I want to drive this home first." As he said this, he stroked his prick, which was already growing hard and splendid. He walked up to me, and we embraced and kissed. Bob's finger sought out and entered my asshole while our tongues intertwined passionately. He whispered, "I've missed you, Johnny, and I've *really* missed fucking your ass."

"I've dreamed of you fucking me so much, Les, and your mouth on my dick. I hope you're gonna fuck my brains out."

"I'm going to fuck you so much in the next three days you're never going to stop smiling. Get down on your knees and show me how much you want me."

I knelt on the rug in front of him, and he held my head and drove his throbbing prick deep into my mouth as he fucked it savagely. After a couple of minutes, he dragged me to the bed, and we threw ourselves on it, on our sides, in position for sixty-nine. I took him in my mouth again, and he swallowed my prick to the hilt. We rolled around and clasped each other tightly while we made frantic love to each other. Often, as he sucked me, Les played with my asshole, and was soon fucking it with his fingers. He released my cock from his mouth long enough to ask, "Are you ready for me to fuck you?"

"God yes, Les, *shove* that big thing all the way in me, and fuck me like no one else ever has." (It was a nice thought, but not likely to happen, considering the fat ten inches of steel-hard cock that the *fuckmaster* Hal Weltmann had hammered in me so unforgettably.) I knelt on the bed and Les positioned himself behind me as he lubed us up, and soon I was thrilled with his huge prick entering me. He grasped my waist tightly as he drove his shaft, and I humped backwards to meet each savage thrust. Les thrilled me with the kind of strokes only a superbly endowed stud like he can manage. The ferocity of his love-making, the length of his strokes, and the bulk of his prick combined to deliver a fuck of epic proportions. I was almost delirious with passion as he fucked—not since Hal had last sunk his colossal shaft into me had I felt the *animal* sexual delirium Les awoke in me at that point. After a long and unbelievably satisfying time of this perfect fucking, Les unceremoniously pulled himself out of me, rolled me roughly onto my back, and knelt straddling me—masturbating his glistening, throbbing monster prick in my face.

"Here's your first surprise Johnny—hope you like it." And with that his prick began to shoot a copious load of come all over my face, into my mouth as I opened it, on my hair, and generally all over. As he was discharging, he cried, "Here it is, Johnny—you've been hungry for this for a long time."

"God, Les—that's wonderful. Oh, *yeah*. Shoot all over me—I've wanted your come for so long."

He continued to milk every drop from his cock as he shook it, and finally took me in his arms as he lay down over me. "I'm going to come in your ass—I'm going to come in your mouth—I'm going to fill you up with come the next three days." He scraped come off my forehead and chin, and had me suck it from his fingers. He lapped it from my chest, and kissed me so I could suck it from his tongue. It would have tasted wonderful if I had sucked him off only an hour earlier; considering I had waited six or seven years for it, it was the ambrosia of the gods.

"Jesus, Les, that was a wonderful surprise. When did you finally start doing that?"

"Almost a year ago. I'll tell you all about it, and I want to do all I can while you're here to make up for all the loads you gave me that I couldn't return."

"God, I've got a load right now that I've gotta give you."

"I want it inside me, Johnny." And Les went down on me as I lay on my back and he was soon sucking my prick as hard as he could. I held his head tightly while I fucked his mouth, and he murmured his delight as he sucked. Soon he stopped, moved up to straddle my body, as he said, "And here's your other surprise." With that he positioned the head of my prick at his sphincter, and sat down on me hard—taking my cock all the way inside him. "God, Johnny, *fuck* me—fuck my ass at last." I hadn't seen him apply any lubricant, but he was ready for me.

I didn't *talk* about the wonder of what was happening—*finally* fucking the man who had first fucked me—I just reveled in the experience. Les began as wild a ride on my prick as I've ever known, and when it became obvious I was nearing orgasm, he shouted, "*Shoot* your hot come in me. Fuck me. *Fill me up, Johnny—I love it.*" And I discharged violently deep inside him. "Oh, god *damn*. I can feel you coming inside me—that's so great." He plunged up and down on me, and his tight asshole worked my prick until I had finished my orgasm, and—still impaled in my cocks—he fell over me and drove his tongue into my mouth.

We kissed passionately for a long time, and it turned sweet and tender after a while. Finally, I whispered into his ear. "I've waited so long for that—and God, was it ever worth the wait. You were so hot and so tight—Jesus, Les, it felt absolutely wonderful to finally give you my load that way."

"I've wanted you that way, too, Johnny, you know that. And I'm so glad to finally get your dick in my ass—and to get fucked so *well*. You are a helluva fine buttfucker, you know that?"

"I know I studied *getting* fucked with the all-time master buttfucker—how could I be anything but good at it? But it seems to me you pretty well fucked yourself on me that time. But I'm not complaining, I loved it."

"Next time I'm gonna lay there and take it while you fuck me and really show me how good you are at it."

We kissed again. "Thank you for my surprises—I can't imagine a better Christmas present."

Les grinned and said, "And we're going to play with your new

Christmas presents a lot. Okay?"

"Every minute we can." We kissed and snuggled for quite a while, until we 'came up for air' and Les caught me up on how he had developed his new-found talents.

During the year or so since we had last made love together, Les had graduated from college and entered the Air Force. He had told me over the years about Mac, his fraternity brother at Wisconsin whom he had sex with regularly, and they got even closer as Les's graduation drew near. They were sharing a bed in a hotel room one night at a fraternity convention; both had a lot to drink, and Mac *begged* Les to finally let him fuck his ass. Les had been pounding Mac's ass regularly and Mac had been filling Les's mouth with his come for a couple of years by then. Mac had tried for a long time, as I had, to breach Les's willing-but-reluctant asshole. On the night in question, Mac got Les about half drunk, and finally succeeded in his conquest by basically raping him.

"God, Johnny, it hurt so bad, I begged him to stop, but he wouldn't—and finally his prick slid all the way into me, and he held me tight and told me to relax and work with him. Once it was in, and I relaxed, it felt *great,* and we worked together slowly until finally he was just plain *fucking* me, all stops out. It was fantastic, and felt just as good as you always told me it would. Pretty soon I felt his come shooting inside me, and that was even better. I was sore for a couple of days after that, but by the time I graduated, Mac and I were fucking each other at least once almost every night."

"But the other . . ."

"That came along later. After I went into the Air Force I had to be really careful, but there were a couple of guys I managed to sneak around and have sex with. In Flight School I met Dick—and he really was named right, his Dick was a real monster—and I wanted it real bad. I could tell he liked me too, and when we were finally able to get together on leave one night, we rented a hotel room and I had his prick out of his pants and in my mouth right away. I hadn't sucked that big a cock since Bob Glass. He wanted me to fuck him, and I did—and he was a great fuck, too. Finally he shoved that huge cock of his up my ass, and I've never felt anything so good—by far the biggest cock I'd had inside my butt. I rode him like he was a buckin' bronco, and he fucked me so hard I thought I was going to split in two. Finally, just about the time I felt his come shooting inside me, I knew I was going to come too—and I grabbed my prick and jacked off, and pretty soon it started shooting all over him. Man, you have *never* seen such a big load. That was the biggest thrill I ever felt, I think. His prick was so huge and it felt so great in me, and then shooting like that for the first time . . . Do you remember the first time you shot your load?"

"I sure do, and it felt better than anything else ever had."

"Yeah, well just imagine that feeling combined with an incredible monster prick jammed all the way inside you, and your ass full of hot cum."

"Sounds like absolute heaven to me."

"It *was* heaven, and I think Dick and I fucked each about four times that night, and I got Dick's load every time, and I gave him a couple more loads myself. Now, I really have to be careful—there's plenty of guys screwing each other in the Air Force, but if you get caught at it, you're out on your ass. But I still see Dick once in a while; and I got together with Mac a couple months ago and gave him that same surprise I gave you—'bout flooded out his mouth and his ass, but he loved it."

"God, and so did I Les. I loved every drop of your come, and I love every inch of your cock, and . . . I know you don't want to me to say it, but I'll always be in love with you."

"Johnny—we've talked about that love thing. Sure, you love me, and sure, I love you, but not the same way you mean it."

I had long ago been forced to soft-pedal any talk with Les about being *in love* with him, even when I was desperately so. He said he loved me, but he was not *in love* with me. Somehow, in spite of all we had shared, and the very active homosexual activities we enjoyed separately, he still felt this was a phase we were both going through, and we'd both wind up enjoying heterosexual lives—and while it was wonderful for us to share sexual *ecstasy*, as we so often did, we were still just "great friends." I had long ago resigned myself to a pretense, when with him, of accepting Les's view of things, and while I had continued to be in love with him, I had learned to let him think I too was only 'having fun' when we made love—and we certainly *did* have fun, of course. I had filled him in on my love for Pierce Stonesifer, and later for Joe Corcoran, but I still loved him, as I still loved both Pierce and Joe, and was now mainly *in love* with my sweet young Billy. I agreed we wouldn't talk about love any more—just those three wonderful F's: friendship and fun and fucking.

I told him about my latest love, Billy; he was aghast at the age problem, but when I showed him one of the nude pictures I had taken of Billy at my house, he said, "Age be damned—that's a beautiful boy. And what an ass. Has he got a big prick?"

"His cock is beautiful, and it's long—and he's a great fucker."

"I want to fuck what he likes to fuck." And Les rolled me on my stomach and began another assault on my ass that ended with his monster prick shooting another vast load—this time deep inside my hungry ass. His voice hoarse with passion, Les cried out as he exploded in me, "And next you're gonna fuck me like you do Billy." As a good friend, I naturally acceded to his wishes as soon as he rolled off me: with his legs high in the air and my cock driving into his ass, I filled my first love with another offering as we kissed passionately.

During the three days I spent with Les, we fucked each other's mouths and asses any number of times, and delivered load after load of hot come into each other. We held each other, we kissed and embraced endlessly, but we also had a great time just being with each other in non-sexual moments.

Our last afternoon together, shortly before Les had to leave to catch a train, we stood naked in his bedroom, our arms around each other, kissing sweetly—pricks hard, of course. He told me, "Johnny, you'll always be a really important part of my life. I know you love me, and you know I love you too, in my own way. I want us to do something before we leave that will mean a lot to me. I'm going to suck you off, and I want you to suck me off—and neither of us will swallow until we can kiss and combine our loads and swallow them together. It's like a blood oath, but in *come*—pledging our friendship and our . . ." A quick kiss and a grin here. "...Okay, our *love*. I wasn't able to do this with you earlier, Johnny, but I can now, and I really want it. Will you do that with me?"

"I can't think of anything that I want more, or that would make me feel more *honored,* Les. I love you, and we'll always be a part of each other." I led him to the bed, and we lay down on our sides to suck each other in sixty-nine. We sucked long and slow, we sucked deep, and we murmured in love and satisfaction as we held each other tightly around our waists, and each caressed the other's ass as it drove his prick into the other's mouth. Soon the sucking and humping began to get frantic, and without saying anything, I shot my load into Les's loving throat. He began to fuck my mouth frantically, and soon I was rewarded with the powerful spurts he gave me.

We released each other and knelt on the bed facing each other. We embraced and looked into each others eyes, and slowly our mouths met, and we passed our joint love-offering back and forth for a long time—quite a mouthful, actually. Finally, Les put about half of the wondrous mixture into my mouth and broke our kiss, looking soberly into my eyes for a long time. Then he nodded solemnly, and we both swallowed slowly, savoring the combined product of our efforts. Still looking into my eyes, he took my head in his hands. "I really love you, Johnny—you'll always be a part of me."

I held his head as he held mine. "And I love you, Les, and at least a part of us will be together wherever we are."

Then we kissed very tenderly—in real *love*, rather than passion.

Les released me and grinned. "So, when you get back to Texas and fuck that pretty ass of Billy's you're going to be fucking him for me, too. Right?"

"Right—and wherever you wind up sticking that monster cock I love so much, I'm going to be in on the fuck."

Les was a wonderful guy, a treasured friend, a magnificent sex partner, and an invaluable asset in my life—and he'll always be a part of me, and I of him. And I'll always be in love with him.

But I was ready to return to the boy I had recently fallen in love with, and probably the only one of my lovers whom I knew was *in love* with me. He was the only one who regularly held hands with me when we were unobserved, or who kissed me and told me he loved me when we were *not* having sex.

9

TRUE CONFESSIONS

A minute or two of silence, and then, quietly,
"I'm really glad you let me fuck you, Phil."
Phil laughed aloud, "I don't remember you givin' me much choice."

Returning to Antares a couple of days before the New Year, I was concerned about what I should tell Billy. Was it better to let him know of my lovemaking with Les, or should I keep it to myself? I felt guilty about my infidelity to him, but it had been with *Les,* after all, who was someone I would always love, and who was so much a part of my entire sexual *self* that a part of him had always been with me every time I had sex—our joint communion of love on the last day we had been together had really only reinforced that feeling on my part. That was probably sheer rationalization of my desire to fuck with wonderful Les, I don't know, but it *had* happened, and there was no denying that—at least not to myself.

I phoned Billy as soon as I got back, of course, and his boyish eagerness to get together was both touching and exciting. "I can't wait to see you, Pete. You're not going to believe how much I've missed you."

"I know how much I've missed you. When can I show you how much?"

"How does tonight sound? I can't talk long right now—my Mom's in the next room—but I'll come over right after supper, if that's okay." I agreed it was fine. "And Pete . . . have the shades pulled, and don't be wearing much when you answer the door, okay? I'm going to be pretty eager."

"Billy, the only things I'll have on when I answer the door will be a smile and a hard-on. How's that?"

"I'm smiling and hard already. See you soon."

Shortly before seven, the doorbell rang. I was already naked, and I stroked myself to a hard and stood behind the door to open it. A grinning Billy came in and slammed the door behind him. He approached me and took my prick in his hands, saying "God, I love you." as we embraced and kissed eagerly.

We continued to kiss as Billy undid his shirt, kicked off his boots, and dropped his Levi's to the floor. I pulled his tee shirt over his head as he dropped his shorts, and he entered my arms again, fully naked, and we ground our hard pricks together while we fondled each other.

I took Billy's hand and led him to my bed. We lay down and kissed hungrily, and were soon locked in passionate sixty-nine, driving our hard cocks deep into each other's throats. Our frantic hands explored each other, and each of us fucked the other's ass with his finger as our sucking grew more frantic, soon culminating in each of us filling the other's mouth with a hot load of come. We lay locked together this way for a long time, savoring every drop as our pricks softened and our caressing grew tender. Finally we broke and put our arms around each other for a long session of sweet, affectionate kissing.

"God, Billy, I've missed having your sweet dick inside me—and this wonderful body and beautiful ass."

"In case you haven't noticed, that sweet dick is hard again. What shall I do with it?"

I rolled on my back, and put my legs in the air. "Fuck me, Billy—fuck me as hard as you can." He greased us up and drove his prick into me fiercely and began a really *wild* fuck—a great deal of panting and cries of passion on his part as well as mine, culminating with a delicious eruption deep inside me. As he knelt there, with his cock still hard and throbbing within me, I began to masturbate.

Billy said, "Wait, Pete." and pulled his prick out of me, wiped the Vaseline and come from my ass and smeared it over my prick and moved forward to impale himself on me. He drove himself downward and began a wild ride. "I wanna fuck myself on you, Pete."

With cries of "I love it." and "Come in me." he bobbed up and down while I humped upward into him, and soon I could not hold back, and was shooting inside my magnificent young lover/stud again.

His head was thrown back, and his eyes closed as he continued to ride me, now slowly and sensuously. "Oh God, Pete . . . oh, God I love you so much." And as I looked in adoration at his angelic face, I realized he was crying.

"Billy, what is it?"

He looked down at me, with tears streaming from his eyes as he blurted out, "Pete, I fucked with another guy while you were gone." And he fell on top of me, and sobbed into my shoulder as I held him and patted his back. I was hurt, I was shocked—but I was also painfully aware of being guilty of the same transgression myself.

"Billy, it's all right. Everything will be okay—don't cry, now. I love you . . . you love me, that's all that matters. We'll work it out."

"Can you forgive me, Pete? You don't hate me?"

"Of course I forgive you. I love you Billy—I could never hate you, you must know that. C'mon, quit crying, and tell me about it."

He calmed down, blew his nose on one of the 'come towels' towels I always kept stacked next to my bed, and dried his eyes. "You know Phil Baker?"

"Phil Baker. You mean he was the one . . . " Billy nodded and buried his head against my chest. My cock had slipped out of Billy's ass by that time, and we lay on our sides, embracing. I was amazed. *Phil Baker*: senior class president at Antares High, captain of the football team, basketball star, Homecoming King; very tall, enormous muscular body, short, curly blond hair and a reasonably attractive face; all-around high school *stud*. "Billy, of course I know Phil. God, I'm really surprised, but I can see how you'd *want* to fuck with him."

"I didn't start out wanting to, Pete." And Billy told me how it had happened:

Phil had become increasingly friendly toward Billy that year, often stopping to talk with him after football or basketball practice, and often standing next to him as they showered. Billy was, of course, awed by this most popular senior *god,* and flattered by his apparent interest in lowly sophomore Billy Polk. On a number of occasions Phil had asked Billy to have a Coke with him, or to go to the movies, and they had done so. Billy said that Phil often let his leg press against his own as they sat in the movies, and sometimes he casually draped an arm around his shoulder when they were together. Billy was not just flattered by Phil's attention, he was aroused—he had often had to turn away from the handsome blond giant with the biggest cock Billy had ever seen hanging between his legs, to hide his own erection—and because of that, he had never said anything to me about it.

Shortly after I had left for Indiana, Billy went to a movie with Phil, who asked him to 'sleep over' at his house afterward. He agreed—flattered, nervous, and excited about what *might* happen, all at the same time. They retired to the one double bed in Phil's room, dressed only in their briefs. They talked a long time, lying side-by-side on their backs. Phil had switched off the lamp next to his bed, but there was still ample light-spill from the bathroom that it was not completely dark. Phil's leg pressed against Billy's as it had done so often when they had sat together in the movies. Soon Phil rolled to his side and propped himself up on one elbow. He put his hand on Billy's stomach and asked him if he ever "fooled around."

Billy, knowing full well what he meant, gulped "What do you mean?"

"Aw, you know," Phil replied, "playin' with your pecker with another guy." Billy's reluctant reply was almost a whisper, "Well, yeah—sometimes."

Phil moved his hand down and cupped Billy's crotch—encountering the raging hard-on that had sprung up instantaneously when Phil had touched his stomach. "You want to play with mine? Yours sure feels like you're ready to play." He took Billy's hand and guided it to his own prick. Billy was surprised to find that Phil had pulled his shorts down—when, he did not know—and his prick was bare and fully erect as Billy's hand encircled it.

["And God, Pete, you wouldn't believe how big it was—and he has incredibly big balls, too."]

Phil pulled Billy's shorts off, and began to play with that sweet, long cock I loved so much. "Jeez, Billy, I've seen your pecker in the showers plenty, and you've got a nice one, but Godamighty, it's really big when it's hard." Billy was by this time stroking Phil's prick eagerly.

["I'm really sorry, Pete, but I was so excited, and I was horny, and Phil . . . well, gosh, he's Phil Baker. And his prick was really big and hard—and it felt wonderful."

"Billy, I couldn't have resisted temptation either, I'm sure. Go on, tell me everything."]

Phil switched on the lamp next to the bed, and smiled at Billy. "You're so damned good-lookin,' Billy, I wanna see you while we fool around. Okay"

"Sure," Billy gulped. "And I wanna see you. You're the best-lookin' guy in school, Phil, everybody knows that."

They played with each others' cocks for a long time, and finally Phil bent over Billy and began to lick his balls and kiss his cock. "You ever have a guy take your dick in his mouth? It really feels good . . . you want me to show you?" Without waiting for an answer, Phil opened his mouth and began a long, *serious* blowjob. Billy reversed his body and began to suck Phil at the same time. He had to stretch his lips to take Phil's cock inside his mouth, and could only take about half of its length initially—but as things progressed, he applied the lessons I had taught him, and was soon sucking most of the enormous shaft.

Billy said nothing as they fucked each others' mouths, but Phil often paused long enough to urge him to suck harder, or to comment on how much he enjoyed eating Billy's cock. Phil rolled on his back and told Billy to fuck his mouth extra hard. Billy knelt over Phil's head and plunged himself deep into his throat, while Phil's lips drove up and down his cock, As Billy neared orgasm, Phil stopped sucking long enough to say, "Keep fuckin' me—it's really exciting."

"But I'm getting ready to shoot my load," Billy panted.

"Don't stop—just keep fuckin.' I want you to come in my mouth."

Billy thrust himself savagely into Phil's throat and said, "Here it comes, Phil—I'm gonna fill you up with come," and after a few minutes of hard fucking, he delivered his hot load into Phil's hungry throat. Phil murmured in delight, swallowed Billy's come, and continued to suck as he caressed Billy's still-driving ass. Billy stretched out next to Phil, and they lay on their sides, embracing, each fondling the other's ass, with Phil's hard prick pressing into Billy's stomach.

"I swear, Billy—your come tasted really good," Phil whispered into Billy's ear. "I'll bet you've never had anybody blow a load in your mouth, have you? You can tell me, Billy—I won't tell anybody else, just like I know you won't tell anybody about me suckin' you off. You ever get a mouthful of come like you gave me?"

"No. No, Phil, I . . . " Billy said, but then said, quietly, "Yeah, I have."

"Will you take mine, Billy? God, I've wanted to eat your dick all this year. It's all I can do to keep standin' there when I'm next to you in the shower—I've wanted to kneel down and suck you off every time. You've got a really sexy prick—and your ass looks good enough to eat, too. But I've been dreamin' about you suckin' my dick just as much" He eagerly fondled Billy's perfect young ass as Billy confessed he wasn't just willing to eat Phil's come—he *wanted* it.

Phil stood next to the bed while Billy sat on the edge of it to give him a blowjob. Phil held Billy's head tightly as he fucked his mouth long and hard, and Billy feverishly caressed the muscular ass driving the huge dick into his throat. Finally, with a barely suppressed shout, Phil came, filling Billy's eager throat.

["God, Pete, his dick is so big, and he fucked my mouth really hard—and he shot so much come some of it leaked out around his cock before I could swallow it."]

They cuddled for hours, but Phil did not return the kisses Billy gave him on his neck, and all over his face, and when Billy made to kiss Phil's lips, he averted them. Before drifting off to sleep, Phil crouched over Billy and sucked his cock again until Billy was near orgasm. Phil rolled to his back and had Billy shoot into his open mouth from a couple of inches away, so they could watch.

["And after that, Phil lay behind me and held me tight—and his prick was pushing up against my ass. I just couldn't help myself, Pete: I put a

lotta spit on his prick, and backed up on it—it was so really huge, it hurt going in, but once he was all he way inside me, it felt fantastic, and I started fucking myself on it. And then Phil rolled me on my back, and I put my legs up on his shoulders while he fucked me. It took a long time, but it felt great, and when he blew his load inside me, it felt like he'd exploded."]

Phil lay there with his flaccid prick still inside Billy. "Gosh, I never wanted to do that to anyone more than I have since I first looked at your pretty ass in the shower, Billy. Thanks for lettin' me fuck it—you're even better than I ever hoped for." They rolled to their sides and went to sleep with Phil's cock still inside the sweet young boy he had just fucked—but whom he had not yet kissed.

The next morning Phil acted as though nothing sexual had happened between them.

Billy concluded his narrative by saying, "He acted kind of like things were just like they were the day before. He was nice, and still acted just as friendly, but . . . I didn't know what to think. I knew I enjoyed it, though, Pete, but I knew I was cheating on you—and I love you, Pete, and I don't want to do anything to make you not love me. I'll understand if you don't want to make love with me anymore."

"I'll always want to make love with you, Billy—and I'll always love you, and I forgive you. Billy, I . . . " I had to tell him. "Billy, I *have* to forgive you, because I've got to ask you to forgive me, too." A puzzled look. "I've told you about Les, the guy with the big prick who was the first one to fuck me?"

"Yeah, your best friend in high school—the one who couldn't let you fuck him, and who never came?"

"That's the one. I visited him in Chicago last week, and he had a couple of surprise Christmas presents for me."

"Did you . . . "

"Yeah, we went to bed together, and he gave me my presents there."

Billy looked at me for a long, silent moment. "He let you fuck him, didn't he?"

"Yes he did, Billy, and he also filled my mouth with come, and filled my ass with come, and shot come all over me—that was the other present."

Billy surprised me. Instead of being angry or acting hurt, he giggled and did his Groucho Marx leer and eyebrow-wiggle: "Pretty hard to wrap presents like that, isn't it?" Then, very seriously he kissed me and asked, "Do you still love him, Pete?"

"Of course I love him, Billy, I always will—but I love you, too, more than anything in the world. In spite of what people say, there's no reason you can't love more than one person."

"As long as you still love me, too—that's the important thing."

"I will always love you, Billy, and I will always want to make love with you. How do you feel about Phil?"

"I really like Phil, but I don't love him."

"Do you want to have sex with him again?"

"I . . . I don't know, Pete. It was fantastic, and I really enjoyed it—but not as much as I do with you. Besides, he'll probably never say anything again. He's pretending we didn't do anything together that night."

"If he does ask you, and if you want to, you do it—just don't stop loving me, or making love with me. And only tell me about it if you want to. I don't own you, Billy—I don't *want* to own you. I just want to love you." We fucked and sucked and cuddled and kissed, and Billy had to go home. It had been a wonderful homecoming, in spite of the cloud of our mutual unfaithfulness. I felt more in love with my young lover than ever.

New Year's Eve we each had parties to go to, and would of course have to stay at them until the new year began, but we agreed that I would be home before midnight Mountain Time, an hour later by our local time, and Billy would join me by then for the short period of time we could spend together before he had to get home. In keeping with the tradition of "whatever you're doing at midnight on New Year's Eve, you'll do all year long," we wanted to 'ring in' 1955 in bed together, making love.

As local "one o'clock" chimed—midnight for folks in Mountain Time—Billy's prick was in my mouth, about to deposit a hot load, and I had just shot a large wad into his. As per an agreement we had made, Billy did not swallow my load until after he shot his, and we were able to mingle our loads in our mouths and share the combined offering, just as Les and I had done the week before. I had told Billy of Les's and my pledge sealed in come, and Billy was eager to solemnize *our* love and commitment to each other in the same way, and particularly at that special time. I was happy, and thrilled to oblige this sweet, beautiful boy.

Into the new year, and into the second semester, Billy and I found time and opportunity to make love often—and with unremitting intensity. Neither he nor I seemed to lose the thrilling *edge* of fucking and sucking one another, and our kissing and cuddling was an unflagging blend of passion and tenderness. Every time his long prick penetrated my ass I felt the most wonderful kind of warmth and excitement, my throat seemed bottomless as he drove his shaft as deeply into it as he could, I gloried in the feel and taste of his balls as I sucked them, and every time his eruption filled my mouth with hot come it tasted more wonderful than the time before. On the basis of our 'pillow talk,' I knew Billy felt the same way toward me.

We also made it a point to be seen together often in public, in innocent and explicable settings, so his presence around my house would seem unremarkable to people in town, and even Joe Don, exercising his bulging crotch on my car or my desk as usual, didn't seem to insinuate he thought anything was "going on." It was not uncommon for someone to say something to me, or to ask me something about Billy, knowing that we were close; I never felt there was any suspicion or accusation in those comments or questions, except on the part of one person. Not surprisingly, that was Phil Baker.

I had come to view Phil in a totally different light after Billy told me about their encounter. I knew him, of course—this was a very small school—but only to greet casually in the hallway or on the street. Knowing he liked fucking butt and eating cock, I found him much more interesting. I had not thought of him before as particularly good looking, but in my new view he was much more attractive—certainly his body had always been striking. While I was not usually drawn to his large, very muscular sort of body, I couldn't help but admire it; given a choice, I would elect a trim, lightly muscled body—just like Billy's. Phil was quite tall, probably about 6'3", and was very large: an extremely broad chest and narrow waist, with huge muscular arms and shoulders, and a well-rounded, ample, but perfectly formed ass. Phil's bodily charms were normally displayed to great advantage in very tight tee shirts and Levi's—the standard uniform for cocky young men in Antares, Texas in the 1950's. Knowing from Billy's report that Phil's bulging Levi's contained an especially large cock, I must admit I began to find myself drawn to him, but in spite of what I knew had gone on between him and my young lover, I had no particular occasion to speak with him at any length.

Around the end of January, Billy had to go with the basketball team to a tournament, and would be spending two nights at a motel in Waco. He told me Phil had suggested they room together. "Pete, what do I do? I know he's going to want to fuck me—he hasn't said anything about it, but I'm sure that's why he wants to room with me. What do you want me to do?"

"What do you want to do, Billy? If he wants to fuck you, do you want him to?" He hesitated a minute, then began to reply, but I stopped him. "Be completely honest, now; I know you love me, and you know I love you, but I can see why Phil excites you. Hell, he excites me—but that doesn't mean I don't love you and want you just as much as ever."

"You mean you want to fuck with Phil, too?" I smiled, and Billy realized what he had just admitted. Then, with a sheepish grin: "I mean, *do* you want to fuck with Phil?"

"I guess that answered whether *you* want to fuck with him or not." He began to remonstrate, but I stopped him. "No, that's okay—I've *told* you. But yes, I think fucking with Phil would be fun. He's got a fantastic body, and judging by what you tell me, his prick must be terrific—but I don't think that's going to happen. Besides, if I'm fucking with anybody in Antares, it's going to be with my very own lover." I kissed him. "Billy, if Phil wants to fuck with you, and you want to fuck with him, do it. But do something for me, will you?"

"Of course, Pete—anything. What is it?"

"Remember all the details, and tell me absolutely everything that happens—and I'll pretend I was there with you when I hear about it. Okay? Deal?"

"Deal, Pete. But shoot, he probably isn't going to want to do anything anyway."

I snorted. "You want to make a bet?"

Billy laughed. "No, I *don't* want to make a bet—I'd be better off betting I'd lose the other bet." Then in a thick foreign accent: "I think Meestair Baker vants to sink his big cock in ze mysterious und beautiful Billy Polk's butt-hole again."

I laughed, and matched his accent. "Und I think also zat you are right. Und *zo do I*.," and we began to wrestle and play around, ending up, of course, with me sinking *my* cock in the mysterious and beautiful—the *very* beautiful—Billy Polk's luscious butt-hole.

A few weeks later, as Billy was getting ready to board the bus for Waco, he dropped into the Band Room as I was working at my desk. "I'm gonna miss you, Pete—but we'll make up for it when I get home"

"Don't forget, if Phil . . . "

"If it happens, I'll remember every little detail."

"Don't forget to tell me about the *big* details, too."

"I'll tell you everything. Gotta run." Then, whispered: "Don't worry, I love *you.*" He grinned, winked broadly (*God, how cute.*), and walked out the door.

I watched his perfect ass as he left—wondering if tonight it was going to be filled by Phil's big prick, and desperately wishing it was gripping my own cock at that very moment, as it had so wonderfully done only the day before.

For the next two nights I was torn between worrying about Billy being treated properly by Phil—if, indeed, Phil was going to *treat* him at all—and by jealousy over his being with someone else. I was equally filled with excitement while I imagined the scene between my hot young lover and the big blond with the magnificent build and the huge prick. Excitement won out most of the time, and I masturbated several times in the next couple of days visualizing Billy's beautiful ass and Phil's reportedly huge balls swinging below his big cock as he drove it into it. It would be dishonest to say I didn't also fantasize about Phil hammering that prick into my own butt, and thinking about those huge, muscular arms holding me while his extra-large balls supplied me with a full load of hot come.

Monday morning, Billy was back in school. In Geometry class he waggled his eyebrows and grinned impishly as he began to leave at the end of the period. He started to walk out, and I wondered if he was going to say anything about the weekend, but he turned back and came up to my desk, laughing. "Thought I wasn't gonna say anything about it, huh? I've got *lots* to tell you. Tonight?

"Tonight it is."

Shortly after dark, Billy was at my house. He came in and we kissed for a long time. "Well, tell me about it—did Phil . . . "

"Are you *sure* you want to hear about this? Gee, I don't think I should tell a nice, young innocent guy like you."

"If you don't tell this innocent young guy, he's going to kick your beautiful, tight butt."

He pulled me to him and whispered in my ear, "How about sticking your dick in my beautiful, tight butt? I'd really prefer that."

I laughed and tousled his hair as I led him back to the bedroom. "Your wish is my command—but just tell me, is that beautiful butt as tight as it was when you left town? Or did Phil show you some butt-stretching exercises?"

"Hey. My butt is still tight."

"You mean Phil didn't . . . "

"Pete, Phil fucked me so much I couldn't see straight." I gulped—I had expected it, but it still hurt. He took me in his arms, "But every second his prick was in me, I was wishing you were with me . . . really. I'd be lying if I said it wasn't fun with Phil, but I just wanted you there too—God, the three of us could have had an incredible time."

"Okay, you promised—I want a blow-by-blow report."

"Get your clothes off and I'll give you a blowjob-by-blowjob report—and I'll even give you a blowjob while I do it. Come on, don't look so serious—I love you, and I just did what we agreed was okay."

"I know Billy—it's just going to take me a minute, okay?"

"I understand. But look, Pete, you and . . . ah, Les . . . fucked each other's brains out last month and you still love me, right?" I put my head on his chest and nodded. "And Phil and I fucked each other's brains out, and I still love you, so everything's going to be fine."

"Wait, you said you and Phil fucked *each other*. You mean...?"

Billy grinned hugely. "Wait until, you hear."

I smiled back, "I can't wait—tell all."

"I will, but just remember that every time I was inside Phil or Phil was inside me, I wanted you there with me—I wanted to be in you at the same time, or have you in me at the same time. Right?"

"Right—go ahead, but don't forget about that blowjob while you tell me."

"I'll suck your nuts dry." Sweet young Billy was getting pretty raunchy.

During the telling of Billy's adventure with Phil, he delivered the promised blowjob, and accepted one from me also—properly timed to underscore the climactic moments (pun intended). Gleaned from Billy's report, the story is as follows:

Billy's expectations were heightened when they checked into their motel room: there was only one bed, so whatever happened, he would be spending the night in bed with Phil again. Phil made no remarks of a suggestive nature as they unpacked, and then went to eat with the team. Following the game, which they won, they hung around another of the motel rooms with some of the other players, and wound up back in their own room alone around 10:30 at night. Billy said he had to take a shower before going to bed. Phil said he'd shower when Billy finished.

Billy had been in the shower only a few minutes when Phil joined him. His big, exciting body dwarfed Billy—and the heat of the shower steam and the sight of Phil's massive cock hanging down aroused Billy, who turned away from Phil, to hide his erection. He was soaping his shoulders when Phil took the bar from him and said, "Here, I'll wash your back for you." Billy relinquished the soap, and Phil began to lather up his back, working his hands around to Billy's stomach and chest, and down his sides. Soon Billy became aware that Phil's prick was fiercely hard, and the tip of it was pressing between the cheeks of his ass. Billy bent down, reached backward between his legs to take Phil's massive balls in his hand, and he began to massage them. Phil pressed up against him, so that his big prick-head was now poised at Billy's asshole. He moaned in pleasure, and put both arms around Billy to hold him tight. Billy released Phil's balls, and stood erect, reaching behind him to grasp Phil's big cock. Phil immediately began humping Billy's fist. "Oh God,

Billy, that feels so good."

Billy turned around and put his hands flat against Phil's massive chest and looked up at him as he played with his large nipples—Phil towered over Billy by six inches. Phil took their two pricks in one hand and began to masturbate them together while he reached around Billy to caress his ass with the other. Billy's voice trembled as he asked, "You wanna fuck my ass again?"

"Jesus, yes, Billy—more than anything."

"On one condition."

Phil grinned. "Sure, Billy, anything—what?"

"You're not going to pretend tomorrow that it never happened—like you did before."

Phil's grin faded, and his hands took Billy's shoulders as he stepped backward to look into the younger boy's eyes very seriously. "Billy, I just didn't know how to handle it before. Sure I remembered what we did, but I didn't really know how you felt, or what you felt about me."

"I thought you knew I had a wonderful time with you, and I loved it when you fucked me. And I want to do it again, Phil. I've dreamed about doing it again, but I want to know it means something to you."

"It means a lot to me, Billy. Let me fuck you again, let me suck you off again. I'll show you how much I appreciate it." He sank to his knees, and with the water streaming over his head, he began to suck Billy's cock with real enthusiasm. Billy held Phil's head and fucked his mouth happily. After a few minutes, Phil stopped and looked up at Billy. "Stay right here for a second." He got out of the shower, and returned only a few seconds later, holding a jar of Vaseline. He held it up to Billy. "I was really hopin'."

Billy grinned and said, "Your prayers have been answered," and took a gob of the lubricant and massaged it into his ass, then turned his back to Phil and said over his shoulder, "Put your big prick in me, and fuck me for all you're worth." He leaned over and spread his cheeks.

Phil positioned his cock-head against Billy's asshole and, with his hands on Billy's waist, began to drive himself slowly, but inexorably into that tight orifice. Billy moaned in pleasure, "Oh God, that feels so good. Fuck me Phil . . . shove your prick all the way in me and fuck me hard."

Once he was completely in, Phil held his arms tightly around Billy's waist and fucked rapidly and deeply, moaning in pleasure. Billy gasped his thrill, and both boys encouraged each other to greater heights of passion. Soon Phil stood up straight, grasped Billy's shoulders tightly and pressed his upper body down as he slammed his prick all the way in and held it there. "Here it is, Billy. Take it." he cried, and Billy felt massive spurts erupting inside him.

Billy had been reaching behind to hold Phil's ass while he fucked him, and he stood to lean back against Phil's broad chest, remaining fully impaled. Phil nibbled on Billy's ear and resumed his humping as Billy whispered, "Nothing in the world ever felt so good." He turned his head, hoping Phil would kiss him. But Phil only grinned at him.

Billy turned, so that Phil's cock slipped from him. He put his arms up around Phil's shoulders and smiled into his face. "And you're gonna remember it tomorrow?"

"I'm gonna remember it always, Billy." He pulled Billy toward him, their lips close together, obviously meaning to give Billy the kiss he had wanted a moment earlier. Then he caught himself, and pulled back a bit.

Billy reached up and pulled Phil's head back down to him and said, "Do it—I want you to." and Phil leaned down and drove his tongue into Billy's mouth. They necked for a long time—still under the shower, which was beginning to get cold. Phil turned off the water, and said they needed to get out and dry off. Before doing so, however, he again took Billy in his arms and said, "I won't lie to you, I've fucked a buncha other guys before, but I never thought I'd *kiss* a guy like that—but everything about you makes me hornier'n I've ever been, Billy."

"Let's dry off and get in bed, Phil. You've fucked me and you've kissed me, but we've got a lot left we can do."

Phil cupped Billy's hard cock and balls and kissed him quickly. "And we're gonna do it all."

"Not just once, I hope." They dried each other off—with slow and admiring application of the towels, then headed for the bed. "I'll bring the towels and the Vaseline," Billy said, "I've got a feeling we'll need them." He had no sooner gathered them up than Phil put one arm around his back and one arm behind his knees and picked him up without any effort. Grinning into Billy's face, Phil kissed the younger boy and carried him to the bed.

Phil lay on his back on the bed as Billy knelt over him and straddled his chest. Phil smiled, "Fuck my mouth 'n just drown me in your come." Billy pulled Phil's head up and thrust his long prick deep into his anxious throat. Phil sucked savagely, and Billy drove himself frantically, and after only a few minutes Phil's mouth was flooded with Billy's hot offering. After Phil had sucked the last precious drop from him, Billy sat back on his heels and smiled down at him. "Was that what you had in mind?"

Phil tried to speak with a mouthful of come, and some of Billy's massive orgasm leaked from the corners of his mouth as he did so. He swallowed and said, "Best ever."

They held each other and kissed and embraced for a long time. Billy asked Phil to tell him about the "bunch of other guys" he had fucked.

"Well, there's been a few guys in school—mostly on the football team, and even the . . . " He caught himself before he went on. ". . . and someone else, who really likes to suck me off, or have me fuck him in the butt. But usually it's when I go into the city. [When someone from Antares talks about 'the city,' he is referring to the city of Lubbock, Texas.] I usually go by the bushes near the men's room in the park, and there's always at least a coupla guys there who want to suck my dick or take it up the ass. Hell, Billy, it wouldn't be polite to turn 'em down." he giggled. "And a lot of the time they insist on giving me money, and . . . well hell, why not take it?"

"Do you ever suck them off, or let them fuck you?"

"I almost always suck 'em for a while, and if one of 'em is really good lookin', or really *hung* . . . yeah, I'll take a load in my mouth then if he wants me to." He grinned, But hey, none of 'em ever gave me a load as sweet as that one I just got." And he kissed Billy again.

"But you don't let anybody fuck your ass?"

"No, I can't do that."

"Have you ever really tried? Honestly Phil, you can't imagine how great a prick feels inside you, and especially when it's a big one like yours, shooting a big load in there."

"I know it's gotta feel good—it sure sounds like you're havin' a helluva time when I fuck you—and most everybody I fuck seems to feel the same way. But no, I haven't really tried. I just don't think I could do that—but I dunno, maybe one of these days, huh?"

They soon found themselves wrapped in sixty-nine, and Billy filled Phil's throat with come again shortly before swallowing a huge load the latter delivered. They kissed, and were soon asleep in each other's arms.

The next morning, Billy woke and went in to pee. When he returned, Phil lay there wide awake, spread-eagled on the bed, with his huge prick pointing skyward. "I reckon this is a piss hard-on, but you might wanna do something about it." Billy reached for the Vaseline and spread it liberally on the throbbing shaft before positioning his asshole over it. Slowly, with both of them murmuring delight, he settled down and rode the wildly bucking Phil's cock until he was rewarded with another thrilling inner eruption of Phil's load. "Oh man, Billy, that was the best ever. Stay on me and let me beat you off." Billy continued his wild ride as the other's eager fist serviced him, and he soon shot his huge first-of-the-day load all over Phil's chest.

Phil scooped Billy's come from his chest and ate it from his fingers, then pulled Billy down on top of him and kissed him passionately. "Man, what a way to start the day. And I *am* going to remember what happened last night—*and* this morning."

"What about tonight?"

"And tonight too, I hope. If it's possible for me to fuck you harder than I already have, or if you can give me a bigger load to eat than you did last night, we'll try for it. Okay?"

"That's a deal," Billy said, and they necked passionately for a long time before getting dressed and meeting the rest of the team.

They lost their first game that day. The coach felt both Billy and Phil were seriously "off their game," and insisted everyone take a nap in the afternoon before the early-evening final game. Billy and Phil did as he said, and agreed to keep their hands off each other until after the last game, so they could get rested—for the game, and for the post-game activities they had planned in their room.

And the post-game activities that night were perhaps even hotter than the night before. As soon as they finished dinner and 'hanging out' with the rest of the team (they won their game that night), they locked their door and stripped in a frenzy, and were immediately wrapped in each other's arms, kissing passionately. Phil backed Billy up and laid him on his back on the bed. He began kissing and licking Billy's chest, and soon worked his way down to his hard prick. Licking it all over, he went farther down to lick and suck Billy's balls, and Billy was soon telling him to stop or he would come too soon. Phil engulfed Billy's prick in his mouth and he sucked fiercely while he caressed Billy's chest and stomach. Billy soon cried, "Phil, I've gotta come."

Phil managed to mutter "Do it." around Billy's driving cock.

Billy levered his body upward with his feet to shove his prick deep into Phil's throat and deliver a huge load to the hungry athlete. Phil slurped and sucked and licked and swallowed, and generally reveled in the taste and thrill of Billy's orgasm. Billy held his head as he calmed down. "God, Phil, that felt wonderful."

"It tasted even more wonderful," Phil moaned. Billy kept his legs spread as Phil moved up over him and kissed him deeply, while with his finger he began to plumb the tight opening of his partner's hot ass. He greased up that entrance to heaven, and was soon driving his big cock deep into it. Billy's legs were wrapped tightly around Phil's waist as the latter began a fierce assault, shouting his delight at the tightness and feel of Billy's ass, and accompanied by Billy's cries of appreciation. He reached his arms under Billy, and with Billy's arms wrapped tightly around his neck, he picked him up. Phil stood, with Billy still impaled on his prick and his legs and arms holding his body. They kissed long and hard, tongue-fucking each other's mouths while Phil walked around, carrying his magnificent burden. Finally Phil sat on a chair and they continued their frenzied kissing, while Billy continued to ride Phil's driving cock until it exploded in him in a series of copious spurts of hot come. Still locked together, Phil carried Billy to the bed, and they stretched out and snuggled and kissed for a long time.

"I can't believe you never kissed a guy before, Phil—you're as great a kisser as you are a fucker."

Phil smiled, "I've never been with anyone I thought was as sexy as you are—and kissing you is almost as great as fucking you. There's nothing quite as good as fucking you, though—your ass is the prettiest thing I've ever seen, and the hottest thing I've ever had my dick in."

Billy began to play with Phil's ass, running his hands over its contours, and gently fingering the twitching hot hole. "You know, you've got a hot ass, too, Phil. It's so round and solid—man it feels great." Phil knelt on all fours over Billy and continued to kiss him while he wriggled his ass and enjoyed Billy's appreciative exploration. Billy said, "Stay just like that," and began to slide his body down under Phil's. He sucked Phil's large nipples, and continued to play with his ass as he licked his stomach, and when he reached Phil's balls, he sucked them eagerly, all the while continuing to probe his asshole gently.

Billy slid all the way out from under, and now knelt and looked at Phil's generous, muscular ass—which Phil offered for display as he put his arms and face down to the bed. Billy caressed Phil's ass and kissed it. "God, you've got a great ass," and his finger renewed its probe of Phil's asshole. Phil reached behind himself and spread his cheeks. "Do you like my asshole, too?" Billy held the cheeks of Phil's ass in his hands as he moved closer. "I especially like your asshole," and he began to lick and kiss Phil's ass all over, but gradually moved in toward the center, and began licking his twitching hole.

Phil panted, "Please, Billy, eat my ass."

Inserting his tongue as far into Phil as he could, Billy began to tongue-fuck him passionately.

"Oh, Jesus, Billy, that feels incredible—that's what Coach loves to do.

Fuck me with your tongue, Billy. *Fuck me.*" Phil was apparently so wrought up he failed to realize what he had just revealed.

Billy ate Phil's ass for a long time, and Phil gyrated his ass and humped along with him for maximum effect. Finally Billy stopped, and whispered in Phil's ear, "If you think getting fucked by my tongue feels good, wait until I put my prick in there."

"Billy, I don't think I can take it."

"Phil, I'm going to fuck you—and you're going to love it as much as I love that big dick of yours inside me." Billy had already begun applying Vaseline to Phil's asshole, and had a full finger probing it already.

"I've never . . ."

He positioned the tip of his cock at Phil's sphincter. "Phil, I'm *gonna* fuck your ass, understand?"

"God, yes, Billy—I want you inside me. Do it. But . . . "

"I'll take it easy; just work with me, and I'm going to show you how wonderful getting fucked is. Back up onto me." Phil wriggled his ass, and gradually backed up to Billy's insistent prick, which slipped past the opening. Billy pressed forward, gently, but insistently. Phil had cried out in pain when Billy's cock-head first breached his hole, but by the time Billy's entire cock was buried inside him, he was crying out in ecstasy.

"My God, Billy, that feels incredible. Fuck me, baby—fuck me with that beautiful big prick." He reached behind and held Billy's ass as Billy began his fuck. "Fill my ass, Billy—I love your prick. *Drive* that hot ass of yours."

Billy showed no consideration whatever for the fact that this was Phil's first fucking. He fucked hard, and deep, and for a very long time, and finally shouted in triumph as he delivered a load of come into Phil's thrashing ass. "Take my come in your ass, Phil—this is what it's all about."

Their passion gradually subsided, and they eventually rolled over on their sides—Billy's prick still sunk inside Phil's ass. Phil gasped, "Billy, Jesus . . . I could feel your come shootin' in me. It was even better'n when you shot it in my mouth."

"Phil, I'm sorry I forced you . . . I just *had* to fuck your ass."

"No . . . thank you for forcin' me. It was like nothin' I've ever felt. Jesus, your tongue fuckin' me was great, but when your whole prick was in there, I thought I'd gone to heaven, until you shot your load in me, and then I *knew* I was in heaven."

Billy pulled out and Phil rolled over so that they could hold each other. "I know it hurts right at first, but God, there's nothing as thrilling as feeling a prick filling your ass." He laughed, "You see what a great favor you've been doing those guys in the park . . . and me, too."

Phil laughed. "No wonder they were all so happy." He continued to thank Billy for his wonderful offering as Billy went down on him and began a long and expert blowjob, that ended with Billy's finger driving deep into Phil's ass again as the latter shot a seemingly endless load into the adoring mouth.

They cuddled and kissed for a very long time. Phil told Billy about his sexual experiences, and at Billy's request paid special attention to the guys he had fucked in Antares. Phil wouldn't identify anyone, however.

"But you know, you already slipped up and mentioned Coach," Billy said.

"I know," Phil said, "and I hope you'll forget I mentioned him, okay?" Billy promised to keep the secret. "But unless I fuck up again, I'm not gonna tell you any one else's name," Phil said. "Some day I'm gonna tell somebody else about the wonderful, beautiful, hot, *hung* stud that first fucked me. You don't want me to tell 'em *your* name do you? But I sure will tell 'em how great you were, and how much I loved it."

Phil asked Billy about his sexual experiences. Billy admitted that except for some 'fooling around,' he had only had serious sex with one guy. "And I can't tell you who that is, either."

A silence. Then Phil asked, "Was it Mr. Harrison?"

Billy's heart skipped about four beats. He didn't say anything for a bit—unable to, really. Finally he said, "I told you, Phil, I can't tell you who it was. But why do you think it's Mr. Harrison?"

"Well, you and him are always hangin' around together, and, well . . . he's a nice guy, and you never hear of him dating. I mean, it just seems like he might be the one. And I wouldn't blame you—hell, if I saw him in the park in Lubbock, I'd fuck him, and I think I'd suck him off, too, I think he's pretty sexy."

"Has anyone ever said anything?"

"No—no. Everybody seems to think it's nice that you're friends. Hell, *I* think it's nice that you're friends. But I know if he was my friend, I'd try to fuck him, and get him in bed. Frankly, I kinda thought about it anyway—but I never had a chance to do anything about it. Maybe I still will."

"Phil, I don't think . . ."

"Oh hell, Billy, I'm just kiddin'. I don't know if you and Mr. Harrison are fuckin' each other, and I don't even wanna know. That's your business. *I'd* wanna fuck him, and he seems like a smart enough guy that he should wanna fuck you. I don't care, and even if you tell me you two are fuckin' all the time, I wouldn't say a word about it. Look, I trust you enough to tell you about all the guys I fuck with; I know you won't say anything. And believe me, I won't say anything about you. Man, I'm glad you've got somebody to fuck; I sure wish I had known as much as you do when I was a sophomore."

"I'm glad I've got someone to fuck with, too, Phil—he's really great, and we have a wonderful time, and please don't ask me who he is. But I'm glad I've got you to fuck with sometimes, too."

"That goes double for me—and I wanna fuck you again in just about three minutes. Hey—does your . . . friend know you fucked with me?"

"Well, yeah, I told him I got fucked by someone else around Christmas time, but I didn't tell him who it was." Billy was not a liar, generally, but sometimes it's best to bend the truth a little.

"And he didn't mind?"

"I think he really *minded,* but he said he didn't own me, and wanted me to be happy, but not to stop loving him."

"You guys . . . *love* each other?"

"Yeah, Phil we do. But look, I just can't talk about it too much, okay?" He took Phil in his arms and kissed him. "Can I fuck you again, or do you hurt?"

"You'd *better* fuck me again. Whoever your friend is, he and I are the luckiest bastards in the world—we both get to fuck Billy Polk, and get to have Billy Polk fuck us."

"And I'm mighty lucky to have two really hot *studs* to feed me their come and drink mine."

Phil knelt on all fours. "Why don'tcha show me how lucky I am again." Billy was soon plunging his long prick deep inside Phil's ass again, and Phil seemed to be feeling no pain from having been fucked for the first time only shortly before. He bucked and humped, and did all he could to meet Billy's profound thrusts in counter-motion. He made Billy slow down. "I wantcha to fuck me for a long, long time—don't come too soon, you feel just great in there." Billy pushed Phil down onto his belly, and assumed a gentler pace and lay flat over Phil's body as he drove his prick just as deep as before, but slowly and very sensuously. Phil put his hands behind him and felt Billy's humping ass as he reveled in his penetration. "God, Billy, your ass is so fine."

"Your ass is the one that feels really fine," Billy said as he continued his slow fuck. "I love to fuck butt—and I'm going to love filling your hot one with another load of come."

"I'm really looking forward to it. But, stop fuckin' me for a minute." Billy pulled out, and Phil rolled on his back. "Get your ass up here where I can really play with it for a little while." Billy turned to face Phil's feet, and straddled his chest—his ass only inches from Phil's face. Phil caressed it and murmured about how smooth it felt, and how beautiful it looked. Taking Billy's hips in his hands, he drew him even closer, and began to kiss and lick his ass—all around the perfect globes of his cheeks, in the crevice between them, and finally kissing his asshole very tenderly. Billy reached behind himself to pull his cheeks apart, and Phil inserted his tongue into Billy. Billy's ass began to writhe, and Phil put his arms around him to draw him close, and drove his tongue in and out of Billy's tight asshole as far as he could. Billy began to work Phil's tongue with his sphincter muscle, and Phil's tongue fucked and licked while he grunted in lust.

Billy drove his ass back against Phil's tongue rhythmically. "Oh my God, that feels so wonderful. Fuck me with your tongue, Phil. Oh God, Phil—eat my ass. *Eat my hot fucking ass.*" And Billy fell forward and took Phil's throbbing prick deep in his throat and sucked hungrily and drove his tightly-closed lips as far up and down the considerable shaft of it as he could. Soon Phil's grunting became frenzied as he continued eating Billy's ass, and Billy drove his lips all the way down Phil's shaft until all of it was—miraculously—buried inside. Just at that moment, Phil shot another big load into the mouth that was so eager for it. Billy gagged and sputtered as Phil's come shot out of his prick while he continued to drive it deep in the hungry throat. Billy managed to control his gag reflex, and continued to suck until he could swallow. Finally, when he had drained every drop, Billy licked up what little come had spilled out onto Phil's pubic hair and balls. He began to suck Phil's big balls greedily, and the latter continued to feast on his delicious meal of hot, writhing sixteen-year-old ass, still voicing his delight as best he could with a tongue busily exploring it.

"That's so good, I could almost come just feeling you do that," Billy panted, "but I wanna fuck your ass some more." He raised up and turned his body to kneel between Phil's legs.

Phil raised his legs and rested them on Billy' shoulders. "Shove it in me again," he panted, "and just fuck my brains out." Billy drove his prick all the way into Phil with one violent thrust. Phil cried out in pain and happiness. "Oh yeah, Billy. Yeah, fuck me hard. Jesus, baby, you are such a fuckin' stud."

The two grunted in passion for only a few minutes more until Phil thrilled to the feel of the beautiful young stud delivering ample evidence of his lust in violent spurts. Billy fell on top of Phil, and still locked together that way, they kissed and cuddled for a very long time.

"Jesus, Billy, what an incredible weekend this has been. I never kissed a guy before, I never got fucked before, and I sure never thought I'd ever be eatin' ass. But with you, it's all fun, and . . . I dunno, just *right* somehow. I never fucked *anybody* who turns me on the way you do, Billy. I think I could be as happy as anyone would ever needa be if I could spend every night with you like this."

"Phil, I told you I'm in love with . . . well, with my friend. Fucking with you has been wonderful—and I hope we're not through *yet* for this trip—but it can only be once in a while. He knows I'm probably fucking around right now, and he says that's okay if I really want to, and he can stand me fucking with someone else once in a while if I still *love* him."

"Does he know me, and that you're roomin' with me?" Billy nodded. "And he figures we're prob'ly fuckin' together, right?" Another nod. "Jeez, Billy, I dunno if. . .well hell, I guess it doesn't matter if he knows it's me. If you and him are fuckin', he sure as hell can't say much about me fuckin' guys, can he? I guess it doesn't make any difference if he knows."

"No, it really doesn't, Phil—and I might as well tell you that he thinks you're really sexy, too, and thinks getting fucked by you would be fun."

Phil grinned. "Well, that's nice to hear. And you know, I bet I'd like to fuck him and suck him, and maybe even kiss him and get fucked by him—and maybe even eat his ass too."

Billy laughed, "I'll bet you'd both like it. I'd like to be a fly on the wall when you did it, though."

"How about bein' another body in the bed when we did it? How would you feel about that—all three of us together? Wouldn't that be hot?"

"There's no doubt it would be hot as the devil, but I don't really know how I'd feel about that, Phil. Besides, you've got lots of asses to fuck and guys to suck with already."

"Well Billy, my hot, beautiful little fuckbuddy—I mean *really* hot and *really* beautiful—you think about it. Who knows what'll happen? Just be sure that I can get together to fuck with you at least once in a while, okay?"

"That's a guaranteed *deal* Phil. Now let's get at least a little sleep."

Phil kissed Billy and held him in his arms, whispering into his ear, "Promise me I can fuck you again in the morning before we have to leave for home."

"I won't let you out of bed until you have—and until I've plowed that hot butt of yours, too." A minute or two of silence, and then, quietly, "I'm really glad you let me fuck you, Phil."

Phil laughed aloud, "I don't remember you givin' me much choice." Then, again quietly, "I'm glad I got fucked too, and I'm extra glad it was somebody like you—no, that it *was* you. You're really the best, Billy."

Some long, tender kissing between admiring fuck-buddies. The warmth of shared embraces. Moving together in sleep, and then waking to raging hard pricks driven again and again into adoring mouths and assholes—with hot, extra-large morning loads sating the appetites of the two magnificent young studs. What a way to end an unforgettable weekend.

As Billy finally came to the end of his promised detailed account, we were both incredibly horny. We locked ourselves in sixty-nine, and each sucked the other's cock dry, but before he left we had sufficiently recovered that we each rode the other's shaft. Billy began to recount the feel of Phil's huge cock fucking him as he rode mine, so I described the sensation of being plowed by Les's thrusting monster as I rode his.

It was a wonderful homecoming, and rather than feeling the encounter with Phil had created a rift between us, I honestly felt that my sweet young lover and I were closer than ever.

A few nights later, Billy presented his perfect ass for my admiration as he knelt on the edge of my bed and I stood behind him, his asshole right at the level of my hard cock. I was reaching for the Vaseline when Billy asked, "Pete, will you do something for me before you fuck me?"

I leaned over him and enclosed his waist in my arms, and said into his ear, "I'll do anything for you, Billy, you know that. What do you want?"

"Please eat my ass again, Pete. It felt so incredible when you did it before, and Phil's tongue-fucking almost drove me wild—I really would like for you to do it to me again."

"It's an *honor* to eat your ass, baby. You should have told me—I'd be thrilled to eat it any time. How's this?" And I knelt and began to kiss and lick his ass all over, and he began to wriggle it excitedly as I zeroed in on his hole.

He reached behind and spread his cheeks and moaned, "Tongue fuck me, Pete. Eat my hot ass for me." I drove my tongue deep into his asshole and feasted for a very long time on his perfect butt. Billy was very vocal in expressing his enjoyment of my efforts. Finally, he pulled away and said, "Lay on your back and let me sit on your face." I did as he wanted, and he lowered his perfect, rounded ass over my face. I held his waist as he positioned his asshole directly over my tongue, and I resumed my feast as I again began to assault his twitching, lovely hole with my driving tongue. He moved his ass side-to-side, forward-and-back, and up-and-down so that I could service him all the better. All the time he moaned in ecstasy and encouraged me to tongue-fuck him *deeper* and *faster*. Soon I felt his come splashing all over my stomach as the sphincter muscle of his ass worked my tongue fiercely. His hand scooped up his come and spread it on my cock, and he jacked me off while I continued to thrill to the taste and feel of my young lover's asshole—and he leaned over at the last minute to take my cock in his mouth so he could eat my load.

Finally, we both calmed down and held each other as we cooed our love and his enjoyment of what I had just done. "That's a feeling like no other, isn't it?"

"Actually, Billy, I don't know. No one has ever eaten my ass."

He held me tight in his arms and drove his tongue deep into my mouth and we kissed very passionately for a very long time. Finally relaxing his grip, Billy raised himself and looked into my face and smiled *very* sexily. "I want to be the first person who ever ate your ass. Can I fuck you with my tongue Pete?"

"Billy, everything I've ever done with you has been wonderful and exciting. Seeing your beautiful body naked the first time, kissing you the first time, jacking off with you, sucking with you, fucking with you, coming in each other's mouths and asses, eating your ass, our love for each other especially—everything has been more than just wonderful, it's been an *honor*. But I can't think of anything that would make me feel more honored than that."

His smile turned into a grin as he put a finger on the end of my nose and laughed, "Roll over and get ready to be *honored* like you've never been before." He kissed me, and used his hands to roll me on my stomach.

I had not been basically 'into' *butt munching* in the past; I could remember only three guys before Billy who had been so *beautiful* that I wanted to explore almost every possible act with them: Pierce, my second big "love," whose asshole I eagerly fucked with my tongue, since he wouldn't let me do it with my prick; Hal, whose facial beauty was almost as impressive as his incredible cock, and who again would let only my tongue into his hot bottom; and Hal's perfect lover, Dan, whose adorable, round little ass was a lovely as any I had ever seen, and whose asshole I first ate while his lover's monster prick invaded my own in its uniquely thrilling way. Billy's luscious ass had been my fourth. [I had even, as reported, tasted the arcane delight of getting pissed on by Billy—something I had never thought of doing with anyone else. Thirty or thirty-five years later I read a book by Larry McMurtry, entitled *Anything for Billy*. It would be the perfect title for my biography.]

If I had had any idea of how amazingly thrilling what I was about to experience could be, I would have been begging every one of my sex partners to eat my butt, and made sure I provided the same ecstasy for them.

Billy began by kissing the back of my neck, and then slowly nuzzling and licking his way down my back until he was kissing the cheeks of my ass feverishly, his hands accompanying with impassioned caresses. He pulled the cheeks of my ass far apart as he planted a slow, sweet kiss directly onto my asshole. "My sweet lover, Pete—God I love you so much." Then the very tip of his tongue began to flit lightly around the muscular opening. As more and more of his dancing tongue invaded me I began to experience an indescribable thrill. The feel of the bulk of a prick sliding in an out of my ass had from the first been intensely exciting—the larger the prick, and the longer the stroke increasing the excitement in exponential proportion. The size of a cock like Hal Weltmann's, and the incredible strokes its length made possible when wielded by a virtuoso *fuckmaster* like him, had seemed to be the ultimate thrill. Now, when Billy's tongue began to invade me, I felt even closer to heaven than I had when Hal first plumbed my depths with his prick.

Three things, I suppose, accounted for the unbelievable sensation Billy now awoke in me. First, even though it was much smaller than his prick, his tongue was much hotter in temperature, and felt moist and *alive*, and therefore seemed more intense an intrusion. Second, all one can do with a prick is shove it in or take it out, however wonderful those motions may be. But as Billy's tongue darted around and thrilled me with its elastic undulations and stimulation all around, and in and out of my asshole, the constantly changing, quick movement in all directions was breathtaking. Finally, it seemed to be the most incomparably *intimate* thing a man could do to another man, and I felt Billy was using his tongue, but not speaking with it in words, to express some combination of "you are incredibly exciting to me," "I want to show you how much I want to make love to you by performing the most personal act I can imagine," and "I love you more than I can really show."

I was quite literally delirious with passion. I guess I don't really know how long Billy performed his ministrations—it was too short, it was eternal, it was beyond any experience I could think of. My verbal expressions of appreciation and adoration for my young lover as he ate me must surely have been incoherent. After a very long time—or perhaps it was after a short time, I was so rapt I cannot really say—Billy rolled me over and took my cock all the way into his mouth with one gulp, and sucked fiercely as I grasped his head and fucked savagely. Although I had shot my load only a short while before, it was a matter of only a dozen or so strokes before I began a violent orgasm that seemed endless, and one of the most exultant moments of my life. I may have delivered a small load of come into Billy's worshipping mouth, or it may have been a huge load, I have no idea—I only know I was responding as intensely as I could to what I felt was the most profound expression of both love and passion I had ever known.

Billy kept my prick in his mouth as he reversed his body so that his throbbing prick hung down over my mouth. I reached up and caressed his driving ass while he fucked my mouth as hard as he could, and delivered his own seemingly endless eruption of love in me. We lay for an eternity, holding each other tight, with our spent pricks lovingly buried in each other. Finally we broke, and as I took Billy in my arms to embrace him and kiss him, I broke into uncontrollable tears. "Pete, what's the matter." Around my sobs I managed to get out, "Nothing at all, I'm so happy I don't know how to deal with it. My God, Billy Polk, I love you more than you could possibly ever know."

Billy smiled at me, and tears clouded his eyes also. "I know exactly how you feel, John Harrison—I love you the same way." We probably spent an entire hour, caressing very gently and kissing very sweetly—and saying nothing in words, yet saying everything in the way we held each other. How could a *sixteen-year old boy* be so wise and so eloquent in sexual expression? What incredible stroke of luck aligned me with a youngster who combined his irresistible, precocious sexual maturity with a sophistication wise enough to understand and maintain the necessary "face" we had to put on outside the bedroom? And how could he seem (no, not "seem"—surely *be)* so ultimately *innocent* while we engaged in such fiercely passionate sex? I had no idea, but I was eternally grateful to whatever power it is that grants us our fortunes.

And here's a remarkable thing: although I applied the same standards of grading to Billy as I did to everyone else in my Geometry class, he got the third-highest score on the final exam that semester, and *earned* an "A" in the class (in the 1950's, the fall semester normally ended in mid-January). Looks, build, charm, endowment, sweetness, intelligence *and* ethics. Oh—and the cutest ass I'd ever seen. What a guy.

10.
VISIT FROM A TEEN-AGE FUCKMASTER: PHIL

This magnificent, big-cocked, unbelievably horny, young giant stud
carried me to my bed . . . about to become the altar upon which Phil
and I would worship each other—the very altar where Billy and I
shared the same rite. Fortunately my sexual 'religion' allows for the
worship of multiple gods.

While I was surely nonplused, I can't honestly say I was surprised
when Phil Baker showed up at my door one night not too long after that.
It was about 9:30, I had just taken a shower, and wore only a light
bathrobe when I answered his knock. "Mr. Harrison? I'm Phil Baker."
"Of course, I know who you are Phil. What can I do for you?" I was
trying to appear calm, but my heart was beating rapidly; what did his
appearance here mean? Did he want to fight me for Billy? Did he
possibly want sex with me?
"I need to talk to you for a little while," he said. "Can I come in?"
"Sure, come on in and have a seat." He came in. Every time I had seen
Phil at school or around town, he had struck me as *big*, but here in the
confines of my living room he seemed *huge*. He may have been a high-
school boy, but he exuded such an air of complete masculinity that my
heart beat even faster. I freely admit that I hoped he was going to
embrace me in those powerful arms and press me to his enormous chest
while he told me he wanted to fuck me, but I said only, "You want a
Coke?"
"Actually . . . you got a beer?"
"Sure, but . . . well, I guess you are old enough to drink beer, aren't
you?" He nodded, and I got a couple of beers out of the refrigerator and
gave him one. A high school senior was, at that time, usually old enough
to drink beer; why I would have been worried about giving alcohol to a
high school senior, considering what I was doing to a high school
sophomore, is beyond me. "Let me put on some clothes, Phil, and we'll
talk."
"You don't needa put anything else on—you're fine just like you are."
I seemed to sense a hint of a possible unspoken subtext: *Probably no*
clothes at all would be more appropriate, and my heart began to
pound—but it was surely only my imagination. Phil took off his letter
jacket and threw it on one end of the sofa, and sat down on the other. He
had been wearing only a white tee-shirt under his jacket, and his glorious
chest and magnificent arms and shoulders filled it out to
perfection—with his large nipples clearly discernible and delicious-
looking underneath the taut fabric. He stretched his very long, muscular
legs out—encased in extremely tight Levi's—and rested his cowboy
boot-clad feet on the coffee table. He raised his ass a few inches, and
gathered his balls up into his crotch—making it bulge even more
temptingly than it had been—and took a drink of beer. He was only
moderately handsome, but his body was stunning. I sat across from him
in an easy chair, and waited for him to open the conversation; where that

conversation was going to *go,* I was not sure—although I knew where I *wanted* it to go.

"Mr. Harrison, how old are you?"

"I'm twenty-two, Phil. Why?"

"Well, I was nineteen a few months ago; that means I'm only three years younger'n you, and it seems a little strange to be callin' you *Mister*—especially since I don't have you for a class or anything. Is it okay if I just call you John?"

"Well sure, Phil, I wish you would, but at school if we talk, or you talk about me, it's still best to call me Mister Harrison—you understand."

"Sure. *John* it is when we're alone, then. So, anyway, let me get to the point . . . John."

I grinned, "Fire away . . . Phil. What can I do for you?"

"Look, this is pretty awkward, but . . . look, I know you and Billy Polk are really good friends, right?"

"Right—I think Billy is really a terrific guy. So?"

"Okay, look—I'm gonna ask you to never say anything to anyone about what I wanna talk with you about, okay?" I agreed. "And if I'm completely outa line, and all wrong about this, please don't get mad at me, willya?" I agreed I wouldn't—heart racing, knowing what would come next.

"I know Billy's only a sophomore, and I'm a senior, but I really think he's terrific, too. And I've got real close to him lately, Mr. . . . John. Look, I'm really trusting you now . . . I mean I've got *really* close to Billy lately. Close as you can get, I guess. Are you followin' me?"

"Phil, I'm not stupid, and I'm sure as hell not shocked; I'm pretty sure I know what 'close as you can get' means in this case. It's fine, I understand. Go on."

"Has Billy said anything to you about him and me?"

"Phil, Billy tells me a lot of things. Some of those are things he doesn't want to share with anyone *but* me, you understand? If he told me anything about . . . well, about what I think you're talking about, I'd have to respect his confidence."

"I can see that, but . . . Oh hell, I'm just gonna come out and ask you, and hope you don't get mad."

"I promise you I won't get mad no matter *what* you ask me, Phil." I got up and moved to the sofa to sit next to him; I was glad his jacket was draped over the other end—it made my sitting close to him seem relatively normal. "Go ahead."

"Well, I know that Billy's seein' someone, and I . . . " He took a deep breath. "Look, Billy and I have fucked around some lately. You know what I mean?"

"I know what fucking around is Phil, and I sure as hell don't blame you. I'm going to trust you too, okay?" He nodded. "I think Billy is an incredibly attractive guy, and I sure don't blame you for being attracted to him—I understand it completely."

"Well, someone else is fuckin' around with Billy. He won't tell me who it is, but I know you and him are together alla the time. I've never heard about you datin' any girls, and I've watched lately, and I don't think Billy's seein' anyone *but* you. So, I've been puttin' two and two together, and . . .well, here it is." He took a deep breath. "Are you and Billy fuckin' around?"

"Phil, do you know how much trouble I could be in if people found out Billy and I were . . . well, more than just friends?"

"Sure I do, 'course I do, but you know I'm not gonna say anything. Hell, I just told you I'm fuckin' around with him . . . oh hell, not just fuckin' around—I've been *fuckin'* him, okay? Still sure you're not shocked?"

I smiled at him, and put my hand on his leg "Still not shocked at all Phil."

He reached down and covered my hand with his. "He toldja all about it, didn't he?"

"Phil, Billy is a lot of things to me, and me to him. One of the most important of those things is that I'm his best friend. He tells me everything, and I tell him everything. Yeah, I know about what happened around Christmas, and everything about Waco a week or so ago. And I understand, I really do. It's fine, Phil, I don't think any the less of either of you because of it. Billy told me everything you and he did and said, because he promised he'd tell me. Phil, he even told me about your trips to the park in the city."

He smiled slowly as his hand began to squeeze mine. "I gotta admit, I've had some incredible fun in the park. But you still haven't answered my question, really, so let me put it another way. Okay, you don't think bad of me for what happened between Billy and me, but do you feel . . . well . . . envy?"

"Okay, Phil, yeah—I feel very envious of you. But I envy Billy a lot, too." I smiled at him, "I felt very envious of Billy when he described what you guys did together."

Phil moved my hand up to his bulging crotch. "I was really hopin' you were gonna say that. I felt sure you and Billy were . . . well, lovers, I guess is the word. That's the word he used. I envy you havin' that with Billy, but . . " He reached up and put his hand behind my neck. "I envy Billy, too. I really think you're an attractive guy, John. His other hand began to stroke my knee. "I promise I won't say anything to anyone—not even to Billy, if you don't want me to." His hand moved up the inside of my leg and into my bathrobe; he put it around my very hard prick.

I put my hand behind his neck and leaned in to him as I began to squeeze his basket—he was fully as hard as I was. With my lips only an inch from his, I whispered, "We can talk about Billy later. Looks to me like it's just John and Phil right now."

Phil kissed me gently, squeezing my prick as he did so, and then his kiss turned passionate. I responded with equal ardor, and after a few minutes he 'came up for air'. "Just John and Phil, yeah—and I think that's gonna to be an interesting combination." He leaned down and took off his boots and socks, and smiled at me. He stood and continued smiling as he began to unbutton his Levi's. "Just John and Phil."

He pushed the coffee table about three feet toward the center of the room, and continued unbuttoning his pants. He stepped up on the table—it was, fortunately, made of strong wrought iron—and faced me, and his smile was very seductive. I began to stand, but he said, "No, sit right there while I get us in the mood." He started to slip his Levi's down, but then he stepped off the coffee table, and walked over to me. He raised me to my feet, opened my bathrobe, slipped it from my shoulders, and dropped it to the floor. I was completely naked, my prick standing straight out from me. He grinned and squeezed my balls gently. "I wanna watch you watch me." Then he gently pushed me back onto the sofa, got back on the coffee table and resumed his interrupted striptease.

It was truly difficult to believe Phil was only a high school student. His body was very, very large. At 6'3" he weighed, I later learned, 215 pounds—but there wasn't any suggestion of fat involved in that, just pure, exciting muscle. Standing on the coffee table, he actually *towered* over me, and I felt I was kneeling at an altar as he began to shed his clothes and reveal his magnificent body—and the seductive way he shed them made the illusion and the excitement that much more intense. Phil smiled constantly, well aware of his endowments and the virtuoso level of his eroticism.

He began by very gradually working his Levi's down to his knees—turning around just as his basket began to come into view, so that I couldn't quite see the treat I knew was in store for me, according to Billy's report. His ass, covered by his Jockey shorts, was ample—the shorts stretched *very* tightly over the two perfectly rounded globes that Phil was now undulating sexily. He reached a hand down inside the back of his shorts—exposing a bit of the crack of his ass in the process—and began to play with his asshole. He looked back over his shoulder. "This really feels good, John. You like whatcha see so far?"

I had stood, and was stroking my cock. I stepped forward and with the other hand I reached up between his legs and cupped his balls through his shorts—they were *massive*. "I love what I'm seeing."

He grinned, "Now you just sit down and watch me show it all to you. And stop playin' with your dick—that's my job tonight." He turned around and used his hands to pull the fabric of his shorts tightly over his cock, outlining it as it bulged hugely to the side. I was eagerly awaiting the sight of this in the flesh. "Here's what *you're* gonna have to work with. Look good?" I nodded eagerly. "I thoughtcha might like it." He sat down on the table and stretched his legs forward. "You can finish takin' my pants off before you sit down." Once his legs were free, he turned on his stomach, used the full extent of his arms to elevate his upper body, and his rounded ass began writhing seductively as he dry-fucked the table, murmuring delightedly, "Mmmmm. God, I feel horny tonight." He knelt on the table and turned to face me where I again sat. "I can see you're feeling a tad horny yourself."

He began to pull his tight tee shirt up, exposing his flat stomach, rippled with muscles. Although he was a very large man, his waist was probably no more than thirty inches, and his shoulders and chest seemed even more massive than they actually were because of that. Even his navel was sexy—a small, perfectly formed 'outie.' Finally he had the shirt over his head and threw it on the floor. He flexed his chest and shoulder muscles for my approval; his heavily muscled arms were huge, his bulging tits were solid and well rounded, and his copper-colored nipples were quite large, located a bit farther to the outside than one would have normally expected—something I found particularly sexy. He looked down at himself admiringly, then looked up at me and grinned. "Still like it?"

I stood and walked up to him. He still knelt on the table, and our faces were on a level. "If I liked it any more, I'd be shooting my load right now."

He put his hand behind my neck and pulled my head to his. "Now, we're gonna have plenty of time to see to that." As he kissed me passionately, driving his tongue hungrily in and out of my mouth, I remembered what Billy had told me.

I reached up and held his face in my hands. "*Goddam*, Phil, you flat-out know how to kiss. But Billy told me he was the first guy you ever kissed."

Phil grinned. "Well, that's right, but I've had plenty of practice with girls, you know—and besides, I'm a really fast learner." And he shoved his tongue so far into my throat I could suck it like a cock—which I did, to his obvious delight. Our arms were holding each other tightly. Finally we broke.

I whispered into his ear. "Billy told me he did something else to you for the first time." I ran one hand down his back and into his shorts, and teased his asshole with a finger. (*God, his ass felt magnificent*—even *epic.*) " Can I hope to be the second one?"

Phil laughed. "Hell, John, it's too late for that—you'll hafta to settle for 'bout number five."

"You *are* a fast learner, aren't you? I guess you've been to the park recently."

"Well, I gotta admit I did make a little trip over there the other day—but that was for number three and four. One of 'em was one of my regulars—and boy howdy, was he ever surprised."

"So number two was . . "

"Number two was somebody you'd know, let's put it that way. Hell, what's the difference what the number is—I'll bet I'll be losin' count pretty soon. Hey, when I get a new toy, I believe in usin' it." He wriggled his ass deliciously, and my finger pressed very hard against his sphincter, almost entering it. He ran a hand down my back, put a finger up against my asshole, and began to murmur as he worked it all the way into me. "But you can bet you're gonna be number five." He kissed me again, and I began to kiss down his face, his neck, and his huge shoulders, and began to suck one perfect nipple as I squeezed and tweaked the other. His finger left my asshole, and both of his giant arms pressed my head to his chest. "Oh man, you're gonna be a helluva good lover aren'tcha?" I changed nipples. "Shit, you're gonna be one helluva good *fuck*, too, I bet."

I knelt and sat on my heels, looking up in awe at his magnificent broad chest and muscled arms. No high-school boy, this—this was a true man, whose body was a shrine of sheer masculinity. His upper body looked as breathtaking as the romanticized paintings of exceptionally virile men that adorn women's historical romance novels—but Phil was alive, in the magnificent flesh, and standing here before me, offering his stupendous body for my pleasure. I had never before knelt before a man whose body alone thrilled me so much that I actually trembled, but there was no doubt Phil's body evoked that response in me, and made my heart pound in my chest.

I reached up and explored his magnificent physique, running my hands worshipfully over his massive chest, and putting them inside the back of his shorts to feel his firm, generous buttocks, often kissing and sucking on the hugely bulging crotch of his shorts, and the prodigious, cloth-covered tube of hard meat running to the left of his crotch and pressing his shorts from inside. This man, this *stud*, could do anything to me he wanted. I stood and drove my tongue deeply into his mouth as we embraced, and he began to suck it as I had his, as if it were an eager cock. "I want to be a *great* fuck for you Phil—but I'll bet you're going to be an even better one."

"Let's just see if I can't be the best fuck you ever had."

"I've had some mighty good ones."

"You're fixin' to get a *fantastic* one." And he again drove his tongue into my mouth for me to suck. After a few minutes of feverish kissing, he pushed me away. "C'mon now, sit back down there and let me finish showin' you the goods." I did as I was told, and he again stood on the table. He faced me, and his big prick was clearly outlined in his tight shorts as it lay completely to one side; he rubbed his hand back and forth over it as he thrust his groin as far forward as he could. "This baby's gonna go so far down your throat and up your butt, you're gonna think you're in heaven."

He again flexed his massive chest and arm muscles, then put both hands behind his head and began to undulate his hips very slowly and with maximum erotic effect; he was a *tease* of the very first water, obviously. Then, with hands still clasped behind his neck, he turned around, and the undulations of his ass grew more pronounced. He put his hands at his waist and leaned far forward, *offering* his wonderful rounded ass to my view, and then he began to simulate the motions of the very deepest possible kind of fucking—pressing his ass as far back as he could make it go, then as far forward as he could; the total effect was unbelievably sexy.

"My God, Phil. Jesus."

He looked over his shoulder and grinned. He slowly slid the back of the waistband of his shorts below his ass, exposing the smooth, golden globes and deep, tantalizing crevice to me. *(Exactly as Billy had done when he first presented his adorable ass for my admiration, out at Rodman's Pond.)* "You might like it even better this way." And he held his shorts there as he resumed his erotic 'air fuck' with renewed vigor. His bare ass was amazingly muscular as he drove it back and forth, and I could see his lovely pink asshole nestled deep within the tempting crevice when it opened to its widest in backward thrusts. Finally he leaned all the way forward, and tugged his shorts down to drop them to his feet. He continued to lean down as he stepped out of them, and with his hands he spread the cheeks of his ass wide, and offered his treasure. "Look good enough to eat?"

"Jesus, Phil—*yes.*

He stood erect and again smiled over his shoulder. "Hell, you ain't seen the main course yet." He reached down and picked up his shorts. When he turned around, his hands held the shorts over his groin. "First maybe you oughta see where the good stuff gets made." He continued to conceal his prick in his shorts, but he exposed his balls for my delectation—and by God, they were truly delectable. They hung down a long, long way in the pendulous, ample sac, but in addition, the balls themselves were *enormous*. The skin was light-colored and slightly fuzzy, looking to be almost hairless, and—there's no other word for it—perfectly beautiful.

"They tell me this is a pretty good set."

"My God—Billy said you had big balls, but . . . "

He pulled his covered prick high, so that his balls protruded slightly. "I thought you might like 'em. You know, maybe a little lickin' and suckin' on these babies might be fun before we show the main feature." He began to rotate his hips, and his mighty ball-sac swung temptingly. "I mean, if you think you might like to have a taste." I stood and put my hands on his waist, and began to caress his hips, then moved them behind him to feel the muscular swelling of his fantastic ass. He "humped" gently as I did so. All the time I looked up at his face as he towered over me, smiling sexily. "Come on, lick me, John—I wanna feel your hot tongue on me." I bent to start kissing him on either side of his groin, and began licking and kissing as I moved in toward his balls. Finally, as I began to lick the underside of his prodigiously filled ball-sac, he seized the back of my head with the hand not covering his prick and pressed me to him. "Oh, yeah. *Yeah*. Come on and suck my hot . . . fucking . . . nuts." His gentle humping became rather frenzied as I opened my mouth and took the incredible bulk of his balls into it; it was a *considerable* challenge to my oral capacity, but I met it with the assistance of good will, the magnificent feel of Phil's muscular ass writhing in my hands, his frenzied exhortations, the almost painful stretching of my mouth, and (I guess) the grace of God. It was clear the young stud was appreciative of my efforts.

Phil's balls tasted and even smelled wonderful—it was obvious he had showered very recently, apparently preparing himself for exactly what we were doing. The frenzy of his comments inspired me to unusual heights of sucking accomplishment (*"Oh* fuck, *that feels so good." " Suck my big balls, John—they're filled with hot come just for you. "*, and the like). I felt his driving ass, ran my hands up and down his massive, muscular thighs, and rolled his huge balls around in my mouth as I sucked—and as I did so, I could not imagine why I had not long ago decided Phil Baker prime material for seduction. (Yes, but *who* was seducing *whom* here? Who gave a shit—*I wanted to fuck with Phil Baker.*)

Phil grabbed my hair with one hand, and fiercely pulled my mouth away from his balls. He knelt on the table, put both of his huge, thrilling arms around me, and planted a deep kiss on my mouth. I held his head tight with one hand, put the other up between his legs, and frantically explored his ass while we tongue-fucked each other's mouths. Then he released his grip, looked into my eyes and said, "Now go back and sit down again. It's show time." I did as I was told, and when I sat down and looked back up at Phil, he was standing on the coffee table again, with his back toward me, and his ass looking glorious—statuesque. His hands were on his hips and he smiled back at me over his shoulder. "Hang on to your hat and get a load of what's goin' down your throat and up your butt tonight."

He turned around slowly, and his breathtaking prick stood absolutely straight out in front of him—parallel to the table. It was not the longest I'd ever seen—although not far from it—but certainly one of the fattest: *major meat*, in any case.

[I can provide exact dimensions of Phil's endowment here, because at a later time I measured it: it was about eight inches long, a bit longer than the one Jim had plowed me with almost nightly for a full year, and was five inches in circumference. By way of comparison, Billy's proved later to be only slightly shorter than Phil's, but slightly under five inches in circumference; Billy's prick actually looked longer than Phil's, since he himself was quite a bit shorter, and his cock was thinner; it looked considerably longer in proportion. Using that as a yardstick—which is an interesting word to use in this context—I would estimate that Les's prick may have actually been almost nine inches long, and I knew Hal's was just a shade over ten.]

The absolutely stunning eroticism Phil had brought to the final presentation of his cock made it seem even more desirable than it might otherwise have been—but a cock that size would have been *very* desirable under any circumstances. I was thrilled at its size, of course, but my delight was amplified by the fact that it was a stunningly *beautiful* prick as well—light-colored (like his balls), very smooth and unmarked, with a lovely light purple cock-head unusually large in proportion to the fat, delectable long shaft.

I was speechless at the beauty of Phil's prick. I stared for at least thirty seconds as he stood there smiling and offering it to me. Finally, I was able only to whisper reverently, "Jesus, Phil."

He kept his hands on his hips and grinned at me. "I guess you like it, huh? If you like lookin' at it, you're gonna *love* eatin' it and takin' it up your ass. Whaddaya think—you want this beauty all the way inside of you or not?"

I sat there transfixed. "I want it as far inside me as it will go."

"Hell, John, it's gonna go *way* far insidea you—and I'm gonna fill you up with all the come you ever wanted." I began to stand; he waved me back down. "Just keep watchin' for a minute—let me finish my show. It's gonna make this big ol' cock taste even better when I finally shove it down your throat."

He began to rotate his hips slowly, and his prick began to sway ponderously, side-to-side and up-and-down in mesmerizing circles—made even more tantalizing by occasional intense forward thrusts, which made the massive shaft jump and bob wildly. Continuing his movements, he stepped off the table and gradually approached me, so that his prick continued its erotic dance only inches from my face. Finally he stopped completely, his prick still bobbing lightly. I was staring at the luscious cock-head in front of me when Phil took my head in his hands and forced me to look up into his face. "Open your mouth, and take this big prick inside that hot fuckin' throat—I got so much jizz I wanna give you." I opened my mouth and he shoved his dick unceremoniously into it, with no more of the erotic teasing he had displayed to that point. The fuck I had been hungry for since I first put my hand on his leg a half-hour earlier was finally under way.

In spite of the ferocity of Phil's initial thrust, I didn't gag, and locked my lips around the base of his shaft, with my nose buried in his pubic hair, and I began to suck deeply as my hands reached behind him to grasp his buttocks. His muscular ass writhed under my caress as he drove his cock in and out of my mouth in very long, slow strokes. "Oh, fuck, John ... God, that feels so good—eat my cock." His hands now held my head lovingly. " Ooooh, baby, make love to my big fuckin' dick."

I held his ass in my hands and gloried in its fluid muscular motions as his thrusts grew more excited. I looked up while I sucked, and was thrilled all over again at the vast expanse of his magnificent chest. I began to caress his rounded breasts, and tweak his nipples. He groaned, "Yeah—play with my tits." and drove his fabulous prick violently into my mouth. He almost pulled it out with each backstroke, and drove it as far as it could go into my throat with each forward thrust. Although my lips held his shaft as tightly as I could, my throat was wide open to accommodate him, and I never gagged once as he assaulted me with one of the most memorable mouth-fucks I had ever known. His huge balls were slapping against my chin while I murmured my delight and he groaned a passionate litany of appreciation, "God damn, John, you're a good cocksucker." and "Jesus, I love fuckin' your hot mouth."

Finally, his tempo increased to a frenzy, but the thrilling length of his strokes abated not a whit as the first few spurts of his load began to shoot into my adoring mouth. Then he seized my head and pulled it in to him savagely. He shouted in incoherent lust as he planted his cock as deep inside as me he could, and spurt after spurt of come splashed against the back of my throat. After he came, he resumed his mouth-fuck, less frenzied, but still driving his prick *deep* into my throat while I greedily swallowed every precious drop of his massive orgasm. His hoarse cries became wonderfully coherent: "Jesus Christ, John, eat that load. Swallow all that hot come—you love it, baby."

He unceremoniously jerked his prick from my mouth and leaned over to kiss me. Still in the throes of lust, he basically used his tongue to continue his mouth-fuck. He panted into my mouth, "Godamighty, my come tastes good, doesn't it?" Finally, his sexual frenzy abated and he stood, put his arms around my head, and pressed me to him. I continued to sit there, circling his hips with my arms while I kissed and licked his stomach and his only slightly less engorged cock.

We stayed in this position for some time, with no word said. Finally Phil said very quietly, "That was fantastic, John—I could tell how much you loved it, too. I don't think I ever got sucked off better'n that, or that I ever gave anybody a bigger load. Jesus, you're great." I know I can give a fine blowjob, and I know Phil's load had been an uncommonly huge one, but I suspect he was exaggerating. However, a little hyperbole in the cause of expressing appreciation for lovemaking is always nice to hear.

I stood up and we held each other tightly. I looked up into his eyes as I said, "I've never taken a load that thrilled me any more than that, Phil. If you got dressed and walked out that door right now, and I never saw you or touched you again, I'd always remember you as one of the hottest men I ever had sex with."

Phil smiled slowly. "But I'm not goin' anywhere tonight. I'm gonna fuck your pretty ass just as hard as I fucked your mouth, and I wanna suck your cock and I want you up my butt, and we're gonna do it all night." He kissed me slowly and lovingly. "Okay with you?"

"God, Phil, that sounds so wonderful. But . . . do we have that much time? When do you have to be home?"

"We got all the time in the world. Look, when I came over here tonight, I didn't know for sure if what I thought about you and Billy was true or not. I knew that if it was, I wanted to get you to make love with me like you do with him—like *I* do with him. But even if it turned out it wasn't true, I was gonna try to suck you off, and to get you to fuck my butt—even if you didn't want me to fuck you. I'm not here just about Billy—I've wanted to fuck with you for a long time. To tell the truth, I kinda hoped I'd run into you in the park some day."

"If I'd had any idea how hot you are, and that I would have run into you there, I probably would have been in that park a long time ago."

"I'm here now—and I don't need to be home at all tonight. I told my dad I'm sleeping over at a friend's house, and I even left my truck way down the street so no one would see it here, 'cause I was really hopin' that I wouldn't hafta leave here at all tonight. I wantcha to fuck me, John, and I wanna fuck you. I wanna go to sleep with my dick up your ass, 'n I wanna wake you up with a blowjob. How d'ya feel about all that?"

I ran my hands over his massive chest and looked up at him as he towered over me (*God, but he was a* huge *stud.*). "I want all of it, Phil. And I want you to hold me in your arms all night."

He laughed. "Just as long as I can leave my dick up your ass at the same time, okay?" He reached down and put an arm behind my knees, put another one under my arm, and *picked me up* like I was a child. My arms circled his neck as he pressed his lips to mine and kissed me sweetly. "Where's your bed? I want that cock of yours insidea me." This magnificent, big-cocked, unbelievably horny, young giant stud *carried me* to my bed, as though I were a child. If I felt like a child at that moment, figuratively, I was looking forward to some serious figurative child abuse. I remembered Billy's vivid account of Phil carrying him to their bed in the motel in Waco, and we kissed hungrily as he carried me to my bed this time. I was hungry to experience the same things Billy had when Phil had deposited him in bed this same way. To be sure this would be the bed where Billy and I regularly pledged each other our love, but it was also the place where Billy had told me of his experiences with this same exciting young *fuckmaster*, and where my interest in him was first piqued.

My bed was also about to become the altar upon which Phil and I would worship each other—the very altar where Billy and I shared the same rite. Fortunately my sexual 'religion' allows for the worship of multiple gods.

I had never experienced the kind of erotic prelude to sex that Phil had provided for me. In retrospect, it seems impossible to believe that a nineteen-year-old could be so *aware* of his sexual power, and such a consummate master of the art of seduction—and with Phil it *was* art, of the highest order. On the other hand, my beautiful young Billy was developing more than just a bit of this ability—in two or three years' time, when he would be Phil's age, he might be even *more* accomplished. I wondered if there might be something in the Antares water supply. Still, as promising as young Billy was, I didn't see how even he could become more seductive than the giant stud who now carried me into my bedroom, smiling down at me like a lover. If I *had* blamed Billy for succumbing to Phil's charms when I was gone at Christmas time—and I hadn't, of course—I would certainly have understood now how helpless he must have been when Phil decided he wanted to have sex with him.

Phil stood next to my bed, still carrying me. "I wanna keep this bed hot tonight. I don't plan to let your mouth or your butt get much rest—and you damned sure better keep mine busy, too."

I smiled up at the sexy giant holding me in his arms, feeling like a schoolboy again. "I want my cock inside you, or your cock inside me all night long."

He kissed me and grinned. "I'll bet I can even think of a way we can be in each other at the same time, don't you? How does a really good, hot sixty-nine sound to you?"

"It sounds like heaven, and I can hardly wait." He lay me down gently on the bed and knelt over me to kiss me. My arms went around him, but he stood up abruptly. "Wait right there, I'll be right back," and I watched his massive nude body leave the bedroom. (*Jesus Christ, what an exciting ass.*). He was back in a few seconds, carrying the letter jacket he had been wearing when he came in. He grinned and reached in the pocket. "Got something here I was really hopin' we'd need tonight." He pulled out a huge tube of K-Y Jelly, the classic alternative to Vaseline in affairs of the heart as well as affairs of the hard.

I laughed and pointed out the economy-size jar of Vaseline that stood next to my bed—open and ready for action, as always. Phil put the K-Y back in his jacket and threw it on the floor. He dipped a finger into the Vaseline and said, "I think I want a little right now." He took a generous glob on his fingers, lifted a leg and massaged it into his asshole. "Jesus that feels good." He turned around and leaned forward, so that I could see his finger busily fucking his asshole. "Look good?" I conceded that it looked wonderful. "Feels great, too—but it's gonna feel a lot better when it's your dick doin' this to me."

He pulled his finger out of himself and turned around to scoop up some more Vaseline. I lay on my back watching him. He grinned and growled, "Getcher legs up and spread 'em." I did as I was told, and he reached beneath my balls to massage the lubricant into my asshole. He began driving his finger as far into me as it would go. "God DAMN that's a hot asshole." I spread my legs farther apart and moaned in delight as he fucked me with his finger. With his other hand he was stroking his big prick. "And it's gonna be tight as hell for this big ol' cock, isn't it?"

"Shit, Phil, any asshole would feel tight to a big cock like that. I can't wait to feel it inside me." I raised my legs high and spread them far apart. "Give it to me, Phil—shoot another load in me, but this time in my ass."

He knelt on the bed, between my legs, and with one huge thrust drove his prick all the way inside me. It felt *wonderful*. He shouted, "Oh ... you feel *so* good. So *damn* good!" And he began to drive into me as deeply as he could, at a frantic pace. "Gonna fuck your pretty ass, and fill you up with my load."

I put my arms around his neck and locked my feet behind his back. "Fuck me Phil—make love to my ass. Give me another big load." He leaned forward, still fucking savagely, and put his arms under my shoulders to hold me while he drove his tongue into my mouth, seemingly as deep as his prick was plumbing my ass. While we enjoyed a frenzied ballet with our tongues, he lifted my whole body up and leaned backwards, so that he was holding me off the bed, still impaled on his thrusting cock. I put my feet on the bed, on either side of his legs, which gave me the leverage I needed to ride up and down Phil's thrilling monster. He met my downward plunges with fierce upward jabs of his cock, and we continued to tongue-fuck each other in a frenzy of lust. Soon Phil gasped into my mouth, "Take it again, baby. Take this hot load." Then, even though he had delivered an enormous load to my adoring mouth only a short while before, his cock again began to discharge multiple, violent spurts inside me. He almost whimpered in passion as he continued to fuck and I continued to ride.

We gradually slowed down, and I came to rest, still impaled on his prick as he knelt there. "I can't believe it Phil—I think you fed me as much come in my ass as you did in my mouth."

"That was such an incredible fuck. Godamighty, John—you are one hell of a piece o' ass, *and* a great cocksucker. How'm I gonna decide if I like fuckin' your ass or your mouth better?" He removed his cock from me, leaned forward and gently lay my body back down on the bed. He stretched his huge, sexy body on top of me and kissed me for a long time. Then he looked into my eyes and grinned. "I hope you're not gonna decide whether you like me fuckin' your ass or your mouth better with just one try at each. I'm pretty sure I'm gonna hafta take several tries at both of 'em before you can decide. How does that sound to you?"

I smiled back and stroked his hair and ran a finger over his lips and his nose. "I *think* it's gonna be a tie—it is so far, but we've got all night to keep trying to decide. I can't believe you could shoot two huge loads like that into me one right after the other. Jesus, how often can you come?"

"I don't really know—a lot. It kinda depends on how . . . inspired I am."

"Do I inspire you, Phil?"

"You just keep count and see—if you don't *inspire* me to at least five or six loads tonight, I'll really be surprised."

I ran my hands all over Phil's magnificent body, particularly caressing his perfect muscular buttocks and his massive, low-hanging balls, and fingering his asshole. "Jesus, Phil, you are one hell of a *man*."

"You're a helluva man, too. You've gotta be a real man to take my prick the way you did—in the mouth *and* in the butt. A lot of guys can't do it, or they complain it hurts, or something. You just swallowed it, and sat on it, and enjoyed every bit of it like a real man." He kissed me again. "And I'm gonna take you like a man, too. Christ, I've already fucked you twice, and I haven't even started to get you off yet." He grinned very broadly, "My mama would be shocked. 'Where are your manners, Philip?' I can hear her now."

"I think you mama would be *real* shocked if she could see you now."

"She'd be a lot more shocked if she could see me in a coupla minutes." He reached for the Vaseline and applied a liberal amount to my cock. "Man, that feels good, John." Then he raised himself up and knelt over me, reaching behind himself to guide my cock to his asshole, and settling down firmly on it. "Oh God. Talk about a *man*. Your cock feels fantastic in me." He began to undulate his ass and ride up and down. His eyes were closed, and he was actually licking his lips while he fucked himself on my prick. He murmured his delight, and although his riding was slow and deliberate, he was giving himself the maximum stroke my prick would allow. A few times he overestimated, and my prick pulled out, but he immediately sat back down on it. "I think gettin' fucked feels even better'n fuckin,' don't you?

I was running my hands over his ass, his awesome shoulders and chest, and tweaking his nipples all this time. "I know getting fucked by *you* feels about as good as anything I can imagine—but what you're doing right now is *real* close."

He continued to ride for quite a while, and I drove upward into his ass as deeply as I could. He was so *large* and exciting to watch as he rode me. The sight of his enormous chest and trim waist, his massive muscular legs on either side of me pistoning his body up and down, and the sensation of his very tight asshole holding my prick as it slid up and down inside, combined to make me near delirious with joy. Finally he drew himself up off my cock, and faced the end of the bed on all fours. "Fuck me from behind—I like it that way best."

I knelt behind him and drove my cock back into his tight asshole, which he immediately began to wriggle and hump. "Fuck me as hard as you can—I wantcha to fill me up with come." I held his trim waist in my hands and gazed in rapture at the vast expanse of his body while I drove myself as hard, and as rapidly, and as deeply as I could—and Phil's formidable ass shoved backward to meet every thrust. In a few minutes, with a lot of grunting and panting, I discharged my load into him, and he almost shouted, "Oh God, I can feel your come shootin' insidea me. That feels so fuckin' *hot*." I fucked until I was exhausted, and we fell forward, flat on he bed, me on top of Phil and my prick still inside his asshole, which continued to work it gently.

"Was that good, Phil?"

"That was as good as it gets. Jesus, John—thanks for that load. I love you fuckin' me. Your prick feels just . . . I don't know, just *right* insidea me."

"I wish my prick was as big as Billy's."

"You both feel fantastic in me. I wish he was here right now, so you could both fuck me."

I snickered, "Yeah—so you could fuck both of *us* is what you really mean."

He stayed under me, but rolled on his back, pulling my cock from him. He looked up at me and smiled. "Yeah, I'd sure wanna fuck botha you, all right—but I'd damn sure want botha you to fuck me, too." Then he grew very serious. "Do you think . . . Jesus, John, can you imagine how wonderful that would be?"

"Yes, Phil, I can imagine. But tonight it's just John and Phil, remember? We both love to fuck Billy, and we both love for Billy to fuck us. But . . . well, I actually *love* Billy, and . . ." I smiled. "Look, let's talk about Billy some other time, okay? Tonight's the night for Phil and John to fuck each other, and that's all we need to think about right now."

"Right. But, I wanna think that tonight is only the *first* night Phil and John fuck each other." I wanted to think that too, and assured him we could plan a lot of time together if he wanted, if we could work it out without hurting Billy.

We snuggled and kissed and caressed for a long time. Phil talked about growing up in Antares, sexually very precocious, having his first orgasm shortly after his eleventh birthday—blessed with a large cock, and from the start learning that there was a considerable demand for it. He had seriously fucked butt only a few years later, and had been plugging happy backsides ever since. He received his first blowjob even earlier than that, but didn't take a load down his own throat until he was almost seventeen. I told him, "I can't believe how long you waited to take a cock up your butt—surely you could see how much other guys enjoyed it when you fucked them."

Phil admitted he had long thought about getting fucked, but somehow felt it was something less than manly—even though he loved to suck cock. "And then I started really noticing Billy about six months ago. He's got the cutest ass, and even his prick is cute. I finally got where I wanted him so bad, I just *hadda* have him, and . . . well, you know what happened. Then, down in Waco, I enjoyed fuckin' Billy so much that I wanted to do anything that'd please him. And he really didn't give me much choice, anyway. He just flat-out told me he was gonna fuck my ass, and that I was gonna like it!" He held me tight. "And he did fuck me, and it hurt for a few minutes, but then, boy howdy did I ever like it." Nothing was said for a long moment, before Phil went on. "I really think Billy's as cute a guy as I've ever fucked. And I know you guys are . . . together, but . . . well, just let me share the fun some, okay?"

"That's a promise, Phil—you're a helluva man, and a helluva good fuck."

More kissing, caressing, cock-stroking and ass-play. I was especially fascinated with the enormous set of balls I often cupped and rolled about in my eager hand. "I really loved it when you sucked them," Phil said. He knelt over me, facing my feet, and his big cock hung down in my face as I gazed lovingly at his ass and his massive balls. He began to suck my prick, and I took his in my mouth to worship it. He said, "Suck my balls, too." Again I stretched my mouth to the limit and serviced his nuts at great length, playing with his cock all the time, and enjoying the wonderful blowjob he was giving me. We rolled over so that my prick hung down into Phil's mouth while I continued to suck his fat shaft, holding my lips very tightly around it, and driving my head as far up and down as his cock would allow—quite an amazing distance, actually. His tongue danced over my balls and my cock, and he finally took my cock all the way into his throat. We rolled onto our sides, each sucking the other deep and hard, our arms around each others' hips, and fingers seeking the entrance to twitching assholes.

Eventually things grew more and more frenzied, our fingers fucked deep into each other, and each was rewarded—not quite simultaneously, but almost—with hot, creamy evidence of the other's passion. Phil's load was again copious. I kept it in my mouth, rolling his softening prick around with my tongue, bathing it in its own emission, while Phil apparently swallowed mine. Finally I reversed my body and lay next to him while we embraced. As I kissed Phil, I passed his load of come into his own mouth. Surprised, he began to say something, and then simply said "Mmmm." and we passed his offering back and forth for a while until I swallowed it.

"God, you're hot John." He snickered, then. "I love the taste of my come—no wonder everybody wants to eat me."

"I'm ready to suck another load out of those wonderful big balls already."

"Hey, give me a coupla minutes. But you can bet there's gonna be plenty more for you. And don't be surprised if I slip your next load back to you from my mouth. I thought that was really hot."

More kissing, more caressing, more small talk and endearments, and me on my back with Phil's huge prick driving into my eager ass again in missionary position, as we kissed feverishly. With fierce forward thrusts he buried himself as deeply in me as he could, and froze there while he delivered yet another forceful, thrilling eruption. After a few minutes, he collapsed onto me and I held him tenderly, playing with his hair. "You must have an endless supply of come. Every load you've given me has been huge."

"Like I said, that's 'cause you inspire me."

I laughed. "Yeah, and maybe it's because you like to fuck butt."

"You might have a point there.' Then he reached down and began to fondle my hard cock. "And you've got a point here I'd like to drain again." He went down on me, and as I held his head he delivered a superb, magnificent blowjob—draining, as promised, my 'point.' He rose to kiss me, and I knew what was coming: we swapped my load back and forth for some time before he swallowed it and grinned. "That *does* taste fine, doesn't it?"

"Not half as good as yours, Phil."

We eventually went to sleep, Phil, lying on his side behind me and—as he had said he wanted—with his prick planted deep inside my ass. His tremendous, thrilling arms held my chest, and my hands lay behind me on his ample, muscular ass. I felt warm, protected, completely at peace, and extremely well *fucked-out* in the strong embrace of this giant young sex machine.

In the morning, I got up and went to pee. As I was standing there relieving myself, Phil came into the bathroom, yawning, with his cock huge and hard, standing out in front of him. "I don't know if this is a piss hard-on, or just a plain-ol' hard-on."

I took it in my hand. "Whatever, it sure is one *helluva* hard-on."

I stood behind him, holding his cock, and directed it at the toilet bowl. "I want to hold you while you piss." He laughed and said he doubted he *could* piss while I was holding him, but I worked his cock gently—my own nestling just under his ample ass cheeks—and eventually, the piss began to flow, and the feel of the strong stream coursing through his fat shaft was an extremely sexy sensation. Finally, I shook the last drops off his prick, which was still quite hard. He turned and took me in his arms and we kissed—rather chastely, both of us well aware of how *un*-sexy 'morning breath' can be. My arms were around his waist, my head rested on his massive chest as I licked his nipples, and his huge arms held me tight. He whispered into my ear: "Fuck me again." Then he turned around, leaned down and spread the cheeks of his ass. "Do it, right here."

I spit on Phil's exposed asshole, and on my own prick. As he held his cheeks apart, I roughly inserted myself into him and fucked furiously. He had to stoop a bit to accommodate me—he was about five inches taller than I, after all—but he managed to hump and meet my thrusts perfectly, reaching behind himself to pull me as tightly in to him as he could. After no more than five minutes I was erupting inside his hot ass. He worked my prick and murmured his appreciation. Eventually he let my prick slip from him, turned around, closed the seat of the commode, and sat down on it. His huge prick stood straight up from his lap. He smiled up at me as I stood over him, drooled a generous supply of spit on his prick, and then spit into one hand as well. With that hand he sought my asshole and began to moisten it; with the other he drew me to him. "Sit on it, John—I can tell your ass is hungry for my big dick."

I stepped forward and straddled him. Cradling his head in my hands, I lowered myself onto his cock, and slowly sat down until every inch of it was far inside me, and my buttocks rested on his pubic hair. We kissed as I began to ride him gently. Forget morning breath—our kissing was as hot as the fuck I knew I was about to get. I clenched my anal sphincter as tightly as I could while I fucked myself on him. My feet were planted firmly on the floor, so I had ample leverage and balance to service the thrilling organ that completely filled my ravenous ass. I was in ecstasy as I forced my ass as far down onto him as I could, wriggled it a bit, then began a slow pull upward on his prick, squeezing it as I ascended, and taking the very tip of his prick almost to the exit point before beginning a slow descent all the way to his lap again. His enormous arms circled my body and he murmured his delight and encouraged me with soft, sexy comments: "Make *love* to my dick, baby! Take me to heaven with that hot ass ... Christ, John, my prick feels three feet long when you ride it like that."

Only the last remark elicited an intelligible response from me: "It feels three feet long to me, too—like thirty-six inches of red-hot Phil Baker dick." Otherwise I simply moaned in wordless ecstasy and thrilled to the ride.

The slow pace allowed us to delight in this ultimate "lap dance" for a seemingly endless time. We were both in heaven, but eventually he began to approach orgasm, and started humping his ass upward to drive his cock into me and meet my downward plunges. I picked up the tempo of my ride, unfortunately decreasing the length of the stroke, but that was more than compensated for by the vigorous fucking he began to administer. Soon I was literally bouncing up and down at a fever pitch, and Phil held himself up off the commode and fucked my ass savagely from below. Finally, his arms reached up from behind and yanked downward on my shoulders, locking my asshole to his frantically driving cock, which now began to *fountain* an explosion of come inside me. My arms were clasped around his head and I shouted with joy as I gloried in his eruption, and he grunted and panted and moaned in utter abandon, his ass still humping his prick into me in rapid, short jabs.

We sat this way for a long time, as Phil's humping finally diminished, and we both relaxed from the extreme tension we had experienced during his massive, glorious orgasm. Finally we sat there motionless for some time, his prick still feeling very large inside me, his fine arms holding my waist and his head pressed against my chest while I kissed the top of it.

I whispered, "I don't believe I've ever felt a bigger load of come shoot in me," I took his head in my hands and looked into his eyes gravely, "and I don't think I've ever been fucked so thoroughly or so thrillingly. Thank you, Phil . . . that was the fuck of a lifetime."

He smiled, and we kissed very sweetly before he replied, also quietly. "It's up to you, but I'd like to fuck you that hard as much as you'll let me."

"But I do have a lover, you know, and . . . "

"Well, I'm not sayin' that I wanna give up fuckin' other guys, don't misunderstand. Hell, I'll prob'ly fuck a coupla guys in the park this week-end, and I've got sort of a date tonight with . . . well, with 'number two,' if you know what I mean." And he grinned hugely.

"I know who you *mean* by "number two," I just don't know who he *is.* And hey . . . it sure was an honor to be 'number five'."

"Number five felt great in me—just as fine as when number one got my cherry."

I wiggled my ass on his cock. "Mmmm . . . Billy."

Phil pressed his face to my chest again. "Yeah, that sweet Billy. I think his ass is about as pretty as anything I've ever seen, but he can really fuck butt like a champ." I had to agree. "John . . . do you mind if I fuck with Billy once in a while?"

"That's up to Billy, Phil; I don't own him." I smiled at him. "And I sure couldn't blame him. Look, I fucked with you, and I'm gonna fuck with you again, right?"

He laughed loudly. "Oh yeah. You're gonna fuck with me again all right."

"Okay, and Billy and you have fucked, and will fuck again. That's not to say that I don't love Billy, or that he doesn't love me. I don't *love* you, Phil . . . "

Another laugh. "You just love fuckin' me, right?"

"I love fucking you, and even more, getting fucked *by* you." I wriggled my ass again; his cock had grown back to the huge size it had been when he erupted in me earlier. He put his arms around me and stood up, picking me up bodily, still skewered on his prick with my arms around his neck. He carried me into the bedroom and lay me on my back on the bed, never allowing his prick to slip from my ass. With my legs now spread far and high in the air, he delivered another thrilling fuck, a very protracted one, ending in another palpable—though admittedly somewhat diminished—orgasm in my thrice-fortunate and ultimately blessed asshole. He had fucked me twice, both times to magnificent orgasm, without ever withdrawing from me. *My God, what a stud.*

As he relaxed and we fell on our sides—my legs still wrapped around him, and his prick still in me—he whispered, "You are one hell of a fuck, John."

"And you are one hell of a man—one hell of a *stud*, Phil."

We cuddled and kissed a while longer, and got in the shower. We played with each other there, of course, but I believe Phil's cock needed a rest—it didn't even get hard. Mine was like a rock, however, and at one point he knelt before me and sucked me to climax as the water played over us. With my come in his mouth, he stood, and we again swapped a load back and forth between us. Finally he swallowed it, took my face in his hands, and smiled as he began to sing a commercial jingle popular at the time: "Mm-mm good, mm-mm good. That's what Johnny's soup is, mm-mm good." A really big grin. "When can I get another bowl of *Cream of John Harrison Soup?*"

"Any time you come around to give me some *Cream of Phil.*"

He laughed. "I'm gonna be around, believe me, and ol' Phil's gonna have a whole *lotta* cream for you."

We eventually got cleaned and dressed—both needing to be at school shortly. Phil made me promise to give him another 'piece of ass' soon—a promise I was not at all averse to making. He added that he would not put any real pressure on Billy to fuck with him, but he still hoped I didn't mind my young lover going to bed with him again if it was agreeable with Billy. I reiterated that it was up to Billy. He urged me to think about the possibility of the three of us getting together for a threesome sometime soon. I told him I'd discuss it with Billy—it seemed like a really exciting idea to me, but first I had to be sure things were okay with Billy about Phil and me having sex.

"So you're gonna tell Billy about our gettin' together?"

"Phil, I have to—but I want to, also. If that's okay with you."

"It's fine with me—will I get a good review?"

"Billy will get so horny when I tell him all about it, he's gonna want to get in your pants again right away."

"That sounds great—but don't forget to tell him I want *both* of you in my pants; one at a time is great—both at the same time'd be even better."

I walked him to the door. Just before opening it, I reached inside his letter jacket and put my arms around him to hold him so we could share one final kiss. He leaned down and we kissed for quite a while. I thought it strange that his arms were not around me, until he stepped back, and grinned as he looked down at himself; he had unbuttoned his pants and pulled them down in front so that his huge balls were exposed and resting on his shorts, which were gathered below them. His lovely cock was arcing out from his balls, and although it wasn't fully hard, it was a long way from soft. "You wanna kiss this baby goodbye?"

I laughed. "God, Phil, you are really something." I knelt and began to kiss and lick his prick, which immediately came to full erection again. He took my head in his hands, forced his cock into my mouth, and began to fuck me hard and deep. "God, John, but I love fuckin' your mouth." I sucked happily for quite a while as he continued to drive himself into me. Finally he pulled his cock from my mouth and raised me to my feet. "If I don't stop now, I'm gonna come again—and I really want to, but I've got a date tonight, and he's gonna want me to give him some good stuff, too. Look, if I get too horny this afternoon, though, I may stop by your office and letcha suck me off, if that's okay."

"Phil. No. I . . ."

He laughed and kissed me quickly. "I'm just kiddin.' I know better, *Mr. Harrison*. But I do want to blow a big ol' load in you again *real* soon—or two or three, or maybe half a dozen." He began to push his prick back into his Levi's as he looked up at me, winked broadly, and smiled. "You have definitely not seen the last of this baby."

Impulsively, I fell to my knees and dragged his pants back down, causing his big, hard cock to flop into my face, and exposing the muscular ass I found so thrilling, and which I began to kiss and caress as I turned his body around. I buried my face between the glorious, golden, velvety, *magnificent* globes of that divine treasure called "Phil Baker's Ass." I licked and kissed my way all over his buttocks and all the way down as far as I could, and then began licking back up in the crevice. Soon I sought the entrance to that tight chute that had so recently welcomed my prick, and he leaned forward so I could drive my tongue as far as I could into that perfect pink gate to heaven. It was an added thrill to know that a considerable amount of my come still remained in this torrid man, and that I still harbored a *very* considerable amount of his emission in my body. I tongue-fucked him as deeply as I possibly could, and he moaned with passion, used the musculature of his sphincter to *clamp* my tongue tightly as I fucked through it, and pulled his cheeks far apart and humped his ass back toward my mouth in total abandon. "Jesus Christ that feels incredible. Get your prick out and fuck me right now."

I stopped my invasion of his twitching asshole, stood up, and put my arms around him from behind. My hands reached beneath his tee shirt and played with his tits as I whispered into his ear, "I just wanted to give you a sample of what you've got waiting for you the next time we get together."

He turned around and sank his tongue into my mouth before he grinned, "It better not be too long, okay?"

"Pull your pants up, Phil, and get out of here, or I *will* start to fuck you again. Save it for tonight—you'll need it." I held his shoulders and looked into his eyes. "Just be very aware of this: you have the most magnificent, thrilling body I have ever held in my arms, and I'm very eager to feel it there again soon . . and when you hold me in these incredible strong arms of yours, I *adore* it—it's almost as wonderful as when you bury that monster prick inside me. And I've had some really big pricks inside me, Phil, but yours is one of the best—and your *balls*. My God, Phil, your balls are the biggest, most thrilling ones I've *ever* seen, much less played with, or sucked, or drained dry, or . . . well, *tried* to drain is more accurate, I guess. It's no wonder you gave me more come than anyone I've ever been with.

"Look, I love Billy, Phil, but I also think that you are an incredibly thrilling man, and I appreciate you very much, and want to make love with you often. Okay. Sorry about the long speech; I guess you've already figured out you impressed me, huh?"

He wrapped those massive arms around me and held me tight for a few minutes, without saying a word—knowing how I enjoyed being in his strong embrace. Then, very quietly: "Thanks, John." As he tucked his hard prick back in his pants—with difficulty, given a huge, hard prick and very tight Levi's—and buttoned them, he said, "When I'm swappin' blowjobs and fucks with my friend tonight I'll be thinkin' about what we did here—and about what you just promised me you've got waitin' for me."

"I sure would like to know who your friend is."

He laughed again. "I'll just bet you would. But you do know him, and I'll even give you a hint: he's hot as hell, but he's pretty damn young—'bout Billy's age." He kissed me quickly and opened the door. "Thanks a million, John. You are a helluva stud. This was the greatest fuck of my life."

"So far."

"Yeah, so far—maybe we can top it next time." He grinned, winked, and flipped a salute as he turned and started off. Watching his rounded ass undulate in his tight Levi's as he walked up the driveway I hoped to see it kneeling bare in front of me again very, very soon—and I thought that although I had not considered Phil to be particularly handsome before, he now struck me as almost beautiful. Amazing what a fantastic body, a big hard prick, and huge balls all working together to deliver a masterful fuck can do to one's perspective.

Phil had come in my mouth twice, and had filled my ass four *times with his magnificent discharge; I had blown three loads into his mouth, and two more up his butt. In less than nine hours he had come six times and I had come five—and he was almost ready to come again just before he left. My God in heaven, what an incredible experience.*

I somehow knew that Phil would be rejuvenated by the time night came, and would be driving that big, luscious cock deep into his friend, the mysterious 'number two,' to deliver another barrage of his huge, thrilling loads. I had to admit to a lot of curiosity as to just who it was that Phil would be fucking that night—a *very* lucky lad who would also no doubt be firing a return barrage inside that precocious, but incredibly accomplished teenage fuckmaster.

11.
A MOVEABLE FUCK

Phil put his arms around Billy from behind, and lay his cheek on his shoulder as he buttoned his shirt. "Shit, you're gettin' ready to go, and I was gettin' ready to come."

In school the next day, I passed a set of homework papers back to my Geometry class, and had taped a note to Billy's asking him to see me after class for a minute—I needed to talk with him. He managed, as he often did, to be the last to leave. As he approached my desk, he grinned suggestively. "Are we just going to talk, or what?" He waggled his eyebrows *a la* Groucho Marx, and in a passable imitation of that immortal comedian added, *"Talk* would be fine, but I think I'd rather *what."*

I laughed. "I'd like to do both, but *talking* first—you may not want to *what* with me after I tell you what I've got to tell you."

His face fell. "Is it serious, Pete?"

"I'm just going to need a little forgiveness, I think. Confession time again."

"Oh, oh. Same kind of confession as Christmas?" I nodded. "I hope the serious part is that you just did it—not that you found someone else to be serious about."

"I just did it, Billy—I sure as hell didn't plan it, and it was just fun, nothing serious—and it damned sure doesn't make me feel any different about you."

He smiled. "Pete, you know how I feel about you, and you know I'll forgive you. We're okay—we'll talk, and . . . look, let's meet and talk about it tonight—but not too late, so we'll have time to *what* afterward. Wait—when did this happen?" I told him it had been the previous night, and that morning. "Wow. An 'all-nighter,' huh? You're not too *worn out* to do more than talk, are you—it wasn't *that* good, was it?"

"Billy, it was great, but nothing is so good I don't want to be with you. I *fucked* last night—we *make love,* remember?"

"We'll do both tonight. Are you going to tell me all about it?"

"You want a *blow-by-blow* description?"

He laughed. "Something like that—but I want to know the rest, too . . ." and then I was treated to a fairly good Edward G. Robinson imitation, *sotto voce:* "Not just the blowjobs, see? Okay?" Then back to the wonderful Billy Polk voice I loved" "You're not going to shock me are you?"

"No, most of it's going to seem . . . well, *familiar* to you."

He didn't say anything for a few seconds. "Phil. Right?" I nodded again. "I *knew* he was gonna figure it out and put the make on you. Pete, I think I know Phil well enough to be sure he's not gonna get serious about either one of us." He grinned, "He's workin' up to getting all three of us together; he suggested it, you know."

I grinned back at him. "He suggested it to me too—and after last night, I'm thinking it might be a whole helluva lot of fun."

"He's something, isn't he? Hey, I've got to get to my next class. Tonight?" I agreed. "Okay, I want to hear *everything*—and then maybe we can . . . *replay* some of the highlights, just you and me."

"I can't wait—and look, when you leave the room, do me a favor—would you walk real slow?"

"Why . . ."

"I want to watch that cute ass as long as I can."

He snickered. "It's yours—you know that; tonight you can watch it all you want, and you can do anything else to it you want." He winked and turned around and left.

But he *did* walk slowly. And I did watch it. And it really *was* cute. Just after he turned the corner and disappeared from sight, he put his head back in the doorway to grin and wink at me. Cute ass, *adorable* boy.

Billy rang my doorbell around 7:00 that night. I opened it, and he stood there leaning against the door jamb, wearing his letter jacket—opened to show his white tee-shirt—with Levi's and boots. "Same costume you saw last night, right?" I laughed as he entered and shut the door behind himself.

I asked, "Is that his standard uniform?"

"Oh, yeah." He took me in his arms and kissed me. "Tell me all about it—and I want to hear every little detail. And I especially want to hear the big ones, too." He took his jacket off and threw it on the sofa as he sat—unwittingly duplicating Phil's entrance of the night before, except for the welcoming kiss.

As I began to tell about Phil's visit in as much detail as I could, Billy began to do his best to re-create it for me. My hand on his leg—his hand moving mine to his crotch—denuding me and mounting the coffee table—dry-fucking the table, and all the rest. Finally, after our kissing and groping, Billy bared his pretty ass, and held his balls up for me to suck before finally exposing his lovely long cock. He more or less duplicated Phil's dancing-cock display before stepping down from the table and beginning to fuck my eager mouth exuberantly. He was adamant about re-creating Phil's filling my mouth with hot come, but when we got to the part about Phil carrying me to my bed, he laughed and declared he'd pass on that.

From that point on we were mostly just Billy and John—no more Phil, although occasionally, when prompted by Billy, I would describe how Phil and I had done something the night before, and Billy occasionally made reference to the way he and Phil had done it. We kissed passionately and at length, we rode each other's cocks, we each knelt to take the other's prick deep in his ass, we fucked each other in the missionary position (so wonderful to be able to see his beautiful body and kiss him while we fucked.), we sucked each other's cocks in all sorts of ways, and we blew our loads into each other as we lay in sixty-nine. What we did *not* have time to do, nor possibly had the stamina to do, was equal the frequency of orgasms Phil and I had given each other—but before Billy went out the door later that night, we had each taken three loads from the other.

We lay together snuggling and comparing notes on the thrill of Phil's magnificent body and his fucking technique. By the time we were through, we both agreed we wanted Phil there with us soon, so we could share in worshiping his glorious body, fucking his statuesque and beautiful ass, and sucking his thick, driving cock or taking it in the ass. Billy said he would talk to Phil and set it up.

"Billy, I'll understand if you and Phil alone want to . . . "

"Pete, I want to fuck Phil and have him fuck me, but if possible, I want to do it while you're there to share it with me—and I want to watch you fucking him, and him fucking you. Look, I love you, and . . . well, lots of times I feel like you and I are almost like one person when we're making love, and that one guy—you and me—that's who I'm gonna tell Phil is the one who wants to go to bed with him next."

Billy could not, as Phil had, spend the night with me. As he was getting ready to leave, I told him about my last couple of minutes with Phil—tongue-fucking his ass by the door. He took my hand and led me to the door. He had already put his clothes on, but he now undid his pants and shorts, dropped them to the floor, and turned around to present his adorable bare ass for me—if possible, maybe even sexier looking than usual, since he was otherwise fully clothed. He leaned over and spread his cheeks, without saying a word. I knelt and made love to his perfect asshole as thoroughly as my tongue would allow. He squirmed and moaned in joy, finally saying, "I don't care what happened at this point with Phil—spit on your cock and my ass and fuck me while I stand here." I did as I was told, and put my arms around him from behind, and played with his muscular chest and fine tits under his tee shirt as I gently put myself into him. We made very slow love standing there, Billy turning his head so we could kiss, undulating his ass to heighten the thrill I felt as I drove my prick deeply into him. Finally, as I began to get excited, he put his hands back and pulled my ass in to him, leaned over, and said, "Fuck it hard and fill me up, Pete." I drove myself into him as savagely as I could, and erupted deep inside the heaven of my young lover's body. Long minutes standing there—my prick still inside him, his hands holding my ass and my hands holding his waist tightly.

Finally he stood and turned around as my cock slipped from him. He took my face in his hands and kissed me very tenderly. "I love you, Pete. I'm so proud that you love me, I wish the whole world could know, so in a way I'm glad that Phil knows—and is probably going to *share* us soon, so at least there can be one witness to how much I belong to John Harrison." Then as he leaned over and began to pull his pants up, he looked up with a sudden lewd grin and said, "and we can both get fucked by that big ol' cock again."

I laughed. "Count on it. Set it up—but don't call him tonight, he told me he'd be fucking someone else—someone I know, he said, someone who's about your age."

"Hey, I'm my age. But it *ain't* me—I'm fucked out tonight."

"Anyway, if you want to, set us up with Phil soon—it'll be fun." Then I too grew very serious as I took *his* face in *my* hands. "But always know that even if Phil Baker's cock is up my ass, or in my throat, it's Billy Polk I love."

"I know, Pete. I'll always know."

We kissed, and in the very spot where early that same day I had said goodbye to one of the hottest men I had ever known, I said good night to the very sweetest one I could ever hope to know. Which was better in bed? Jesus, how could you tell? They were both master lovers in their own ways, and the thought of sharing my bed with both of them soon was exciting and interesting . . . very interesting indeed, and very, *very* exciting.

As it turned out, and without either of us planning it, both Billy and I were to have sex one-on-one with Phil again, separately, before the three-way get-together we decided we wanted to pursue.

Separately, but on the same evening.

The first part of that evening I learned about from Billy the day after. The adjectives concerning Billy's beauty and accomplishments I have added to the account, while those about Phil are Billy's own:

At basketball practice, Billy told Phil he wanted to talk with him, so Phil suggested he come by his house that evening and they could take all the time they wanted. Billy didn't think sex was in the offing, since they would be meeting at Phil's house. As it turned out, Phil's parents were at the house when Billy arrived there on foot, but they were just going out, and would not be back until around ten o'clock. A few minutes later, the two wound up in Phil's bedroom, sitting next to each other on the bed, with the house all to themselves. Considering what I knew of Phil—and Billy's attraction to him, of course—it was surprising they didn't start fucking at once, but Billy insisted they talk. He told Phil he knew about his encounter with me, that I had told him everything about it—and while he wasn't really angry with Phil, it just *annoyed* him. "The thing with . . . Mr. Harrison and me was private, Phil. I told you I couldn't tell you who my lover was because I didn't want you to know—nothing against you, I didn't want anybody to know."

"He could really get in a lot of trouble, couldn't he?"

"He really could, and it would just be *wrong* if he did. I was as anxious to make love with him as he was with me—maybe more so. We were both willing and, well, I guess . . . eager. And we really do love each other, Phil."

"I know, and I wouldn't want anything even a little bit bad to happen to either one of you—and I won't *do* anything that's gonna hurt you. But shit, Billy, you know how horny I am, and . . . well, you and I had such great hot sex together, and I knew you were havin' sex regularly with somebody, and . . . I just figured it had to be John—Mr. Harrison—and I'd wanted to have sex with him myself, so I thought, hell, why not check it out? Are you pissed off at me for fuckin' with him?"

"It really just bothers me, I guess. But, no, I'm not mad about that. I might be a *little* mad about you going over to his house to see if he was my lover, but I know what a great fucker you are, and I know how much . . . Mr. Harrison likes fucking, and . . . well, you and I fucked, and I told him all about how terrific it had been, so I sure can't blame him for checking it out, can I?"

"It *was* terrific with you 'n me, wasn't it? But it was really terrific with John, too. And by the way, you guys are fuckin' each other's brains out, and you still call him *Mr. Harrison*? What gives?"

Billy laughed. "I call him *Mr. Harrison* at school—he's my teacher, after all, and I'm only a sophomore. Calling him *John* seems . . . I don't know, *wrong*, somehow, but I really don't know why."

Phil said, "I asked if it was okay for me to call him by his first name when we weren't at school, and he said okay—after all, he's only three years older'n me. So what do *you* call him? I know you don't call him Mr. Harrison when he's suckin' you off."

"I call him a special name, which I'll tell you, but it's only for me to use, okay? He's John to you, he's Mr. Harrison at school, and with me . . . well, he's Pete."

"Pete?"

"No explanations, Phil. I'm not even taking any questions. It's just strictly between me and Pete, okay?"

Phil laughed. "Fine with me. So—did he say how he liked his meeting with me?"

"You know darned well how he liked it—he said it was *unbelievable*, and he could see how I *couldn't* have turned down sex with you."

Phil put his hand on the inside of Billy's leg. "Would you turn down sex with me now?"

"Your parents . . ."

"Won't be back for a while—I know we have at least a coupla hours when we could fool around safely." Phil clasped Billy behind the neck, drew him close, and kissed him passionately. "Whaddaya think?" Billy's arms went around Phil, and he returned his kisses. They fell back on the bed and began necking and groping. Phil whispered in Billy's ear. "Show me your pretty ass and tell me what I can do to it."

Billy got off the bed and stripped off his clothes completely, then got back on, and stood astride Phil's head, facing his feet. Phil ran his hands up along Billy's legs and gazed in rapture at the perfect, rounded little ass he and I both adored. "Jesus, Billy, that looks good enough to eat."

Billy smiled down at him over his shoulder. "That's a good idea, Phil." He gradually lowered himself until his asshole was directly over Phil's mouth. Phil grasped Billy's waist and drew him down onto him before feasting on Billy's asshole. Billy's tight hole clutched Phil's plunging tongue, and both boys were delirious with passion. Billy rolled off. "Off with the clothes, Phil, and give me something to eat too."

Phil stripped quickly and the two rolled together on their sides in sixty-nine, and began to suck each others' cocks and finger their assholes. Billy began to lick and suck Phil's huge, succulent balls, and Phil sought Billy's. Soon each mouth was at the other's asshole, and a lengthy dual tongue-fuck had them both groaning in ecstasy. Billy abandoned Phil's ass and wolfed down his big prick again. Phil followed suit with Billy's cock, and their ecstasy climaxed a few minutes later as each filled the other's mouth with massive spurts of semen. They lay clasped this way for a long time, snuggling and playing with each others' asses, while swallowing and savoring each other's offering, licking and kissing still-hard pricks and drained balls.

They lay head-to-head, and caressed and kissed until each was hard again. Phil knelt on all fours, facing away from Billy, and told him to watch. He wet his finger and began to fuck himself in the ass with it. Looking back over his shoulder he asked Billy, "Look good?" Billy's finger joined Phil's and the two plunged together as Billy declared it looked wonderful. "Then *fuck* it, Billy—give me another big load." Billy rammed himself into Phil, using only spit as a lubricant, and fucked hard, fast, and deep. He had come only fifteen minutes earlier, so he fucked his partner fiercely for a very long time before he drove himself all the way in and held himself tight, shuddered, and delivered another helping of his hot liquid love to the lucky Phil's ass. That Phil had enjoyed it as much as Billy was clear from his cries of joy, and the frantic bucking and humping that accompanied Billy's thrusting.

They again fell into each other's arms for a few minutes of quiet kissing and hugging. Then Phil rolled Billy onto his stomach, and began to worship the younger man's rounded, perfectly formed and perfectly beautiful ass. He gently ran his hands over the twin, velvety globes as he kissed them, then began a kissing and licking campaign that ended with his tongue again deep inside Billy, whose humping and writhing suggested a level of delight he confirmed with his impassioned vocal cries urging Phil to ever more urgent adoration.

Billy raised his ass as far as he could; Phil knelt behind him and lovingly inserted himself into the entrance to heaven. He was fucking Billy very gently and slowly, and as deep as he possibly could—with both of them murmuring their delight—when noises from the living room indicated that Phil's parents had returned sooner than expected. Billy immediately pulled away, but Phil said, "They won't look in here. Please don't make me stop, baby." He was caressing Billy's ass and stroking his cock. "Oh Billy, I've gotta finish fuckin' you."

Billy was about to give in and accept Phil again—against his better judgment—when Phil's mother called as she walked by the closed bedroom door, "We're home, Phil. Is Billy still here?"

Billy, thoroughly *spooked* now, was putting on his clothes quickly as he called out, nervously, "Yes ma'am, Mrs. Baker, I'm just getting ready to go."

Phil put his arms around Billy from behind, and lay his cheek on his shoulder as he buttoned his shirt. "Shit, you're gettin' ready to go, and I was gettin' ready to come."

Billy turned and kissed him quickly as he laughed, "There'll be another time—in fact, that's one of the things I came here to talk with you about. Put your clothes on and give me a ride home—I'll tell you on the way."

As Phil drove, Billy told him that the three-way fuck he wanted was going to happen. In the interest of a *spectacular* fuck, however, Billy decreed that none of us was going to fuck anybody, or even jack off for forty-eight hours before we got together. Phil agreed without reservation. "Hell, I'll have that much extra come to give you guys—but it sure is gonna be hard to keep this hard cock in my pants and outa my fist for two whole days."

"It'll be hard on all of us—*literally*—but we'll be that much more *ready* when we do get together."

Phil laughed, "I don't see how much more ready I could be than I am right now. You don't know how much I want to finish fuckin' that beautiful ass of yours. Here, feel this thing." Phil unbuttoned his Levi's and pulled his hard cock out, which Billy played with as they sat in front of his house. "C'mon Billy, sit on my lap and lemme finish fuckin' your pretty ass."

"Phil, I've got to get in the house, or my mom'll wonder what I'm doing. How does Saturday night sound? I'll see if Pete is free, and I'll tell my mom I'm staying with Joe Don—he's covered for me before."

"Yeah, he's covered a few times for me, too."

"Oh, yeah? I didn't know you and he were friends."

"Sure, Billy, we're real good friends."

"Phil, you and Joe Don . . . no, never mind, I don't even want to ask. Anyway, maybe he'll cover for you Saturday night too."

"Okay, that's Saturday night, unless you tell me that ain't gonna work out. And you're really gonna make me quit gettin' my rocks off starting Thursday?" Billy laughed and said he was. "How about doin' at least *somethin'* for me right now, before you go in? Please, Billy—at least suck me off, huh? Don't make me go home and jack off."

Billy laughed. "Phil, I've gotta go in. Hey, here's what you can do—and it's okay with me if you want to. You go over to Pete's . . . Mr. Harrison's house, and if he's free, tell him my plan. See if Saturday night, *all* night, is okay for really hot sex with you and me and him—and the *shooting-your-load-curfew* starts Thursday afternoon. Then, if he wants to finish getting you off . . . " He laughed again. "And why do I think I know what his answer to *that* is gonna be? Anyway, he can have the load you were about to give me when your folks came home. How does that sound?"

"I'd rather finish fillin' you up, and *then* go to see him, but . . . oh, hell, kiss this thing goodbye and I'm on my way to John's house. I sure hope Saturday night's good with him—I'm lookin' forward to watchin' you two together almost as much as I am to fuckin' the both of you."

"I find that pretty hard to believe."

"Well, I said *almost* as much."

Billy kissed Phil's cock and stuffed it back in his pants, kissed him on the lips, and told him to let him know the next day if Saturday was going to be the big day. Then he was gone.

My doorbell rang shortly after 10:00 that night. I answered it, to find Phil standing there in his usual uniform, but holding his letter jacket in front of him, rather than wearing it—strange, since it was cold out. "Phil. Come on in, what's up?"

"Hi. Anybody here?"

"Only me."

He stepped inside and said, "Here's what's up." He dropped his coat, to reveal that he had unbuttoned his Levi's, and had them pulled down below his balls—he was wearing no underwear. His cock was hard (of course–this was *Phil.)* and he was stroking it slowly. "I really need some help with this."

"Christ, Phil, what if someone had been here?"

He grinned. "That's why I was hidin' it. Can you help me with it?" I was already playing with it with one hand, and squeezing his huge balls with the other. "I just had this thing up the prettiest ass in town . . ."

"That's gotta be Billy."

"Of course—the prettiest ass in Texas, prob'ly. Anyway, I was fuckin' Billy in my bedroom, and my parents came in."

"Shit, Phil, they caught you guys fucking?"

He laughed. "No, nothing like that, I keep my bedroom door locked—have since I was twelve. But here I was, way up inside Billy, fuckin' like crazy and just about ready to start fillin' him with my load when they came in the house. It shook Billy up so bad he wouldn't let me finish. He told me to come over here and finish inside you—and he said I should tell you it was okay with him if you wanted me to." He took my head in his hands and planted a deep kiss. "And it's sure okay with me—guess you can tell."

I released Phil's cock as I kissed back, and put my hands down the back of his Levi's to play with his ass. "My butt's nothing like as pretty as Billy's, but I'd sure like to take that load in it," I put a finger in his asshole, which he began to hump, "and I'd like to give you one back."

"That'd be terrific. I got a big load of Billy's in my butt right now, so we wouldn't need the Vaseline—and I think I two loads would be four times as good."

"Your math may be screwed up, but your heart's in the right place. Let's go to the bedroom." I led him there, and we both stripped; as we stood by the bed, Phil took me in his arms. After some passionate kissing and fondling, he used his hands to turn me around.

He whispered into my ear from behind. "Grease up—I wanna fuck you while you stand here." I reached into the Vaseline and greased my asshole and Phil's cock, which he proceeded to drive all the way into me with one sudden thrust. It was so sudden, and I wasn't prepared, so it hurt a bit—but *God*, it felt wonderful once he began shoving it in and out. He held my waist in his hands and fucked me savagely, grunting in passion. "Gotta put this load up a hot ass." I bent over and braced myself on the bed to withstand the shock of his violent slams against my ass. I could hear his balls and belly slapping against me as he drove his big cock rapidly, and with strokes of absolute maximum length. In just a few minutes I felt his come exploding. He continued to fuck hard and fast for a long time after he shot his load. He pushed me forward to lie flat on the bed, and he fell heavily on top of me, as his excitement only gradually began to subside. He kissed my ear. "Shit, but that felt good. Oh God, John, I love to fuck your ass."

I turned and held him. "You gonna fuck my mouth, too?"

He laughed, "Well, Billy ate a load a while ago, seems only fair I give you one—all of a mouth-fuck for each of my hot studs, but only half of a buttfuck apiece."

"I'll bet Billy fucked your mouth too—I tasted something mighty sweet when you kissed me."

"God *damn* that boy is something—his come tastes as sweet as his ass, doesn't it?"

"Everything about Billy is sweet." Phil continued to lie on top of me, while we snuggled and kissed. Phil told me Saturday was going to be "three-way night" right here in my house, if that was okay. I agreed that it was not only okay, it was going to be great.

"It sure is gonna be hard not to get my load for two whole days, though."

"What do you mean?" He told me about the moratorium Billy was imposing on orgasms after Thursday afternoon. I had to laugh. "Billy is by far the youngest of us, but he seems to take charge a lot of the time—and I love it."

"The thing is, I don't think I've gone two days without fuckin', or gettin' sucked off, or jackin' off since I shot my wad the first time—when I was eleven."

"Damn, Phil—eleven?"

"Yep, and I jacked off at least two or three times a day after that, and got my first blowjob and fucked my first butt a coupla years later. I didn't give anybody a blowjob until I was in high school, but I could see how much fun everybody else was havin', so I just had to join in. 'Course I didn't take a dick up my butt until Billy fucked me in Waco; Jesus, I can't believe I waited so long. Anyway, even on days when I'm sick—like with flu or something—I still jack off a coupla times."

"You're incredible, Phil—seeing you around school, I never suspected you were such a . . I don't know, a total *fuck machine*. But I sure am glad I found out."

"Mmmm . . . me too, and if I don't get your dick up my ass soon, I'm gonna bust." He rolled off me, and knelt on all fours, with his ass high in the air. I tongue-fucked him and feasted for a long time on his magnificent balls before I drove myself in and fucked him almost as hard as he had fucked me. We were both temporarily exhausted after I shot in him, and lay locked together, snuggling, for some time.

"Phil, the first time I fucked you, you said I was number five. What number are you up to now?"

He turned around and laughed. "Why hell, if I had many cocks stickin' *outa* me as I've had stickin' *in* me lately, I'd look like a porcupine. One afternoon in the park last week, *three* guys lined up behind me and each one shot his load in my ass." I groaned, and he laughed again. "Hell, it was only fair—they'd been bent over lined up in fronta me right before that, and I fucked all three of them first."

"You shot your wad in three different asses in a row?"

"No, actually, I didn't come in the middle one—musta been tired—but I pretended like I did, and he seemed to have a helluva good time anyway."

"Christ, Phil, you're not a fuck machine, you're a fuck *assembly line*." He went on and detailed at great length the specifics of his astonishingly busy sex life—which led me to ask him how he had put off seducing Billy for so long.

"I had my eye on him for a long time—he's cute as a button—but I never thought he'd be willin'. Then I just got where I could *not* look at that pretty ass of his another minute without tryin' to get in it. Then finally one day in the shower I got to see his long cock hard, 'n it was just as cute as his ass, and I *hadda* make my move."

He said he normally jacked off either before getting out of bed or during his morning shower. During the day he usually managed to keep his dick in his pants, although he admitted that for years he had enjoyed occasional locker-room fucks and blowjobs during off-hours and study hall periods–with many different students, and even with the coach. He swore me to secrecy about the coach, and I didn't tell him that Billy had already told me about his 'thing' with the coach—a pleasant, if unexciting, married man with three children and a pretty wife. If there wasn't anyone to have sex with, Phil usually jacked off twice before going to sleep, but he managed to find someone to fuck with about three or four times a week. He said he probably *averaged* four or five orgasms a day.

At that point, we both were so hot talking about his sexual adventures that we clasped each other in sixty-nine, and ate each other's asses and came in each other's mouths. After another rest, he resumed his incredible story when I asked him to tell me about the park in 'the city' he frequented for sex.

His activities in the park were unbelievable—usually getting his load two or even three times with different, anonymous guys, and taking a load or two in the process. He declared he was very particular, though, and turned down a lot more offers in the park than he accepted. I asked him why, aside from his fabulous build and good looks, he thought so many guys "came on" to him in the park. He laughed again, "Hell, I walk around in the bushes with my pants pulled down below my balls, and my hard dick wavin' in the breeze."

The fact that Phil had not been caught, arrested, or infected was as astonishing as his sexual drive. That he found time for his school work was equally amazing. He had average grades, but if he had not been devoting so much time to sex, he probably would have been Valedictorian as well as President of his class.

During this long account, Phil had been getting dressed, having to go home—it was after midnight. I asked him if he ever screwed girls. "Nah, but I prob'ly will some day. I date, 'n all that, but nothin' serious yet. You c'n fuck with guys and not have to put up with all that bullshit girls wanna give you. Hell, I'll probably give up fuckin' guys and get married some day—I wanna have kids." He was bending over putting on his boots as he said this, but looked up and winked. "But I've still got a lotta guys to fuck and suck with first."

He stood, and in his skin-tight tee-shirt and bulging Levi's he looked almost as sexy as he did when he was naked. He put his hands on my shoulders and smiled as he looked into my eyes, "I'm sure fuckin' a girl will be fine, but right now when I get down between two spread legs, I want to find a big stiff prick waitin' there for me, and it's hard to imagine anything better than stickin' my dick inside a good-lookin' guy." The smile turned into a grin. "Like I just did. And just tell me honestly, can you think of *anything* more tempting than Billy's ass?" I confessed I considered the aforementioned article of anatomy to be one of the Wonders of the Modern World. He took me in his huge arms. "And Saturday we're gonna watch each other fuckin' it and eatin' it, and . . . shit, I'm gettin' so hot I want to get undressed and fuck you again. Whaddaya think?"

"I think if you don't leave neither of us is going to get any sleep tonight." I kissed him hard. "Now get the fuck out of here."

At the front door, we kissed and swore to practice abstinence beginning Thursday afternoon. Phil grinned at that, "But I bet I can line up somethin' to fuck *early* Thursday afternoon."

"Your young friend, perhaps?"

"Well, he's right here in town. Hey, this was a great night, John: started out fuckin' one hot guy, finished up with another—finest kind. Saturday night is gonna be fantastic—'n I'm gonna *drown* you guys in come." He was out the door.

What an incredible man. If I had not experienced the sexual exploits I had already shared with him, I would have thought his account of his sexual activities was mostly braggadocio and bullshit. But I suspected it had been true.

12.
TANGO FOR THREE, AND TEA FOR TWO

As I looked up at him, his body appeared to be a model for the
Colossus of Rhodes—"with conquering limbs astride from land to
land," and all that. What the Colossus didn't feature (as far as we
know) was the huge, throbbing prick that stood straight out from
Phil's magnificent body..

I had laughed at Phil for declaring he would at least find someone to
fuck Thursday afternoon before we began our two day fast in preparation
for Saturday night. Billy had also laughed when I told him Phil's plan,
but we both agreed it made sense, so during lunch period on Thursday
I took Billy home with me, and in the forty-five minutes we had, I sucked
a copious burst from him, and then had him kneel on the side of my bed
as I worshipped his perfect ass first with my tongue, and then with a load
of come delivered with maximum love and *drive*. This wonderful
exchange was capped—after a brief respite, while we snuggled and
kissed—by my wild ride on Billy's prick and his delivery of another load
to tide me over until Saturday.

As we drove back to school we saw Phil's truck pulling in at the far end
of the parking lot. He got out, the passenger door opened, and Joe Don
Griffith emerged; the two headed into the main building. Phil had not
seen us. Billy and I looked at each other and we both broke into laughter.
"For $64,000 dollars," Billy said, "can you guess the name of another
sophomore that just got a load of come up his butt? I'll bet I'm
right—does that surprise you, Pete?"

"Oh . . . I imagine they just went out and got hamburgers for lunch
instead of eating in the cafeteria."

He snorted. "Yeah—sure. I think somebody just had Phil Baker's dick
for lunch after six months of watching the famous Joe Don Griffith *desk
fuck*, I'm pretty sure we're right. So Joe Don's another one of us who
love Phil's big ol' cock. How about that? Anyway, it looks like Phil *is*
planning to honor our curfew for Saturday night."

"It's gonna be a night to remember, Billy."

"That it is. Gotta get to class—thanks for taking me to lunch, Pete."

"Best lunch I ever ate—and thank *you* for feeding it to me so . . . well,
so forcefully."

Billy Polk, the famous celebrity impersonator, supplied a pretty
convincing Jimmy Durante: "You ain't seen nothin' yet, Kid."

Thursday night was not difficult to get through—I'd left a pretty
sizable load in Billy that day, after all—but Friday, and especially during
the day Saturday, my anticipation of our planned threesome made me so
horny I could hardly keep my hands off my dick (Billy and Phil later
confessed to the same problem). I kept busy with the routine of my non-
sexual activities.

And I did still *have* non-sexual activities to engage in. I'm sure the
reader suspects that exercising my raging libido consumed all my time,

but I still performed my teaching duties, socialized with friends (non-sexual interactions, except when Jim came to visit), shopped and cleaned house, went to movies, and all the minutiae of living—I even found time to direct the Methodist Church choir. I had a substitute lined up to perform my church choir duties that weekend, however, since I planned to be worshiping at *two* altars on Sunday morning—named Billy and Phil. As music director for the church, I usually picked out the hymns to be sung, and one I had chosen for that Sunday was "Come to the Church in the Wildwood," so that during the service, when the altos, tenors, and basses would be accompanying the melodic line of the hymn's chorus with the reiterated chant "come, come, come, come, come," etc., they would unwittingly be urging Billy, Phil, and me on to the greatest heights of sexual ecstasy. I didn't really think we would need their urging, though. My irony was wasted on the congregation, of course, but it broke Billy and Phil up Sunday morning around eleven as I told them about it while we were still thrashing around naked in my bed.

I was primed and ready when, at 7:00 Saturday night, my two hot partners arrived—on foot, and both panting. Billy had eaten supper at Phil's house, and the two had ostensibly left for Joe Don's to spend the night. They left Phil's truck parked in front of Joe Don's house, in case their parents happened by. Joe Don had been apprized that he needed to cover for both of them, probably assuming it meant the two of them were going somewhere to fuck for the night, although they assured him they had separate destinations.

I wondered to myself if Joe Don believed Phil and Billy were headed for separate destinations. How would he feel if he thought they were going off to have sex together? Since he was apparently having sex with Phil himself, he surely knew him well enough to doubt that Phil Baker would be going off to spend a Saturday night with a beautiful boy and *not* have sex with him. If he felt about Phil as I knew I probably would in his circumstances, he'd be mighty jealous of Billy (of course, if he had any sense, he'd also be jealous of Phil.). There was a slight possibility Billy had just made an enemy—but since Joe Don himself was obviously fucking with Phil, I didn't really think he would make any public fuss.

On the way over to my house Phil and Billy talked about Joe Don—a conversation later related to me by Billy, who said he had to bite his tongue to keep from coming right out and asking Phil if he was fucking the subject of their discourse. Billy told Phil he thought it sure was a coincidence that Joe Don covered for both of them.

"Now I think Joe Don's cute as hell, and you know how horny I am, but if you're really tryin' to find out if I'm stickin' it to him, you know I couldn't say anything about it to you, don'tcha? Hell, I'd never tell him about what *we* do unless you wanted me to."

"Well, you told Pete about it, didn't you?"

"Well yeah, I did—and I guess I shouldn't have, but . . . but God *damn* I'm glad I did—look where we're headed right now. Still . . . well, all right, you gotta remember I was tryin' to get Mr. Harrison in bed, too—so if *you* wanna try to put the make on Joe Don, I guess it's okay for you to tell 'im what you and I do together."

"I don't know, Phil, there's something about that argument that doesn't quite seem right, but forget it—right now we're both glad about what the three of us are going to be doing in about ten minutes."

"Billy, *glad* isn't anything like strong enough to account for the way my Levi's are stickin' out—here, feel this baby." He took Billy's hand and put it on his bulging crotch. "Feel good?"

Billy pulled his hand away quickly. "Phil, quit it. I know it's dark, but still . . . . And besides, who says I wanna put the make on Joe Don? I've got all I can handle right now."

"Yeah, okay—but you didn't answer my question. Does it feel good?"

"It feels great, you know that—let's just wait until we get to where I can *see* it too. And *suck* it. And mine is just as hard as yours, but you're not gonna feel it here in public," and Billy started running, pursued by a laughing Phil. Thus, their arrival at my house short of breath—the beginning of a long night and morning of total, abandoned, no-holds-barred, hot *sex* with me and two *("Not one, but* two—*count 'em, two.")* beautiful, oversexed high school students.

We wrapped our arms around each other, and each kissed the other two passionately, and for a long time—we all instinctively knew we were not going to rush anything this night, that we could take the time to savor every exciting sexual nuance. With our three heads together following something of a three-way kiss (lots of dancing tongues), Phil said, "I can't believe we're finally together—this is gonna be so fuckin' hot. And I haven't come since noon Thursday." Billy and I traded amused glances at that point. "So if somebody doesn't take my load soon, it's gonna go off by itself."

"I think we all feel that way—I know I do, but let's don't rush anything," I said. "I think we ought to do something special here at first. I know my load's going to be *huge,* and Billy's going to shoot bucketloads, and Phil threatened to drown us with his, so we need to really *share* this extra-big first load each of us has built up—it would be a shame to give it all to just one of us. Past that, I want at least one load from each of you guys filling up my mouth, and another shooting inside my ass tonight, and I hope it's gonna be more than one."

"You're gonna get at least that from me," said Phil, "prob'ly more—and Billy, if I don't give you at least one mouthful, and fill the prettiest ass in Texas up a couple times, too, you can . . . I dunno what."

Billy giggled. "Maybe we'll fuck you if you don't. And hey, I'm with you guys. I'm gonna stick my cock so far down your mouths you'd be screaming for mercy if you weren't being flooded out—and I wanna blow loads in your asses neither one of you's ever gonna forget."

They both looked at me. "My turn? Okay. I don't know how I could keep up with you two guys, but I'll sure as hell try." I took Billy's neck in my hand and looked into his eyes. " I know I want the guy I love to suck my balls dry, and to feel my love for him exploding all the way inside his beautiful butt." I kissed Billy, then turned my attention to Phil. "And I'm gonna fuck your face until I give you plenty of evidence of just how hot I think your mouth is, and I will flat-out fuck that sexy ass of yours and give you every drop I can."

"Jesus, that's enough talkin' about it," Phil said. "Let's go in there and get naked and *do* somethin' about it. I've got a load I can't keep much longer." We laughed and broke our huddle to head for my bedroom.

They threw their coats on the sofa, but once in the bedroom Billy—my *take-charge* teen-age lover—took charge. "I think even getting undressed has gotta be special tonight—I've never been with more than one guy at a time before. I know you have, Pete. And Phil . . ."

I laughed, "Shit, Phil fucked the entire tenor section of the Mormon Tabernacle Choir in the park one day."

Phil acted shocked. "No I didn't—one of the guys was out sick."

"Well, anyway," Billy continued, "this is gonna be my first time, and I want every minute of it to last, and I want it to be, well, *meaningful*, and . . . I don't know . . ."

I put my arms around him from behind. "How about *mouth-watering?*"

Billy turned around in my embrace to grin, "That's close enough. Okay, look, Phil—Pete told me about how you stripped for him in his living room *the night you decided it was absolutely necessary that you fuck my lover.*" Phil giggled at that. "So get up there on the bed and show me, too—then Pete and I will each give a show."

"Okay, but I wanna go last. I wanna *come* first, but I wanna *strip* last, so I don't hafta wait before you guys start doin' whatever it is you're gonna do to me when I'm through."

"Fair enough. Pete—up on the bed and show us what you're gonna give us." I demurred, but gave in rather easily.

Phil said, "Don't you guys do anything yet—I'll be right back. Gonna get a beer."

I took Billy in my arms and we kissed tenderly. "This is going to be a lot of fun, but never forget for a second that no matter how *hot* Phil is, I love you—very much."

"That goes for me, too—you know that. I'm gonna get just as wild as either of you guys, and I'm going to want Phil to do all sorts of things to me—just like I want you to do 'em to me—but you know your love is the most exciting thing of all."

Phil was back with beers for him and me, and a Coke for Billy. "Okay, stop the sentimental crap and let's get dirty. Get up there and give us a show, John."

I slipped out of my shoes, kissed Billy and then Phil, and stepped up on the bed. They settled down on the floor to watch, backs to the dresser and legs and arms draped all over each other. Phil clapped loudly and made a megaphone with his hands as he called out raucously, "Hey buddy, show us your dick." He and Billy dissolved in giggles.

I won't attempt to describe my strip act—I thought it left a lot to be desired—but my spectacularly hot audience of two seemed to enjoy it, and certainly applauded the shedding of every article of clothing, and every bit of my anatomy as it was revealed. The biggest hand came as I knelt on all fours, facing away from them, humped my ass as deeply as I could, and at the same time drove my second finger in and out of my asshole energetically. My audience got in the spirit of things at that point, and I was treated to three fingers—mine, and one from each of the spectators—fucking me at the same time, just as eagerly, and as deeply as they could. I later rotated my hips and made my cock bob and dance as I 'worked the house,' and gave each of the two hungry mouths I found about four or five deep thrusts with what I knew they would both be servicing much more completely in a short time. I acknowledged the tumultuous ovation I received with deep bows—facing away from the audience to show them where I hoped they would soon be expressing their appreciation in a more palpable way.

It was Billy's turn. I joined Phil on the floor—naked, of course—and Phil began to play with my prick as Billy took off his boots and got up on my bed; I made Phil stop, advising him it wouldn't take much for me to come, so he settled for having me sit on his hand so he could give me something to ride while we watched my spectacularly beautiful and sexy young lover treat us to a preview of the delights he would be offering us this night. Phil's finger in my butt felt so good, I offered to perform the same service for him, and he was happy to accept the return favor. He had to undo the buttons on his Levi's to make room for my hand, but he seemed eager to accept my offer—and judging by the way his sphincter muscles clamped my finger when I inserted it, he enjoyed mine as much as I was enjoying his.

From his place on the altar where all three of us would soon be worshipping each other—which is to say, my bed—Billy put his hands behind his head, and thrust his pelvis forward as he announced, *a la* Mae West, "Hang onto your hats, boys—Billy Polk is gonna show you whatcha got comin' tonight."

He slowly removed his shirt, with plenty of hesitation and sexy leers as each button was undone, leaving his upper body covered still with his tee shirt—which he pulled on from behind to stretch it tight. His impressive abdominal and pectoral muscles were clearly—and temptingly—delineated, and his waist looked particularly slim contrasted with his chest. He drew the bottom of his tee shirt up and put it behind his head, leaving his tanned chest framed by the white of the material still stretched over his shoulders. He ground his hips suggestively as he played his hands up and down his sides, around his stomach and chest. He tweaked his nipples, and cupped his tits to show them off. Then his hands found their way to his crotch, and he humped slowly as he massaged his bulging basket. Mae asked us, "Ya like it, boys?" We stamped and cheered, and would have applauded, had we not each had one hand busily engaged in another gratifying pursuit.

As I watched Billy, I was enormously happy and proud that we were lovers. He was unbelievably erotic as he stripped, but at the same time his sexy display—through the unlikelihood of one who appeared to be so sweet and vulnerable being so sensuous— seemed to call attention to his youth and his wholesome joy in sharing himself with us. How could one consider anyone *wholesome* who removed his clothes in the sexiest possible manner purely to gratify the appetites of two horny men finger-fucking each other while they watched, two men with whom he planned to practice the extensive cocksucking and buttfucking his display inspired? In fact, you needed only to know Billy to realize how very wholesome he was. Compared to Phil and me—both of us young, but confirmed sensualists—Billy was a model of naivete. He *loved* sex, as we all three obviously did, but in Billy it seemed (no, I am sure it *was*) an expression of joy in living and youthful affection as he enjoyed the pleasure he provided his partner even more than he enjoyed gratifying his own.

Billy undid his Levi's, and gradually dragged them below his hips as he moved his ass from side to side; he lay on his back, put his legs high in the air, removed his pants, and threw them to us. We cheered him on. Still on his back, and with his feet planted far apart, he levered his body upward and began to hump the bulging crotch of his shorts, seemingly trying to fuck the ceiling. Then he flopped back down, rolled over, and continued humping—this time seeming to fuck the bed. He ground his buttocks in the most suggestive way possible, and moaned in simulated passion as he did so—or perhaps in only partially simulated passion. Then suddenly he stopped and got on all fours, facing away from us. Over his shoulder Mae West announced, "Billy boy here is gonna get this butt filled with really hot cock tonight." As he said this, he reached behind and lowered his shorts, so that the velvet globes of his adorable little ass and his irresistible pink hole were exposed. Then he lay flat and fucked the bed again, this time raising his perfect, now deliciously bare ass as high as he could with each simulated stroke. Finally, he rolled over, raised his legs, and pulled his shorts off. He concealed his cock and balls in his hands as he stood.

Smiling suggestively, he stepped off the bed and walked up to Phil where he sat on the floor. He put his cupped hands inches away from Phil's face. "Ya want a little taste of whatcha got in store?" (yes, it was still Mae West) and he released his cock, which protruded parallel to the floor as Phil engulfed it in his mouth. Both of Billy's arms went around Phil's head and pressed it to him as he delivered six or eight deep thrusts into his eager mouth. Then he pulled out, took Phil's face in his hands to administer a quick kiss. "Keep that thought." he said, and it was Billy, not Mae, who delivered that line. Then, with his prick wagging deliciously, he *oozed* over to me and rested the tip of his prick on my lips. The immortal Mae was back with us: "Go ahead, big boy, try a little sample." He took hold of my head and slid his prick *very* slowly, deep into my throat. Then, just as he *s-l-o-w-l-y* pulled it back almost to the point of withdrawal, he re-inserted it in the sexiest *slow motion* imaginable, and cycled it in and out that way for a delicious few minutes while my hands caressed his undulating buttocks. Finally he stopped, leaned over and kissed me very sweetly and whispered quietly in my ear, "I love you, Pete."

I've never known exactly what it means when it is said that someone "beams" at another; nonetheless, I'm sure that's what I did at my sweet young lover as he stood and smiled down at me.

He put his hands on his hips and posed for us, his long, beautiful cock jutting straight out from his trim body. Mae's final announcement ensued: "That's all boys, if ya liked whatcha saw, how about givin' me a hand?" Phil and I freed our hands and applauded madly. Billy silenced us, "No. I meant for both of you to *really* give me a hand" As he said this he was running his hands over his chest and down his stomach, cupping his cock and balls, and then up between his legs to his ass, and back to his chest. Phil and I needed no further invitation. We sprang to our feet and began giving Billy our hands, running them over his exciting young body as he laughed. He gave both of us a quick, friendly kiss, and pulled me down to the floor with him. "Okay, Phil, get busy—looks like you're the only one with clothes on around here." We held each other as Phil shed his boots and prepared to take his turn.

Billy's was 'a hard act to follow,' to use a not entirely inappropriate vaudeville expression, but, not surprisingly, Phil provided a breathtaking demonstration of his eroticism. Some of what he did I had already seen as he had performed his seductive show for me in my living room earlier, but much of it was new. He first spent a good deal of time flexing his muscles and pulling up his shirt to reveal his truly impressive stomach and chest musculature, along with considerable gyration of his hips, and thrusting of his pelvis. As he faced away and rolled his hips, his ass was a mouth-watering sight, encased by tight pants that emphasized, rather than hid, the generous, perfectly rounded shape of his buttocks.

He looked back over his shoulder and grinned at us as he made a great show of unbuttoning his Levi's, and slowly pulling them down enough to expose his ass, still covered by his shorts. Then he leaned all the way over and pulled his shorts down as well—presenting the impressive spectacle of Phil Baker's naked ass for our appreciation. We clapped and whistled, and he reached back to spread his cheeks as far as he could, and wiggled his ass temptingly. His asshole looked good enough to eat—Billy and I agreed on that, and both determined to do exactly that later on.

Phil pulled his shorts up over his buttocks, and lay on his back to remove his pants, as Billy had—feet toward us. Once that was done, he raised his legs in the air, and again exposed the perfection of his muscular ass for us to enjoy when he doffed his shorts. He rolled to his stomach and pulled his knees up, so that he was kneeling with his face on the bed and his majestic bare ass high in the air. He finger-fucked himself for a few minutes before he stood, facing away from us, and began to hum a mindless ditty and rub his hands all over his body while he performed a seductive kind of dance—especially marked by swiveling hips and pelvic thrusts. As he danced, he gradually turned to face us, revealing that his prick and balls were covered by the tee shirt that he was stretching down over them; there was no hiding the size and beauty of his endowment—emphasized by the masking shirt.

He turned away, and pulled his tee-shirt over his head, then turned back, concealing his prick and balls in his cupped hands. He stepped off the bed, over to Billy. He leaned down and kissed Billy, came over to me, and did the same, still coyly hiding his cock and balls. Then he went back to the bed, and knelt on all fours on it, facing away from us. His legs were spread as he knelt, so that hanging down low beneath his buttocks and the tantalizing crevice of his ass, were the two huge globes of his astonishing balls. He wriggled his hips from side to side, so that his scrotum swayed freely. Looking over his shoulder, Phil smiled, "Anyone want to take a little lick on these big balls? They're never gonna be this big again, 'cause I don't think I'll ever be able to go this long without emptyin' 'em again."

Billy and I stood and approached the kneeling giant stud. Billy put one hand on Phil's back, and caressed his ass with the other. "After you, Pete." I moved in and licked and sucked Phil's balls avidly—not something that could be done very gracefully, given our relative positions, but I did my best, and both Phil and I groaned our enjoyment. I stopped sucking and buried my face in Phil's ass to tongue-fuck him for a moment before 'yielding the floor' to Billy. As my young lover leaned over and began the delicious feast, my hand wandered to *his* ass and caressed it as he licked; once again, both licker and lick-ee expressed enjoyment vocally.

Without turning around, Phil said, "That was the appetizer, now you get a little sample of the main course." And with that he used one hand to present that "main course" (as had also referred to it the night he had first offered himself to me) by pointing his cock far behind him, under his balls. Billy moved in and put one hand under Phil's prick, and held it as he began to suck. I suppose I should have been made uneasy by the sight of my lover kneeling at the ass of a sexy stud, while he feasted on his big prick, but it looked indescribably exciting. I caressed Billy's ass and reached through his legs to play with his balls and prick while he sucked Phil. Billy stopped. "Now you, Pete." As I took Phil's prick in my hand and closed my mouth over the big cock-head offered to me, Billy played with *my* ass, but kept his face only inches away from mine, and he watched closely and murmured his encouragement as I began to suck in earnest. "That makes me so hot, Pete. Eat it like I'm gonna eat yours, and you're gonna eat mine. Oh God, that is so sexy." Phil's cock tasted wonderful, and his big balls felt wonderful pressed up against my forehead. Finally Phil made me stop, and he stood up on the bed.

As I looked up at him, his body appeared to be a model for the Colossus of Rhodes—"with conquering limbs astride from land to land," and all that. What the Colossus didn't feature (as far as we know) was the huge, throbbing prick that stood straight out from Phil's magnificent body. "That's enough show, guys, somebody's gotta take this load, or I'm gonna lose it."

I stood, and pulled Billy to his feet to kiss him lightly. "Let's eat some cock." We both moved in, and without any particular planning, we worked very well together to service Phil's hot meat. We licked and sucked his balls and we took turns driving our mouths down onto his shaft until the cock-head was deep in our throats. Billy put his mouth at the side of the base of Phil's prick and told me to do the same. We provided a sheath which Phil fucked into while we sucked and licked up and down his big shaft, with our lips often meeting over it, and our darting tongues often meeting under it along the way, and each time we both found the pulsating head, we held it between our two mouths as we kissed.

Phil was moaning in ecstasy as we ended a particularly vigorous dual traversal of his monster and were locked in a kiss including the head. "Keep kissing, I'm gonna come." He seized his cock, and with just a few strokes he directed his emission over Billy's and my mouths as we kissed, on our foreheads, our cheeks, and our noses. Phil's orgasm seemed endless—he was almost *shouting* with total abandon as he continued to bathe us in his hot discharge.

"Take my fuckin' load—oh God, take my come. Fuck. Fuck, you guys—I'm gonna come all over you."

In truth, I never saw a bigger load. Billy's face and mine were virtually covered by it, but we kept kissing and gradually opened our mouths sufficiently to let some of the generous hot gift drip into them. Finally, with Phil panting from exertion, and his still huge, come-covered prick resting on our noses, we began to lick the formidable shaft again, and to suck every drop from it. Phil had a hand on each head as we continued to service him, and said hoarsely, "Oh God, that felt so fuckin' good. You guys're terrific."

Neither Billy nor I had yet made a move to clean off the come that dripped from our foreheads and eyebrows onto our cheeks, and even onto our chests. Of course, when it had dripped within tongue range, we managed to eat what we could. Phil stepped off the bed and stood between us, one massive arm around each, grinning hugely. "You guys are fuckin' *covered* with it. Here, let me help you." He licked a generous amount of come from my face and kissed me so that I could suck it from his tongue. He did the same for Billy. Then I licked some from Billy's chest and gave it to Phil, and so forth, until all three of us had managed to lick up and literally *share* all of Phil's plentiful offering. We huddled, hugged and kissed for quite a while, until Billy and I declared we also needed to relieve the pressure of a two-day buildup of come.

Phil volunteered to do what he could to take both of us at the same time. "It would be so hot if both you guys could shoot at the same time—what a load that would make." He knelt, and did his best to suck our two pricks at the same time. However enjoyable this might have been, it was not especially efficient, so he began to alternate his attentions; while he did so, he caressed our asses, and Billy and I held each other and kissed passionately. Finally, he lay down on his back on the bed. "Both of you get over my face and shoot your loads in my mouth."

Billy and I knelt next to him and masturbated frantically, as Phil moaned his pleasure and excitement. "Shoot in me—fill my mouth up with your loads. Give it to me, guys." Billy soon began to heave with passion, and his lovely long prick delivered an extended series of huge white spurts into Phil's open mouth. Billy was moaning in ecstasy, and I was nearing orgasm, but I had the presence of mind to cry out, "Don't swallow, Phil—keep it for us all." as my cock began to shoot copious jets of my own emission into the eagerly waiting receptacle.

Phil closed his mouth and savored our gift with a delighted "Mmmmmm." while Billy and I shook each other's cocks to get every drop of come from them. Phil sat up, and put his arms around us; we each kissed his cheeks, and he turned his head toward me and kissed me—depositing a considerable, delicious ration of Billy's and my joint offering into my mouth, then turned his head and did the same for Billy. He pulled away, looked at both of us, and nodded. Billy and I swallowed with great ceremony, and it was clear Phil had retained his share to swallow. The three of us looked seriously at each other for a few moments before we broke into simultaneous grins and began to hug and kiss, as Phil declared he didn't think he had ever taken a bigger load in his mouth than either of us had given him, "And Jesus, guys, *two* of 'em at the same time. You damn near drowned me."

"What a way to go."

Since some spatters of our loads were still on Phil's face, not all having gone into his mouth, I licked his face clean, and the three of us hugged and rested for a time, knowing that with the release of our first, built-up loads past us, we could now devote ourselves to a more leisurely pace, which would enable us to savor every minute of this special time together.

During our ensuing lovemaking, watching Billy and Phil together did not bother me, as I thought it might—I felt secure in Billy's love for me, and knew that the lust he felt for Phil did not threaten our loving relationship. The physical difference between the two was such that as they held and kissed each other, embraced and penetrated each other, I marveled and thrilled at the contrast between two such different—but equally stimulating—young men. Phil was seven inches taller than Billy, and outweighed him by something like eighty pounds. His massive body and superb muscles were that much more exciting to see when compared to the younger and trim—though very well-built—Billy, who seemed almost dwarfed by Phil. As a result my young lover appeared that much sweeter, and more vulnerable to me. Looking at them together, Phil thrilled me with *excitement,* while Billy thrilled me with *love*—although he excited me a great deal, too.

However, it was interesting to note that the younger, much smaller, less experienced Billy often seemed to dominate and direct Phil when they made love together. Billy fucked Phil's mouth or ass with an assurance, and often even with a savagery, that made it perfectly clear he was the dominating, virile *stud* who was in charge of their mating at that point—and the huge, ultimately masculine Phil obviously enjoyed succumbing to Billy's mastery. When Phil fucked Billy in return, he usually did so with a care and gentleness he never exercised when he fucked me; at those times he was clearly the aggressive, commanding partner—and I thrilled at being dominated by such a formidable, well-hung *fuckmaster.*

In a way, Phil was the perfect model for a man I would like to be fucked *by*, and Billy was exactly the type I most wanted *to* fuck. None of that is to say that I didn't *adore* getting fucked by Billy, and fucking Phil—it was *all* wonderful, and something of the "best of both worlds." The juxtaposition of the two physically differentiated master lovemakers provided me with further stimulation; an additional stimulating contrast was that both were so young, and yet seemed so sexually mature—particularly amazing considering Billy's relative lack of experience.

I was a very lucky man that night, making love with *two* golden, muscular, beautiful young men with boundless sex drive and magnificent endowments, which they eagerly and tirelessly shared with me.

Detailing every permutation of our sucking, licking, kissing, and fucking that night and the following morning, with cocks, tongues or fingers, would involve such a lengthy narrative, that I will only describe some memorable moments—"snapshots" of my memory, so to speak, cross sections of a three-way lovemaking marathon that was as astonishingly satisfying as it was prolonged.

Snapshot: Billy kneels on the edge of the bed, with only his toes hanging off the side. I can see only his hands as they rest on the bed, since my view is blocked by Phil. I stand behind Phil and study, kiss, and caress his epic ass as he humps deeply—the crevice between his golden, velvet buttocks closing and opening widely as he slowly, but inexorably drives his big cock deep into Billy's ass. The slow tempo belies the depth of his endlessly repeated plunges into my young lover's adorable body. His hands hold Billy's waist, and he groans his satisfaction, in counterpoint to Billy's feverish cries of, "Oh, fuck me Phil—stick that big prick in me as far as you can. Harder, Phil. Harder. Oh God, that feels so *fine.*"

I stand and move to the side, where I can appreciate the beauty of Billy's fine, trim body as he humps his ass backwards to meet each profound thrust of Phil's organ—which looks enormous as it is almost entirely revealed each time he draws back from Billy to prepare for another of the long strokes of penetration that are proving so stimulating to both. Phil looks like a giant fucking a small and vulnerable boy—but a boy who is enjoying himself enormously. Billy's head hangs down as he revels in the ecstasy of receiving this driving cock deep inside, and I caress his back and kiss the nape of his neck, causing him to turn his head and look up at me, his eyes glazed with the delirium of the master-fuck he is receiving. "Pete—this feels so good; I love Phil's cock in me, but I want you inside me even more. Phil *fucks* me, but you *love* me this way." Phil hears none of this, as he is completely rapt in his assault on the receptacle he is so amply filling. Billy and I kiss, and he tells me to kneel in front of him on the bed so he can suck my prick. I eagerly take my place in front of him and he opens his mouth to me as I hold his head firmly, and repeatedly drive myself all the way into the warmth of his throat, past the tightly-clasped lips that provide me with as much pleasure as the enormous suction he is exerting.

I lean forward and with my hands explore the wonderful country of Billy's back, finding my way finally to the twin mounds Phil is so eagerly dividing with his expert ministrations. Billy's ass writhes under my touch, and Phil's hands leave Billy's side to move up my arms to my shoulders; he pulls me in to him, and we kiss tenderly at first, but the interplay of our tongues becomes extremely feverish. Billy takes a big cock up his ass and sucks mine, while I glory in the feel of his service, and tongue-fuck the mouth of the hot young man driving himself fiercely into my lover's perfect body.

Snapshot: Phil's cock feels enormous as he drives it repeatedly into my ass. My entire body is suffused with an excited warmth that is intensified by the sight of his massive chest heaving with passion as I look up at him. He holds my legs high, and I spread them wide to accommodate his deep thrusts. I remember the glorious sight of his ass when I watched him fucking Billy, and I picture to myself how fine it must look now as he drives himself into me. Billy lies on his side next to me, stroking my prick. He often kisses the head of it, then kisses his way down its shaft, up my stomach and chest, and delivers his sweet kisses to my eager mouth. He holds his face over mine and smiles down at me. "Do you want me to fuck your mouth?" I declare I can think of no better accompaniment to my grateful reception of Phil's thrusting than the additional receipt of Billy's wonderful shaft in my mouth.

Billy straddles my head with his legs, uses his hands to pull my head up from the bed and hold it upright as he drives his cock into my mouth. I open my throat as best I can, and am able to take him all the way inside me; his pubic hair is under my nose as I suck gratefully, and he provides short, rapid humping movements to stimulate me to further oral worship. My hands hold his perfect, muscular buttocks as they dance so gracefully, and I pull his body as tightly in to me as I can. He murmurs his love both for me and for my cocksucking technique. I hear Phil say, "Spread those pretty cheeks for me, John," and I use my hands to expose Billy's lovely pink hole for him. Phil continues slamming his enormous cock deep into my ass.

Soon Billy is panting, "Oh god, Phil, fuck me with your finger." I feel Phil's wrist between my fingers as they separate Billy's cheeks, and it is clear his digital penetration is thoroughly appreciated. Soon Billy calls for more fingers, and he releases my head, lets it drop, and falls over my face, still fucking my mouth with real fervor. "Do it, Phil, do it hard." Phil steps up his tempo, and I am rewarded with a flood of hot come splashing against the back of my throat as Billy moans in abject ecstasy. I swallow and savor every drop, and once Billy has calmed down a bit, I gently suck him until he is obviously completely spent—all the time Phil's enormous cock keeps hammering relentlessly into my ravenous ass.

Snapshot: I lie on my back and look up at the perfection of Billy's ass—two magnificent curved surfaces framing the tight pink pucker guarding the entrance to heaven. His balls rest on the bridge of my nose, his long prick hangs down into my mouth, and I suck it happily, moving my head slightly back and forth, up and down, to service him; my hands reach up and hold his narrow waist, explore his back and the velvet surface of his buttocks, and occasionally pull his ass downward to drive his prick deep into my throat. My own cock is tightly held in Billy's mouth, and he drives his head up and down on it while he exerts tremendous suction, and his contracted lips grasp it firmly as they slip over the surface. Inside his mouth, his tongue plays over the shaft and head of the throbbing organ I lovingly offer him, and I repeatedly thrust my pelvis upward to feed his eager hunger. We both murmur our delight in guttural moans.

My legs are held high, bent at the knees; Billy's hands grasp them mid-thigh. I can feel Phil's large hands holding the sides of my ass, and his hot breath tickles me as he licks it generally, but concentrates more and more on saluting the crevice and asshole with his tongue. Finally, his hands spread my cheeks wide, and the delicately dancing tip of his tongue teases the muscular ring opening into the orifice he has so recently *filled* with the huge tube of erected flesh both Billy and I have been worshipping this night. Finally, his whole tongue penetrates thrillingly, and he continues his wonderful licking, but this time inside me—and this hot, moist, naked, quivering muscle is thrust in and out very rapidly, and delights me with the sinuous movement applied when he plunges it to the greatest possible depth, and holds it there.

Phil's superb tongue-fuck ends abruptly, and I feel him moving on the bed; soon his massive body looms in sight, and my head is clamped between his muscular thighs as he kneels—his smiling face and broad chest forming a perfect backdrop from this angle for the huge cock that protrudes so tantalizingly, directly over my forehead. His large hands rest on my arms as they encircle Billy's torso. He leans over, and his hands feverishly explore the younger man's back and sides, and then with one hand he caresses the perfect ass that delights my vision, while with the other he applies lubricant up and down the considerable length of his prick, and cups and rubs his throbbing purple cock-head with his palm to lubricate it equally. His lubricated finger probes gently into Billy, then two fingers, then three, and he moves in closely, so that the tip of his massive prick is at the entrance to Billy's body. I watch from no more than three inches away as he very gradually drives the vast bulk of his cock past the tight muscle, and it disappears into my lover—slowly, inexorably, seeming to go on forever. Billy backs his body to meet Phil's forward thrust, and he stops his sucking for a moment to encourage his penetrator. "Oh God, Phil—fuck me with your big cock."

Billy and I continue to suck each other avidly as Phil begins his slow, profound fuck, and his enormous ball-sac first rests on my forehead and then my nose as he thrusts. The huge shaft of his cock *glistens* and is golden and silken-smooth as it enters and exits Billy. I see the muscle of Billy's asshole disappearing into his body as Phil thrusts his monster prick deep inside, but emerging and grasping the shaft tightly, and even following it for a short time as it is stretched back. Phil's movement is slow and loving, and the length of his stroke is astonishing. I watch his prick enter, and *enter*, until it is completely buried; then it slowly emerges—inch after glorious inch of it—until I actually see about half of the head withdrawn before it starts its passionate plunge back in.

Billy's finger is now fucking my ass in the same tempo Phil employs on his, but he continues to service my prick with his mouth, and the sight of the glorious penetration occurring inches from my appreciative eyes does nothing to stop my service of Billy's long prick, which drives deep into my throat every time Phil's cock achieves maximum depth of penetration. The tempo increases, until it is frantic—and Phil's stroke shortens with it, until he is humping wildly, but his entire prick stays buried. With hoarse cries, his body freezes, and Billy releases my prick to pant, "Come in me, Phil—shoot your load for me." With a huge cry of passion, Phil obviously does what Billy wants.

Billy and I continue our mutual oral lovemaking as Phil's orgasm subsides, and he lies quietly over Billy, still buried inside him, and murmurs "Jesus, Billy, you're a great fuck." Finally he stirs, and begins to pull out. I watch his still enormous shaft withdrawing, and it glistens even more now—still wet with lubricant, but shining now with his come as well. As it slowly leaves the hole it has been filling, a sizable amount of Phil's discharge comes with it, and drips onto my nose as I watch

Billy's puckering hole gradually return to its normal size. Phil's cock—still large, but now relatively flaccid—flops onto my forehead and leaks come onto it. I can contain myself no longer, and discharge into Billy's loving mouth.

Very quick snaps:

(1) We form a kind of equilateral triangle as we lie on our sides on the bed; each worshipping mouth has a prick to suck, and each prick is driving deep to provide maximum satisfaction. The pattern of John-sucks-Billy, Billy-sucks-Phil, Phil-sucks-John is occasionally changed to provide maximum variety of *who* sucks *whom*. All participants perform superbly, and appreciative comments abound.

(2) Billy kneels at the side of the bed, where I stand, eagerly driving my prick into his ass. Phil stands behind me, pressing his big prick against me and adapting to my rhythm, so that he enters me gradually and is soon fully inside—and fucking me as avidly as I am fucking Billy; coordination is difficult, and involves careful choreography of our cocks and asses, but the pleasure more than compensates.

(3) Billy now lies on his back at the side of the bed, and Phil stands next to it. Billy's legs are high in the air, and as Phil thrusts himself into the adorable asshole presented to him, Billy's legs circle his waist. Phil fucks for a long time—his large, but muscular and perfectly-formed ass humping deliciously for my visual delectation—and finally he leans over to put his arms beneath Billy's body and pick him up as he stands again. Billy's arms are around Phil's neck and his legs are locked around his body, he is completely impaled on the enormous shaft, and they kiss noisily and wonderfully. I kneel behind Phil, spread his cheeks, and tongue-fuck him.

(4) Billy is lying on his back; Phil straddles his body—facing the beautiful young man whose cock he is riding, whose pelvic thrusts are driving his wonderful long cock upward into Phil's ass. Phil's head is thrown back, his eyes are closed in rapture, he licks his lips, and he bounces up and down rapidly and ecstatically. I straddle Billy's face, facing Phil, and feel Billy's arms encircle me as his tongue licks and invades me deeply, incessantly, and thrillingly. I lean slightly forward and put my arms around Phil, who opens his eyes and smiles at me, enfolds me in his enormous, muscular arms, and himself leans forward to kiss me. We kiss passionately as he bobs up and down on his exciting mount, and Billy fucks both of us simultaneously—me with his tongue, and Phil with his prick.

(5) Billy and Phil lie on their sides in sixty-nine, each cock deep in the other's throat, and each beautiful ass humping marvelously to drive it there. I lie on my side and eat Billy's ass as he humps Phil, and then tongue-fuck Phil's epic ass as he humps my young lover. I put my cock as far into each ass as I can, and hold it there, allowing the recipient's humping to stimulate my act of adoration.

(6) Billy lies flat on his stomach, his legs spread wide, and I lie on my stomach between them, with my face buried deep in the crevice of Billy's perfect ass; my tongue drives deep into him, and he writhes his buttocks appreciatively and tells me how wonderful it feels. Phil straddles my legs, and lowers himself; his huge prick invades my asshole and begins

to move in and out—gently at first, and then very fast and deep—and his massive body presses heavily on my back, as his deep thrusts are accomplished by movement of his pelvis alone. Although the ecstasy I experience as I eat Billy's undulating ass and receive Phil's savage penetration is overpowering, I still picture the sight of Phil's ass as he fucks—it must look exciting beyond belief.

Snapshot—a long exposure: I want to do a creditable job of sucking two cocks at once, so I have directed Billy and Phil to lie on their backs, facing away from each other. Phil spreads his legs very wide, and Billy's are raised and spread slightly. Each has his ass-cheeks pressed tightly against the other's, their ball-sacs nestle together, and their hard pricks lie up against their bellies. I kneel next to them and take their two cocks together in one hand to masturbate them simultaneously. I lean over and take both into my mouth, stretching my lips painfully—but the sensation is very exciting; the two shafts are of identical length, but Phil's is considerably fatter. I move my head up and down rapidly, and fuck my own mouth as deeply as I can with the twin treasures. Both of my partners express eager appreciation for the unusual sensation, and urge me to continue. In truth, it is not very successful, however fine it may feel for them or for me; I am unable to achieve very good suction, and my tightly stretched lips must do most of the work of stimulation—but my tongue assists, as it licks and dances over the shafts and heads of the two young, exciting pricks filling my mouth.

I stop sucking, and pause to lubricate their cocks and my ass generously, and then face Phil to straddle them, positioning my asshole directly over their parallel shafts. I hold them tightly together, and stimulate myself with the two heads, then I press myself down onto them, wriggling their cocks and my own ass, trying very hard to allow them both to penetrate me together, and feed my overwhelming hunger for these two young love-gods. It is very painful, and try as I might, I cannot take them together. They are both panting how very hot it would be if they could fuck me at the same time. "I'm sorry, guys, I guess I'll have to take turns." I drop Billy's prick, and plunge my ass violently down over Phil's—which feels wonderful as I bob up and down, and he humps upward as best he can. After a few long, delirious moments of this, I raise myself and Phil slips out, but I immediately move backwards and seize Billy's prick and position its tip so that I can plunge myself quickly and firmly down onto it. Phil's prick was considerably more filling, but I love Billy so much that riding his is equally as exciting, and I ride it with complete abandon. After a few minutes of this delicious invasion, I again take Phil, and alternate between riding these two splendid mounts for some time.

I am thoroughly, *wonderfully* impaled on Phil's prick, and resting for a moment with my ass planted firmly on the pubic hair at the base of his invading monster. Phil says, "I have an idea. Billy, get on your knees." Billy extricates himself and kneels next to us. "See if you can get a finger or two inside John's ass along with my prick." I lean forward, exposing the base of Phil's cock as it skewers me. I raise myself an inch or two, and feel Billy's finger work its way into my ass along with the massive bulk of Phil's dick; It feels very exciting, and I urge him to continue.

Phil fucks me gently and carefully with his prick; Billy fucks me with his finger at the same time, but a lot less gently. "Give me two fingers now."

I feel Billy's single finger recede, immediately replaced by two, and the sensation is unbelievably stimulating. Billy apparently locks his hand around Phil's shaft as I ride the combined bulk of it and the two fingers as though it were one gigantic prick.

Phil is enjoying this almost as much as I. "Can you take both of us this way, John?"

I moan, "Stick your cock in me too, Billy, I want both of you fucking me." Billy removes his fingers, kneels behind me, and very slowly begins to insinuate the head of his cock into me, next to the Phil's shaft; it is painful, but as the first time I felt a single cock penetrate my ass, the pain is replaced by an unbelievably strong euphoria. Phil's legs are widespread again, and Billy kneels between them as he gradually slips his entire prick inside my already thoroughly filled hole. Now the two began a slow dual fuck that is unquestionably the most thrilling thing I have ever experienced. I hold perfectly still, and my two young studs work slowly and carefully to coordinate their deep penetration without either slipping out—sometime driving in simultaneously, sometimes alternating their thrusts.

Finally their tempo increases, and Billy cries out, "Oh God, I've gotta come." Phil ceases his motion, and Billy's prick slides up and down Phil's shaft inside me, and soon I feel a thrilling eruption. He continues to move up and down while Phil pulls my head down and kisses me passionately as he tells me to ride his prick carefully so that Billy will stay in. At the same time, he begins to hump upward, in a rapidly increasing tempo that soon leads to the explosion of his load inside me. My ass, Billy's prick, Phil's prick—all are bathed in the wondrous dual discharge; my lips are pressed to Phil's mouth as our tongues writhe together, and Billy's arms encircle my waist, and his face is pressed against my back as he expresses his love for me.

We lie thus for a long, memorable time. Finally, my passion is such that I need release. I disengage from my dual penetrators, raise Phil's legs high and drive myself into his ass; he puts his hands beneath his body to support himself, allowing me to caress his chest and stomach as I fuck. I feel Billy's arms encircle me from behind again, and I reach around to pull his body tightly to me as I begin to discharge my load into Phil.

Interspersed between, before, and after these incidents, were countless actions of love and lust, of fucking and sucking, of caressing and hugging, of licking and kissing. Aside from the occasional time when one would be using the bathroom, we were a tightly-knit trio of lovemakers. We did sleep, off and on, and we had a rather hilarious nude breakfast together, as well as a couple of extremely inefficient (but terribly enjoyable) three-way showers—and one of those showers included a three-way pissing contest that almost got out of hand.

Each of us got fucked and sucked simultaneously; each of us sucked while fucking. Each of us deposited at least one load in each of our partners' mouths, and at least one more in each of their asses, in addition to the 'pressure-release' masturbatory orgasm we each experienced at the beginning of our encounter. We were together for a delicious and delirious seventeen hours; Billy and I each had six orgasms—Phil had nine. The four-way sex I had experienced with Hal, Dan, and Jim had been the wildest sexual encounter of my life up until that time—Phil and Billy shattered that record for me.

Our hugging and kissing as they left around noon on Sunday was tender, and we were all exhausted. Billy and I told each other how much we loved each other, but we also confessed to a lot of love for Phil at that point. Phil's exit line surely expressed all our feelings: "I really love you guys—*and I've never had so much fuckin' fun in my life.*"

And I think I spoke for all of us when I added that I had never had *so much fun fuckin'* in my life.

The ecstatic threesome we enjoyed that week-end was undoubtedly the highlight of my year at Antares; it was by no means, however, the end, or yet even the wind-down of my sex life there.

Billy and I continued to share our love regularly, and if anything our devotion to each other had been strengthened by the marathon sexual adventure we had shared with Phil. Rather than pretending it had not happened, which would have been a reasonable course of action to follow, we recollected and re-lived parts of it—both of us marveling at Phil's endurance and his sexual power—and it invariably stimulated both of us to greater heights of passion.

On two separate occasions, Phil called me quite late at night and asked to come over; I welcomed him into my bed, of course, and both times he was an almost insatiable stud. In the space of a couple of hours we would virtually run the gamut of sexual possibilities, and each accept multiple orgasms from the other.

On the second of those meetings, Phil demonstrated his voraciousness when he finished exploding a load into my ass while he was fucking me missionary style, then immediately mounted my cock to ride it to my own climax inside him—after which he dismounted, promptly raised my legs, and re-entered my ass for another fuck, culminating in a second palpable eruption inside me in the space of about thirty minutes.

I told Billy about the two visits from Phil, and he relished the details and re-enacted the more exciting ones with me. Phil also had sex with Billy again one weekend when I was out of town, and the two went to a movie together. That evening after the movie, having no other place to go, Billy took Phil out to Rodman's Pond, and in the moonlight, on the site of his first lovemaking with me, fucked and received Phil as he had me.

Phil had not known about the place before, and suggested that it might be a good place for the three of us to get together for another threesome—during daylight hours. He told Billy, "It would be so fuckin' hot to screw with botha you guys again out there, in broad daylight." Billy agreed with him that it would, and I had to admit it sounded wonderful to me as well. Consequently, the three of us spent a glorious Sunday afternoon that spring by the side of the pond.

The water was too cold for swimming that day, but the sex was too hot for words. Our pond-side threesome duplicated much of the activity we had enjoyed in my bedroom, even including the double penetration and combined orgasm of Phil and Billy's cocks into my hungry ass. Phil tried to take Billy and me into his asshole at the same time, and we did manage to both get in at one point, but it proved to be awkward under the physical conditions (a blanket on the bare earth, rather than a bed) and we had to abandon the idea. Phil had, however, thrilled to the feel of our brief joint tenure inside him, and said he wanted to be sure to try it again in my bedroom. Neither Billy nor I demurred, and although we were in the middle of our second triple fuck at the time, we agreed to a third.

Quite a bit of our sex play that afternoon was conducted while standing, given the circumstances, and our lovemaking didn't last as long as it had before, but it was fully as intense and enjoyable, and something about the three of us completely losing our inhibitions with each other under the brilliant blue Texas sky added excitement to an already unbelievably exciting experience; this same added fillip had graced my sexual encounters here with Billy.

The three of us were actually together a few days before our next, and—as it turned out—final threesome, but we did not have sex at that time. It happened fairly late one afternoon when Billy and I had decided to go out to Rodman's Pond to see if it was warm enough yet to swim, and also—whatever the water temperature—to make love there. As we got within a mile or so of the pond, we saw a truck parked there; we were both a little irritated—after all, we had never before encountered anyone else out there to keep us from doing whatever we wanted. "It must be Mr. Rodman," Billy said. "He's the only one who ever comes out here. But he probably won't stay long." As we neared the pond, Billy recognized the pickup. "That's Phil's truck."

We pulled in and parked. Phil was stretched out on a beach towel; next to him, on another towel, was Joe Don Griffith. They were both wearing their Jockey shorts, and welcomed us with apparent warmth. "Hi." Phil said. "We wondered who was comin' out here—we're just gettin' some sun." Billy declared we had come out with the same thing in mind, and we too stripped down to our shorts, and spread out on the blanket we had brought.

We all chatted casually, both Billy and Phil referring to me as 'Mr. Harrison' when they addressed me—Joe Don called me "Mr. H," as usual.

Joe Don didn't act as though there was anything strange about Billy and me being out here together. He looked extremely good. His body, like Billy's, was slight, but he also had good natural musculature. His butt looked very cute in his shorts, and his crotch bulged appealingly, as it always did when he massaged it on the corner of my desk. Surprisingly, neither Billy nor Phil made any veiled comments fraught with sexual innuendo, and Joe Don stayed pretty quiet.

Phil declared it was time he and Joe Don got back to town, that they had had plenty of sun for one afternoon, and they prepared to go. As they dressed and picked up their towels, I spotted something on the ground, and picked it up when no one was looking. Joe Don had already climbed in the passenger side of the truck as I stopped Phil to give him what I had picked up. "Phil, I think you dropped your toothpaste" I handed the tube of K-Y Jelly I had seen on the ground. This very large, muscular, handsome, ultra-macho *stud* blushed quickly, then thanked me. With a *very* big grin he winked at me, got in the truck, and drove off. I told Billy what I had found, and we broke up with laughter. Our laughter over, we tried the water and found it cold, and proceeded to do what we had come out here to do: make passionate love to each other in the great flat expanse of Texas countryside, on the very spot where we had first consummated our passion and planted the seeds of our love.

Phil called me that night and told me that he had said nothing to Joe Don about his relationship to Billy or me, although he did say that Joe Don had asked him if he knew if there was anything 'going on' between Billy and me; Phil had told him he knew nothing. He added that Joe Don had been very concerned that we might have suspected they had been 'doing something' at the pond. I told Phil that Billy and I had known since two days before our first threesome that he had been having sex with Joe Don, and that we had already discussed it, and agreed it was no one's business but theirs. Phil was relieved, and snickered. "Aren't you gonna ask how it is?" I told him I'd been curious as to *how it was* for a long time, but that it was strictly curiosity—I was not interested in sex with Joe Don. Phil snorted, "Yeah, sure. Take Billy or me out of the picture, and then what? You'd be sniffin' around Joe Don's cute little ass just like I do. Well, anyway, I'll tell you how it is—it's *great*. Joe Don is hot as Billy, but he's just afraid to show it—except to me. And he really shows it to me., too. I'll bet he'd be glad to show you if I suggested it."

I laughed, "No thanks, Phil. Joe Don's a nice guy, but I've got all I can handle right now."

"Well don't forget, you and Billy promised to handle me again soon."

I laughed to myself at Phil's assessment of Joe Don's timidity about showing his interest in sex to anyone but him. It was clear Phil hadn't observed Joe Don doing his famous 'desk fuck'.

Our third (and last) Billy-Phil-John encounter took place again in my bedroom one evening shortly before the spring semester ended—and while it lasted only around four or five hours this time, the three of us explored each of the other two to the fullest possible extent. As we experienced it, we all suspected it would probably be the last time the three of us could be together that way for a long time—if, in fact it would ever happen again. Phil was going off to college in a couple of weeks, and I had to return to summer school to finish my degree and face induction into the military as soon as I graduated. Rather than casting a pall on our love-making, it led us to exceptional sexual abandon—each of us fucked and sucked and kissed like there was nothing else of interest in the entire world.

That night I was lying on my back while Phil rode my cock, and Billy knelt between my legs and pushed Phil's upper body down onto me, saying "Kiss him, Phil." As Phil leaned over, Billy shoved his prick inside Phil's ass, where it pressed tightly against mine. Phil cried out in surprise, but in a moment was eagerly riding our two cocks together, gasping his enjoyment. He apparently enjoyed it as much as I had when he and Billy had double-fucked me again, earlier in the evening. I particularly enjoyed the sensation of Billy's orgasm flooding Phil and bathing my cock while I continued to fuck him.

Phil and I sufficiently hymned the joy of what we had experienced that Billy was persuaded to try it—but although he tried eagerly, he simply could not take both Phil and me at the same time. Every other possible sexual thing the three of us could think of to do we tried and accomplished.

We also had a lot of *fun* together. Billy was clever and amusing, Phil was clever in a rather clumsy way, and we enjoyed each other's company as we were enjoying each other's bodies that night. Phil took a great deal of teasing about his relationship with Joe Don, and took it with the best of grace.

At one point Billy seemed to get very serious, and told me he had to confess something to me. I sensed his gravity, and got serious too. "Whatever it is, Billy, you know I love you."

"Well . . . well, I don't know how to say this, but . . . but, well . . . *I think Phil is hot for my ass.*" He dissolved in giggles, and Phil plunged his face between the cheeks of Billy's ass and ate with huge, comic slurping sounds.

When the time that both needed to get home had almost arrived, Phil ceremoniously had Billy and me kneel side-by-side on the edge of my bed, our toes hanging over the side. He told us he wanted to watch us hold each other and kiss while he fucked us. Billy and I embraced and kissed as well as we could, given the circumstances. Phil drove his cock deep into Billy and fucked savagely for a few minutes before drawing out and plunging into me and giving me the same thrill. Then, after a few more minutes, he was back in Billy, and so on. Finally, his body tensed, and he shot a huge load into me. After a few minutes frozen like that, he leaned over and kissed my back and murmured, "John, in my own way, you know I love you." Then he withdrew his cock and put it—still fully erect—into Billy. He added, "And I love you, Billy." as he began to fuck ferociously again, still rotating between Billy and me, this time culminating, after a very long siege, in a joyous orgasm inside my young lover. He remained inside Billy for quite a few minutes, also playing with my ass, and added, "You know, the thing I really love about botha you guys is the way you love each other. I'm really jealous of that, and I admire you both, and well . . . oh, shit, I'm just not built that way I guess. Keep it up guys—you're both great guys, and you're both great fucks." He laughed and backed away from the bed.

Billy and I stood, and the three of us embraced silently for a long time. Before they began to dress I kissed Phil and told him, "In a way you're a part of our love, Phil—Billy's and mine. We both love you for that. Thanks, Phil . . . and we both love you for your monster cock and that hot ass, too—you're a *fantastic* fuck."

A day or so after final exams, I had just come home, and Joe Don Griffith telephoned. "Have you finished gradin' the Geometry finals yet,

Mr. H.?"

"I have, Joe Don, and . . . "

"Well, what I really mean, I guess, is, have you actually turned in our grades yet?"

"Yes, but, . . . is there a problem? You did fine, Joe Don—I turned in a 'B' for you, and it was a good, solid 'B' at that."

"Oh, I figured I did okay, but I wanted to ask you about somethin' else, and I needed to be sure . . . Look, Mr. H., can I come over to your house and talk to you for a few minutes?"

I was sure this had something to do with Phil, and Rodman's Pond—and probably Billy, as well. "Sure, Joe Don, come on over." He hung up, and appeared at my door a few minutes later; I invited him in. He looked extremely good—his Levi's were as tight as ever, and he wore a very tight white tee shirt, which emphasized his tan, and showed his trim body off very nicely. Still not unusually handsome, but—I had to admit—terribly *sexy*.

He sat on the sofa, and came right to the point. "Mr. H., the reason I wanted to be sure you had turned in our Geometry grades was that I want to talk to you about somethin', and you might get pissed off at me about it."

"Joe Don, I doubt seriously that you're going to piss me off, in the first place, and besides, what would that have to with you grade in Geometry? If you came over to tell me you cheated on the exam, I *would* go back and do something about your grade, but that would be about the only reason. Is that it?"

"Gosh no, Mr. H.—no. No, I want to talk to you about somethin' . . . personal, I guess you'd say."

"Does this have something to do with Billy and me finding you out at Rodman's Pond with Phil Baker a while back?"

"Yeah, it does. I . . . well, Mr. H., how well do you know Phil? It seemed to me when you guys ran into each other out there, that you were pretty well acquainted. I mean, of course you *know* him—Antares is pretty small—but . . . well, he's not in any of your classes."

"Well, yes, Joe Don, I know Phil pretty well, I guess."

"But not as well as you know Billy."

"No, not as well as I know Billy. I guess everyone knows that Billy is . . . Look, Billy's my student, but he's also a friend. And that has nothing to do with his work in Geometry, Joe Don—nothing. Billy got an 'A,' but he worked hard for it."

"Oh, I know that—I mean, Billy helped me with Geometry stuff sometimes in study hall, and he always knew it. No, I didn't mean to suggest you gave Billy anything he didn't earn."

I said, "So, what are you really getting at?" *As if I didn't know.* "Look, why don't you just get to the point. You're not going to piss me off, your grade's already been turned in, and as you know, I'm not coming back this fall—Uncle Sam's going to have me working before then. So, even if I did get pissed off, so what? And just to break the ice, Joe Don, anything we talk about here—I mean *anything*—will be strictly between you and me, if that's the way you want it. So—ask me . . . tell me. What?"

"Okay." He took a deep breath and jumped in. "Do you know what Phil and I were doin' at the pond when you saw us there?"

"You said you were getting some sun, as I recall."

"What did you *really* think we were there for?" I hesitated. "Go ahead, Mr. H., tell me what you really thought. Whatever you say, it isn't gonna make me mad."

"Okay, Joe, Don. I thought when I got there that you and Phil had been fucking. Is that what you expected me to say?"

"Yeah, it is, and . . . well, that *is* what we had been doin' until we saw you comin' up the road. I *think* I know how you feel about that, but I don't know for sure. How *did* you feel about it?"

"I didn't really feel anything about it, Joe Don; I just felt we were intruding on you guys. But whatever you and Phil do together is strictly up to the two of you—none of my business at all."

"Have you ever done anything like that, Mr. H.?" This was a serious question, and was marked by none of the sexual suggestiveness his speech so often connoted. Before I could frame an answer he quickly added, "And remember, this is strictly between us, like you said."

"Okay, Joe Don . . . yes, I have done that before."

"And have you done it out at the pond?" I nodded. "And that's why you were comin' out there that afternoon, wasn't it—to do it again?"

"Okay. You've told me what you did out there that afternoon. Now as long as you never tell *anyone* my answer . . ." He swore he wouldn't, ". . . that's what I went out there to do that afternoon: me and Billy—like you and Phil. I'm not surprised you figured it out, under the circumstances, but . . . well, why are we talking about this, Joe Don?"

He laughed nervously. "You know, I'm not really sure. Part of it is that I *want to* talk to someone about . . . about Phil and me, but there isn't anyone I can talk to about it. And part of it is . . . oh hell, Mr. H., I'm just gonna say it. Part of it is because I really would like to fuck with you, too."

I looked at him for a long time before I answered. "Joe Don, I don't know what to say."

"Just say *yes*. You know how I've been practically wavin' my dick in your face all the time—just never took it out of my Levi's. And, well, I've seen you look at it like you thought it might not be all that bad."

"Oh hell, Joe Don, I'll admit it looked very tempting every time you parked it on my desk, or my car—and *humped* it. You really kinda *displayed* it for me, didn't you?"

He smiled. "Yeah, I guess I did. You really turn me on, Mr. H. But I think you knew that, didn't you?"

"Honestly, Joe Don, I didn't. I knew you were teasing me, but I didn't really think you meant anything by it . . . I thought you were just being sexy."

"No, I *did* mean something by it—I was just afraid to say anything to you. Then I saw how you and Billy were gettin' to be really special friends, and knowin' how Phil and I were special friends . . . well, anyway, I figured you probably wouldn't be interested in me anyway."

"Normally, I would be interested, Joe Don. You're a very attractive guy, but . . . well, I feel something very special about Billy."

'Hey, I understand, Mr. H. Billy's a really good lookin' guy, and a terrific person, too, and I feel the same way about Phil that you do about Billy."

"You mean you're in love with Phil, is that it, Joe Don?"

He paused a moment, and then exhaled deeply. "Yeah, that's it. And I know Phil really *likes* me—we have an incredible time together—but I also know he plays around all the time. Hell, he even tells me about it."

"He tells you who he plays around with?"

"No—I've tried to get him to a few times, but he won't say. He even says there are a couple of guys in Antares he messes around with some. Mr. H., don't get mad, but . . . well, is it you and Billy?"

"I'm not really going to answer that, Joe Don. But tell me, what if I *did* say it was?"

"It'd be okay."

"But there's really no need for you to know, is there?" He shook his head. "So, okay, let's don't even go into that. Tell me about you and Phil."

He recounted being attracted to Phil when he had been in eighth grade—the older boy was already very well developed, and growing into star-athlete status in the high school. When Joe Don had entered high school, and got on the football team, he began to try to stand near Phil when they showered. Finally, Phil began to notice him, and once, when Joe Don was unable to hide an erection, Phil playfully grabbed it and said something about his "growing up." He then asked Joe Don if he thought his cock would grow up like his own, which he began to stroke until he also had an erection. Joe Don had taken hold of Phil's hard cock, and was hooked from that moment on. The moment had passed as a casual sexual lark. "I'll tell you, Mr. H., I'd seen a lotta dicks before, but I hadn't ever seen or felt one that big—and I'd never wanted anything as much as I did Phil's great big ol' cock. I'd never sucked dick before, but I knew I wanted to suck him off."

Soon Phil began to befriend Joe Don, and halfway through his first freshman semester they had sex in the back of Phil's truck. Their lovemaking was strictly oral at first—sucking and licking—but soon graduated to serious kissing as well. *(So much for Phil's protestations to Billy about never having kissed a guy before.)* Phil gradually sold Joe Don on the idea of taking a cock up his ass, and they tried many times before Joe Don was able to accommodate Phil's huge shaft. But by the end of the semester, Phil was fucking the younger boy regularly, and Joe Don was completely in love. Phil didn't take Joe Don's dick up his ass until a year later. I smiled to myself as he told me that, and I discovered that Joe Don had been 'number two' on Phil's list of guys who had fucked him—with Billy as 'number one', and myself as 'number five.'

In essence, Joe Don said he was in love with Phil, but he knew that his older love-object fucked other guys—and he felt he could tolerate the situation if Phil would continue to make love with him.

"Joe Don, Phil seems to be a pretty wild, free spirit. But he's a nice guy, and you're lucky to have him to yourself as much as you do, I think. And I'll bet in his own way, he loves you, too."

"I know. He tells me he does, and I'm lucky for that. I guess I just have to settle for sharing him."

"So why are you here, wanting to fuck with me? Is this a way to get back at Phil?"

"No .. no, I .. I just want to go to bed with you once, too—like Billy does, and like *I think* Phil does. I know I'll probably never have the chance again, and I know it wouldn't make any difference to Phil—damn it. Even so, I'd never tell him about it, and even if I did I wouldn't tell him *who*. And I'd sure never say anything to Billy about it." He stood, walked over to the chair where I sat, and put his hands on my shoulders. "Mr. H., take me to bed. Just once, make love to me."

"Joe Don, I don't know if we should . . . "

"But do you *want* to?"

I reached out and took his waist in my hands and pulled him in to me. "Yes, Joe Don—I want to."

He smiled, leaned down, and kissed my lips very sweetly. "Then *do it*, Mr. H." He took a step backwards, pulled his tee-shirt over his head, and began to unbutton his Levi's. "Make love to me—I've been wanting you to all year." He threw his shirt on the floor, and dragged his Levi's to his knees. He was wearing no underwear, and his hard cock popped out of his pants as it was released, and stood out straight from his body. It was not as long as Billy's or as fat as Phil's, but it was certainly large enough to be very satisfying. and it was extremely pretty—smooth and white, circumcised, and bobbing temptingly. He stood there, hands on hips, while I admired him. Then he turned around and showed me his ass (very, very *cute*), and said over his shoulder. "Anything you want, Mr. H.—it's yours if you want it." He turned and stepped back in to me, so that his prick was bobbing only about three inches from my mouth. "I hope you want it."

I knelt before him, reached between his legs, and moved one hand up until I was fondling his ass, then with my other I drew him in to me, took hold of his prick, and looked up at him. "I want it very much. Give it to me." Then I guided his prick to my lips, opened my mouth, and took every inch of it into my throat as I began to suck it.

His hands cradled my head and he began to fuck my mouth vigorously. "Oh God, that feels so good. Oh, suck my dick, Mr. H.—eat my cock." He slowed his tempo, but increased his stroke as much as possible while he fucked—almost withdrawing on each backward motion, and plunging all the way in until his pubic hair pressed against my nose and his balls slapped against my chin. I kept my head immobile, and he accomplished this entirely by humping his ass. My hand still pressed against his ass, and my finger sought his asshole while he humped—it was soon deep inside the warm, undulating chamber. My other hand caressed and squeezed his balls while he fucked my mouth.

His tempo increased, and he soon began to moan. "Oh shit, I can't hold it back—can I shoot in your mouth?"

I stopped sucking only long enough to say, "God yes, Joe Don, give me your load."

I was rewarded only a few seconds later by a massive eruption of his hot, creamy come in my throat, and his hoarse, delirious cries of "Eat my come. Oh God I wanna fuck you. Take my hot load." He continued to grasp my head, driving his now-softening cock slowly, deep into my throat for a very long time as he thanked me. "That was so hot, Mr. H.—Jesus Christ, that was wonderful." Finally, still holding my head, he pulled back, and knelt with me. "Thank you." We kissed very passionately for quite a while, until he said, "Will you do the same thing to me?" He put his arms around me tightly. "I want you to fuck my mouth and give me your load, too."

I stood, and pulled him to his feet. "I don't know if I can give you as big a load as that one, but I'll do my best if you want it."

He sat to remove his pants and his boots, "Yes sir, Mr. H., I want it bad." As soon as he was completely naked, I took his hand and led him to my bedroom. He sat on the bed and watched as I undressed, and once I had finished, he knelt in front of me and began to suck my prick. Holding Joe Don's head in my hands to keep my dick inside his mouth, I pulled him along as I gradually backed up and lay down on the bed, so that he was now kneeling over me, sucking hungrily. I locked my legs around his neck as he sucked, and drove my cock upward into his mouth. His cocksucking technique was superb.

"Jesus, Joe Don, you suck cock like a champ."

He stopped for a minute, and looked up at me. "I learned from a champ. Phil is a genius at cocksucking." He grinned, before he resumed his work, "And I'll bet you know that."

I moaned my enjoyment, and clasped his head tightly in my hands. His hands roamed eagerly over my chest and stomach, and soon I could not hold back. "I'm going to come Joe Don—take it." As I began to shoot into his mouth, he sucked that much harder and murmured his pleasure.

After a few minutes we both calmed down, and he moved up between my legs to lie on my stomach. He whispered, "That tasted so good—and you were so hot." Then we kissed and caressed for a very long time.

As he lay in my arms, I whispered, "I hope you can come for me again."

"I can come as many times as you want me to. I know I want a lot more than just one load from you."

We lay there and talked for quite a while, and I discovered Joe Don was not the sexually assured stud his pose suggested. He was rather shy and eager to please, and until today had never had sex with anyone but Phil. A year of Phil's tutelage had, however, created a master fucking machine. And true to his word, he produced orgasm after orgasm for me. His second one coincided with mine while we lay locked in sixty-nine, and simultaneously bathed each other's tonsils with our discharge. He blasted his third one all over me as I lay on my back while he rode my cock wildly, masturbating all the time until I erupted inside him. He came in my ass once as I knelt before him on the bed to receive his voracious thrusts, and another time while I was standing, bent over slightly to accommodate his apparently insatiable appetite to fuck—after which I turned around, bent him over, and returned the favor just as passionately. He also delivered a palpable load into me as he sat in a chair and I sat on his cock, riding it joyfully while we kissed.

He was sweet, he was hot; he was a raging stud when he fucked me, and an appreciative receptacle for my cock, however he took it. He seemed like an unusually large and masterful boy when he held me and drove his cock fiercely into me, but small and vulnerable when I held him and kissed or fucked him.

It was almost midnight before he left. He reiterated his delight at finally making love with me, and his oath that this evening's encounter would remain a secret between the two of us. "I'd like to do it again, Mr. H.—maybe it can happen."

"I don't know what the next two years are going to hold, Joe Don, but I really enjoyed this, and I'm glad it happened. Keep on *loving* Phil, Joe Don—I'll continue to love Billy. Who knows what's gonna happen? I know I'd *like* to be with you again sometime, somehow."

"I'll always remember it, Mr. H. Thanks for tonight—and thanks for being a good teacher. I'm sorry you're going away."

Out of a high school male student body of fewer than fifty, I had fucked—and been fucked by—three of them. It *must* have been something in the water. As it happened I was to have sex with Joe Don again, but that would be some time in the future.

I prepared to move back to campus for summer school and the completion of my degree. I was hoping to get through the summer before my draft board called me for induction, but I knew it would be close. Billy had to begin working for the summer on the Rodman ranch, and he would basically be busy sunup to sundown every day except Sunday, and there was no getting around it. We faced a long summer of being able to see each other only once a week at best, followed by my absence during Billy's last two years of high school. Neither of us wanted to face the reality of that as we spent our last night together before I moved away. Joe Don covered for Billy, and we spent that warm, starry night locked together in love, and sleeping in each other's arms out at the pond where we had first tasted the mutual excitement that led to our love.

The next morning, we made love to each other slowly and sweetly, and our kisses were extra long and poignant; we knew we had reached a difficult point in our relationship. We swore our devotion to each other and agreed that we would meet as often as we could during the summer. What the fall might hold, neither of could say. I would be in the Army (or so l thought at the time), Phil would be off to school at Texas Tech, in Lubbock (the temperature of the city park would no doubt reach new heights.), and Billy would be left in Antares. I told him he needed to find someone else to play with.

"Pete, I don't want anyone else. The thing with Phil just happened, and it was fun, but I don't see that kinda thing happening a lot in the future. I know I'll see Phil now and then when he's home, and I feel pretty sure we'll get together and fuck—and it will be great, and lots of fun, but it'll just be fun. It's you I want to be with."

"What about Joe Don? He's going to be missing Phil too, you know."

"I know, and . . . well, maybe. I mean, Joe Don's cute, and he's sexy, but it would just be . . . I don't know, different somehow. I love you, and Phil was sort of a . . . a hero to me, I guess, and when he wanted to fuck, I just couldn't say no. I honestly don't know what I'd say if Joe Don told me he wanted to go to bed with me."

"Well, I'll be willing to bet he asks you sooner or later—probably pretty soon—so you'd better think about what you want to tell him. And Billy, if you *want* to have sex with Joe Don, do it. He's a nice guy, and you're a horny guy who isn't going to have Phil or me around much—you've gotta do something."

"I guess I'll just have to wait and see what happens. But what about you? I know you're not going to settle for jacking off for the next two years."

I laughed. "Hardly. I know I'm gonna have to find other guys for sex—we'd both know I was lying if I said I wouldn't. I *am* going to be jacking off a lot, though—thinking about holding you in my arms, and feeling you inside me. Jesus, Billy, I love you so much. But look, we've got this summer, and we'll be with each other as much as we can. Then for a couple of years we're both just going to have to see what happens. I know that whatever happens, I will always, *always* love you, Billy."

"And I will *never* stop loving you, Pete."

"But things do happen, so let's make the most of the summer, do what we have to do for the two years after that, and see where we stand when I get out of the Army and you get out of high school. However things wind up after that, we'll always still love each other, and we'll always have the memory of one *helluva* great year together, at least."

"You know, I'm seventeen years old, and I've already got what is *absolutely* going to be the best year of my life pretty well behind me." He snickered, and the cute, sweet, funny *Billy Polk the Great Impressionist* added Greta Garbo to his repertoire: "Is soch a greeeaat tragedy, I sink I vant to get focked just vunce more zis morning."

My Bogart impression in answer was just as convincing, I thought. "I'll fuck ya kid, but yer gonna have ta fuck me back."

Both Greta and Humphrey got their wishes.

13.
THE LONG, *HOT* SUMMER: EARL AND SHANE

I sat up. "Hi. I'm glad you're here—I'd decided you weren't gonna be able to come." Earl was as he said, "I'm gonna be able to come, all right—a lot." He was groping his bulging crotch. "I got extra-horny driving over here thinking about it. This whatcha want?" I reached for him and assured him it was exactly what I wanted.

Although the time between Sundays, when I could be with Billy, seemed terribly long, the summer still passed by quickly. Sometimes Billy drove down in his mother's truck to be with me on Sundays; other times I went up to see him, and Mrs. Polk usually fed me lunch on those days, and treated me as if I were Billy's older brother—not realizing I was more like her son-in-law. On those Sundays I drove to Antares, Billy and I invariably wound up making love out at Rodman's Pond. On two of the Sundays he drove down to see me we went out to the secluded place in Arroyo Grande State Park where I had made love with Dan Chrisman, and once we drove up to Palo Duro Canyon to make love in a remote alcove of that natural wonder—sex outdoors with Billy felt especially liberating and thrilling to me.

I had told Billy about both Dan and Hal Weltmann, of course, and had shown him their pictures in my college annuals. He agreed that Dan was about as beautiful as it was possible to be, but he thought Hal was fully as attractive. My description of Dan's body and of Hal's dick intrigued him further. He regretted that there was no chance of his meeting either one of them, much less our engaging in a threesome with either of them, or—most desirable of all—a foursome with both, like the one Jim and I had experienced.

I believe Billy was jealous of Dan when I told him about how I had *worshipped* him out at Arroyo Grande, but he seemed to accept it after I worshipped him in the same way—in exactly the same spot. But he was jealous of me when I described the way Hal fucked me with his monster meat. He told me when he was studying pictures of Hal, "I hafta admit, Pete, I'd like to see what I could do with ten inches of dick." I admitted I would like to demonstrate for him what *I* could do with Hal's ten inches, and then watch while he followed my example.

I lived in an isolated garage apartment that summer, so I had no need to explain why Billy and I locked ourselves in my rooms during his visits, nor was the sometimes noisy exuberance of our lovemaking even noted.

I had other visitors on weekdays as well—mostly one-night-stand tricks I picked up somewhere. Jim Corcoran was back in Oklahoma for the summer, but he came to visit once, and we naturally resumed our "fuckbuddy" relationship for a few nights. Another was Earl Jensen, but it took a considerable amount of persuasion before I got him in my bed.

Earl was about six feet tall, with a large body, but well-built and handsome, a Nordic *hunk* with extremely light blond hair who had attracted my attention well before I left campus the first time and moved to Antares. He had an air of sexiness about him, and a slow, soft, hoarse manner of speech that seemed even sexier. He had been a freshman during my last year on campus, and I had lusted after him from the time I met him. He laughed off my first few attempts to proposition him—he thought I was kidding. Later, when the sexual innuendo had grown much more blatant, his laughter turned nervous, and he frequently blushed.

He didn't wear tight pants, so I was unable to guess what he was hiding inside them with much certainty—except that he had a nicely rounded, ample ass. The fact that his crotch didn't bulge inordinately didn't necessarily mean anything; I had several times encountered boys whose crotches promised nothing special, but who proved to be more than adequately hung. On one very memorable occasion I had convinced one of those boys with an indefinable bulge, but with an adorable face and cute ass, to go to bed with me—which proved to be a one-time-only 'toss in the hay,' I regret to say. When he stripped off his shorts, he reeled out a fat cock that grew to something close to nine inches as soon as my hands and mouth began working on it.

One night during his freshman year, Earl and I had gone to a drive-in movie, and I finally put my hand on his crotch and asked him if he'd give me some dick.

"Aw, Harrison, quit kiddin' around," he said, and he moved my hand away. I assured him I was dead serious, and groped him again. He let my hand stay this time, and as I continued to plead my case, I felt his cock grow and stiffen under my hand until it became clear Earl Jensen was packing *major meat* in his pants.

He moved my hand away again. "Shit, Harrison, you gave me a hard-on. You shouldn't be doin' that." He continued to remonstrate, and I continued to urge, until he allowed me to open his fly and pull his cock out, which took considerable maneuvering—it was a *lot* of cock. And even in the dim light from the movie I could see it was a lot of *beautiful* cock. I began to stroke it and Earl laughed nervously, "What am I gonna do with you, anyway?"

"Why don't you let me suck you off?"

"Jeez, you don't wanna do that."

But I was already leaning over and opening my mouth—and having to open it wide.

I sucked for a while, and Earl sat immobile as I did so, occasionally moaning how good it felt. I was hampered by his clothes, so I stopped sucking and began to unbuckle his belt. He didn't object as I pulled his pants and shorts down to his ankles, and he spread his legs so I could resume my work. Judging by the eight-inch dick Jim was regularly feeding me at that time, and the ten inches Hal was occasionally giving me, I estimated that Earl had around nine inches of fat cock—with a lovely big set of balls to supply it with ammunition.

When I had returned to my sucking, and opened my throat to take all of Earl's dick inside, he finally showed signs of life. "Oh Jesus, Harrison," he gasped, and his hands seized my head and began to drive it up and down his shaft as he began to fuck upwards into my mouth. I played with his balls and fondled his ass while I sucked, and he grunted and groaned in ecstasy. After about ten minutes he pushed my head down, burying my lips in his pubic hair and held it there as he panted, "I've either gotta get something to blow my load in, or you're gonna have to swallow it."

I managed to mumble around his big shaft, "Give it to me." and he started to fuck my mouth again, with renewed vigor.

In only a few minutes he wrapped his arms around my head and began to fuck my mouth with fierce, short jabs until he raised his body off the seat and froze in position, crying, "Yeah—here's my load." His hot cream began to flood my throat so generously I had to swallow to keep it from overflowing my mouth. His thrusts had resumed after he finished ejaculating, but as he calmed down and sat down again, they grew gentler, and he released my head and began to caress my shoulders. "Godamighty, Harrison, that felt so fuckin' good," he whispered.

I stopped sucking and sat up to look lovingly at him. "You can't imagine how good it felt to me."

He turned to me and smiled, "Nobody's ever taken all my dick in her mouth before." He chuckled, "Or, I guess I might's well admit it, in *his* mouth either—but I've only let a coupla guys blow me before." He ruffled my hair, "But guy or girl, you're the best so far."

I was still incredibly horny, and was groping myself as I panted, "Ever fuck a guy in the ass?"

" Jesus, Harrison, you actually want me to fuck you in the ass?"

"Oh yeah, Earl, it would be fantastic." I was groping myself frantically by then.

"Well, it ain't gonna happen. Hell, take your dick out and jack off and calm down. You got a han'kerchief to jack off in?" I did—and I did.

When my orgasm was nearing, I turned slightly to face Earl, and reached over with my left hand to pull his head in to me while I continued to stroke myself. I gasped, "God, Earl, you're so fuckin' hot, and your dick is so big—and Jesus, your come tastes so goddamned good." and kissed him on the lips. Surprisingly, he did not avert his lips, but he didn't return my kiss or open his mouth to admit my tongue, either. I continued to kiss him, nonetheless, until after I had discharged into my handkerchief.

He sat there for a minute more, then patted my back gently and pulled his lips away from mine. "Y' okay now?" he asked. I was not only okay, I was happy, but still I was disappointed that it had been so one-sided.

Earl did not shy away from me after that, nor did he avoid being with me alone, even in situations where further sexual encounters might have been possible. He was still friendly, but he never allowed me to do more than rest a hand on his leg occasionally. I pleaded for a return engagement, even reminding him that he had declared me the best blowjob-artist he had encountered. He promised me that someday he'd let me have it again, but all to no avail—he always gently, but firmly, declined. He had not come through on his promise to give it to me again by the time I left to go to Antares, nor had he when I returned to campus for visits during the preceding year, even though I had seen him a few times, and invariably renewed my pleas.

It was without much hope of success that I propositioned Earl again when I encountered him on campus one day early that summer. He was living at home—the small town of Dimmitt, Texas—and working there for the summer. He was only passing through town the day I spotted him; he had stopped on campus to go by the Registrar's office to straighten out some scheduling problems for the fall semester.

He greeted me warmly, as always, and we went to have a Coke. I asked him to stay, and maybe go to a movie that night. Although Dimmitt was less than an hour's drive away, I suggested he spend the night with me.

"Naw, I've gotta be at work early in the morning. Besides, you know what would happen if I spent the night with you, Harrison." He grinned, "I'd hafta fight you off, wouldn't I?"

I grinned back, "Well, I could suck you off while you fought me off."

"It ain't that I'm not horny—I am—but I really can't stay," he said.

"You remember you promised me that someday you'd give it to me again?" I asked.

"Yeah, reckon I do," and he chuckled as he added, "and I remember you give a damn fine blowjob, but I can't do it tonight."

I reached under the table and put my hand as far up his leg as I could reach. "When, Earl? I promise I'll do anything I can to make it enjoyable for you."

"Oh hell, okay. Look, call me some night soon, and I'll figure out when I can come back over."

"And spend the night?" I asked.

He laughed, "Okay—and spend the night. I bet you'll wear me out, though."

"I'll do my best," I said, and he gave me his home phone number.

I called him on Monday of the next week, and he promised to come to my apartment after work on Wednesday evening.

I remember that Wednesday afternoon and evening very well, for two reasons: it was when I started reading *The Grapes of Wrath* for the first time, which began my lifelong love for the writings of John Steinbeck, but I also clearly remember the excitement of anticipating Earl's appearance to make love with me. Fortunately my mind was so taken with the book, that I only occasionally began to wonder *when* Earl was going to show up. As it began to get dark—around eight o'clock—I began to suspect Earl might not be going to make good on his promise. When I could no longer see to read out in the front yard where I had spent the afternoon, I went up to my room and flopped on my bed. I tried to continue reading, but my disappointment and frustration diverted my thoughts too much to concentrate on Steinbeck. At some point, I fell asleep.

"Harrison, wake up." I heard Earl saying as he shook my shoulder. The bedside lamp was still burning, and I glanced at my watch—it was almost ten o'clock. "Sorry I'm so late—Momma and Daddy made me go to church with 'em, but I got here soon's I could."

I sat up. "Hi. I'm glad you're here—I'd decided you weren't gonna be able to come." Even in my foggy, just-wakened state I had the presence of mind to avoid voicing the less diplomatic thought that first came to mind: *I figured you decided not to come.*

Earl was grinning as he said, "I'm gonna be able to come, all right—a *lot*." He was groping his crotch. "I got extra-horny driving over here thinking about it. This whatcha want?" I reached for him and assured him it was exactly what I wanted. "And since I was so late gettin' here, I'll stay all night, and you can have it all you want. Sound good?" He didn't bother to wait for my obvious reply. "I'll hafta leave by about six o'clock to get to work in the morning," he said, as he sat on the edge of the bed to pull off his boots and socks, then stood to doff his shirt and pants. I had been wearing only my shorts, and I slipped them off while Earl was undressing. He stood there wearing only his skimpy white briefs, his enormous cock obviously hard and ready for action, bulging to the side and clearly outlined by the thin fabric.

I was stroking my cock as he casually slipped his shorts down, and his prick sprang out, bobbing magnificently not a foot from my face. It looked even bigger than I remembered it. His massive body looked equally desirable—naturally muscled, although not particularly defined. He had especially well-rounded breasts, with unusually large nipples. The hair over his cock was light blond, and aside from the blond patches under his arms, his body appeared to be hairless. He put his hands on his hips and whispered in his always-ultra-sexy voice, "Look good enough to eat?"

I slipped off the bed and fell to my knees in front of him, saying, "God yes." and engulfing his fat shaft in my mouth while I fondled his meaty ass.

Earl held my head and fucked my mouth as he murmured his satisfaction. "That feels so fuckin' good, Harrison. But don't go gettin' me off too soon. We've got all night, so take your time and enjoy it—just like I'm going to." He pulled my head off his dick and tilted my face up to look at his. He smiled down at me, "And I promise you I won't hafta stop at one or two loads if you want more."

"I want all you can give me, Earl."

"I don't think I ever blew more'n about five loads in one night, but the way you suck cock, I might just break my record tonight." He shoved me to my back on the bed and knelt over my chest. I looked up in awe at the monster cock throbbing over me, and he fell forward over me, placing his hands well above my head to brace his body. His cock now hung down in my face, touching my lips. "C'mon Harrison, eat my dick." I opened my mouth and obeyed his instructions.

I played with his ass while he lay over me fucking my mouth savagely, often driving his cock so hard into it that I gagged. Each time I did, he would mutter "Sorry," but would continue his brutal assault nonetheless. He also rolled us to our sides, and he cradled my head in his hands while he fucked my mouth, and he rolled onto his back so he could watch me crouch over him while I sucked his cock. He often held my head immobile and told me to stop sucking for a few minutes at a time, so that he could delay his orgasm, but he never removed his cock from my hungry mouth. He offered continuous encouragement for, and appreciation of my efforts.

After something like forty-five minutes of cocksucking, my lips were stretched, and my mouth was tired. Fortunately, he was ready before I had to call a temporary 'time out' to rest my mouth. I was on my back and he was kneeling over me again when he finally said, "You ready to take my load?" I nodded my head and murmured assent. "I wanna watch you eat my come, okay?" he asked, and pulled his cock out of my mouth, then rose to his knees as he began to masturbate fiercely. "Open your mouth wide," he panted, and I had no sooner done so than thick, white come began to course from the end of his huge cock-head. It did not shoot out, but *flowed*, so that he was easily able to direct all of it into my open mouth while he continued to masturbate. The flow was interrupted several times before it again began to course. Every drop of his enormous orgasm went into my mouth, and just as I finished swallowing, he shoved his prick back inside and seized my head to press my lips tightly against his belly. He rolled us to our sides and caressed my head as he moaned, "Jesus Christ, Harrison, that was fantastic."

He finally pulled my body upward and smiled into my face. "Best goddamned blowjob in the history of the world." We embraced, and I played with his ass again, which he was grinding lazily, rubbing his soft, but still huge prick against my own painfully hard one. He let me kiss him, but again he wouldn't open his mouth to allow my tongue inside.

I spent a lot of time kissing and sucking his particularly exciting breasts and nipples, which seemed to please him a great deal, considering how he murmured his satisfaction and how his prick regained its size and rigidity. We embraced and ground our cocks together again until I knew I was near orgasm. I whispered, "I've gotta get off, Earl."

He released me and rose to his knees, rolling me onto my back. "You want me to get you off? It's the least I can do after that incredible blowjob." He positioned himself between my legs, and leaned over. I thought he was going to start sucking my cock, but he only watched it from fairly close-up as he masturbated me. He stopped and grinned at me. "Will you suck my balls while I get you off? I love that." He re-positioned his body so that he crouched over me in sixty-nine, with his large ball-sac and still-formidable cock hanging down in front of my face. I reached under him to play with his magnificent tits while I took his balls inside my mouth to suck—and it was a challenge to get them both in. He panted his enjoyment, and stroked my dick all the harder. I was hoping I would feel his mouth engulfing my cock, but it wasn't to be.

Soon I could hold back no longer, and I muttered around the mouthful of balls, "I'm gonna come, Earl."

He cried, "Yeah—shoot it, Harrison." and continued to play with my dick, but also played with my balls as I began to erupt. He whistled his appreciation, "Wow, big load. You really needed that, didn'tcha?" He laughed, and turned so that his face was directly over mine. My come was dripping from his chin and his nose, and his forehead and cheeks were covered with it. I had apparently missed his eyes, and a single fine rope of white come intersected the line of his lips. He grinned at me, "You flat-ass blew a load. You gonna clean me off?"

I took his head in my hands and licked my come from his face, while he whispered in that sexy voice, "Yeah, you like that come, dont'cha, Harrison?" When I had finished, I kissed him again, and he still kept his lips closed. But after a minute he pulled away and looked into my eyes briefly before he smiled and said, "Oh, what the hell." Then he leaned down and kissed me, and his tongue drove deep into my mouth, as I discovered that Earl Jensen was as great at kissing my mouth as he was at fucking it.

We lay together, necking, and embracing for a long time. Earl put his cock between my legs, and fucked me that way lazily while we fondled each other—and he caressed my body as extensively and as eagerly as I did his. Between kisses, he told me, "I've got plenty of blowjobs from guys in the past, but I've never actually gone to bed with one of 'em—and I damn sure never did this with a guy before."

"You never had sex with a guy who wanted you as much as I do," I told him.

He chuckled, "Maybe that's right—you sure as hell wanted me, didn'tcha?" I agreed, and he added, "You ready to want me again?" His cock was by then fully restored, and his leg-fucking had grown serious.

I rolled him to his back, and after another prolonged period of licking and sucking his swelling breasts and prominent nipples, I knelt between his legs while I started to suck his cock again. He held my head and fucked upward into my mouth. I stopped sucking, and leaned over to kiss him. There was no hesitation this time—he kissed me passionately. While I was kissing him, I reached over to the large open jar of Vaseline I kept ready near my bed, and lubricated my ass. I rose to my knees and smiled down at Earl as I straddled his waist and lubricated his cock. He looked surprised, but then he began to smile as I positioned his cock-head at my asshole and began to wriggle. "You sure?" he asked. I nodded, and began to settle down. I watched his face as his prick entered me, and by the time my ass was nestled tightly against his pubic hair and all nine inches of his fat, hard cock were buried inside me, it was clear he was in ecstasy.

Earl didn't speak as I rode up and down his prick, but he moaned and groaned in joy as he thrust upward to meet my downward plunges. He pulled my head down and we shared rapturous kisses while he fucked me. As we were kissing, he rolled us over and rose to his knees, so that he was fucking me missionary style, with my legs resting on his shoulders. "Goddamn, Harrison, you are one hot piece of ass. I never thought I'd fuck a guy—but I love it."

It was very evident he loved it—and he fucked me for a full hour, again resting at times to prolong his orgasm, and occasionally changing positions. He seemed to be most excited when he knelt behind me and fucked me dog-style, but when his orgasm approached, we were lying on our sides, and he lay behind me in spoon-fashion, fucking me and masturbating me. "I'm gonna come." he shouted, and rolled to his back, pulling me on top of him—my back lying on his chest and stomach. He humped me wildly as he came, and although I couldn't feel it erupting inside me, I learned when I went to the bathroom later that he had given me another very large load. While I lay on my back over him, he continued to masturbate me, and only a minute or two after his own orgasm, he brought me to mine. I blew my load straight up, and it fell back down to coat Earl's hands and my stomach. He brought his hands up to my mouth so I could suck them clean.

Earl fucked me once again before we drifted off to sleep, and I awoke later to find I was lying on my face and he was between my legs, beginning to put his cock up my ass again. He fucked me for a long, ecstatic period before he came this time, and I returned to sleep with his cock still inside me.

It was just getting light outside when he shook my shoulder. "Harrison, I've gotta leave for work soon. I cleaned my dick off—you wanna give me another blowjob before I leave?"

I wanted to, and I did—and he seemed as appreciative as he had been when I took his first load the night before. I had been crouching over him when he filled my mouth, and after I swallowed, I rolled him to his stomach. "I wanna look at your pretty ass while I beat off," I said, and he murmured contentedly.

I kissed and licked his ass, and he wriggled it in pleasure. "Feels good," he breathed, but when I buried my face between his ass cheeks and put my tongue inside him, he began to gasp in passion. "Jesus Christ, John, eat my ass." It was, incidentally, one of the few times I ever heard him call me by my first name, and the first time since he had shown up the night before.

I tongue-fucked him for some time before I rose to my knees, and without asking his permission, I decided I was going to fuck him, if possible. I slathered Vaseline on my prick, and then lubricated his ass. He obviously knew what was going to happen, but he didn't say anything—although I think he was holding his breath. I positioned my cock at his sphincter, and steadily pressed until I was completely inside him. He never uttered a sound in protest, and if he was in any pain, he gave no sign of it. Once I began to drive in and out, he began to moan quietly, "Yeah, fuck my ass, Harrison. Give me your dick."

I fucked him for a long time, changing positions twice, and he seemed to enjoy taking it dog-style the most—as he had apparently most enjoyed giving it that way. But I was fucking him missionary style, with his feet locked together behind my back, when I began to ejaculate. I seized his head and held it tight while I fucked his mouth with my tongue and erupted inside his hungry ass He gasped around my tongue, "Jesus, I can feel your load shooting in me."

After we had calmed down, Earl looked up at me and smiled. "I can't believe that happened."

"Did you like it?"

"Shit yes, Harrison. It was great—now I can see why you were havin' such a good time while I was fuckin' you. But look . . ." he grew serious ". . . this is strictly between us, right? All of it." I swore I would keep our secret, and he smiled again. "So, if you want my dick again," and he kissed me lightly before he continued in a whisper, "or if you want my ass again, you better keep your lip zipped."

"I want your dick again—and I sure want your ass again, too, if I can have it."

"You got it, Harrison. Now I've gotta jump in the shower and get ready to go to work. C'mon in and wash my back."

We got in the shower, and almost finished without incident, but when

Earl was scrubbing my back, I felt his hard cock poking my ass, so I turned around and knelt so I could suck him off. He didn't take any breaks to prolong his orgasm this time, and fucked my mouth for a solid ten minutes before I felt his delicious come flowing again. When he had finished, he raised me to my feet and kissed me passionately. "I like the taste of my come on your tongue." We kissed for a few more minutes, then he sank to his knees and said, just before opening his mouth to suck my dick, he said, "Shit, I let you fuck me, and I loved it—might as well see what suckin' a cock's like."

He sucked for a long time, and I was forced to confess that I didn't think I would be able to get another load for a while. He confessed that he had enjoyed it, and was looking forward to picking things up right where we were stopping that morning—and soon.

When Earl visited the second time, we didn't pick up right where we had stopped the first time, as he had said he wanted—but it didn't take us too long to arrive at that point. He surprised me by locking his lips to mine the minute he came through my door, and after a prolonged session of extremely passionate kissing, he told me he wanted to get fucked again—so I obliged, of course. Once I had blown my load in his ass, he confessed that he had been looking forward to that eagerly since our earlier meeting, and that he was almost as amazed at the fact that he had let me fuck him in the first place as he was at the discovery that he had enjoyed it so much. After he plowed me in return, we snuggled and kissed for a long time before he picked up where we had left off the time before: he went down on me and sucked me off, savoring my discharge for a minute before swallowing it. He looked up at me and grinned, "Tastes even better'n my own."

Earl came over to visit four or five times a month that summer, sucking cock and taking it up the butt as eagerly as I did. I presume he may have continued to have sex with women, but considering the stories he told me about home-town guys who he fucked and sucked off that summer, and the ones who fucked him—including one who had, according to Earl, two more inches of dick than he did—made me wonder how he could have had the time and energy for straight sex also.

Before I left for military service, I suggested Earl look up Jim that fall if he was interested in continuing to share the kind of sex play we engaged in with a master of the sport. Jim wrote later that he and Earl had hooked up, and were having a helluva time.

Although the Internet is the primary resource for information on any college or university campus today, in the 1950s the school's Library served that purpose. I certainly found that to be true when I was an undergraduate student, but the location I most frequently sought when I went looking to find something in the Library was not in the stacks or the card catalogue, but in the third-floor Men's Room. I wasn't looking for information at those times—I was looking for dick. Just as the Internet is one of the main venues where gay men hook up with tricks today, bathrooms in college libraries were (and still are) a principal place to discover men—young and old—who might be interested in playing around with other men.

Over the course of my four years on campus I had picked up any number of sex partners at the third-floor Men's Room in the Library, some of them extremely satisfying ones, but I had never met anyone who proved to be anything more than a casual one- or two-night stand. Jim had experienced somewhat better luck during the year we roomed together, probably owing to his greater boldness in propositioning prospective tricks.

The summer I returned to campus to complete my degree I used the Library as I had before, but the exhaustive (and exhausting) sex I shared with Billy on Sundays, and soon began sharing with Earl mid-week, made my cruising for sex in the Library less important to me. Still, just as I kept my eyes open and my antennae alert for signs of sexual interest on the part of boys all over campus (I met the cutest and most insatiable guy I ever picked up for a one-time fuck in the Cafeteria line, for example, and several extremely satisfactory one-night stands developed with guys I shared classes with), I frequently repaired to the Library when I was horny.

On one of those visits early in the summer, I spotted someone working at a third-floor table in a clear line-of-sight to the notorious Library Men's Room. It was someone I had been hoping to hook up with, but hadn't expected to discover there, although knowing what I did about him, I wasn't surprised that it was where I finally encountered him. He was Shane Vaughan, football star, reputedly as big a fan of Hal Weltmann's cock as I was, and the one whom Hal claimed wielded a cock even bigger than his own. Naturally I sat at the same table, and struck up a conversation in the universally approved 'library whisper.'

I noticed that Shane kept glancing at the Men's Room door, and he must have noticed that I was doing the same thing. For once I was glad that nothing was happening in that quarter, which might have distracted him.

I introduced myself, and told him we had a mutual friend in Hal Weltmann. Shane's face lit up. "Is Hal back? I thought he graduated."

"No, he's gone, I'm afraid. I really miss him."

"Yeah, I miss him, too," Shane responded. "He's quite a guy."

"I've never met anyone like him," I said. "And according to Hal, the only guy around here who's anything like him is you."

As I was to learn, Shane was not especially perceptive, and what I had just implied took several seconds to sink in. When it did, Shane smiled as he said, "That was nice of him to say that," and his smile turned into a leer as he added, "And if you're talkin' about what I think you're talkin' about, it's true."

"Knowing Hal as well as I do, that's pretty hard to believe." I decided to take a bolder approach. "So tell me, Shane, where can a guy go to get a blowjob around here?" Shane was taken by surprise, and began to stammer a reply, but I cut him off. "Or, for that matter, do you know where a guy can go to *give* a blowjob?"

His eyes narrowed slightly, "What did Hal tell you about me?"

"He said you were the best-hung stud he'd ever met, and he only told me that because he thought you and I could have a great time together."

Shane relaxed, and chuckled, "Fuckin' Hal. Lookin' out for me, huh?

Are you . . . " he looked around, to be sure we were not being overheard ". . . well, might's well say it, you hung anything like Hal?"

"Jesus, Shane, nobody's hung like Hal—except you, from what I hear. I'm sorta average, but Hal always had a good time with me—I've got other talents. So anyway, you haven't answered my questions—where can a guy go to get a blowjob around here, or give one?"

He grinned, "He could go to my place." He began to gather up his books as he added, "Cmon."

I followed Shane to a rambling, well-appointed private home out at the Country Club, where he was living that summer. He explained that it belonged to a Mr. Warner, a middle-aged man who had asked Shane to house-sit that summer while he toured Europe. There was a fairly large swimming pool out back of the house, enclosed by cement-block walls, and completely private. We went directly to the pool area when we arrived.

"You wanna swim?" Shane asked. "I figure you can see you don't need a swim suit."

"Are you gonna get in?"

Shane grinned and took me in his enormous arms. "I sure as hell hope I'm gonna get in—and I don't mean the pool." It clearly wasn't necessary, but he patted my ass as he said the last, to let me know what he really meant.

I put a hand behind his neck and drew his head down until our lips were almost touching, and I whispered, "You can get in anything you want to get in, far as I'm concerned," and we kissed. He was not at all hesitant about kissing, and for a presumably insensitive jock, he was a wonderful kisser. Our hands explored each others' bodies—his was massive, even larger and more muscular than Phil Baker's.

He pulled his tee-shirt over his head and said, "Suck my tits." His chest was nothing short of awesome, and I worshipped his rounded breasts and surprisingly small and dark nipples as my hands played over his broad shoulders and huge arms. "I love to get my tits sucked," he gasped.

I said, "I hope you like gettin' something else sucked," and I reached down to grope his cock. It was down his left leg, fully hard and straining for release. Hal had not lied about its size—it was *stupendous*, both in length and girth.

"I love gettin' that sucked best of all," he whispered. Then he put his hand down the back of my pants and inside my shorts. His finger began to tease my asshole. "Well, there's a coupla things I like even better. You wanna fuck my ass? I sure hope so, 'cause I'm gonna fuck yours, if you can take it." By then his finger was halfway inside me—which was uncomfortable, since we were not lubricated.

"I love Hal's cock up my butt," I said while I was sucking and licking his tits, "and he doesn't hold back an inch when he slams it in me. I've been wanting to try yours since he told me about it—I'm sure I can take it."

"You're sure as hell gonna find out tonight," he said, and kissed me hard. "Let's get naked." He took me by the hand, and led me to the diving board at the end of the pool. There was a round table next to the diving board, with a stack of towels and several large tubes of K-Y jelly on it—each partially used—and a canvas bag in a chair next to it. Shane indicated an empty chair and said, "Throw your clothes there." He sat on the diving board to remove his boots. I was wearing loafers, and kicked them off. We were both wearing white athletic socks, and we left them on until we did some between-fucks swimming later on.

I slipped out of my shirt and pants, then my shorts, but Shane was paying no attention to me. He had quickly pulled his Levi's off—he was wearing no underwear—and mounted the diving board. As I turned to look, he was standing on the diving board, hands on hips, and grinning down at me over the biggest, most awesome cock I had ever seen.

I approached him, looking up at his spectacular body. It was *deja vu*. I had knelt before Phil Baker and stared in wonder at his huge and magnificent body, and again I trembled and my heart pounded with excitement as it had then. Given the fact that the cock jutting out from his glorious body was about two inches longer and even fatter than Phil's impressive meat, my awe increased exponentially. Phil was quite a bit more handsome than Shane but at that point I was considering only Shane's breathtaking body and cock.

It was obvious Shane liked to show off his body and cock, and was justifiably proud of them. His tone of voice suggested he was bestowing a great favor when he looked at me smugly, and said, "It's all yours tonight, John." Then he turned around and exposed his large, muscular ass. He leaned over and used his hands to spread his cheeks, as he looked back and added, "Even this."

I ran my hands up the inside of his legs, and with one began to fondle his balls while I caressed his ass with the other. I put one finger all the way inside his asshole, and he stood erect, squeezing his ass-cheeks together, and trapping it inside. He said, "Wait'll you see what I can do with your dick in there." He relaxed his ass, but began to hump it gently as he worked my finger with his sphincter. This was a talented asshole. He began to turn around, and I pulled my finger out just before his cock slapped against my face.

"My God, Shane, it *is* bigger than Hal's."

"Yeah, but there's nothin' like Hal's dick, You haven't really been fucked 'til you had that up your ass."

"I've always felt that way, too," and as I took Shane's cock in my hand, I added, "but I think this is gonna set a new standard." I was only able to encompass Shane's dick with my thumb and middle finger by squeezing it tightly—and it was so gloriously hard, I could barely compress it enough to do so.

Shane's hands took my head and pulled it in to his cock. I opened my mouth wide to admit it, but found I had to stretch it even wider before his cock-head could pass my lips. I stretched my lips as far as I could to admit it, but once it was in my mouth, I was able to relax somewhat, since the shaft was very slightly smaller. Shane was apparently used to his cocksuckers being unable to cope with all of his endowment, since he was very gentle at first. I sucked and played with his balls—which were normal-sized, but seemed small in comparison to his immense cock. He cooed his enjoyment and fondled my head as I drove my lips up and down his shaft. It took some time before I was able to take most of it in my throat, although I never was able to completely deep-throat it, but once I was comfortable with it, Shane fucked my mouth voraciously, relenting just a bit each time he caused me to gag.

Pulling his cock from my mouth, Shane complimented me on my cocksucking—he told me no one had ever been able to deep-throat him all the way, and only a few others had come as close as I. He spread towels over the diving board and lay on his back on it, saying "Let's sixty-nine." I stood over Shane's head, straddling the diving board, and fell forward over his body to resume my feast. He took my cock inside his hot mouth with one gulp, and used his tongue to heighten the effect of his very accomplished cocksucking technique. He often took my balls into his mouth along with my cock when he sucked—having spent some time sucking Hal Weltmann's prick made that relatively easy for him.

Shane specified that he wanted me to save my first load to give to him when I fucked him, so we spaced our cocksucking out, leaving ample time for kissing and resting—and my stretched lips *needed* the rest. During one rest, he whispered, "Fuck me," and rolled to his stomach. I stepped over to the table and opened a tube of K-Y. I lubricated myself, then applied it to Shane, who murmured contentedly as I pushed my fingers all the way inside him to get him ready. He rose to kneel on all fours as I straddled the diving board again, standing behind him and positioning my cock at his asshole. He grunted "Fuck me hard." and thrust his ass backward so that he completely impaled himself on my cock. "Aaaaaahhh. That feel so *fuckin'* good."

I fucked him as hard as I could, as deeply as I could, and as rapidly as I could, but he still begged for more. He never let up thrusting his ass backwards to meet my forward thrusts, and after about five minutes of frantic fucking, I cried, "I'm gonna come, Shane."

"Yeah, baby. Fill me up with come—I love it." As I erupted deep inside him he moaned, "Oh shit, yeah—I can feel you coming. Give it to me." I stopped fucking, once my orgasm was spent, but he continued to fuck himself on my cock. "C'mon, John—keep fuckin' me. I've gotta have it."

"Shane, I'm gonna have to take a rest before I can fuck you any more. That took a lot out of me."

"Get that bag over there on the chair," he panted. I pulled my cock out of him, and brought the bag to him. He was now sitting up. "Put it down there," he said, gesturing to the side of the diving board. He reached into the bag, and pulled out a long, bubblegum-pink object. "Fuck me with this," he said as he handed it to me. I took it from him.

I was holding in my hand an extremely lifelike rubber replica of an enormous cock, probably close to a foot long, with a handle-grip about five inches long on the end of it. I knew what it was, of course, but I did not at that time know it was called a 'dildo,' even though that name for such a device had been used for hundreds of years. "Jesus, Shane, where'd you get this?"

"I'll tell you later. Grease it up and shove it up my ass, and fuck me with it." He returned to his kneeling position and as I greased up the dildo, he said, "Use lotsa stuff on it." I applied the K-Y liberally, and as I began to insert it, Shane again shoved his ass backwards to accept it all—a *lot* more to take than I had been able to give him, even more than Hal had given him, I estimated—but he gloried in it, and fucked himself on it as eagerly as I fucked him with it, taking the entire shaft and even an inch or two of the handle-grip inside him at times. He took the dildo from my hand and held it in place while he rolled to his back and spread his legs as he raised them. "Fuck me again." I took hold of the dildo handle again and fucked him hard and deep, and he seemed to be in heaven. Finally, his chest began to heave, and he cried, "Suck my dick—but keep fuckin' me." I bent over him and stretched my lips wide again as he humped up into my mouth. "Fuck me—please!" he gasped, and in a moment his cock began to fill my mouth in furious spurts that almost caused me to gag, but I managed to contain all his discharge, and swallow it. I had stopped driving the dildo into him, when he began to ejaculate but he told me to resume fucking him with it. I did as he asked, but as he calmed down, I lessened the force and depth of the dildo's penetration. Eventually, he put his hand down over mine where it held the dildo, and whispered, "You can stop now. Jesus, that felt so good."

He pulled the dildo out, and sat up, pulling his softening dick from my mouth. He kissed me, and sucked my come-covered tongue, then whispered, "Great fuckin', great suckin'. Give me a little while, and I'm gonna fuck the shit outa you, if you want."

I asked him again where he had obtained the dildo, which he called a 'rubber dick' when I fumbled for a word to describe it. He laughed and apologized. "I'm sorry I hadda use that. You've got a great dick, and you fuck like a pro, but I just gotta scratch way down deep where it itches. That's what's so fantastic about fuckin' with Hal—that big dick of his can get all the way down there to satisfy the itch without any outside help." He went in the house to get us some beer, and then explained how he came to have the dildo.

Mr. Warner, owner of the house, was an admirer of Shane's amazing cock, and wanted a replica of the fabulous organ Shane regularly plowed him with. Warner was a wealthy and extremely generous contributor to the athletic program at the college, and one of the many privileges he enjoyed as a result of his generosity was free access to the locker room before and after games and practices. That privilege allowed him far greater enjoyment than he could derive from just watching the games; he enjoyed watching the *players* most of all, not as athletes, but as participants in his sexual fantasies, and in the locker room he often saw them naked, the way he always saw them in his dreams, but in the flesh—the abundant, muscular, delicious flesh.

Most of the athletes had watched Warner watching them in the locker and shower rooms, and were aware of his appetites. Some learned that parading their bodies for his enjoyment earned them small gifts of money, and those gifts were larger if they also displayed and manipulated hard cocks for him to see. Only with exceptionally handsome, physically stunning, or very well-hung athletes did the man offer more than a simple gift of money. He first tried to win their confidence—thinking, foolishly, that the athletes had no idea why he was wooing them—and when he thought he had it, he offered considerable sums of money if they would have sex with him; they almost always agreed to the arrangement. At any given time over the years, a dozen or more young athletes were enjoying his lesser gifts, and three or four were regularly having sex with him for money—although Warner was discreet enough that each of those who was selling his sexual favors to him thought he was the only one doing so. Shane's awe-inspiring body and prodigious endowment had captured Warner's attention right away, and by the third game of his freshman season, Shane had begun taking Warner's money for sex, and the two had been fucking each others' brains out ever since. Shane received a hundred dollars every time he spent the night in Warner's bed; converted to turn-of-the-twenty-first-century money, that would be the equivalent of twelve or thirteen hundred dollars.

Apparently unlike some of the others Warner was paying for sex, Shane actually enjoyed screwing with the older man, who was not only generous, but who was also well-hung himself, sucked cock like a champion, and enjoyed being fucked by Shane as much as he enjoyed fucking him. They became something like friends in addition to maintaining their "john and rent-boy" relationship, and Warner shared confidences about whom he was fucking with—and Shane didn't really abuse those confidences when he hooked up with some of Warner's other "boys" on the side for purely recreational, non-profit sex.

Exactly *why* Warner wanted a dildo patterned after Shane's cock was not exactly clear, although Shane said he suspected he wanted it so he could fuck himself with a believable Shane Vaughan stand-in any time he wanted. Warner commissioned a noted sculptor to create the replica—a close friend who was well aware of Warner's appetites, having shared a bed with him on any number of occasions when they were in college together. The sculptor drove over from his studio in Taos, New Mexico to begin the work of crafting the lifelike dildo. He originally planned to do a life-cast from Shane's erect cock, but it didn't work—Shane lost his hard-on each time they began the casting—so he took endless measurements and photographs of Shane's cock from all angles while Shane was getting fucked by Warner, and his enormous cock was at his most impressive.

"My dick is biggest and hardest whenever I've got a dick up my ass," Shane admitted. He also admitted later what I came to suspect when he fucked me: that probably the main reason Warner wanted the dildo was that he needed something like that to keep Shane's cock huge and hard while he got fucked by it.

The sculptor returned to Taos to produce his commissioned work. The painstakingly detailed replica of Shane's cock was originally sculpted in some medium Shane did not know—he thought it may have been wax—and then a mold was prepared to make rubber castings. Warner had a half-dozen copies of the dildo, Sean himself had three, and the sculptor had kept a few for himself. All this was some thirty-five years before the popular Doc Johnson dildos began appearing on the market—cast live from the better-hung among famous porn stars, heralded by the popular Jeff Stryker model.

Shane was proud of his dildo, and justifiably so. I compared the dildo to the original and it was an amazingly exact reproduction of the model for it. Shane especially enjoyed the idea that he was fucking himself with his own cock, and he was pleased that Warner had taken one with him on his European trip.

"But I want the real thing up my ass," I told him when he had finished his account. He grinned and promised me I would get it as much as I wanted. By that time I was ready for it, and so we spread mats on the concrete apron around the pool to resume our lovemaking. Shane lay on his back, held his arms up to me, and said, "Get down here and fuck my mouth while you suck my dick."

I knelt over him in sixty-nine, and opened *wide* again. We double-sucked happily for several minutes before Shane moaned, "Why don'tcha ride my dick?" I was more than hungry to do just that, so I reversed my body and grinned down at him while I reached for the K-Y he had thoughtfully placed near the mat. He grinned back, "Yeah, I wanna fuck that pretty ass of yours."

It had been a long time since I had taken Hal's monster cock up my ass—the closest to Shane's I had ever had—but Earl had been plowing me regularly (had, in fact, fucked me only the night before), so I was reasonably ready to take the astonishingly huge shaft I greased up after I prepared myself for it. I *hoped* I was ready, at any rate. I *knew* I wanted it, and I trembled with anticipation as I held the shaft tightly in my hand and positioned my asshole at the tip, and then began to wriggle back and forth to admit it.

I was so hungry to get fucked by this matchless cock, that I had no trouble whatever in taking it inside, and it felt nothing short of sensational as it began to slide into me, but once the head and an inch or two were inside, it began to go limp. Shane gripped his cock hard and tried to force it farther inside as he humped upward, but it was not working. He reached over his head to get his dildo, which he had also placed in readiness next to the K-Y. "Turn around and fuck me with this while I fuck you." That was when I suspected Warner's main reason for having the dildo fashioned.

I kept Shane's cock inside me as I revolved my body on it. He spread his legs wide, and bent his knees while I applied more K-Y to his still well-lubricated asshole. I began to insert the dildo, and he moaned and gasped his encouragement, and as it went in, I could feel his cock growing and stiffening inside me. I fucked Shane's ass with the dildo, and as I bobbed up and down on his real cock, it entered me in its entirety—and what an entirety.

Being held in Hal's arms, impaled on his ten-inch monster cock while he kissed me passionately and fucked me profoundly with it, kissing him and looking up at his incomparably beautiful face while he murmured words of ecstasy, had provided the most thrilling moments of lust in my life. With my ass pressing against Shane Vaughan's belly and his even more challenging ass-reamer thrusting upwards into my ravenous ass came close to setting a new record for thrill. Later, when I knelt on all fours while Shane fucked himself with his dildo and hammered his cock into me brutally, unsparingly, I thought I had gone to heaven.

Shane fucked me for at least a half-hour, in all imaginable positions, usually fucking himself with the wonderful replica of what he was shoving into me, but having me do the honors when I was in a position to do so. He was screwing me missionary style when his orgasm began to approach. He abandoned the dildo to put both arms under my shoulders and raise them as we kissed feverishly, and in a moment I could feel his orgasm exploding deep inside me, in four or five palpable spurts. He rolled us to our sides once he had calmed down somewhat; his kisses became tender, and he whispered, "Keep sliding the rubber dick in and out—it feels so goddamned good." His cock had wilted somewhat inside me, but it regained at least some of its full glory as I did what he asked. I was still painfully horny—I had almost had an orgasm when I felt Shane's cock begin to erupt inside me—and I was working Shane's shaft with my sphincter, humping up and down on it. He chuckled, "Feels like you need to get off again." I agreed it was something I needed to do very soon.

Shane pulled his cock out of me and rolled to his stomach—the dildo still protruding from his ass. He looked back over his shoulder and whispered, "Putcher cock in there with the rubber dick." He rose to his knees to afford me access. I would have preferred to pull the dildo out and fuck him solo, but it was an interesting challenge. I put the protruding handle beneath my balls, and began to enter him above it. I was able to work my cock all the way inside him next to the dildo, but only with considerable difficulty. Still, with Shane gasping encouragement, I managed—and once I was all the way inside, it was extremely stimulating to feel my cock sliding up and down against the lubricated rubber shaft while I fucked him. Shane seemed to be more than just stimulated. He humped back and forth and ground his ass around my dick while I slammed into him, moaning his excitement. Double-fucking Phil had been more fun for me, but of course I had been fucking along with Billy's dick at the time—and this rubber substitute wasn't going to be drowning my cock in come while I fucked alongside it.

He ceased his humping and looked back over his shoulder while I took a brief rest. "God *damn* I like a two-dick fuck. You ever had two guys fuck you at the same time? It's fantastic." I admitted I had—remembering the wonderful feel of Phil's and Billy's cocks driving into my ass simultaneously the night of our first threesome. Shane went on, "I don't get a chance to get two cocks inside me at the same time very often—but I love it when I can. Gettin' fucked with my rubber-dick inside me at the same time is a pretty good substitute."

"You get that a lot?" I whispered into his ear as I lay over him and began to fuck in earnest again.

"Damn near every time," he gasped, and resumed his humping and grinding around the two shafts buried inside him, until at last I shot into his ass.

I later asked Shane if Hal had double-fucked him with the dildo, or with someone else, but he said he doubted he could take *that* much dick up his butt, but he had never tried—he had been fully satisfied with Hal's tremendous dick all by itself. Moreover, since Hal wouldn't allow himself to be fucked, Shane had never had the occasion to bring his rubber dick out when they were together.

We fucked each other again later that night, before going to bed, and did so again the next morning. Although we spent some time sucking each others' cocks, neither of us was really interested in sucking the other one off instead of fucking. Shane most wanted to get fucked and double-fucked, and I saw no reason to get him off any way but by taking him up the ass, since nothing in my experience up until then was comparable to that—although a few years later I knelt on a pool table in a San Diego sailor bar during my special twenty-fifth birthday party while a sailor with eleven full inches of cock (certified on-site with a ruler) spared me not one of those inches as he fucked me mercilessly in front of a crowd of twenty or thirty sailors and Marines, several of whom had blown their loads in me before the huge-hung sailor did, and several of whom fucked me afterwards, and almost all of whom lay or knelt on that pool table and got fucked themselves at some time during that wild night (that, however, is part of a story that I fear I will have to save for another book).

I spent quite a few more nights with Shane and his famous rubber dick out at Warner's house that summer, and on one occasion we even managed to make love without recourse to his hard-rubber inspiration. We had been to a movie, and were going to Warner's house to fuck, when Shane pulled into the public cemetery just past the town limits. He said he was unusually horny that night, and wanted to stop off there, so we could spend a little time warming up at a place that held especially happy memories for him. He drove to the back of the cemetery, and parked where his car would not be seen from the highway. He removed a tube of lubricant from the glove compartment and we made our way to a grave-site with a cement bench.

He explained, "This is the place Hal and I had sex for the first time—the night we met. We sucked each other off, and then he bent me over that bench and fucked me twice before we went back to my place for an all-nighter. Greatest night of my life."

We had been stripping while he told me this, and were soon naked, although he had put his boots back on—me, my shoes. The moon was bright, and his huge naked body, with his monster cock standing straight out from it and bobbing gently, was breathtaking. He squeezed a generous glob of KY Jelly from the tube of lubricant, and liberally applied it to his cock before reaching behind himself to smear some on his ass. He grinned at me as he apparently finger-fucked himself and said, "Turn around and bend over. Tonight you're Shane, and I'm Hal—and I'm gonna fuck you 'til you squeal."

I bent over the bench, and braced myself as Shane applied the lubricant to my ass. He positioned his cock-head at my sphincter and panted, "C'mon, baby, give me that hot ass." And he shoved, and impaled me on his entire mammoth prick with one fierce thrust. I almost screamed in pain and surprise, but as soon as he began driving himself in and out of me, in fierce and extra-long strokes, I gave myself over to his lust, and cried my enjoyment and encouragement loudly enough to wake the dead who were sleeping all around us.

Apparently the location, and the memory of what he had shared there with Hal, inspired him sufficiently that he did not need his rubber dick.

He fucked me savagely, often pausing to avoid orgasm, managing to fuck me for a good fifteen or twenty minutes before his discharge. Once he began his fuck, he obviously forgot that I was supposed to be Shane getting fucked by Hal, since he gasped, "Goddamn, I wish you were Hal—Jesus, why didn't he let me fuck him?" Moments later, I apparently *was* Hal in his fantasy, since he accompanied his lengthy, glorious fuck with grunts of "God, I've wanted to fuck your pretty butt for so long." and "Yeah, take my cock, Hal." and "This is what it feels like when you shove that big dick of yours in me." and culminating in a scream of "Take my load, Hal." as I felt his huge load exploding deep inside my body.

I rose to my feet, and put my hands behind us to fondle Shane's ass as he continued to hump into me, kissing and nibbling on my ears and neck. He panted and gasped Hal's name repeatedly for a few moments, then, after a brief silence, he whispered, "Sorry, John, I know you're not Hal, but I've dreamed of fucking him so often, and I guess I just got carried away."

I tuned around to embrace him, pulling his cock from my ass. His huge arms went around me and he leaned down to kiss me for a long time. "Shane, I *was* Hal, and you gave me the fuck of my life."

He grinned down at me, "And no rubber dick." Another kiss. "You must be 'bout ready to get off, too." He pushed me back so that I lay on the bench. He straddled the bench and lowered his asshole down on my cock. He had his eyes closed, and he smiled dreamily as he looked up at the moon and fondled his tits while he rode me, pistoning his massive legs up and down, his still almost fully erect cock flopping thrillingly.

I gazed up at his glorious body and said, "I'll bet you *really* wish I was Hal now."

He opened his eyes and smiled down at me. "Yeah, that would be great—but you're fine, John. I love you fuckin' me just like I enjoy fuckin' you." He rose, disengaging himself from me, and stood. "Stand behind me and give it to me the way I gave it to you—just the way Hal gave it to me right here that first time. But I know it's gonna be you—and I really want you.

I stood, and Shane leaned over the bench, and in far too short a while I was erupting inside him, and as he felt me coming, he panted, "Give it me, John—just like Hal." At least he was aware who was fucking him. But I didn't mind, really—fantasizing about the presence of Hal in our midst was probably as exciting to me as it was to Shane.

We left the cemetery, and went to Warner's house, and shared another few rounds of particularly gratifying sex before I left the next morning.

Once, toward the end of that summer, I picked up a cute student in the library, and since it was an especially beautiful, warm evening, took him out to the same bench in the cemetery to have sex. He laughed when we got there, "Man, this is the same place I got fucked the first time by the biggest prick I've ever seen, a coupla years ago." I played dumb, but wondered whether it had been Hal or Shane who had preceded me in the young man's attractive and tight ass—surprisingly tight, since he had entertained Hal or Shane there at least a few times.

I recommended Shane contact Jim or Earl for possible fun and games that fall. From Earl's later report, I learned that Shane was able to enjoy all of Earl's nine inches along with his rubber dick—and upon Shane's recommendation, Earl became the only non-athlete among those part-time 'employees' whom Warner welcomed into his bed to benefit from his generosity. Shane's preoccupation with his rubber dick put Jim off, for some reason, and they only had sex together once.

Sex with Shane was great fun, of course; enjoying the biggest cock I had ever had until then assured that, but—except for the one time—the necessity of having to use his rubber dick as an aid in our lovemaking lessened my enjoyment somewhat. But *only* somewhat.

The high watermark of passion in my life at that point was still sex with Hal Weltmann, and late that summer, that same *Stud-of-all-Studs* came to call.

14.
PILGRIMAGE TO A SUNDAY WORSHIP SERVICE

He had intentionally left a day early, hoping to find me for an
en route fuck for old time's sake. Of course the thought crossed my
mind that he might have been just as happy to have found Shane, or
perhaps just anyone who would appreciate his talents, but ... I was
not about to look a gift horse in the mouth—especially when the
"horse" was a thoroughbred stallion like Hal, with his glorious horse-
dick..

I was in my apartment studying one afternoon when I answered a
knock on the door, and found the incomparably handsome, sublimely
sexy, and astonishingly hung Hal Weltmann grinning at me.

"Hal–God, what a great surprise. Come in and close the door."

"Hi. You're hard to find, you know that? I heard you were back here
this summer, and I was passin' through, and really wanted to see you
again. I hope you're alone."

"If I had anyone with me, I'd run him off, you know that—it's really
good to see you. Sorry if I was hard to find, but I'm going to be even
sorrier if I don't *find you hard.*"

He took me in his arms and kissed me, and our tongues intertwined
passionately. "You know about how long it'll take me to get hard around
you." He ground his pelvis into mine, and I reached down and caressed
his monster prick through his trousers.

"Speaking of hard."

"It *does* seem to be ready, doesn't it? You been missin' that big ol' dick
of mine?"

"Jesus, Hal—I've been dying to get your cock in my hands again."

"Well, there's only a belt buckle and a zipper between you and it—but
I hope you're gonna let me put it in a few places besides your hands." He
stepped back and pressed down on my shoulders until I was kneeling
before him. "Take it, John—you haven't had this baby in your mouth for
a long time," he said as he groped his bulging crotch.

I reached up to undo his belt, and pulled his slacks and shorts to his
ankles. His gargantuan prick bobbed up as it cleared his shorts. "My
God, Hal—it's even bigger and prettier than I remembered it."

He put his hands on the back of my head and pulled me in. "See if it
tastes just as good." I opened my mouth eagerly, and he slowly drove the
monster shaft deep into my throat. I gagged at its length and mass, but
soon adapted, and relaxed my throat to the point I had his entire prick
inside me—no mean accomplishment with a challenge like that. He
murmured in delight and humped slowly and shallowly as I moved my
lips up and down his entire length, exerting as much suction as I could
provide. As I sucked, my hands caressed his writhing ass, and his
murmurs turned into groans of pleasure as I teased his asshole with a
fingertip. He cried, "Oh shit, that turns me on." and began to hump his
cock savagely into my throat.

After a few minutes of this absolute delight, he pulled his cock from my mouth. "Whew, we better take it easy, or I'll be coming."

"But I want to eat your load—you know that."

"Yeah, but we've got lots of time. Well, I guess we do—is there anything you need to do tonight?"

"There's only one thing I need to do tonight." I began licking his prick, up and down the shaft, and sucking his balls.

"I can even spend the whole night if you want."

I stood and took him in my arms. "*If* I want? Jesus you know the answer to that." We kissed again for a long time, my hands exploring his butt, while he unbuttoned my shirt. We were soon both naked, and Hal knelt and began to suck my cock and play with my ass. I caressed his head dreamily and said, "I can't believe you're here with me again—and I can have you for the whole night."

He stood and enclosed me again in his arms. "And it's gonna be just you and me." His cock slipped between my legs as he stood, and he fucked me that way while we kissed passionately and I fondled his writhing buttocks. "We've never had a whole night together, have we? But we do now, and I want to do everything with you as many times as we can. Guess you can tell I'm horny as shit."

He led me to the bed. I threw off the spread, and we lay down and caressed and necked for a long time. Finally, with Hal lying on his back, I knelt and straddled him. "I want you to fill me up like nobody else can." I dipped into the open economy-sized jar of Vaseline next to the bed, and prepared us both. I had been riding Earl a lot lately—probably a good nine inches of fat, hard meat—and had only a few days earlier got plowed for the second time by Shane's dildo-fortified monster cock. Shane had Hal's length, and even more bulk to offer, but drinking in Hal's facial beauty, and knowing what an insatiable stallion he was, I knew I was in for the ultimate thrill again.

His hands held my sides as I settled down over his stupendous cock, and he gently undulated his ass and humped. Finally, every throbbing, thrilling inch was deep inside me, my ass was resting on his pubic hair, and I felt the incredible warmth and satisfaction that only being completely impaled on a really big cock can provide—and studying Hal's smiling, gloriously beautiful face amplified those feelings of warmth and satisfaction. I wriggled and ground my ass around my sex-god's matchless and monstrous shaft, and Hal urged me on. "Jesus, that feels good. I love fuckin' your ass. You really love it, too—I can tell."

"Hal, anybody sane would love getting fucked by you—I'm so glad you want me."

"Christ yes, I want you. I want you to ride me like you would a rodeo bronco." I began to comply. "And I'm gonna fill your hot ass with the biggest load you ever got." He humped and bucked frantically, I rode up and down the entire length of his unbelievable shaft, stroking my own cock as I did so, and we were both almost shouting with ecstasy when his body went rigid, and he levered it up from the bed with his heels and back while I felt the thrill of his orgasm beginning to explode deep inside me. He pulled my head down and sank his tongue into my mouth as I continued to ride, and he continued to fuck. Finally he relaxed his body, and whispered around my tongue, "You about ready to come?" I assured him I was very close. "Get up here and let me watch you blow your load in my mouth."

I regretfully let his still formidable prick slip from my ass as I knelt over his face and masturbated. He cheered me on *("Give me your load, John—shoot in my mouth.")* and soon I was spraying his face and shoulders with my orgasm, yet managing to direct most of it into his open mouth and onto his waving tongue. He swallowed eagerly, and licked his lips. "Jesus, that was hot. I love to see you come on me." He scooped my come from his face, and licked it off his fingers.

We lay together and cuddled and talked for a long time. His strong embrace felt almost as good as the sensation of his massive cock pressing into me and his probing finger gently teasing the hole he had so recently filled with the liquid evidence of his manhood. He caught me up on his life since we had last been together.

He had taken a job with an insurance company (everybody in the 1950's seemed to be selling insurance) and was doing well—of course I, personally, would have bought just about *anything* he might be selling. He was on his way to a district seminar in Albuquerque, where he was to spend a week. He had intentionally left a day early, hoping to find me for an *en route* fuck for old time's sake. Of course the thought crossed my mind that he might have been just as happy to have found Shane, or perhaps just anyone who would appreciate his talents, but it was me he had found, and I was not about to look a gift horse in the mouth—especially when the "horse" was a thoroughbred stallion like Hal, with such a glorious horse-dick.

Hal was living with his beautiful lover Dan Chrisman, and the two were happy together. "Dan never messes around, and I swear I don't know why I want to—he's such a hot lover, and his ass is about as cute 'n as hungry as they get." He grinned, "Still, I can't help spreadin' the wealth a little bit."

"Thank God you spread some my way. I have really missed that fantastic dick of yours. I've never had anything that thrilling inside me."

"Shoot, I'll bet you been gettin' a lot of 'em, though, haven't you?"

I told him about my lovemaking with Earl and Shane. He laughed when I told him about Shane's rubber dick. "Guess I'll hafta visit ol' Shane next time I'm in town, and check it out. I bet you loved gettin' fucked by that big cock of his, didn'tcha?"

I laughed, "Yeah, I did—but so did he. Only dick I've ever seen to compare to yours, Hal."

"Butcha like mine the best, right?"

"Absolutely—it's just as big, and I don't have to be fucking you with a rubber dick to keep you hard. But mostly, you're best, because you're you—you're Hal Weltmann. I was hot for you long before I came into my room that night and found Jim sucking you off. Then when I saw how much dick you were feeding Jim, I was completely hooked. There's nobody like you Hal—hung and sexy as anybody could want, but just as beautiful as a god, too."

He kissed me very tenderly and whispered, "Thanks, John. I know I don't deserve that, but I know you feel that way, and it makes me feel good. And I know how you feel, 'cause I feel that way about Dan—he may not be hung like me or Shane, but he's as sexy and as handsome as any guy I've ever seen." He laughed, "So, I wonder why I wanna fuck around behind his back? Oops, better put that some other way—I get behind his back and fuck him all the time."

"Lucky Dan." I chuckled. "And he's about the only I guy I know who may be as beautiful as you are—'cept maybe Billy."

"Billy? Okay, who's that?" he asked.

I told him all about my adventures with Billy and Phil, and even Joe Don. I had promised Joe Don I would never tell anyone about our meeting, and I hadn't until then, but who would Hal ever tell? Hal asked if I had any pictures. I showed him pictures of the three in the Antares High School annual, and then the nude photos I had taken of Billy the fall before.

"Jesus Christ, he is *cute*. And what a pretty little ass. Man, I'll bet you love fuckin' that. No wonder you're in love with him. I wish I could see his prick in these pictures; is it nice?"

"It's beautiful, and nice and long—nothing like yours, but really fine."

"Well now, there ain't many like mine, are there? I think his ass might be damn near as cute as my Dan's—hell, *he's* damn near as cute as Dan. God, I'd like to fuck him." When I told him Billy's age, he wasn't at all bothered, and he didn't caution me about playing with fire, either. "Hell I picked up a kid a coupla weeks ago, and I fucked him twice before he told me how old he was—and he was two years younger'n your Billy is." Anyway, you think Billy would let me fuck him? Would *you* let me fuck him?"

"Hal, Billy does what he wants to. If he wanted to fuck with you, that would be okay, I guess—it would be his decision; I sure would be jealous, though."

"Hell, John, I'd want you there, too." He held me tight and whispered into my ear, "Wouldn't you like to watch this big ol' pecker of mine slidin' into that pretty little ass? And then when you got real hot watchin', I could suck your cock while I fucked his young butt. Wouldn't that be hot?" I had to admit the thought made me very hot indeed—so hot that I had turned around and taken Hal's prick in my mouth again, and sucked eagerly as he took mine, and we carried a passionate sixty-nine to full conclusion—each delivering another mouthful to feed the other.

We dressed and went out to eat, then returned to my room for a full night of *epic* love-making. I knelt for him to take me from behind, and another time I lay on my back while he kissed me passionately and fucked me even more heatedly. At one point, when we were embracing, I began to subtly penetrate his asshole with my finger. He said nothing, so I continued, and soon I had my entire finger inside him, and the muscle of his sphincter grasped my finger tightly as he moved himself up and down on it. "Jesus, that feels fine."

"Have you learned to take it up the butt yet, Hal? God, I'd love to fuck your ass."

"Well, I'll tell you. You remember the night you and Jim and Dan and I all got together so Dan could fuck butt for his birthday?"

"Not likely I'd ever forget that—it was probably the most memorable night of my life. You were as hot as always, and Dan was so fuckin' gorgeous—I just wish we'd had the lights on; I really wanted to see how beautiful Dan was while we had sex, and to watch that huge prick of yours going into that cute little ass."

"That's the way it would look with Billy, you know. And you could really see—hell you could get right up there and eat my ass while I fucked him. How'd you like that?"

"Jesus, that would be wonderful. But we're getting off the subject; you still haven't answered my question. Has this hot ass been *breached* yet? Have you taken a prick the way you're taking my finger?"

"Well, I was tellin' you . . . Dan really enjoyed gettin' to fuck you and Jim, and while he loves my dick in his ass, he still wants to fuck butt, and he knows I don't want him fuckin' with someone else, so I finally let him really try mine. We worked for a long time, and we used lots of Vaseline, but he finally got it in, and he fucked the living hell out of me."

"Isn't it great?"

"I gotta admit, it was fantastic. But I made Dan a promise—that I'd never let anyone else fuck me, that I'd save my butthole only for him. He knows I can't help but fuck around some, but that's something I save just for him."

"I understand Hal, and I think that's really nice, as much as I'd like to fuck your hot ass."

"Well you can finger-fuck me some more while you ride my dick, how's that?" It was, of course, fine with me, and Hal seemed to enjoy it even more than I, since he shortly rolled us over and finished fucking me missionary style—slamming his cock into me as deliriously as I remembered him ever doing.

We lay and cuddled and talked again for quite a while after Hal had blown his third load, in my ass. He got up and went to the bathroom, then turned out the light and got back in bed. He lay on his side, his back to me, and I put my arms around him. and played with his chest and kissed his back. My hard prick pressed against the crevice between his cheeks. He raised one leg, so that my cock now pressed against his asshole. He backed up to me and began to wriggle until the tip of my dick was in position to enter him. He humped and pressed backward, and my cock began to enter his ass; it was liberally greased up—he had apparently prepared himself for this. He said nothing, just put an arm behind me to pull me in to him.

I sensed that this was something we would not talk about—he had made a promise to Dan, so this was not happening—he only *seemed* to welcome my dick inside his asshole, he only *seemed* to roll on his stomach so that I was free to plunge into him fully, and he only *seemed* to reach behind and use both hands to pull my ass closer while I fucked him. I said nothing as I held him in my arms and fucked his marvelously bucking ass. Neither of us was able to avoid gasps and grunts of pleasure as I shot my load into him, but still, we said nothing.

I put my arms around his chest, and rolled us to our sides again. We lay there quietly, my cock still in him while I toyed with his fully hard cock. Finally he said quietly, "Gee, I just had the greatest dream."

"I did too, Hal—one of the best dreams I ever had." We drifted off to sleep with me still in him. I woke once during the night to find his huge prick penetrating my ass, and him murmuring his ecstasy in my ear as he worked up another mammoth load to shoot inside my hungry hole—then we went to sleep again, with him still inside me.

In the morning, I rode his cock again, and he sucked me off, then we showered and went out to eat breakfast before he had to leave for Albuquerque. Before he left he made me promise to sound out Billy about the possibility of a get-together. He gave me the address and phone number of the motel where he would be staying for the week. "Maybe you guys could drive over and we could have some time together." I explained that Sunday would be the only possibility, because of Billy's job. "Just be sure to tell him how big this ol' dick of mine is, and how much you love it when I shove it inside you, okay? And tell him I think he's got a really cute ass, and I wanna fuck it like it's never been fucked. Now, I'm gonna hold Sunday open, just in case—you call me either way, though, okay?"

He dropped me off at my apartment, and he leaned over and kissed me full on the lips as I began to get out of the car (pretty wild behavior in Texas in 1955—fortunately no one was on hand to see). "I had a great time—and I hope I'll see you Sunday. And hey, if Billy *does* want to fuck with me, it doesn't mean I'm gonna neglect your hot ass."

"I would hope not. I'm already thinking about it, and I'm hard again. Wanna come in and throw another fuck into me before you hit the road?"

"*Want* to? Oh, yeah. *Can* I?—nah, gotta get going, but I'll give you an extra shot on Sunday, how's that? But be sure Billy knows I'll have *plenty* for him, and that I'm dreamin' about slippin' into that pretty little ass of his to give it to him. Oh man, look at that—I'm gettin' hard too."

He spread his legs and I did, indeed look. His prick bulged down his pants leg, to a point just a few inches short of his knee. I put my hand on it and squeezed; he cupped my hard cock and kissed me again. "Shit, John, come to Albuquerque Sunday anyway, even if Billy won't come along; don't bother to call, just come—but bring that cute little Billy if you can. Either way, I'll know I'll have at least one really hot guy to make love with, okay?"

We set three o'clock in the afternoon for Sunday "I'll be there Hal, and I'm pretty sure Billy will want to come, too." I was still squeezing his huge, steel-hard cock as I said, "He should get a treat like this fantastic Hal Weltmann prick at least once in his life."

Hal laughed. "Hell, everyone should. Thanks, John—see you Sunday at three o'clock." And he drove off. God. An unbelievably handsome man, and his ten inches of fat, driving meat exploding those huge, hot loads in my ass. God, *God*, what an incredible *stud*. My ass still tingled from this morning's fuck, and his come was still in my body—but I was already impatiently awaiting Sunday.

I went inside to call Billy's house and ask his mother to have him call me as soon as he got home from work. She asked, "Is there something wrong, Mr. Harrison?"

"No, Mrs. Polk. I have to go over to Albuquerque Sunday, and I was hoping Billy would go along for the ride."

"I'll be sure to tell him—I know he'll want to go with you. And you plan to eat lunch with us here before you start out."

I really was hoping Billy would go along for the ride—*the ride of his life,* more than likely.

Billy called about eight that night. "What's up, Pete—what are we going to Albuquerque for?"

"You may not want that to be 'what are *we* going for' when I tell you."

"Bet you're wrong. Tell me. And mom's out in the yard, so we can talk."

"You remember me telling you about Hal, the fraternity guy?"

"Yeah, you showed me his picture, remember? The beautiful guy with the huge cock, who got you and your roommate to let that gorgeous blond lover of his fuck you for his birthday. You said he had the biggest prick you'd ever seen, right?"

"Right." I hadn't told Billy that I had recently sampled Shane's even larger endowment, or that I was having sex with Earl regularly; at that point I saw no need to let him know how much dick I was getting that summer in addition to what he was giving me. I didn't want him to think I wanted or needed his love any less than I genuinely did. "And Billy . . . Hal's dick is still just as big as ever."

"Oh, oh. Sounds like you had a visitor."

"He showed up at my door yesterday afternoon, and . . ."

Billy laughed, "And you had to be hospitable, right? It's okay, Pete—I understand; just be sure to tell me all about it on Sunday. But what's the deal with Albuquerque?"

"Well, I showed Hal the pictures I took of you while he was here—and being a sensible guy, he has decided you've got the cutest butt in the world, next to Dan."

"The gorgeous blond—at the birthday party, right?"

"That's the one. Well, anyway, Hal is in Albuquerque for a meeting, and is hoping you'll come over and get together with him. He told me to tell you he was dreaming of fucking you. He knows we're lovers, and he wants me to come there with you, of course. "

"I sure wouldn't even think about it without you, but . . . well, it sounds pretty exciting, Pete. What do you think I should do?"

"Honestly? I think you should go. It's not that I want to watch you having sex with someone else, but I sure enjoyed the threesomes we had with Phil, and it would be *us* with Hal—not just you. I know how thrilling sex with Hal is, and I'd like you to get to experience that—you may never get a chance for something like it again."

"I have to admit your description of him made me think about how hot it would be to go to bed with him, and . . . yeah, I'll go, Pete—if you think I should."

"You don't have to decide right now—think about it, and when I come up Sunday you can tell me. I promised your mom I'd come for lunch—see if eleven is okay with her, since Albuquerque is a three-hour drive, okay?"

"Okay, Pete—but I know I'm gonna want to go and see if you've been exaggerating about this guy. If you haven't been, I think I may be in for the fuck of my life. But Pete, remember I love you, and I want to be at least holding you when I'm with Hal, promise?"

"I promise—and Hal said he wouldn't be ignoring me, so I want you holding me, too."

He laughed. "Can I hold you any way I want to?"

"For sure. And I'm supposed to deliver this message from Hal—he wants you to be sure you know how big his cock is, and how good it feels, and that he's really eager to slip it inside that cute little ass of yours."

"My cute little ass is tingling right now. Just be sure he's not the only one who fucks it Sunday."

"God, I love you, Billy—we'll have a helluva time." We talked a bit longer, and finally hung up. The thought of Sunday was so exciting I could hardly keep my hands off my dick, but needing to 'hit the books,' I abstained—fortunately, as it turned out, since Earl came over around ten o'clock that night and told me that *for starters* he wanted (as he so eloquently put it) to fill my hot ass with nine inches of hard, throbbing cock. Once again, I felt I had to be hospitable, and he *did* fill my ass with his nine inches, and it *was* hard and throbbing, and it *did* prove to be just for starters.

Billy drove my car as we headed for Albuquerque shortly before noon on Sunday; I loved watching him drive (actually, I loved watching him do almost anything—he was so sexy, so truly beautiful). I had brought a college annual with me, to show him the pictures of Hal again. He studied them (only casual attention to the road was all that was usually needed while driving the flat, straight, mostly deserted roads of the Panhandle of Texas), and affirmed his earlier judgment of Hal's exceptional beauty. "Let me see his lover again." I found Dan Chrisman in the index and turned to his picture. "Jesus, Pete—they're both so handsome."

"And Dan has a great body, too, and a really cute ass—but not as cute as yours, in spite of what Hal says. Hal's real tall, and his body is nothing special, but somehow when Hal's cock is exposed, you never think of looking at his body very much."

"Boy, I'm really looking forward to this."

"You're gonna flip your lid. Think Phil's cock, but think about two inches longer."

"I hope I'm gonna be able to take it, Pete—I'm not really sure I can; Phil seems *huge* when he's inside me," he leaned over to kiss me, "Just like you do."

"I think you'll be so excited by Hal, you'll surprise yourself. I wasn't at all sure I could take it when I first saw it, either."

"Hell, Pete, remember I've seen you with Phil's cock *and* mine in you at the same time."

"Yeah, but that was long after Hal really broke me in. Let's talk about something else—I'm getting so horny I'm gonna have to do something about it if we don't." I kissed him. "So, what kind of season are the Scorpions gonna to have this fall?"

Billy laughed. "I don't know—but they tell me their starting quarterback has the cutest ass in the league."

"Who said a thing like that?"

"The captain of last year's team, his Geometry teacher, and a handsome stud with ten inches of dick, who decided that without even seeing it in the flesh."

"I'm gonna haul my meat out and start beating it if we don't change the subject."

We did try to have a serious conversation about what the next two years would hold for us, but we decided it was best to just not think about it, and take whatever happened in stride. Billy mentioned that Joe Don had suddenly been much friendlier lately. "Just a question of time, Billy."

"I know—I'll just have to see what happens about that too."

At Billy's urging, I told him all the details of Hal's visit earlier in the week, and cautioned him not to say anything about my having finally got to fuck his ass. "He says he promised Dan he wouldn't let anyone else do that, so when I fucked him, he pretended it wasn't really happening—and we didn't say anything about it."

Billy grinned. "For something that didn't happen, I'll bet it felt great for both of you."

"Amen, brother Polk."

We pulled up at the motel in Albuquerque a few minutes before three. I called Hal's room from the lobby. "We're here."

"Hey, I'm really glad to hear you say *we*. Am I gonna get to fuck your lover's cute little ass?"

"You better, or we're gonna have a disappointed boy on our hands. He says he's not sure he can take it all, but he can hardly wait to try."

"Neither can I. Room 118—come right away."

"It may take a few minutes after we get there before we're ready to do that."

Hal met us at the door—fresh from the shower, wearing only a towel wrapped around his waist. We came in and Hal put his arms around me and kissed me as Billy shut the door. "Hal Weltmann—Billy Polk."

They shook hands, and Billy put his other hand up to Hal's cheek. Hal was much taller than Billy, but did not seem to dwarf him as Phil did, since his body was much lighter. "God, it's good to meet you, Hal," Billy said. "It doesn't seem possible but you're even more handsome than you look in your pictures. You can't believe how much I've heard about you."

Hal took Billy's face in his hands and grinned. "If you heard it from John, every bit of it's true, I'll bet."

Billy's arms went around Hal, and he turned his face up to be kissed, saying, "And I can't believe how much I'm looking forward to seeing for myself if it's all true."

Hal returned Billy's embrace, and he became very serious as he whispered "Jesus Christ, Billy, you're beautiful." and they kissed for a very long time—first tentatively, but gradually getting quite passionate. Finally they separated a little bit, looking into each other's eyes. Then Billy looked over to me, and extended a hand for me to join their embrace. As I did so, each put an arm around my waist, and we all three hugged and kissed. Finally we broke, and Hal said, "Why don't you guys get naked. I got something for both of you." He reached under his towel and stroked his cock—which was already pretty well advanced in erection—then unknotted the towel and let it fall so that it was draped over his erection, and very *firmly* supported by it. "Come on you guys, I wanna get undressed, too."

Billy walked up to him, and very gently pulled the towel away, exposing the huge, raging erection that was supporting it. He gasped, "My God, Hal—that's the most incredible thing I've ever seen."

Hal grinned crookedly, "It's incredible, and it's edible, and it's all yours, Billy—every one of these rock-hard ten inches." Billy knelt as at an altar, his lips only inches from Hal's cock, and his eyes riveted to the magnificent sight, seemingly almost hypnotized. He whispered, "It's beautiful."

Hal gently put a hand behind Billy's head, and proffered his gargantuan cock with the other as he said, very quietly, "Kiss it Billy—make love to it."

"God, Pete, you told me how big it was—you didn't tell me how beautiful it was."

"I couldn't begin to describe it, Billy—it was easy to tell you how big it was." Hal had not noted Billy's name for me; he would later raise the question, but would be told the subject was off-limits. For the moment, he was as hypnotized as Billy was—mesmerized by the beauty of the young Adonis adoring his cock.

Billy moved in slowly, never taking his eyes from the throbbing head of Hal's dick, and kissed it very gently. His tongue came out, and he began to lick the head, and then kissed and licked up and down the long, fat shaft. One hand held Hal's balls and squeezed them; Hal now held Billy's head gently in both hands as he moaned in ecstasy and rotated his hips. "Ohhhhh, Billy, oh God, that feels so good. Love my prick, Billy—it's all yours, make love to it." Finally, Billy opened his mouth, and very slowly Hal pressed his enormous cock into it. There was no way Billie could accommodate all of it just then, but he did a wonderful job of taking most of it, and murmuring in ecstasy as Hal's groans increased in fervor, "Eat it, Billy, let me fuck your mouth." He began to slowly, but very decisively drive himself into Billy, who now held Hal's writhing ass firmly in his hands.

I have no recollection of having undone my clothes, but I realized my pants and shorts were around my ankles, and I was stroking my cock. Billy gradually withdrew from Hal's cock, and again began to kiss and lick the head. "It's incredible, Pete—it's so wonderful." He looked over at me and saw I was masturbating. He motioned me to join him. I kicked off my pants and shoes, and knelt next to him, and together we worshipped at the altar of Hal's ten-inch wonder—licking and sucking both sides as we had with Phil before. Hal was in ecstasy—but, then, so were Billy and I.

Hal pulled away and raised Billy to his feet. He took Billy's face in his hands and kissed him for a very long time—their tongues frantically darting in and out. Then he held Billy at arm's length. He panted, "I want to see your prick."

Billy removed his shirt while Hal knelt and undid his belt. Dragging Billy's pants and shorts down, Hal marveled at Billy's throbbing erection. "Talk about beautiful. God, Billy, it's big and it's gorgeous. Oh man, I want you inside me." He opened his mouth and drove his lips forcefully down until they nestled in Billy's pubic hair. His hands pulled Billy's ass in toward him, and he sucked fiercely, and audibly, as Billy began to hump and fuck in perfect sync with Hal's driving mouth. Soon their actions became feverish, and Billy began to moan, "Oh God, if you don't stop I'm gonna come." Hal's hands gripped Billy ass-cheeks and used them to fuck his mouth with Billy's dick even harder, moaning, "Mmm, hmmm." Finally Billy cradled Hal's head in his arms, and fucked furiously as he cried out, "Take it, Hal—eat my come." His body was racked with spasms, and Hal sucked greedily and groaned in ecstasy. They froze in that position for some time while they calmed down—Hal's mouth still completely engulfing my lover's beautiful cock. Then Hal sat back on his heels and looked up at Billy. "That was terrific. What a great load. Thank you, Billy—nothing ever tasted so good."

Billy stepped out of his pants and kicked off his shoes. Hal used his hands to turn Billy's body around. He looked closely at Billy's perfect ass, and moaned his admiration. He ran his hands lightly over the twin velvety mounds, then kneaded them gently, and spread them apart, exposing the perfect pink ring where I had worshipped so many times. Hal pressed his face up against Billy's ass and began to lick the sphincter. Finally he drove his tongue as far in as he could, and tongue-fucked to the accompaniment of Billy's passionate groans. I knelt behind Hal and fingered his ass. He pointedly spread his legs and pushed his cock back through them, and tapped it against my hand. I got on my back, and drew myself up between Hal's legs, so that his enormous cock lodged securely in my throat, and I sucked happily while he ate Billy's ass.

Hal stood up, and from my position on the floor I watched his huge cock go between Billy's legs and his arms hold him from behind. He kissed Billy's ear, "Jesus, your ass tastes even better than your load. Please let me fuck you, Billy. I want to put my dick all the way inside that perfect ass—it's so beautiful."

"I don't know if I can take it all, Hal," Billy whispered, "but I want to try." He turned around, and they kissed as I stood and got out of the rest of my clothes. I lay down on the bed; Billy joined me there, hugged me, and whispered, "I love you, Pete. Don't forget I want to be in you, and I want you in me too—not just Hal."

Hal had by then joined us, and he leaned against the headboard, stroking his cock. "Who wants to eat this?" I moved away, and Billy knelt over Hal and began to administer an expert blowjob. His mouth drove wildly up and down Hal's shaft, and the latter humped eagerly. Hal held his hand out to me, and I moved in and he began to kiss me passionately while Billy sucked. Then he whispered, "I want to watch you fuck him while he blows me."

I lubricated Billy and me from the jar of Vaseline Hal had thoughtfully placed by the bed, and knelt behind my lover's perfect ass and slowly drove my cock into him. He humped frantically on my cock as he sucked Hal, who groaned, "Oh, man—that looks so good, John. Fuck him—fuck that perfect little ass, get it opened up for me." Billy stopped his ministrations long enough to encourage me to fuck him harder and deeper; I complied and the three of us enjoyed total delight—I was fucking my lover's hot ass, Hal was getting his big cock sucked masterfully, and my sweet Billy was getting fucked at both ends.

Finally, I could contain myself no longer; my panting signaled Hal to call out, "Fill his pretty ass with come, John.", and I soon erupted inside Billy, who moaned his appreciation and sucked Hal all the harder. Hal said, "You want my load, Billy?" Billy sucked faster and said "Mmm, hmnn." and soon Hal's ass was driving upward from the bed, and it looked as if practically his entire cock was inside Billy's mouth while he fucked it. Hal's hands slapped down and he held his body rigidly off the bed, groaning as he began to shoot his load. Billy murmured his appreciation and swallowed the load as it shot into him. Hal grunted in animal lust as he came, and Billy's ass still held my cock tightly in its grip.

Finally Billy fell to one side, and lay on his back panting. I leaned over him to kiss him, and I could taste the mustiness of Hal's come on his tongue. Hal's arms encircled us both, and we all lay there for a time, recovering from the excess of passion that had brought each of to orgasm already.

Some time later, following a long period of tender caressing, kissing, and mutual compliments between Hal and my lover, Billy was lying on top of Hal, kissing him. Hal's hands moved down and fondled Billy's ass. "I want to fuck your beautiful ass, Billy—I want to fill you up with dick like you've never been filled."

"Oh yeah, Hal—I *want* you to fuck me .. I want every bit of it if I can take it, but you're gonna have to be gentle and patient with me while I try to get all that unbelievable thing inside me." Billy had slipped to the side, and was holding Hal's huge cock as he looked at it reverently. Hal raised himself and told Billy to kneel. Billy knelt on all fours, and looked up at me. "Hold me, Pete." I positioned myself in front of him, and he raised to his knees so that I could take him in my arms. Behind him, Hal was lubricating his enormous prick and studying the luscious receptacle Billy offered for it; he moved in and placed the tip against Billy's asshole, and began to press, at the same time taking Billy's waist in his hands.

I cautioned him, "Please go slow Hal—give it to him a little at a time."

"Oh, Billy—I'm gonna fuck you as *sweet* as anyone has every fucked anyone. Just let me make love to your ass with my dick." Billy began to wriggle his ass, and back up gently, as Hal pressed forward slowly, and began to enter my young lover.

Billy began to moan with passion. "Oh Jesus, Pete, that feels so fine. Give it to me nice and slow Hal—it feels wonderful." I watched over Billy's shoulder as he pressed himself back toward Hal, who continued his gradual penetration with slow, shallow, in-and-out strokes. Soon, with a couple of inches of Hal's cock still not inside him, Billy cried, "God, Hal, I don't think I can take any more—don't fuck me any deeper than that, but fuck me, *fuck* me with that big thing." He held me tight, and Hal murmured his appreciation for the beauty and tightness of his host.

"Just a little more, Billy, I'm almost all the way inside your hot ass now—take all of it for me, you'll love it." He began to move deeper and deeper, while Billy clutched me very tightly and moaned. Finally, Hal's prick disappeared from sight, and his stomach was pressed hard against Billy's back.

"Aaaaaaaaaaaahhhh. Oh God, Pete—it's so fuckin' huge. Hal, you feel so great!"

"I've got it all inside you, Billy, and I'm going to show you how much I appreciate this hot ass." He began to fuck slowly, but with extremely long strokes. Billy's moans increased, and he kissed me frantically as Hal began a real onslaught against his ass. In a few minutes, Billy was driving himself back and forth on Hal's cock, Hal was fucking unmercifully, and both were in ecstasy. "Oh *fuck, fuck*. Your hole is so hot, Billy—Oh God, my balls are slappin' against your ass."

"Billy's cries were animal, and almost unintelligible. "Fuck me, fuck me—fill me up." Billy's head was buried in my shoulder, and I watched, almost hypnotized by the *majesty* of the fuck he was receiving. Hal leaned forward and kissed me wildly and moaned into my mouth as he continued to drive his cock just as wildly, "Your come feels so hot inside him." Then he backed away suddenly and went completely rigid—planted entirely in Billy's ass.

"I'm coming in you, Billy—take my fuckin' load." He moaned, and Billy moaned along with him.

"I can feel it shooting Hal—God, I want you to fill me up with come."

Hal fell on top of Billy's back, driving him from my arms and flat onto the bed as he re-commenced fucking, and obviously gave him every drop of come he could. "That was so *good* Billy—God, you're fantastic. I love fucking your ass." I had positioned myself behind the two—kneeling between their legs, playing with Hal's ass and admiring it as he *still* fucked. I put my face into it and tongue-fucked until, with a great sigh, he rolled off Billy, and away from him, pulling his cock out, and declaring him to be an incredible fuck. "Jesus, Billy—you took me like a champ."

"Pete, I want to take you like a champ, too—right now. Fuck me—put another load in there with Hal's." I knelt between Billy's legs and quickly put my cock inside him, needing no lubrication to enter his still-distended asshole, awash with Hal's hot come. I know I must have felt inadequate after the pounding he had just received from such a gargantuan rod, but Billy seemed to enjoy my fucking him as much as had Hal's. Indeed, he felt as tight as he always did, and his cries were as passionate and appreciative as they had been before.

Hal lay propped up on one arm and watched us; with his other hand he played with my ass, and began to finger fuck me. "Fuck him, John—that looks so hot."

"Give me more back there, Hal." He got some lubricant, and soon had about three fingers driving into me as I fucked Billy. Then he positioned himself behind me, and I felt his monstrous cock begin to penetrate; how it could have been that hard after the fucking he had just administered I could not guess—but he thrust it all the way in, it was hard and it was huge, and it felt unbelievably satisfying. I fucked Billy frantically, and

Hal met each of my backward strokes with a forward thrust of his cock. "Oh baby," I panted into Billy's ear, "Hal's fucking me too."

"Give me your load, Pete. Fill me like Hal did," and his hips moved frantically, and soon I delivered my load into him, accompanied by our mutual cries of delight. I lay buried in Billy, both of us quiet now, but Hal continued his assault on my ass, and only a few minutes later, he shot another load, into me. I could not actually feel the spurt, but Billy confirmed that he had given me plenty of come, because just a minute or so later Billy knelt behind me and drove his cock into me, and again, no lubrication was needed. "Jeez, Pete, your ass is dripping with Hal's come—and I'm gonna give you mine." It took him only a very short while to blow his load, and this time I could not help but feel the strong bursts deep inside me. Hal watched and commented on the utter beauty of Billy's ass as he fucked mine.

We all cleaned up a bit, Billy went down to the soft-drink dispenser and got Cokes, we rested a while, and made casual conversation—mostly small talk about big cocks and hot guys. Billy often stroked Hal's cock while we chatted, and Hal often stroked Billy's cock and his ass. I stroked everything I could find to stroke. Some oral play led to a three-way suck, and we all sucked each other at length—but not to orgasm. At one point Hal said he was almost ready to come while I was sucking him, but Billy told me to stop. "I want that come in my ass again."

Hal kissed Billy. "I was hoping you'd let me fuck you again."

"Hal, you're not getting out of his room until you fuck me *at least* once more—and I want to watch you fuck Pete, too."

Hal grinned and told me to kneel on the bed. I complied, and as Billy watched closely, Hal shoved his cock inside me again, and I was rewarded with his massive perfection filling me to my complete joy. Billy lubricated his own ass, and knelt beside me on the bed. "Take turns, Hal." Hal pulled out of me, and drove himself savagely into Billy, who cried out in pain and surprise, but soon humped eagerly as he received Hal's shaft deep inside him. For quite some time, the incredibly hung *fuckmaster* alternated between Billy and me, until he began to pant, saying, "I'm gettin' close—who's gonna take this?"

I cried, "Give it to Billy, Hal." He pulled out and drove himself into my young lover, and just a few thrusts later delivered his load, with the usual panting and guttural cries of pleasure on both sides. I got to my knees and embraced and kissed Hal—who was still buried inside Billy. "You're a fantastic man, Hal."

"And you're a fantastic fuck, John—and this sweet baby is the best fuck of all." He pulled out from Billy and fell on his side laughing, "Whew, I gotta take a break." He held out his arms to Billy, and the two embraced and lay there. I lay behind Billy, and my arms reached around to encircle both of them. I got up to get a drink, and returned to the bed, where they still lay wrapped in each other's arms, kissing. This time I lay behind Hal, and took a gob of Vaseline with me. I quietly greased up Hal's asshole as he lay there, and neither of us *said* anything as I slowly slid my prick into him, although we both murmured satisfaction.

Hal continued to hold Billy while I fucked him. His ass met my thrusts, and the force of my slamming into him was certainly transmitted to

Billy's body, since he and Hal embraced the entire time. At one point Billy grinned and winked at me over Hal's shoulder, in effect saying *This isn't happening, right?* I had already exceeded my customary number of orgasms for even an unusually hot sexual encounter, so I fucked Hal for a long, long time before I climaxed. My arms were locked around Hal's chest, and I was playing with his nipples when I finally shot my load into him, and I kissed his ears and bit his neck as I did so. Hal moaned his pleasure, but said nothing.

We lay that way for some time, until Hal rolled to his other side, pulling my cock from his ass. We embraced, and started to kiss. Soon I could feel the wild gyrations of Hal's ass and the jolts of Billy's body slamming against Hal, and could even hear Billy's belly slapping against Hal's ass as he fucked him. It was clear that another *"This-is-not-happening-to-Hal fuck"* was well under way. Billy caressed my head and grunted in passion as finally he shot into Hal after a long siege. Hal whispered, "Oh God, John—no wonder you love this kid. Billy's wonderful." just after he took Billy's load—the only thing he said the entire time the two of us fucked him. The three of us lay there for a long time—silent, spent, appreciative of the wonder of our lovemaking.

It was getting late, and Antares was still three hours away, so our time had to end. We showered quickly, and—under the circumstances—fairly efficiently. Before we began to dress Hal declared he wanted to fuck Billy just once more, if that was okay. Billy was certainly agreeable, as was I, and we moved back to the bed. Remembering how I had watched Phil fuck Billy while I lay below him, I got on my back on the bed, and had Billy kneel over me in sixty-nine. We sucked each other while I observed the incredibly handsome Hal first kiss, then lick, then tongue-fuck my sweet lover's adorable ass. I was totally rapt as I watched his incredible cock—shining with lubricant—enter, and enter, and *enter* Billy's asshole, from only a few inches away. Finally Hal's balls rested on Billy's ass, and the two began an incredibly frenzied, and—if their hoarse cries of passion were any indication—mutually appreciated fuck.

The sight of Hal's enormous cock driving so very deep in—and then pulling on the ring of Billy's asshole as it pulled so very far out—was unbelievably exciting. Again the glistening of his lubricated shaft added to the wonder of the scene, and the sight of the bottom of his cock-head as it *almost* emerged on each incredible back-stroke, the feel of his balls slapping over my nose as he drove in, and the taste and feel of Billy's long cock as he plunged it deep into my mouth while being fucked so masterfully, all added up to an unbelievably erotic total, that soon had me shooting my load into Billy's mouth, and only a minute or so later had Billy's cock exploding in my hungry throat.

Hal's cries soon reached a fever pitch, and he fucked furiously and again filled Billy with his hot discharge and whimpered with delight, while fucking very shallowly for a long time. As he withdrew, I was again rewarded with the sight of hot come dripping from my lover's dilated asshole. "My God, you're a great fuck, Billy."

"My God, you're a great fucker, Hal."

The three of us flopped on the bed and embraced for some time—passionate kisses only slightly outnumbered by sweet ones.

Hal was lying flat on his back as Billy declared he could not leave without having him inside once more: "One for the road." Billy knelt over Hal's head, facing his feet, and sat on his face. Hal kissed and slurped eagerly as Billy and I both played with his balls and stroked his monster cock back into perfect vertical splendor. Billy walked on his knees until his asshole was positioned over Hal's awesome endowment. I knelt between Hal's legs. Billy wrapped me in his arms and slowly lowered himself onto Hal; he began bouncing up and down, riding the magnificent shaft. I backed away to admire the wonderful sight. Billy put his hands on the bed behind him, with his feet flat on it, so that he was almost lying backward over Hal, but with his body held high enough that I could see Hal's huge cock sliding in and out of him; his eyes were closed and he licked his lips as he drove himself up and down the full length of the epic ten-inches of fiercely hard flesh—groaning loudly in abject ecstasy. As he fucked himself on Hal, his own cock flopped up and down frantically—very long, fully erect, and absolutely irresistible.

Soon Hal cried out, "Here it is again, Billy—take my load." Billy continued to fuck himself as Hal discharged, and whimpered in delight—and shortly Billy collapsed with his back on Hal's stomach—the huge cock still in him, and his own prick standing up and throbbing.

Billy disengaged from Hal's prick, and his 'take charge' nature asserted itself. He unceremoniously rolled Hal to his stomach, reached into the Vaseline, and prepared Hal's ass and his own cock. Hal spread his legs, and Billy knelt between them, and the fiction of Hal's *not* getting fucked vanished as Billy told him, "Gonna fuck that hot ass of yours again," and shoved his cock all the way inside Hal with one brutal thrust, and began to fuck savagely as Hal rose to kneel on all fours while he moaned his enjoyment.

"How's it feel?" Billy asked.

"God, it's wonderful. Fuck me hard."

It took a long time before Billy shot his load inside Hal's hungry ass, but both participants expressed their joy loudly and often. Finally, Billy jammed himself as far into Hal as he could, and he froze there, with his ass-cheeks clamped together, and he cried "Take it, Hal."

Hal gasped, "Yeah—give it to me, stud." and his ass ground and humped around Billy's cock, draining every drop from it.

In a few moments, Billy pulled out and moved aside, telling me, "Get in there and fuck him in my come, Pete." He lay down next to Hal and said, "You want John to fuck you, too?" It was one of the few times I had heard him refer to me by my actual first name.

Hal groaned, "Yes. Fuck my ass, John—I love it." I was by that time already fucking him, and it was clear he did, indeed, love it. I especially loved being able to fuck him at last without the pretense of it not really happening. He and Billy embraced and kissed passionately while I fucked Hal for an extremely long time before blowing my last load into him.

The three of us lay wrapped together, exhausted. At last we kissed all around, and dressed. Billy declined to clean up again, kissing Hal and saying "I'm smuggling that last load of yours back into Texas."

Hal snickered. "I think you've got three or four of my loads in there." He took him gently in his arms, and became quite serious. "I'm gonna think of that perfect ass of yours every time I fuck someone, Billy."

" I'll never forget that perfect cock of yours inside me, Hal."

"I'll never forget how good yours felt in me," Hal replied. Then he grinned at me, "Or yours. Thanks for being a great friend, John . . ." He rumpled my hair. ". . . and for being a great fuck. And especially for making it possible for me to meet Billy. You're terrific." And he kissed me, and then kissed Billy for a long time, "And you're beautiful. This was a really special day all around." We all agreed that it had been, and hoped that *some day, somehow* it might happen again.

Driving back to Antares, Billy and I talked about what an incredible man Hal was, and what a wonderful experience we had shared in Albuquerque, but wished we could now spend the whole night together by ourselves—in *love*, unlike the sheer *lust* we had just experienced. As it turned out, we were able to achieve our wish.

Arriving at Billy's house near midnight, we found his mother waiting up for him. She insisted I spend the night. "It's too late for you to drive all the way home tonight. You can just bunk in with Billy—he's got to get up at 5:00 anyway, so you can get an early start." So, in the very room where I had first fucked this perfect youngster, I spent the night wrapped in his arms—and, given the exhausting adventures of the day, we spent the whole sweet, tender night sharing affection rather than sex.

Sadly, a re-match with Hal never occurred. In fact, I never saw him again after our Albuquerque meeting. I had sex with Shane after that, but it would be a few years before I again screwed with any other man as stunningly endowed as he or Hal.

15.
"HAPPILY EVER AFTER" TIME?

He grinned slyly. "Besides, I don't remember 'em sayin' anything about not fuckin' boys in the marriage vows." I could have explained what the "cleave only unto her" part of the ceremony meant, but I thought that would be hypocritical, seeing that I was encouraging him to cleave unto me again just at that moment.

Billy and I savored every minute we could share now. Summer was almost over, and I had been informed that I would be drafted immediately after receiving my bachelor's degree in late August. In a way, I wanted to "store up" as much wild sex as I could before leaving for the Army—well aware how restricted an active homosexual love-life was likely going to be there. Earl was on hand much of the time, and his fine big, Nordic cock continued to be a source of great joy, and Shane's stupendous endowment provided even greater, if less frequent, thrill. When Billy and I could have sex, we did our best to experience all we could—but our tender kissing and caressing was especially poignant.

Following my graduation (my mother was on hand, and Billy had brought his mother) we were able to steal only one last night together. Billy got Joe Don to cover for him, and we spent the night again at the altar where we had consecrated our love, Rodman's pond—making love, telling each other of our devotion, and promising it would continue forever. We agreed that each would have to pursue his own sex life for the next two years, but that it could never substitute for what we now shared.

As the sky was only beginning to get light, Billy had to leave and go to work, and we both cried as we held each other tightly and kissed for the last time until . . . who could say?

Plans frequently take on a life of their own. I wound up being inducted into the Navy, rather than the Army; I spent two years on the west coast and overseas, and saw Billy only twice during that time—on Christmas leave following boot camp, and on another leave a year later, during his senior year in high school. Our reunions were exuberant and passionate, but far too short. We exchanged letters regularly, and told each other all that was happening. True to my prediction, Joe Don propositioned Billy, and the two began a regular, though fairly low-key sexual relationship; each *liked* the other a lot, and enjoyed the sex, of course, but their relationship was as much a shared solace for Phil's and my absence as it was a strong mutual attraction. Phil made it home periodically, and regularly "serviced" Joe Don; he also took Billy to bed, although with somewhat less frequency—but always with the complete sexual mastery he had earlier brought to him, and to me, and to *us*.

Billy began dating a few girls, and by his senior year, when he was elected Captain of the football team, he was suddenly very popular with *all* the girls. More and more he began to narrow the scope of his dating to another former student of mine, daughter of the local bank president; by the time he was ready to graduate, they were very much a "couple," and everyone assumed they would some day marry. She went off to a girls' school, and Billy headed for my Alma Mater, to major in business administration—on the advice of his presumptive father-in-law. Joe Don enrolled in the same school, and the two decided to room together.

Mr. Rodman gave Billy a special graduation present: his summer wages presented in advance as a gift, without any work expected, so he could enter summer school right away and get a head start on his degree. Joe Don decided to accompany him so they could get a head start on their new status as roommates and live-in fuckbuddies.

Long before that I had received a letter from Earl telling me that Shane was stationed at Camp Pendleton, several miles north of San Diego, where I was stationed. He had joined the Marines to avoid being drafted. I looked him up, of course, and we had a large number of very enjoyable meetings. He always brought at least one Marine fuckbuddy with him when we met, and sometime several more; a two-day orgy-cum-gangbang I shared with Shane and seven other Marines was a distinct highlight of my military career.

Shane could not keep his famous rubber dick on base, of course, but he didn't need it when we met—he always had a real live Marine cock up his ass to keep him hard while he fucked me, and I often helped him fuck another Marine by providing the same service. He satisfied his appetite for taking two cocks in his ass simultaneously almost every time we were together—as did a surprising number of his Marine buddies when there was sufficient manpower on hand to accomplish it. I myself never became able to take Shane's monster dick inside me along with another one, but I managed two other Marine cocks at a time on several occasions, and even managed to take four different Marine cocks in two shifts at a 'going away' party Shane threw for me the night I was separated from the Navy—at the La Jolla home of a ridiculously wealthy older man who had a stable of sailors and Marines (including Shane) that he drew on to provide him with sex-for-money on an apparently daily basis, and who acted as *Keeper of the Rubber Dick* for Shane while Shane lived on base. I never saw Shane again after that night.

I was mustered out of the service in early September, and rather than returning to teaching in the Texas Panhandle, I accepted a fellowship to pursue a Master's degree at the University of Alabama. I had only a week back in the Panhandle to visit and get things together for my move to Alabama.

Jim had graduated, and moved back home to Oklahoma, apparently taking Earl along with him, but I spent four nights in Billy and Joe Don's dorm room, where Billy and I made love at all hours, and at great length during that time.

Although he confessed he was finding himself more interested in sex with his girlfriend, and less with Joe Don or Phil, Billy assured me that between him and me it would always be *love*, not just sex, and that he would always love me and want to be with me, and to make love with me whenever he could.

Billy and Joe Don had long before then shared stories of Phil and me, and when I came to stay in Billy's bed before leaving, we did not have to hide what we were doing. Our lovemaking was wild and joyous, and as noisy as it could be in the confines of a dormitory room, and the two times we went out to Arroyo Grande for *al fresco* fucking, we got a lot noisier—once even attracting a spectator, whom Billy spied watching us, with his pants and underwear around his ankles while he jacked off. On my second night in the dorm, Billy asked Joe Don to join us in bed, and we had a very satisfying three-way fuck both that night and the next. My final night, Joe Don insisted on leaving us alone together, and Billy and I spent the entire night kissing and hugging, and fucking and sucking as though we might never see each other again.

We continued to write, but I was not to see him again until I went back to Texas for his college graduation. His relationship with Joe Don had become somewhat like what mine had been with Jim, except that Billy's homosexual lovemaking was limited to regular fucking with Joe Don and a few others, but with gradually decreasing frequency—while Joe Don branched out considerably, and became something of a voracious fuck-hungry stud.

Billy said, in a letter, that he often returned to their room to find Joe Don having sex with one out of the many cutest and hottest guys on campus he managed to lure into his bed—and many of whom then began to court my beautiful Billy eagerly, but most of whom did so in vain. Billy confessed he had welcomed the advances of a half-dozen or so of them, however.

He wrote: *"Most of the guys Joe Don lines up are really hot, and just a year ago I probably wouldn't have been able to resist the temptation to fuck with just about every one of them. You'd flip over a lot of them, Pete—especially one named Steve, who's hung like Hal, and is just about as pretty as Hal's blond lover, if you can believe that. But lately I just don't seem to be all that interested in sex with guys anymore. I know you can't believe that. Don't misunderstand—sex with guys is not sex with you. I'll always want to make love with you, Pete—anytime, and anywhere we can. I swore I'd love you all my life, and I can't think how that will ever change. My prick is incredibly hard as I write these words to you, thinking about what wonderful times we have had together—and I hope we'll somehow always be able to meet and renew our love, if only once in a while. Gotta go and beat off, and I'm going to pretend I can feel you behind me, shoving that wonderful dick up my ass and giving me your load."* He added a postscript: *"It's later—the next morning: Joe Don came in and caught me jacking off last night, and we wound up spending the whole night fucking each other's brains out. Jesus, I wish it had been you."*

Phil had graduated from college and had recently married. He told Billy he was not interested in guys anymore, but I later had good reason to know he continued to provide the masterful service to others that he had given Billy and Joe Don and me. He moved to Houston, and seldom came back to Antares.

I was only able to be with Billy alone for one night when I went back for his graduation, but it was a night of joy and wonder, and as hot a variety of sex as we had ever practiced—even though he told me at that time that he had asked Beth (the banker's daughter) to marry him, and she had accepted. "So I guess I'm going to be an old married man, and we want kids, too—but I will never *not* want to make love with you." He was now the same age I had been when I first met him; he seemed much more mature now, and he had filled out physically (probably ten pounds heavier—but still trim and muscular), but he was still the incredibly sweet boy I had fallen in love with seven years earlier—and whom I would always love. One of the two most beautiful boys I had ever known—Dan Chrisman was the other, of course—was now the most beautiful *man* I had ever known, and his ass was every bit as cute as ever, too.

Joe Don graduated at the same time. He was considerably changed, I thought. His facial features had crystallized in a way that made him strikingly handsome. Much more assured and "in charge," he had developed quite a fine physique through gym work, and was seriously dating one of the varsity football players—an extremely handsome blond quarterback, whom Joe Don told me had "a bottomless throat, a bottomless ass, and a cock to make the angels weep."

"*To make the angels weep?* Christ, Joe Don, Where did *that* come from?"

Joe Don shrugged, "Oh, I dunno—some poem in English, I think." He winked broadly and grinned, "But hey, I guess I'm not an angel, 'cause it doesn't make me weep—just makes me *gag* once in a while when he shoves it too far down my throat. But mostly, it just makes me feel great." He showed me his boyfriend's picture, and I admitted he had snagged a real prize.

Joe Don and his quarterback moved to Los Angeles shortly after that, and neither Billy nor I heard from him. I was astonished six or eight years later to spot Joe Don fucking a very young boy in a male pornographic movie—one of those eight millimeter silent "loops" that preceded the full-length, well-made porn movies that began to appear in the 70's and beyond.

I kept my eyes peeled, and found Joe Don appeared in a number of those short fuck-films, often partnered with his blond lover—who demonstrated that he did indeed have a bottomless throat and ass, and whose cock made me (no angel) weep—but with hunger, and envy of Joe Don. Joe Don looked wonderful in those films (his lover looked *stunning*, for want of a better word.), and he continued to appear in them until the end of the 1970's. He had made the films under a variety of names, so there was no way to trace his "career." Did he go into directing? Production? Sadly, I have no idea what happened to him after that.

[If it seems extremely unlikely that I would have known two *occasional sex partners who wound up making pornographic movies—Dave Elton was the other, of course—I offer no defense or apology. If this were fiction, I would avoid the coincidence, but I am only telling the story of what actually happened. In fact, I also had a fairly short-term live-in lover in the mid 1960s—Richard, who was as beautiful as he was beautifully hung—who went on to star in a loop and one of the very early gay-porn feature films.]*

The magnificent and unforgettable Hal disappeared from my ken also, but I always hoped that he and Dan remained partners in love; surely, two men so unforgettably beautiful and exciting should always be together.

A couple of years later, Billy married Beth, and I served as his Best Man. It was an occasion of real stress for me—the man I loved and most wanted to be with, was marrying a woman. A nice woman, to be sure—but it should have been me. The only slight consolation was that Phil had returned as a groomsman, and Billy had thoughtfully assigned us a room together at the motel where the wedding party was staying. The grin and wink Billy tendered me when he informed me of the sleeping arrangement was so cute, I had a real struggle to keep myself from jumping him then and there. Joe Don had been asked to serve as a groomsman also, but for some reason he was unable to come to the wedding.

Phil and I had an *epic* sex marathon the night Billy was married—preceded by many equally wonderful hours of fucking and sucking and kissing and rimming the night before. Marriage had not dimmed Phil's sexual vigor or his joy in homosexual lovemaking in the slightest, and his cock seemed even more exciting than I remembered it—and I remembered it as very, very exciting indeed. The strength of his erection was still astonishing as he carried me around our motel room impaled on it while fucking me with thrilling force—and the power of the *en route* explosion of come deep inside my body on that occasion was unforgettable. I marveled again at the massiveness of his balls, and gloried in the volume of hot, creamy come they delivered to my adoring mouth and ass so many times those two nights. His body seemed larger and his huge chest and narrow waist even more incredibly *manly* than I remembered, and the sight of that Herculean frame riding up and down my cock was almost as exciting as the feel of his tight ass gripping my shaft so ecstatically. We tongue-fucked each other until either fatigue or the unstoppable desire to replace our tongues with hard cocks made us stop.

At one point Phil inserted two of his fingers alongside his cock as he fucked me. "Remember when Billy and I fucked you together, John?" I remembered it well, and greatly enjoyed the closest simulation to that we could effect at the moment. My reminding Phil that he had enjoyed Billy's cock along with mine led to two of my fingers being bathed in my come as I discharged inside him.

Billy's *physical* presence was missing from that room, but his sweetness, his beauty, his perfect physical endowments, and his fierce sexual power were with us in spirit. We both mused at length about how much we had enjoyed that very *special* man's offerings, and wished he were there to share with us. On a number of occasions those two evenings, when either Phil or I were inserting our cocks into the other somewhere, or delivering a load of come to the other, we said something like, "This is for Billy." Or, "Pretend this is Billy's." Or, "God, I wish Billy were here to do this to both of us." It was the final three-way fuck between Billy and Phil and me—and sadly, the glorious Billy was not even there to share it.

I told Phil I knew about his telling Billy he wasn't fucking guys any more. He laughed, "Well, I prob'ly meant it at the time, and I love my, wife, I really do, but shit, I just love fuckin' butt and eatin' cock too much to give it up. I've got a high-school kid lined up now who can give as good a blowjob as you do, but he hardly ever does it, 'cause he wants my dick up his ass all the time." He ginned slyly, "Besides, I don't remember 'em sayin' anything about not fuckin' boys in the marriage vows." I could have explained what the "cleave only unto her" part of the ceremony meant, but I thought that would be hypocritical, seeing that I was encouraging him to cleave unto me again just at that moment.

That was the last time I saw Phil—but what a send-off. My ass was sore for days—*delightfully* so—and his certainly *should* have been.

My sex life apart from Billy was varied and satisfying. I had more than my share of incredible sex while I was in the Navy, mostly with sailors and Marines: several with cocks that rivaled—and a few times even exceeded—Hal's and Shane's (including Tony and "Jacks"—as well as Shane himself, of course); quite a number with awesome bodies like Phil's or Shane's; a couple with asses almost as cute as Billy's (Hy and Ron); one bed-partner I could easily have fallen seriously in love with (Gordy)—and all sorts of assorted other less spectacular, but almost universally satisfying ones I fucked and sucked, and got fucked and sucked by.

Through three years of graduate school (leading finally to a doctorate) and years as a professor at a major state university in the Deep South, I met and bedded a dazzling variety of hot, beautiful, exciting guys—including fairly extended love affairs with several of them.

Billy and I continued to correspond, but my letters to him had to be very carefully guarded, since Beth would no doubt see them. His letters to me constantly expressed his love, but it was only when he telephoned, on rare occasions when he was alone, that I could tell him how much I still loved him, and wanted to be with him—in love and in bed. He became Vice President of his father-in-law's bank, and was doing very well. The Billy Polks had a daughter in 1965—a beautiful child (he sent a *lot* of pictures), who became the absolute apple of her father's eye.

It was in 1975 that I got a call from Billy, asking me if he could fly out to see me—no explanations, he needed a friend he could talk to. I was surprised and delighted, but I had also been alarmed by the tone of his voice when he called. He flew to Atlanta, where I met him, and we checked into a motel near the airport (he had to fly back the next morning).

Once we were in the room, he took me in his arms and we kissed tenderly for a very long time. It was the first time we had kissed in twelve years. "I've missed you so much, Pete—but I love you as much as ever."

He looked absolutely stunning. He was thirty-seven years old, and was just as appealing to me as he had been at sixteen—even though by that time I tended to favor sex partners *much* younger than myself. He was now strikingly handsome in a mature way. Later, when I saw him nude, I was thrilled and pleased to see that he was still trim and muscular—a perfect *man's* body in place of the perfect *youngman/boy's* body I had worshipped twenty years earlier.

Before our kissing could turn passionate—and I was not yet at that point sure that it *would*—he declared we needed to talk. I mixed him a drink, he pulled off his tie, and sat to tell me his news.

He had learned that Beth was having an affair with another man, and he was not at all sure she loved him any longer; furthermore, he seriously questioned his own feelings for her. "There just doesn't seem to be anything *there* between us any more, but I'm not even thinking of doing anything with anyone else. Pete, the last time I had sex with anyone other than Beth was in 1961. That was the night I told you I was going to get married; that was the last time you and I made love—fourteen years ago."

"I've never forgotten, Billy and I love you just as much now as I did then, you know. I can't lie to you . . . I've been with a lot of different guys since then, and I really loved some of them, but it's always been you I loved most."

"Of course I know, and you have to know that just because we haven't had sex, it doesn't mean that I don't still love you—I do, Pete, I love you with all my heart, and always have. I've ached with the desire to make love with you thousands and thousands of nights since we went to bed together the last time—but I was married, and I had a wife I had promised to be faithful to. And Pete, I was never tempted enough by any other guys to break my promise to Beth. Sure, there were some really cute ones around, and even a few who made it clear they were interested in playing around with me, but I didn't want sex with them. I had a wife, but I loved you also—if I was going to have sex with anyone besides her, I wanted it to be you."

"Does Beth know you've come out to see me?"

"Sure. I told her I needed to talk things out with you. She knows I love you, Pete—she just doesn't know I love you the way that I do. She knows I respect you, too, and that you're the best friend I ever had."

"Are you fighting over this affair that Beth is having? That could really present a problem for Tammy." Tammy was their daughter—now around ten years old. (The name was certainly not one I would have picked, but . . .)

"No. Thank God it's all very *civilized*, and Tammy isn't caught in the middle of any big fights. But what happens if Beth leaves me?"

I had no real solutions to his problem, of course, but all he really needed was a sympathetic ear to pour out his troubles to, and I was more than happy to provide that. Ultimately, he decided that he and Beth needed to try and make a 'go' of things—for their daughter's sake, if nothing else. "I may need a lot of advice and sympathy for a while, Pete."

"Billy, I will always be there to help you if I can. You know how much I love you." I was sitting on the bed, leaning against the headboard. Billy came over and sat next to me, and took me in his arms.

"Make love to me Pete, if you want to. I want to feel you inside me again—no one has ever meant to me what you mean. Phil, and later Joe Don—and even Hal and those guys in college—that was all fun, but I feel like I sort of outgrew that. I've never outgrown loving you, Pete. Please, make love to me."

"Are you sure, Billy? You know I want you—I want to be inside you,

I want you inside me, I want to hold you and kiss you, and be sure you know how very much I love you." He smiled and began to unbutton his shirt; I stood and returned his smile as I began to unbutton mine.

We watched each other disrobe, and when we were both nude, we stood there for a while, holding hands and enjoying looking at each other. We moved together and began to fondle and kiss—first sweetly, and then with savage passion. We ground our hard cocks and pelvises into each other, and our hands lovingly explored the familiar territory of each other's body. Billy turned himself around in my arms, so that his perfect ass nestled against my hard prick. He turned his head so that I could kiss him, and he whispered, "Take me, Pete. I've wanted your prick inside me every day for the last fourteen years. No one has fucked me since you did, and I didn't want anyone else to—but I've wanted you in me all the time. I'm so hungry for your love I don't know what to do." He walked over to the bed and leaned down, putting his hands on it. "No, I'm not just hungry for you, I'm *starving*. Please fuck me, Pete—I want my lover's big cock inside me again." It took me only a few seconds to retrieve the lubricant from my bag, and I soon broke Billy's fourteen-year fast.

How many times we said "I love you" to each other while I made gentle, deep love to this perfect man's magnificent ass, followed by frantic, savage, driving love, would be hard to say. After my eruption inside him, which he greeted with a shout of "Give it to me, Pete. I want you.", we both collapsed forward on the bed and lay there some time, until Billy whispered, "I can't imagine loving anyone more than I do you, Pete. I've missed you so much."

We held each other. Billy continued, "I'm sorta ashamed to say it, but an awful lot of the time over these years when I've been making love to Beth, I've pretended it was you I was with. I never screwed up so bad that I said "I love you, Pete." when I shot my load, but a lot of the time that was what I was thinking. My cock hasn't been inside anyone but my wife in all these years—but I've wanted it in you, too. Oh hell, I might as well be honest, Pete—I've wanted it in you much more than I wanted it in her. I love Beth, and I wanted a family, and Tammy is . . . well, you know what I mean. But it's always really been you I wanted to be with. You know that, don't you, Pete?"

"Of course I do, Billy. And I'm not really ashamed to say that I've been with an awful lot of different guys since we last made love, you know I have, and some of them really meant a lot to me—hell, I *loved* some of them—but no one has ever meant to me what you always have. I couldn't begin to tell you how many times I've jacked off with my eyes closed, seeing your perfect body, and your beautiful face, and your long beautiful prick in my mind—or jacked off studying those pictures I took of you that night. There have been countless nights I've pretended it was you I was making love to; there were times I've had a guy ask me "Who's Billy?" after I finished coming inside him, or he had just shot a load in me. One shipmate of mine was actually named Billy, too, and when I fucked with him it was so wonderful that I could call him by name, and really be calling out to you." My shipmate/sometime-fuckmate Billy was one who loved to refer to himself in the third person as he fucked, fortunately, and the sound of his "You like this big hard prick of Billy's up your ass, don't you?" brought a positive response far more genuine than he imagined. "But Billy, I still love you as much now as I ever have, and there has never been a day of my life since I first went out to Rodman's Pond with you that I wouldn't rather have you in my arms than any other person in the world."

Billy snickered. "Even Hal?"

"Jesus, he was something, wasn't he? But yes, even Hal." If he could snicker at me, hell I figured I could snicker back at him: "But it might be nice to have you in my arms and Hal in my butt."

"I'm just so glad that for the moment I'm in your arms and you're in *my* butt. It's where you belong, Pete." I agreed my errant cock was, indeed in its proper place at that point.

I asked him, "You know where *your* cock belongs, don't you?" He agreed he did, and forthwith made sure it, too, was in its proper place.

Although our lovemaking was only reasonably frantic that night, neither of us slept a wink—almost every minute we weren't having sex we spent sharing quiet, tender affection. His beautiful, long cock was even bigger than I remembered it (had it grown?), and when he drove it deep inside me as I lay on my back and he kissed me, I felt a *satisfaction* in lovemaking I had not known for a long time. The explosion of come that followed a bit later was as exciting and as sweet as any I've ever felt inside me. Hot come shooting from a magnificent stud's beautiful prick, but given with real love—a potent combination.

Our kissing and caressing after each orgasm—and we each had many of them—was as tender as possible, and yet was passionate as well. At one point, when we sucked each other off in sixty-nine, and had offered our loads at almost exactly the same moment, time seemed to stand still. We lay there holding each other without a word for a very long time—mutual *love* filling our hearts.

Shortly before he had to leave to catch his plane the next morning, Billy mounted my cock as I lay on my back, and very slowly and deliberately drove himself up and down, all the while declaring his love for me. After I had discharged into him, he stayed impaled on me, masturbated, shot his load into his hand, and offered the hand for me to eat from it. "My love, Pete." I ate it gratefully, still basking in the wonderful feel of his hot body gripping my adoring cock tightly.

Billy left for Antares, hoping to patch things up. At the flight gate at the airport he told me, "I know we didn't answer any questions, Pete, but I needed to talk with someone about it—and frankly, I wanted desperately to make love with you again after all these years. No, I *needed* to make love with you. You're a wonderful love-maker, Pete. I want sex with you as much now as I did when I first fucked you that night in your bedroom in Antares."

"I'll never forget that night, or any moment I ever spent making love with you, Billy. Please let me know what happens with Beth." And as he prepared to board his plane, we did something very daring by the standards of 1975, and which would probably raise quite a few eyebrows even today: we held each other in our arms and kissed passionately for a long time before he turned to go up the ramp to his plane—and his adorable little ass still looked as cute going away from me as it had in my Geometry classroom in Antares High School twenty-one years earlier.

He returned to Texas, I returned home, and eventually I realized that his marriage was going to break up; by 1977 it was an accomplished fact. He and Beth remained reasonably friendly, and he was able to visit Tammy freely.

It was at that time I finally took a life-partner, who has been—with a few minor, meaningless slips along the way, on both sides—the most wonderful sexual playmate, caring lover, and concerned and sharing friend I could ever have wished for. We have been together for twenty-four years now. It was he who finally convinced me to enter the age of word-processing, and—after I finally mastered the system—encouraged me to set this story down.

As I type these final paragraphs into my computer, it's growing late, and I'm staying up a bit past my usual bedtime to write *finis* at long last. I must wrap it up now, for I know that in only a few minutes my partner will appear in the door to my study—handsome and perfectly built, undoubtedly nude, and probably stroking his considerable erection as he says those words that have thrilled me so many thousands of times over the last two dozen years: "Are you coming to bed soon, Pete?"

Thus: *finis*. "And so to bed."

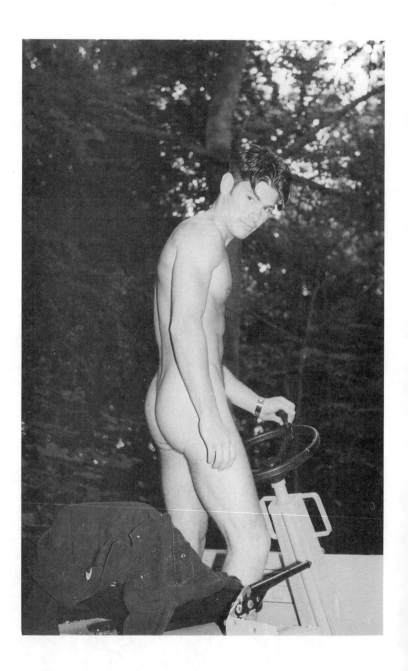

Acknowledgments

Cover model Steve courtesy of David Butt of Suntown Studios, Ltd, London. Butt's fine photographs may be purchased from Suntown Studios, Post Office Box 151, Danbury, Oxfordshire, OX16 8QN, United Kingdom. (http://website.lineone.net/~suntown1.) E-mail at SUNTOWN1@aol.com.

A collection of Mr. Butt's photos, *English Country Lad*, is available from STARbooks Press. *Young and Hairy*, David's latest book, is enjoying huge success currently and is also available from STARbooks Press.

About the Author

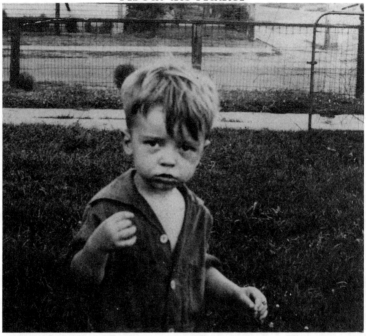

Above, the author, taken about the time he realized he was interested in boys, not girls. He is considerably older now, but in that fundamental respect he has not changed at all.

John Butler retired after a thirty-six year career in music teaching and administration, ranging from elementary and secondary school music, to Dean of Liberal Arts at a major American University, where he also served as Professor and Department Head for twenty-seven years. He has published widely in his primary career field, but his first publication in the field of interest that has occupied his mind since he started fooling around with the little boy next door at the age of nine or ten came with the publication of the erotic novel *model/escort* in 1998. Since then he has also published the novel, *WanderLUST: Ships that Pass in the Night,* as well as the novel "The Boy Next Door" in the anthology *Any Boy Can*—and short stories in the anthologies *Taboo., Fever!,* and *Virgins No More.* All these are currently available from the publisher: STARbooks/Florida Literary Foundation, Sarasota, Florida.
The author welcomes comments or questions through the e-mail address: NotRhett@yahoo.com